A
Game
of
Survival
By
S.L Wisdom And
S.J Noble

CW01429374

Copyright Statement

Copyright © 2023 by S.L Wisdom (S.Salter) and S.J Noble (S.Waldron).

All rights reserved.

The right of S.L Wisdom and S.J Noble to be identified as the Authors of the Work has been asserted by them in accordance with The Copyright, Design and Patents Act 1988.

This book or any portion thereof may not be reproduced or used in any form or by any electronic or mechanical means, including information storage and retrieval systems, nor be otherwise circulated in any form of binding or cover other than that in which is it published and without a similar condition being imposed on the subsequent purchaser, without the express written permission of both authors, except for the use of brief quotations in a book review.

This is a work of fiction. The events described in this book are fictitious; any similarities to actual events and persons, dead or alive, are entirely coincidental.

Paperback ISBN: 9798871655788
eBook ASIN: B0CMXSWKWM

Cover design by Francessca Wingfield

Editing by Ria Hockey at Moon and Bloom Editing.

To survive it is often necessary to fight, and to fight you have to dirty yourself.

George Orwell.

Trigger Warnings

Murder
Non-con
Abduction
Abuse
Torture
Kidnapping
Rape
Drug use
MFM

Chapter 1

Lucille

Screaming, all I can hear is screaming.

"Get her out of here, Linc!"

"He's losing too much blood. We're going to lose him if we don't get the fuck out of here!"

Gunshots and more screaming.

"Lucille! Get up, we have to move!"

"Fuck. Get her up NOW! We have to fucking move!"

"TEDDY! WHERE IS TEDDY!?"

Beep. . . Beep. . . Beep. . . Beep. . .

The pungent smell of disinfectant invades my nostrils, and other than the consistent beeping of machinery that confirms I am still alive, it's the only thing that lets me know I'm in a hospital room. I slowly open my eyes, the blinding light of the room making me shut them again instantly as it all but burns through my cornea's. I take a steady breath and try again, blinking a few times to adjust to the brightness, gradually sharpening the blurred images of my surroundings. The room around me is almost bare with white walls and flooring, a few pieces of hospital equipment and a light blue chair towards the back of the room, in front of a large glass window. It's definitely not Summerlin hospital. I look up noticing there's an IV bag pumping fluids into me and several different things written on the board above my bed but I can't read it properly from my angle. I scrunch my eyes closed again as an almighty thumping pain in my head makes me wish for sleep to swallow me once more. I have to shake it off though, I have no idea how long I've been out. I need to get up now and I need to find Teddy. The thought alone increases the beeping on the vital signs monitor I'm hooked up to and there's a cold sweat breaking out across my body as the memories wash over me, making me want to puke. My baby, I pray to God that he's safe.

I attempt to move but my body hurts from merely laying still, never mind what Vinny did. I attempt to remove the IV from my hand and pulse reader from my finger but I can't. What? Why the fuck can't I move? I gaze down at my arms, the shock at what I see making my head spin. I'm restrained! A thick belt-like strap is fastened around each wrist, keeping my arms securely by my sides. I jerk my arms as hard as I can against the restraints causing a searing pain to shoot through my shoulder but it's no use, I'm completely immobilized against them. *What the fuck!?* This can not be happening. I pull at the restraints again, crying out at the pain ripping through my body. "Somebody get me out of these fucking things!" I scream at the top of my lungs. I can feel the panic rising through my body, my vision is closing in again and I'm finding it too hard to breathe. "HELP!" I scream, my voice cracking at the end as the darkened edges of my vision cave in. Two young female nurses come barreling into the room, immediately rushing to my bedside.
"Oh my goodness Miss, you must be quiet, there are other patients in here trying to rest. Try to calm—" The taller of the two begins before I cut her off.
"Get these fucking things off my wrists right now. I need to get out of here!" I demand, straining as I attempt to pull my hand free once more.

6

"I'm sorry Miss Holland, but we can't remove them. Just try to calm down now or you're going to hurt yourself," she chides.

I turn my head towards the second nurse and narrow my eyes. "You need to let me go, I need to find my son!" I argue, pulling my arms back trying to release myself with little effect. The nurse does nothing but shake her head at me.

"I'm sor–"

"You heard what she said. Take them off." A deep guttural voice cuts her off before she can object any more. I snap my head up, meeting Silas eye to eye as his bulking frame takes up the whole entrance to the room. His eyes are pitch black, jaw fiercely clenched and he looks every bit of the devil I know he can be. His eyes shoot towards each of the nurses who seem to have lost their voices at his sudden intimidating appearance. "Take. Them. Off." He demands, taking a step further into the room.

The taller nurse to my left takes a step back and I swear I actually hear the fear in voice when she objects with a simple, "No."

Silas' eyebrows rise in mock surprise. "I'm sorry. Did you just say no?" He questions, taking another step forwards, cocking his head to one side as he observes her. I watch the nurse swallow nervously before she answers with a sheen of sweat beginning to coat her upper lip.

"I...I...We can not remove the restraints, Sir. She has to be examined by the doctor, and he is the only one with the authority to remove them once he sees fit," she replies, looking to her colleague for support but she only seems to be intrigued by her shoes as she refuses to look up. "You must understand, Miss Holland is restrained for a reason, she could hurt herself, or others if she gets into a hysterical state again" she says, trying to placate him.

Silas' face turns dark, like Lucifer himself has taken hold of his soul as he encroaches on her, slowly like a predator stalking towards its prey.

"I'm the fucking authority here. So I suggest that if you want to keep your fucking job, you will do as I say and remove those fucking straps from her wrists or I swear to the Devil himself that you and your colleague here will not live to see another fucking sunrise. Do I make myself clear?" he growls. His tone laced with malice as he stands up to his full height, squaring his shoulders, all intimidating and absolutely terrifying, sending a shiver the entire way down my spine as I watch on helplessly from my bed.

Neither one of the nurses speaks as they look at each other before rushing towards me at the same moment and fumbling to remove my wrist straps. The release is instant as the cuffs are undone, freeing the bonding that had left marks against my skin. I bring my arms up, stretching them out above my head and the tension in my back fades until I hiss out at the pain through my shoulder again which earns me a scolding look from the taller nurse who I can now see is called Jane from the badge that she's wearing.

"I'll fetch the doctor, Miss Holland," she nods, dipping her head low without looking at Silas as she and her colleague both scurry out of the room.

The silence is deafening as soon as we're alone, ringing loud in my ears as I close my eyes and breathe through my pain. In through my nose, out through my mouth. The bed dips at my side as Silas sits beside me. "Where is he?" Is all I ask, barely a whisper, not even bothering to look towards him, keeping my eyes closed, I can't bring myself to look into his eyes. The silence remains growing increasingly louder with each passing second as Silas shifts uncomfortably before placing his hand gently across my thigh.

"Lucille..." he begins, his voice so low and gentle compared to his previous outburst.

"Please, Silas. Just tell me where he is." I beg, the intrusive thoughts coming back to battle with my insanity. Silas removes his hand and clears his throat. I know the truth before he even says the words, he's gone, they couldn't save my boy.

"We'll find him," he assures me, pulling me into his chest and cradling my head against his body, planting a soft kiss into my hair.

The door to the room opens as a middle aged man wearing a light blue smock shirt with a stethoscope dangling around his neck hurries into the room, quickly followed by Jane and her colleague. I can't begin to process what he says but Silas nods and answers back when necessary as I stare into the bed sheets, my mind a million miles away. I hear words such as "infection" and "stitches" but the buzzing in my head becomes unbearable. Like a thousand wasps are stuck inside, screaming at me to let them out. I can't focus, I can't breathe. I. Can. Not. Breathe. My hands claw at my neck as I gasp for air, I'm sure I'm going to die. Is this it? Is this what death feels like? A heavy weight pressing down on my chest, threatening to squash me under the pressure. I feel hands on me, gentle but rough, so many hands. I don't know who they belong to. I can't breathe. I can't see. The room is blurring, large mismatched shapes all begin to transform into deformed gray beasts with sharp teeth and even sharper claws that seep into my sight, snatching away the light. I just need to lie down, to sleep, to let the nightmare end.

Beep. . . Beep. . . Beep. . . Beep. . .

I'm not even sure if I'm alive anymore. How can I be? My heart has been ripped so viciously from my chest and I have no idea how to get it back. The only thing letting me know that it isn't just some horrible nightmare is the searing pain still burning through my shoulder from Vinny's knife. The flash back of Cole's blood plastered across my body and his own as I watched the life slip slowly from his eyes are haunting my every thought and when I finally give into exhaustion, I'm plagued with nightmares of Teddy, alone and scared somewhere screaming for me to find him. I can't cope. I've come to realize that if the heartbreak from losing my son doesn't kill me, the exhaustion will.

I've been occupying the same chair for the last two days now, slumped against the bed holding onto Cole's lifeless hand, as if I were to let go, he would surely disappear. After my last panic attack, I haven't yet been allowed to leave the hospital, my wound from Vinny's blade became infected so I'm still on a course of IV antibiotics and having to monitor the stitches, but I was allowed to leave my room after Silas threatened to slit the doctors throat if he didn't let me see Cole, and this is where I've been since. I feel like I have nothing left to give anymore. I'm not even thinking straight at this point. I know my thoughts are no longer rational, but if there's one thing I know for certain, it's that this man, mere breaths away from death, is the only man that knows where my son is. And the hope that he survives to tell me how to find him, is clinging to my last little bit of sanity.

My stomach cramps angrily, reminding me that I haven't eaten for nearly three days. How can I when it seems so minor compared to everything else. I don't have time to eat when I need to be there the second Cole wakes up, to be able to find out where Teddy is. The thought alone makes me feel nauseous and I have to lean forwards, placing my head against the cool metal bar of the hospital bed to ground myself, to steady my concentration on the feel of the cold metal against my skin. I take deep steadying breaths, willing the bile in my throat not to spill, letting the waves pass slowly before bringing my head back up and landing my gaze back on Cole. He looks so peaceful when he's sleeping, even when he's hurt. My eyes flicker to the bandages covering his gunshot wounds and a pain physically sears at my chest that he got hurt trying to protect my son. He's here because of me. It was only yesterday that I found out that Cole had received emergency surgery to repair the bullet wounds and needed multiple blood transfusions due to his extensive blood loss. I heard Silas mention internal damage while on a phone call but he walked away from me as soon as he knew I was listening. Turns out I had gone into a complete state of shock by the time we arrived at the hospital and as soon as Cole was taken away, I collapsed into Linc's arms. When I came round, I was lying on a bed with two male strangers standing over me who at the time I thought were attacking me, so I hit out on instinct, subsequently breaking one of their noses, which is why I ended up in restraints, so I've been told. I now know the two male nurses were trying to stitch up my shoulder, but I don't for a second feel bad about my reaction. I blacked out again not long after. In all that time, Cole still had not come round from his anesthesia.

I have sat and tortured myself, constantly replaying every single little detail since leaving the club and writing that note for Silas, to being brought here, just to pinpoint where it all went wrong, to scrutinize my choices in going alone. I should have known it would have been a trap, little did I know to what extent. I should have just let Vinny take me and then this would never have happened. I would never have lost Teddy, at least we would be together, and Cole would not have to die for me. And where was Max when everything was happening? I can't allow myself to believe that he was working against us, he loved Teddy like he was his own, he would never knowingly put him in danger, but where is he? He should be here with me, helping us find Teddy. I have a feeling of dread in the pit of my stomach. I can only hope that wherever Max and Teddy are, they are together somehow so neither of them are alone. My heart cracks open even more at the thought of my little boy all alone with a monster I can not save him from.

I can feel the now familiar pull of the drugs in my system, calming me down as the morbid intrusive thoughts plague my mind. I've come to the conclusion that I must have lashed out more than once after the incident, I'm almost certain the hospital is drugging me to calm me down, to keep me sane, can't say I blame them. Distraught and hysterical, they are the words I heard Lincoln use over the phone two nights ago when he thought I was sleeping. Well that's no longer the case. No, now I'm just empty, broken, a shell of my former self. I have no more tears left to cry, not anymore. Now all I have is a burning hole of despair, cracking open my chest, leaving me with such heartache I don't know if I'll ever survive it.

I can't think of Teddy, the pain is too excruciating. More so than anything I suffered under the hands of my ex husband. I would endure his hands every day for the rest of my life if it meant I'd see my son safe again. My chest aches so painfully, I find myself gasping for breath at the smallest of triggers. I have no phone thanks to Vinny, so no connections. Not that I'd know who to call. I have nobody, I'm alone here despite the guard they have outside the door when they leave to run their business. I guess they're not stupid enough to leave me unprotected while their brother lies close to death in a hospital bed. Not after the attack we all just suffered. This is personal, I can feel it. But why my son? Why me? I try to think back to what Vinny said before he tried to...I can feel it, my throat closing in, my breath becoming weak, my chest becoming tight. I scratch at the skin around my neck as if to loosen the rope that's tightening around me, but my hands are empty. I'm panicking again and I can't stop it from swarming me, my breaths are ragged and my vision is darkening at the edges. The room is disappearing around me. Maybe this is all just a nightmare and Teddy will be here when I wake up.

Chapter 2

Silas

Rain descends outside the windows of my office, colliding with the ground. I find the sound comforting. It reminds me that even nature can shatter just as we can. That everything is ever changing. The feeling of despair is something that I have grown used to, but seeing that darken the light of Lucille's radiance ripped my soul apart.

Looking around the room, everything seems pointless, none of it matters anymore. Remembering the hollowed look on Lucille's face everytime I see her has my chest caving in as she visibly wastes away before me in that hospital. Lucille was hysterical and devastated as any good mother would be. But when I arrived at the hospital, the bastards had her restrained and although I understand exactly the reasons why, they didn't have my authorization to do it and that makes me fucking furious. They will be dealt with in due course. I can see the trauma that has been inflicted on her, it weighs heavy on her soul, like a dark rain cloud clinging to her once bright light. I have a guard stationed at the door to Cole's hospital room at all times, and though I won't admit it out loud, I'm worried out of my mind that she'll do something stupid if Cole doesn't wake up soon, or if, *Dio non voglia, God forbid*, we don't find Teddy. My heart breaks alongside hers every second I have to see the pain she's living in. It's the reason I am here, back at the helm of our syndicate. The best thing I can do is to find Teddy and get our revenge. I need to be a better leader and show our enemies we are a force to be reckoned with. They may have slid in and infiltrated our ranks once but not twice. Over my dead body will I let this go without brutal and justified retribution. We will retaliate and get Teddy back. I just need to find out where they are holding Teddy and what exactly went down with Cole and Ronan. The latter is trickier, only two people know what actually happened outside of that warehouse, one is Cole who is still unconscious and I fear will never wake up and the other is Ronan. The thought of losing Cole is something I try not to dwell on, I can't go down that way of thinking. It won't do anybody any good and I'm not sure the grief I would feel would be easily contained. I fear I would eventually succumb to the darkness that seeps through my body and become the very monster my father created.

Pushing the thoughts out of my mind I look down to my watch. Lincoln and Felix left two hours ago, following some leads on Ronan's men. Since the showdown, they have been working tirelessly to track down anyone associated with Ronan, Felix the tech savvy go to who has been hot on pinning locations down for Ronans known associates, and Linc who has become even more of an unwavering force of brutality than he ever was before. Unfortunately, through all of their efforts, Ronan and his men have seemingly gone underground like the rats they are. Hiding deep in the sewers, only coming up to feast on the vulnerable.

My phone vibrates in my pocket, startling me from my thoughts. Pulling the device into the palm of my hand, I look at the screen, frowning as I see the caller ID. This is a surprise. A welcomed one I must add. I answer without any hesitation.

"Nicholas, brother. How are you?" I greet.

"Silas, I'm good, thank you. Your lawyer, Miss Lewis, has worked her magic." Nicholas says. His voice is

15

hopeful. I don't think I've ever heard him sound that way, I can almost hear the smile as he speaks.

"You're welcome, old friend. I told you I'd sort it. When do you get out?" I ask, even though I already know the answer after having my own update on Nicholas's release paperwork from Miss Lewis this morning. I want to hear him say the news. He is a good man, he deserved every bit of good news he can get. I'm just glad I could bring this day forward for him as someone I know I can trust. Afterall, I don't have many of those in this city.

"One week. They have some paperwork to do but that's the date they have my release set for."

"And what do you plan to do once you are out, Fratello?" I ask, hoping he'll agree to take up my offer of work I laid out for him while we were sharing a cell together in the state jail. We spoke about his future many times but he was not one to look too far beyond his time in jail. He used to tell me he didn't like to dwell on what may never be. I guess I know that feeling now. I can't see past today for fear of what will never be.

"I need to find my sister, but then if your offer still stands, I owe you and I think I could be of use to your team," he says.

"You know Nicholas, I would love nothing more. Get your family sorted, a job will be waiting when you're ready." I assure him.

"Thanks, Si. I gotta go, my time's up. Speak soon." He hangs up before I have a chance to say more. He'll be a valued member of the club on his release. Returning my phone back to my pocket, I allow myself a rare smile and continue to check over the club's accounts. These numbers won't shift themselves.

I've spent the last couple of hours scrolling through spreadsheets, ensuring all the numbers are adding up and checking stock is accounted for when I'm interrupted by a knock at the door, completely caught off guard by the amount of time that's passed by without me realizing. Frowning, rubbing my fingers into my eyes, I grunt for whomever it is to come in.

Felix stands at the door, I raise my eyebrows at him in question.

"Boss, we have someone downstairs who might have some answers for us. Lincoln is starting the interrogation. He sent me to come and get you," he explains.

I nod slowly, pursing my lips as I urge away the headache blossoming behind my eyes. "I'll be down in a moment, Felix. Man the security while we are indisposed. I want to ensure the prisoner has our full attention."

Felix nods, "Yes, Boss," before leaving the room.

I remove my suit jacket and place it on the back of my chair, before rolling up my white shirt sleeves, exposing the extensive designs of tattoos that mark their way up my arms. I don't want to get my designer suit soiled with blood, it's a bitch to get out. Making my way down to the basement to join Lincoln, I can't ignore the tense feeling working its way through my body. I need answers and this might be our only chance to find them. I can feel the red mist descending on me even before entering the room, and I can almost smell the blood before I've spilt it. I hope this individual knows what they've let themselves in for.

Turning the brass handle, I open the door to find Lincoln looming over our guest with his back to me, not failing to notice the way his fists clench at his sides with

17

blood dripping from the knuckles. A feral grin spreads across my face as I watch Linc continue to pummel his fists into the wailing man, undisturbed by my arrival until he spins around, having knocked the man unconscious as we exchange a knowing look. "What's his name?" I ask

"Seamus" Linc spits, lifting his chin towards the body slumping across the floor.

It doesn't take long for Seamus to cough himself back to consciousness and I take up the space Lincoln held before, kneeling to eye level with his semi-conscious body. Now my fun begins. I lose myself immediately to the darkness, the monster our enemies all fear has come out to play. Before I know what is happening, I have our guest by the throat, slamming him into the wall. All of my anger and hatred is surfacing, and I can't stop what happens next. Blood smears the walls, my knuckles are split open and hands covered in thick crimson red liquid. I am barely aware of my surroundings as I look down at the man in front of me. I inflict another blow to my victim's jaw, making it crack on impact. Normally I would feel the satisfaction from the sound but not today, not for the past 72 hours. Not since Teddy was taken. Not since my brother was left for dead by those bastards. I flinch as I feel a hand touch my shoulder. It's as though I'm in a fog and I can't see clearly. I swing my fist only to be blocked.

"Brother, snap out of it. We need him to be able to answer us. Any more hits to his jaw and he won't be able to talk," Lincoln grunt, his voice clearing the fog ever so slightly.

Realizing my surroundings and the person in front of me, I bring myself back into reality shaking his hold from my wrist.

"Sorry, I fell down the rabbit hole again," I chuckle, shaking my head.

Lincoln smirks at me, "And who am I? The fucking Mad Hatter in your Alice in Wonderland? I always thought it was Cole that was the one who needed to be pulled out of the darkness. I guess crazy just runs in your blood."

I can't help but smirk at that comment. I guess we are both a little crazy. Linc leans down where he grabs our prisoners' chin, inspecting the damage. "I have to say Silas, you have really fucked his face up, but it's almost an improvement," Lincoln jokes. Moving towards the side bench he grabs a glass of water and throws it over the Irish fuck, jolting him awake with a groan as his eyes flicker open. I'm surprised he's still alive if I'm honest.

"Wakey, wakey, rise and shine motherfucker," Linc sings. Blood is trickling down the side of Seamus' face. His eyes are swollen and the bruising is already starting to show. I'd be surprised if he can even see us with how badly I've fucked his face up, but at least he can hear us.

"Seamus, it seems you are on the wrong side of things. Unfortunately, I can't guarantee you'll get to leave this room walking but I can give you a quick send off to the next life if you give us the information we need," I say calmly.

"I'm going to hell anyway, doesn't matter the route or speed I travel, so do your worst you Italian cunts," he laughs, spitting a mouthful of blood at us. Before I have a chance to respond or maybe overreact, Linc has pulled a taser from the workbench and zapped the bastard making his body spasm against the cement floor as his teeth grind together and a slow stream of piss spreads its way across the front of his pants.

"Now I don't know about you, but I can keep this up for a long long time, so how about you tell us where they are keeping the boy? Or do I need to resort to paying in kind?" Linc snarls, leaning down to Seamus's face.

Blood and sweat drips from his face as he shows his teeth with a grin. "Pay in kind? I have nothing that you can take to bargain with you fucking idiots. I am loyal to the cause!" Lincoln only laughs as he fishes out a picture from his trouser pocket holding it in front of the Irish bastard's face.

"Do you know this girl? It would be a shame if she got caught up in your mess wouldn't it, Seamus my boy." Lincoln taunts, waving the picture closer to his face. And that right there is everything we wanted. Seamus' face pales and his eyes grow wide as he studies the photo carefully.

"Fuck you! That's my sister. If you hurt a single hair on her head you'll be fucking sorry!" Seamus roars and attempts to scramble to his feet. I would say I'm shocked at Lincoln's strategy to make him give us the information but when the stakes are this high, nothing is off limits. The piece of shit in front of us doesn't know we would never hurt a child.

"Let's see her face, Brother. If she's pretty enough maybe we can auction her off to the highest bidder. If not, at least we can hope she's a virgin. It will bring us a bigger profit if her cunt is still tight and unused." I join in, trying to get a bigger rise out of him.

Seamus glares at us, he's taken the bait beautifully. "Look, just don't touch her please, she's innocent! I can't tell you what I don't know!" He begs, his tears mixing with the blood on his face as he begins to sob uncontrollably.

His choice of words trigger me and I see the curtain of red close down across my vision, taking a step forward. "She's innocent!? Like the boy your boss has taken from his mother!? Tell us what we want to know and she'll stay safe from us. You have my word and you know I don't give that freely." I growl, thrusting his head back to look me in the eye.

"I don't know! All I know is he is not in the city, please!" he chokes. I'm about to pull the gun from my back holster and blow the cunts' brains out for being such a fucking inconvenience when the vibrations of my phone once again catches me off guard. Reaching into my pocket I glance at the screen. Fuck, it's the hospital.

Without a second thought I answer. "What is it?" I bark into the reciever. I gave my number to the doctor overseeing Lucille and Cole's care and told him to call me if anything happened to either one of them while Lincoln and I were away. After threatening to slit his throat he seemed more than willing to do as I asked so he had been filling us in on their recoveries while we have been out trying to locate Teddy. In the beginning I hated the way she looked at me with such hope in her eyes when I had to snuff it out everytime I came back to her with no answers. It fucking broke me. Now I wish for that glimmer of hope because she is a broken shell of the woman I love, I can only hope that finding Teddy will restore her light.

"Yes sir, everything is fine."

"Then why the fuck are you interrupting me, Gerrard? I'm fucking busy here!" I seethe, rubbing my thumb and forefinger into my eyes to relieve the tension that's building.

"It's your brother, sir, he is awake."

I snap my eyes open. "We'll be there as soon as possible, don't let him leave. Where is Miss Holland?" I ask, spinning around to face Linc who's watching me carefully.

"She's still by his bedside, sir," he replies calmly.

"Okay, good. Keep them there." I instruct before ending the call and turning back to the Irish scum with a new sense of excitement coursing through my body. "He's fucking alive!" I exclaim, silently thanking the gods that the mad fucker pulled through. "Looks like it's yours and your sister's lucky day. Goodbye, stronzo."

As soon as the words leave my mouth Lincoln has locked, loaded and squeezed the trigger. Blood paints the walls along with chunks of his skull and flesh, leaving a unique piece of art splattered against the entire room, it's fucking beautiful. I nod to Linc who holsters his gun. "Let's get to the hospital, I'll call for a clean up on the way. Cole has a lot of explaining to do."

Chapter 3

Cole

A low pitched beeping arouses my senses, pulling me from the depths of sleep. My eyelids flicker open as I take in my surroundings, the bright white walls of the sterile room piercing painfully through my skull. It's almost too bright for me to fully open my eyes,instantly forcing me to close them again. That's when I feel her. Her small steady breaths are warm against my neck, she's asleep, that much I'm sure of, clinging onto me while I lay in an unfamiliar bed. I think back for a moment, racking my brain to how I ended up here. My head is buzzing, tingling almost as I try to force myself to remember. Reality hits me like a freight train. A montage of images flash in my mind, Vinny, the warehouse, Ronan, Teddy, it all comes barreling back at an overpowering speed. I remember the intense pain, Teddy shouting at me to help him, the blood, Lucille's screams and then nothing. My eyes fly open. This is a hospital bed, I'm in a fucking hospital. I can feel my heart palpitating rapidly in my chest, as if it's threatening to crack through my ribcage.

Raising my arm on the opposite side to Lucille, I remove the oxygen mask from my face, allowing me to fully breathe in the distinctly harsh smell of antiseptic that's mixed with that horrible artificial fragrance contained in soaps and cleaner. My inhale hurts more than I imagined as the sterile air seems to burn down through to my chest making me wince. The sudden movement has Lucille stirring beside me and I instantly freeze. I want nothing more than to stay in this moment with her tucked at my side, feeling her petite body against mine, concentrating on the way her breath fans gently across my skin as she sleeps. She has no idea how much I need her at the moment but the memories and images of how I ended up here are filtering through my mind once more and they're too graphic to ignore. Teddy. I need to know they got to him in time.

Carefully shifting myself out of Lucille's embrace, I look at the tubes connecting me to several different machines that I am sure have kept me alive until now and as I take one last lingering glance over at my beautiful little mouse, burying the sight of her peacefully sleeping body deep into my core, I suck in a deep breath and begin to rip the wires from my body, setting off multiple alarms and ripping the skin open from my cannulas, causing blood to seep into the crisp white bed sheets. My movement alone would have woken Lucille but the alarming sound of the vital signs monitor blaring out its alert has her sat bolt upright, wide eyed and gaping at me as she takes in the bloodied scene. Her widened eyes snap to mine and it takes every bit of strength I have to look away from her.

"COLE! You're awake!" she exclaims standing up from the bed, allowing me to move away from her. I frown, noticing from the corner of my vision the way her body sways slightly at her sudden movement, but I have to ignore it. I'm not ready to speak with her just yet. I have failed her and her son, what the fuck am I meant to say to make that any better? I can feel her eyes burning into me, following my actions as I continue removing the mass amount of cannulas and monitoring pads from my body, the blood continuing to ooze from each one that I rip out of my skin. Welcoming the brief stabs of pain momentarily easing the anger that's building inside me. "Cole, stop! What are you doing? You'll hurt yourself!" Lucille pleads. Her voice rapidly becomes louder as she panics at my actions. But I continue to ignore her. "Please Cole, stop!" She screams at me.

At the very moment she moves towards me with what I know is an attempt to physically touch me, to deter me from my goal, the door swings open and a nurse comes rushing into the room, flapping her arms around hysterically. "Mr.Salvatore you are awake, I wondered what all this commotion was about," she chirps in an annoyingly high pitched tone "Oh goodness, you have made a mess of yourself haven't you" she tuts, shaking her head as she switches off the alarms.

I glare at her, grinding my teeth together to bite back my retort. The nurse, who's name badge says Rita, looks to be in her late forties, with dark hair that's fastened into a tight bun and brown eyes that remind me of rich soil raises her perfectly shaped eyebrows at me as I pull out the last of my infusion lines, her gaze drifting to the blood trailing it's way down arms.

"Get my brothers, Silas Salvatore and Lincoln Rossi here now or I'll be discharging myself without a single fuck about who tries to stop me." I snarl.

To my surprise Rita gives me an 'I take no shit' look before popping out her hip and pointing her finger towards me. "Keep your voice down, other patients are resting and quite frankly, I don't care for you causing trouble by pulling out your infusion lines and making your demands. I'll speak with your doctor about contacting your brothers, then I'll be back to check your observations and patch up the damage you've caused. Oh and Mr Salvatore…before you attempt to remove the catheter by yourself, I recommend letting a member of staff do that one. I suggest you take a moment to collect yourself. This is a hospital, not a bar." She turns on her heel and leaves the room without waiting for a reply. I was not expecting that, It appears Rita knows how to hold herself. I look under the sheet and sure enough, there's a tube in my cock! Fuck!

Lucille looks at me, her eyes pleading with mine as I finally give in and land my gaze in her direction. I can see the tears there threatening to spill. I know she's waiting for me to speak to her, but I can't. I can't find the words to make this better. I close my eyes, shame making me turn away from her, only opening them to look out at the night sky through the window. I need to wait to speak with my brothers. I cannot face her until I have atoned for my failures.

"Cole please, I need you. I need you to tell me what happened." She begs from her space behind me, not daring to reach out to touch me again. She sounds distressed, broken even, I can hear it in the cracks of her voice, and each word she chokes out sends a crack straight through my heart. I let them take her son. The truth is I don't deserve her or the happiness she brings me if I can't protect the people I love, and I didn't, I let them all down, it's all on me. She's better off without a fucking failure like me in her life. I grit my teeth as I catch her reflection in the dark of the window as she shifts towards the bed, pleading for me to speak with her. Luckily just as she makes her way round beside me nurse Rita saves the day again and enters to do my observations. I watch Lucille break a little more as she silently turns away from us to let Rita do her job.

What feels like hours later, Rita finally finishes checking over my vitals, which she lets me know repeatedly that she is not happy with, but I don't give a shit so I stay quiet while she writes down her notes. She patches me up in several places where I've ripped the skin while removing my IV lines, removes the catheter and checks the bandages still covering my gunshot wounds before leaving me alone with Lucille again, informing me before she leaves the room that the doctor will be with me shortly to give me a debrief on my surgery. The words leave me a little dazed as she says them, though I quickly come to the realization that I probably wouldn't have survived had I not needed some sort of surgical intervention.

As the door closes, the deafening silence screams between Lucille and I but I don't give her the chance to speak first, I need to know if they managed to get Teddy in time before I passed out. "Where is Teddy?" I ask, locking my eyes onto hers. I stand from the bed in a gingerly manner, the pain coursing through my body thrums, screaming in protest at the adjustments but I shove it aside as I watch Lucille's eyes immediately begin to water. Her breaths become shallow and her lip quivers as she tries to stop herself from falling apart. Her body language is telling me the answers I need to know but I have to hear the words to confirm my fears, I have to hear her say it. I want to push her to answer, but the door barges open with my brothers charging their way into the room, locking their eyes on me with what I can only assume is a mixture of anger and relief. Linc immediately engulfs Lucille into a tight embrace as she begins to sob silently against his chest and the sight of it makes my blood boil. Not in jealousy, but in anger. Anger at myself and what I have done and the pain I have caused her. I have to look away from them. Silas turns to face me, fully taking in the patchwork of bandages covering my body before shaking his head, grinning a wide mouthed toothy grin full of relief and pure fucking joy before pulling me into a tight hug.

"Brother, you're a lucky bastard. You had us all scared for a moment. You lost so much blood we thought for sure you were a goner." I shake my head ignoring his comments as I push him off me, trying not to get caught up in the moment. I need my answers.

"Did you save Teddy? Did you get to him in time?" I ask sharply, taking a step back. Silas glances over at Linc who is still holding Lucille as she snuffles quietly into his jacket.

Taking a deep breath he looks back at me. "No, the car took off the moment your body hit the ground. We're doing everything we can to locate him." Anger consumes me. I have already failed Lucille and Teddy, and not only that, I've been unconscious for God knows how long and my brothers still haven't found him. What the fuck have they been doing!? How could they let Ronan get away? And why the fuck are they here with me right now and not out there searching for him!?

"Have you been seen by the doctor? Are you fit to leave? We will find him Brother, we are doing everything, combing through everyone." Silas continues. But the all consuming rage and fear inside me is like a tornado swirling uncontrollably and I can feel the eruption bubbling beneath my skin before it even happens.

"What do you mean you haven't found him?! How long have I been out?" I snap, taking a step towards Silas.

"A little over three days. We've been searching but the Irish are good at hiding their tracks. As soon as you

28

have been discharged, we can start from the beginning, go over everything we know, pull contacts and pull rank with whatever Information you can give us." Silas says, trying to reassure me. Little does he know, it does everything but that. I snap my eyes to Linc, immediately being hit with the memory of Ronan admitting to the murder of his mother. Fuck. I can't divulge that. Not here and not in front of Lucille. I swallow down the hatred rising in me. Closing my eyes and taking a steadying breath, silently apologizing to my friend for keeping this from him. I know at this moment what I must do and I know they might never forgive me for it. But forgiveness isn't something I'm searching for, redemption is the only thing I crave and that's what I'll find.

I glance over to Lucille and tut loud enough so she snaps her head up to look at me. "Have you just been playing house while he's out there in the hands of the enemy?" I smirk.

"How dare you!" She shouts, pushing aside her hurt for anger. "I have been by your side for the last forty-eight hours, praying for you to wake up to help me find my son! What is wrong with you Cole!?" she exclaims, stepping out of Lincs hold. I detest the way she's looking at me right now but this is what I need. I need her to be angry at me. To hate me the way that she should.

I laugh, "I bet you've just been letting them get between your legs. Otherwise he'd be home by now." I taunt motioning to my brother and Linc, the accusation thick on my tongue, tasting sour as I say it. Her face falls slightly but before Lucille is able to respond, a heavy force cracks into my jaw, catching me off guard, making me stumble back into the wall. I laugh as I steady myself, running my hand across the throbbing pain in my face, trying to ignore the pain radiating through my body. Here we go.

"Don't you dare fucking speak to her like that. You may be my brother but I won't hesitate to put you in your place. You will not disrespect Lucille like that," he roars at me, nostrils flaring and eyes narrowing. I can't help but stifle a laugh at the thought of feisty nurse Rita not being happy with all the commotion he's now causing. "If it wasn't for the fact that you've already taken multiple bullets I'd put one in you my fucking self." Silas snarls, causing Lucille to let out a broken cry as she clutches onto Lincoln to keep herself upright. His stare is piercing a hole into my head. He's fucking pissed at me, I've seen that look too many times, but he remains in control of his emotions, probably for Lucille's sake. Internally I'm glad that at least one of us is staying focused and not letting his emotions rule his actions.

"Why are you being so cruel, Cole? Being by your side while you were fighting for your life is the only thing that kept me from falling apart. Silas and Lincoln have been trying to find him. We have to stick together otherwise I'm not sure I'll survive this, I am his mother. How dare you say I have been for one moment thinking of anything but my boy!" she croaks, and as I take a proper look at her, I see the worry etched deep into her face. Her frame is thinner than it was just days before and her eyes are rimmed with deep circles of exhaustion.

"Cruel? Maybe I'm showing you my true self. Did you think of that? Come on Luci, don't be so naive to think that I ever wanted anything more than your tight snatch. Just ask my brothers here, no woman has ever kept my attention for longer than a week, so why would you be any different?" I taunt her. I have never hated myself so much for the lies I'm spewing, it's almost making me want to vomit as I speak to see how much my words hurt her, but it needs to happen. She needs to hate me. "Plus, you have these two lap dogs to entertain you, you don't need me." I add, gesturing towards Linc and Silas once more. "Now if you'll excuse me, I need to get out of this place, I'm feeling a little blood thirsty and I think my brothers would hate for you to see what it is I really crave." I say with a smirk.

Lucille shakes her head, no longer trying to hold back the tears that stream down her face. "Well more fool me for loving you. Why don't you get some rest, maybe that's what you need. Then you'll see clearly." *Fuck, I love you too, Lucille.* I know she's trying to rationalize my abrupt turn in personality but that's not going to work. This is me, I'm dark, twisted and unlovable. I'm a murderer, I'm not good for her.

"Don't worry little mouse, I'm sure you have enough cock to satisfy you without adding mine into the equation." I smile at her, despising the fictitious statements I'm sprouting.

"You fucking son of a bitch." Linc growls deeply as both him and Silas move towards me in unison, no doubt to put me in my place at that last remark. I smirk at them, throwing my arms out to welcome whatever it is they have to give. Pain is my pleasure, and I welcome their violence. But Lucille stops them short. "No. If that is how he feels, let him go. He'll come back to us. He won't leave us to find Teddy without him." Even now she's trying to see the good in me, to paint me to be a saint when all I do is sin. It's no use, there's no saving me now.

"Well boys, I'll leave you to it." I walk past the three of them towards the open door before I hesitate at the final blow I'm about to deliver. "I hope you find your boy, dead or alive." I add looking Lucille dead in the eyes, silently

31

begging for her to forgive me for this, before I leave them all behind me.

I've just ensured she will never be mine again, the nail in the coffin so to speak. She'll never forgive me for what I just said, and so help me God, I pray that she never does because that woman will bring me to my knees. I hear a gut wrenching wail from Lucille as I stand on the outside of the room, fighting against everything in me that's telling me to go back and hold her, comfort her and tell her I'm sorry. But I close my eyes and push forward, without bothering to discharge myself. As I exit the hospital, I make my way to the only place that I can exercise my demons. I'm already going to hell, so why not go dance with the devil?

Chapter 4

Silas

I can't deny that watching my brother storm out of the hospital room like a raging tornado, destroying anything in its path, has me worried, because what I feel right now is way beyond that. I hear a high pitched shriek a little further down the corridor where Enzo just departed and a loud crash of what I can only assume is some sort of equipment a few minutes later. I know I'll have to make amends and pay for the damages. I won't have his pride tarnish my name. I know my brother, he doesn't give up on those that he loves but he also doesn't believe himself worthy of receiving love, and now I'm standing in the wreckage that he's left behind, torn between chasing after him and smacking the ever-living shit out of him for the way he just spoke to Lucille, bullet wounds or not, and never leaving her side again. Her broken cries are what make the decision for me, and I subconsciously move forwards to encompass her against my chest as she completely comes apart between Linc and I. We lock eyes, with our arms wrapped tight around Lucille's body, and an affirmative decision is passed silently between us. We agree that Cole won't get away with the hurt he's caused her.

This anger I'm feeling right now, towards my own flesh and blood isn't something new, though my baby brother has never been the target of that anger before. I've always been so protective of him, tried my hardest to keep him away from the depth of darkness our father possessed, and especially after the incident. It's instinct for me to want to chase him but I know It's not what he needs right now, and from the minute he walked out of that door, he is no longer my priority. Hearing Lucille's gut wrenching cries between us only fuels that anger inside of me, but she is my main concern now and I focus on doing everything I can to remain calm, reminding myself to take deep breaths, to stay focused and control my emotions. For her. I nod to Linc as his eyes cast over mine once more, noticing that he too is battling with his own urges and trying not to let his guard slip. He may be able to keep it up in front of her, but I know he too is as fucked off as I am at the shit that just went down, I can see it burning in the darkness of his eyes. But we won't confess it here, not now, not in front of la mia luce. I lock my jaw, the sheer pressure of tension flowing through my body is sure to crack my teeth if I'm not careful.

 I slowly move myself in front of Lucille and bring my hands up under her chin, lifting her deep emerald gaze to mine, her swollen, tear stained face ripping at my heart already seizing in my chest. I swipe my thumbs across the tears streaking her porcelain cheeks and gently place a kiss onto her reddened lips. The pain through her once bright eyes bores deep into my soul as I pull back to take in her reaction and I swear, for just a second, that it was me who was shot, not my brother, as her broken spirit dares to split me in two. I blink back at the intrusional thoughts, and think carefully about my next words. Where do I even begin to try and explain my brother's actions? She'll never understand, hell I will never understand, I was never in that basement. I never experienced the shit he was subjected to, I could barely fucking look at him for fear

34

of what I might do when the anger inside of me erupted. When we found him, I was so angry at what they'd done to him, but more so at myself for not finding him sooner, I have never fully forgiven myself. It fucked him up and he's never been the same since. I swallow deeply, shoving down the memories as far as they'll go, and hope that what I'm about to say, goes some way to soothing the damage Cole has done.

"My brother has never been very good at accepting love, la mia luce. He believes he has failed you, so in his eyes, he's no longer worthy of you. I'm sorry for the pain he caused you, and you have my word that it will not go unpunished. No man, even my blood, will ever speak to you the way that he just has without reprisal. Now come on, we have a lot to do to find Teddy."

Lucille's whisper of a gasp doesn't go unnoticed as she pulls her bottom lip between her teeth to try and stifle her cries, her heart breaking all over again at the mention of her son. The first few days are always the most crucial when someone is kidnapped, and we've already lost too much time. We need to hurry up and find him before we miss our chance completely.

Focusing my gaze on Lincoln, who has stayed stoic through most of this whole ordeal I clear my throat. "Lucille needs to head home for some rest, then we can make a plan to track down Ronan. He holds the answers now."

Linc presses his lips together into a thin line then nods with a simple, "After you, Brother," at my instruction. I nod again, reassuring myself that this is at least somewhere to start.

We need to get out of here. I need to get an update from the guys I've had tracking Ronan, and Lucille needs to finally get out of this place. If I have anything to do with it, she will never get close enough to stepping foot inside a hospital ever again, not even to go back to her job.

I lean forward, fully pulling Lucille from the hold Linc still has around her waist, noticing the reluctance in the hard lines of his face as he hands her over to me before I effortlessly scoop her up into my arms and walk towards the door.

Lucille slaps my chest as I begin to move. "Silas put me down, a few nasty words spat at me by your brother because he's too damn stubborn to pull his head out of his ass and see the whole picture won't break me, I can walk by myself." The frown on her face as she snarls at me is cute, and I can't help but think Cole is wrong. She's not a little mouse, she is a kitten with sharp claws and if he's not careful, he'll be on the receiving end of those. I make no effort to do as she's asked, I only tighten my hold and enjoy the feel of her body against my own as she wriggles to get free. I'm three times the size of her, she has no chance of escaping my hold but I do enjoy her feeble attempts. The commotion inside Cole's hospital room has the corridor of nursing staff glaring at us as we leave the hospital. The way they whisper to each other behind raised hands is not lost on me or Lucille as she finally settles further into my chest, trying to hide her face. I make a mental note to make sure everybody on this floor gets fired for being so fucking nosey and unprofessional and making my woman feel so damn uncomfortable. Lincoln is following directly behind us as we exit the building and I have to fight back my chuckle at the sound of his slurry of insults aimed towards them all as we leave.

As soon as the humid night air hits us outside, I look down at Lucille who has all the rage of a little puppy burning through her eyes once again at the fact I refused to do as she asked and let her walk on her own. I can't help but smile.

"Have you finished fighting me yet, la mia luce?" I tease as I gently lower her feet down to the ground. Her face is flushed red and I can practically see the steam coming from her ears as Lincoln lets out a low whistle behind and chuckles.

"I think our little love isn't happy with you, Fratello. I'd be careful if I were you, she's a feisty one. I'm going to bring the car around." He turns to Lucille with a smirk on his face. "Try not to lay into him too much, it'll only make him spank you harder later, Love." He winks at her before pulling the keys from his pocket and strolling over to collect the car.

Her cheeks instantly fill with heat that blossoms its way down her neck as she turns towards me, pointing her fingers into my chest and pushing me as she accentuates each of her words. "You. Silas Salvatore. Are such an ASSHOLE!" Linc is right, she will be in for a spanking if she carries on speaking to me like that, as amusing as it is. My cock twitches just at the thought of her thick creamy thighs spread over my lap as I spank her voluptuous ass while it turns the perfect shade of pink under my palm. I swear I'm almost drooling before a sharp slap brings me straight back to the present with her eyes burning into me even more furious than before. I bring my hand to my cheek that is no doubt red from her palm and I grin at her, a foolish, love sickening grin.

"You got all that anger out? I'm not the one that you're really angry at, but I can take your rage if that's what you need from me. I will be whatever you need, because I love you, my light. But that goes both ways, I need to feel

37

your warmth against my body, so that the darkness can not take over and consume me."

I watch as the anger she possessed moments ago ebbs away her eyes begin to glisten with fresh tears that threaten to spill as she brings her hands to my face and places them gently against my skin. "I'm sorry, Silas. You're right, I'm not angry at you. I just can't believe he left. I didn't expect him to react like that after everything. And Teddy, I'm so scared Silas. What if we can't find him?" Her voice breaks on her final question at the harsh reality of it and there's little she can do but give in to her tears once again as they begin to stream down her beautiful face, leaving watery lines in their wake. Pulling my face closer to hers she kisses me with a wild need, I want nothing more than to pick her up and fuck her for all to see who she belongs to but I know that is not what she needs right now. Lucille breaks the kiss as quickly as she started it and smiles at me, "Oh and by the way, I love you too, Silas. But you're still an asshole, you're just my ass hole."

I laugh, "I wouldn't have it any other way baby girl." She turns on her heels and heads over to the car where Linc has been watching our embrace, waiting silently for our moment to be over. He opens the door for her to slide in and before dipping her head she reaches up to plant a gentle kiss on his cheek, thanking him for being so gentlemanly.

He has a big shit eating grin on his face as she disappears into the backseat of the car. "I think I'm her favorite, you know," he says. I chuckle to myself before I slap him playfully up the side of the head and follow Lucille into the back of the car like the love sick puppy I guess I am. Lucille's gaze turns to the window, where she watches the world go by as Lincoln rolls the car out of the parking lot.

The journey home seems to pass by quickly with all three of us no doubt lost in our own thoughts about our current situation and staying silent for the entire ride, only chancing quick glances in each other's directions as if to check we were still there. Lucille's hand is placed in mine, and while I absentmindedly stroke my thumb over her knuckles, I notice how she gives it a squeeze every so often and so I return each one back, hating myself for it being the only little bit of comfort I can give to her in this moment while she's undoubtedly torturing herself with thoughts of Teddy.

By the time we arrive home, Lucille seems to realize that when I said home, I didn't mean hers and as Linc directs the car up to the entryway of our drive her spine straightens immediately. "I need to get some fresh clothes at my place," she announces, still staring straight out of her car door window. She hasn't been back home since Teddy was taken, with most of her time being spent unconscious or by Cole's side in the hospital and It's something myself and Lincoln had planned to avoid for as long as possible.

"I'll send Dario to fetch some things for you if you make a list, or you can take my card and buy a whole new wardrobe for you to keep here." I offer, hoping she doesn't want to go back home away from us so soon. I would hate for her to leave under normal circumstances but right now, I know for a fact that if she was to return home, this nightmare would become all too real for her and she would not be able to cope.

"I want to be able to get my own belongings, Silas. Stop trying to suffocate me, I've stayed away long enough

39

being in that hospital. I will need to face it soon enough," she snaps at me, ripping her hand from my grasp.

Closing my eyes and taking a deep steadying breath. I realize this isn't going to go the way I'd hoped and I'm in for another fight.

"Lucille, I'm trying to protect you. How about you have a shower or a soak in the bath? You can borrow some of mine or Linc's clothes and we'll arrange for you to go back once we know it's safe." I try to persuade her, keeping my tone lighter than I usually would but already knowing I'm on the losing end with the exasperated look in her eyes. If I didn't want my way so much I'd be damn proud of her for standing up to me and showing me she truly is my rightful queen.

"Silas, whether you like it or not, I'm going home today. I need some space to think, to breathe. I need to be around things that remind me of him. I'm lost without him but I'm not afraid of facing this. You can't keep me here against my will!" she shouts at me. Fuck it, the way she tried to defy me was cute at first but I've had enough now, what little patience I did have has quickly been diminished. She needs to understand that my rules are the only rules and she's not going anywhere, especially not in her current emotional state.

I look to Linc before I move, the car now stationary in front of the house, and he knows exactly what I'm about to do before I even do. "Si, don't do it. It's not going to end well for you," he says, trying to persuade me.
Lucille looks between us, confused at what's being left unsaid and without a second thought I grab her and haul her over my shoulder, lifting her out of the car and racing into the house in the direction of my bedroom before she has a chance to object. Her wild protest begins as soon as we reach the front door and she starts smacking me and

kicking out with her legs, fighting me with every step I take towards the bedroom door. Her screams are piercing as she beats against my back but I keep my hold tight around the back of her thighs as I chuckle to myself and slap my hand hard across her ass.

"Silas. Put me down you asshole! You can't decide what I do," she yells as I walk through the door to my room.

"If you are not going to listen to reason and you continue to want to put yourself in danger, then you will stay in this room until myself or Lincoln can talk some sense into you!" I throw her onto the bed and quickly make my way back out of the room while she scrambles to get up. I shut the door behind me as she jumps from the bed and swiftly turn the key into place which earns me a lengthy slur of obscene profanity as she bangs against the wood from the other side. She has everything she needs there with the ensuite and fully stocked mini fridge with food and drinks so I don't feel even the slightest bit guilty about leaving her there. The windows are locked and shatterproof if she were to try to escape again. The only exit is through this locked door, and I won't even entertain that thought until she's calmed down and willing to cooperate. Leaning my back against the door that separates us, I close my eyes and take a deep breath. "I'm sorry, Lucille. We can talk once you are ready, but I almost lost you once, I'm not taking any chances this time."

"I won't forgive you for this, Silas. You can't keep me in here forever," she yells. I slide myself down the door resting on my heels as I listen to her throw the furniture against the door for almost an hour. I wait patiently until the room has fallen quiet and she has no doubt tired herself out. I pull out my phone and bring up the live feed on the security app linked to the camera's we have installed in every room in the house. They're discrete, so unless you knew what you were looking for you wouldn't even know they were there. Only myself, Linc and Cole have access to them and they're very rarely used considering we don't bring many people back here. We much prefer to keep the work that we do as far away from our home as possible. I watch intently as Lucille surrenders herself to her exhaustion and collapses on my bed, surrounded by the destruction she has made of my bedroom. I'm definitely going to need to order a new floor lamp by the look of it, and a new chair. I can tell that she's crying from the way her shoulders shudder against the bed sheets as she buries herself face down into the comforter and I want nothing more than to open this door and hold her, but I know that is the last thing she wants or needs from me right now so I refrain. I continue to watch until she's fast asleep, reluctantly moving myself from the door and making my way downstairs to find Linc.

It doesn't take me long to find Linc, sitting in his personal office. The room is in darkness but his frame is lit up from the monitor lights. His eyes are focused on the multiple screens displayed before him as he types frantically onto the keyboard. I walk in, trying not to disturb him too much. I know when he's in the zone he hates for it to be broken so I flop down onto the leather couch and roll the tension out of my shoulders. His head snaps towards me with a disapproving look etched into his frown lines. "Was that really necessary, Si? She doesn't need to be locked up for fuck sake."

"Maybe not but somebody has to be the villain in all of this and if she wants to continue to act like an irresponsible brat that's exactly what I'll be. Until we know it's safe for her to go back there, she's staying right where I can keep an eye on her. I can't focus on finding Teddy and worry about her safety at the same time." I seethe, exasperated at the thought of Lucille alone on my bed, crying over her missing son. Her son that we still haven't fucking found! I run my hand through my hair and rip it at the roots trying to distract myself from the spiral I'm sure to fall into. I know she will need to go back eventually, but right now isn't an option.

"Cole is already trying to fill the role of villian with that bullshit he pulled back at the hospital, she doesn't need both Salvatore brothers being dickheads to her," he says, trying to be the voice of reason, as always. I know he would have dealt with it differently, but what more can I do with the disobedient flight risk.

"I'm not locking her up forever, she can go back to her place, just not tonight. We need to strategize and plan without impulsive decisions that could get one of us killed. It's already been too long, we need to find him."

I'm not trying to justify my decision because I know I'm right but saying it outloud does make me feel slightly better about the situation. Lucille would be a distraction and we can't afford to have that while we focus on finding Teddy. Linc shakes his head and I know he agrees with what I've done just not how I've implemented it.

"I know that, Fratello. You always try to do what's best. I just don't think she really needed to be carted off and shut away like that. I agree with you it's not safe for her to be roaming around. But she just woke up, her son is still missing and your fuckhead of a brother just completely shattered what was left of her." I sigh at his reasoning, because of course he would see it from her side too and try to defend her wanting to go back home.

"Why do you always have to play the fucking knight in shining armour?" I shake my head and chuckle, rubbing my hands across my face. "I tell you what, you can rescue the princess from her tower but only when I allow it." I joke, earning a smirk from him in return.

"I take it you have the cameras turned on to keep an eye on her?" He asks while glancing back to his monitor and swiping away the hair that's fallen into his eyes.

"Like you haven't already looked in on her yourself. She's exhausted herself from destroying my room. I doubt she'll wake up for a good few hours now. Her body needs the rest." I say, shaking my head. He would have logged in to check on her soon as we left him. Bastard is just as obsessed about her safety as I am, he just isn't as vocal about it.

Linc grunts without looking my way. "Right, well, back to this mess. While you were going caveman on our girl, I combed through the CCTV around Max's apartment, trying to piece together anything we might have missed. I have barely made a dent but I'm not stopping until everything has been sifted through with a fine toothed comb. I've already arranged for Cassandra to do the morning drop off and pick up for Alesso tomorrow but he needs to stay out of this Silas, he already knows too much." He warns, his tone turning a shade darker at the mention of his son.

I lean forwards, but before I get a chance to reply, a knock at the door interrupts my train of thought. Linc is on his feet in an instant before I even have the opportunity to say come in. As if he knew who it already was, Linc opens the office door to Alesso and pulls him in for a swift hug, though I don't pretend not to notice how tight the hold is on his shoulders as he pulls him to his chest.

"Hey Son, is everything ok?" he asks, pulling back to study his face. Linc won't ever admit this but I can see the way his brain is working, he's mentally putting Alesso in Teddy's place, imagining it were him missing instead. He's torturing himself in that way, but it only adds extra fuel to his fire for finding Teddy. We're all a little fucked up in the way we deal with things I suppose.

"Hey Dad, I woke up and noticed the lights on and well, I just wondered if there was any news on Teddy and Uncle Cole," he says sleepily. Of course, there's no he's aware of Cole waking up from his coma, we went straight to the hospital as soon as we got the call from the doctor. The poor kid has been so upset thinking that Cole was going to leave him like his mother did. It's been heartbreaking for us all to see him go through it. Which in turn has been equally hard on Linc, too. I glance at Linc, waiting for him to take the lead on this, it's better coming from his father after all. He straightens up and clears his throat as he leads Alesso into the room, nudging him to take a seat next to me while he kneels down in front of him and reaches out for his hands. I can see the turmoil in his eyes, wondering how much of the truth to divulge, he's too young to understand.

"I had hoped to have this conversation in the morning before you go to school but since you're here now…Cole is awake" Linc begins to explain.

"He is awake? Where is he? Is he ok? Can I see him? Does Luci know?" Alesso jumps up from the couch and blurts his barrage of questions out so frantically it's hard to keep up.

"Woah woah, slow down buddy, let your dad explain before you hurt yourself moving that quick." I chuckle, motioning for him to sit back down.

"He's okay, Son. He just needs some time on his own to go through what happened. He was hurt pretty bad and he needs time to recover. But as soon as he's ready and he's feeling better he'll be here to cook with you, take you to school and whatever else you want to do with him. I promise." Linc reassures him, giving him a gentle squeeze of his shoulder.

"And what about Teddy? Have you found him?" Alesso asks, looking hopefully into his fathers eyes but Linc simply shakes his head giving him all the answer he needs.

"Come on now, let's get you back to bed. It's late enough." Linc whispers, stroking his hands through his hair.

"But Dad–"

"No buts, I have work to do and you have school in the morning, now get back to bed. Cole is fine, Son. He and Teddy will both be home soon."

I give Alesso a gentle but reassuring pat on his back. "Listen to your father, Alessandro. We'll let you know if anything changes." Alesso drops his head in defeat as Linc guides him back through the door to the office mumbling a goodnight as he goes.

I can't imagine what It must be like to try and explain this to a child. A child who has already been through so much in their short life. As I wait for Linc to return, I move to sit behind the desk and pull out my phone checking on la mia luce. She's still sleeping peacefully, her steady breaths rising and falling as she dreams of everything that should be but isn't. Setting my phone on the desk, I bring my head into my hands and give in to the assault of questions firing around in my head. What has gotten into my brother? Where is Max? And how the hell are we going to get Teddy back? I pray to God that when we find him we won't have a repeat of what I walked in on when I found Cole all those years ago. My memories threaten to drown me until Linc walks back into the room and I can shift my focus to something else.

"Alesso okay?" I ask, rubbing my hands over my face.

"No, but he will be. You and I both know he thinks the world of Cole. It's just hard for him to understand. Hell, even I don't understand what the fuck is going on." Linc says, taking my previous seat on the sofa and brushing his fingers through his hair.

"Fuck, I don't know. I hope he doesn't make too much of a mess getting whatever the fuck this is out of his system. He's been in Teddy's situation and we both know how fucking messed up that was. I can't even...I just can't even begin to think. It's no doubt resurfacing all of those memories for him. We need to trust in him that he will come back to us and not push him too far, otherwise I fear he'll do something we all may live to regret." I take in a deep breath trying to calm myself before I continue. "With that being said, I could beat him to within an inch of his life for how he spoke to Lucille today, so maybe it is a good thing he's not around Alesso right now."

"That's true because I'd fucking kill him myself if he hurt him in anyway. The only reason I didn't put my fist through his face earlier was because of Lucille, I don't think she'd have been able to stay standing had I not been holding her. Hopefully you're right and the distance he's giving himself isn't such a bad thing if he can't control himself right now." Linc agrees.

I shake my head, there's no point dwelling on it any longer, Cole is gone and we will deal with him whenever he decides to show his face again. Until then, we have too much to do. "Were we able to track down the dates of when Ronan's next shipment will be arriving? The plan is ready as soon as we know when and where. We can only hope that it has some sort of weight behind it that we can use as leverage to get Teddy back. Or at the very least, we can capture a few of his men and make them bleed until they reveal the locations of their safe houses."

"I have Felix tracking their movements. Hopefully they will slip up soon and the surveillance from Max's place will be able to point us in the right direction, too. We'll get him back, Fratello. Even if it's the last thing I fucking do. My father played a part in this. I won't fucking let him win." Linc grits through his teeth. The level of betrayal felt from his own flesh and blood will undoubtedly go with Linc to the grave. This isn't on him, but I know he's taking this personally. His father betrayed us all in his scheme to get Lucille kidnapped and take over the business. He paid the ultimate price for his sins. But that still isn't enough for Linc. The knock on decisions from others actions have led us to where we are now, and that is deep in the pits of despair. I rise from my chair and grab Lincoln, pulling him to my chest. I hold him tight. I couldn't give a fuck if I'm supposed to be a coldblooded killer, I hold my friend who's been through the depths of hell and back with me and without any words being said I let him know that I love him before leaving him to do what he does best.

There's no way in hell that I'm sleeping anywhere but next to Lucille tonight, I don't care how angry she is with me, I may need this more than she does. To know that she's safe and alive in my arms. The past few days while she's been at the hospital have been nothing short of excruciating, and I am beyond a new level of exhaustion by the time I reach my bedroom. Pulling the key from my pocket, I unlock the door and enter, making sure to lock the door behind me again. Lucille is fast asleep. She looks so delicate, so easily breakable with only a few remaining bruises left on her skin and a wound that will leave a lifelong scar on her shoulder. It angers me instantly at the thought of anybody putting their hands on her precious body and causing her harm. I quietly strip out of my clothes, leaving just my boxer shorts on as I slide into bed next to my sleeping angel. I study her face for a while, the way her lips pout and her long lashes gently graze the tops of her cheeks. She's so pure it leaves an ache so deep in my chest I fear I might choke on it. I can't help myself as I bring my fingers towards her face and gently trace a line over the curve and fall of her cheek as I whisper, "I'm so sorry baby girl," onto deaf ears. I lean forward and plant a kiss on her forehead making sure not to use too much pressure. I stiffen as Lucille sighs beneath me and as I pull back, I notice a small smile pull at her lips as she mumbles something I'm unable to decipher. "That's it, la mia luce, dream pretty dreams." I whisper into her hair, kissing her once more before I let exhaustion take over and pull me into a dark and dreamless sleep with her in my arms.

Chapter 5

Lincoln

The silent reassurance I received from Silas was not lost on me, his unspoken acceptance almost cracked my already fragile state. We wouldn't be in this fucked up situation if it wasn't for my fucking snake of a father. The mere thought of being blood related to that wretched piece of shit makes me nauseous. I absentmindedly pour myself a tumbler of whisky, relishing in the burn it leaves down my throat. I swear on my own life that if I don't find out where they're hiding Teddy, I will, without a whisper of regret, leave a path of death and destruction in my wake so fucking fierce that even the devil himself will be cursing my name.

I shoot back another glass of whisky and slump heavily into my chair. You would think under normal circumstances the first port of call in situations like this would be to go to the feds. But fuck is this anything but normal. They have laws to stick by, for us, all bets are off. Besides, whatever they can do. I know I can do it better, faster and more effectively. I have no reservations when it comes to getting what I need. The memory of charring my fathers body flashes before my eyes, the smell of burning flesh invading its way into my nostrils. I have to shake my head to get rid of it.

I open up the surveillance tabs on my screen and drop a pin into Max's residence. I've run through this footage a hundred times already but I can't ignore the feeling that I'm missing something, just like with Lucille's tampered documents. This is the only place they could've taken Teddy from before he ended up at the warehouse with Vinny. The unease in the pit of my stomach has manifested itself to something of a monster that is slowly eating away at my insides. Felix has already noted that the footage covering the front of Max's house has been altered. From the moment Max got home with Teddy, there's a very subtle but noticeable glitch when you know what you're looking for. But all previous attempts at regaining the footage have been unsuccessful.

I need to look at it from a different perspective. I've been so distracted with both Lucille and Cole in the hospital that I haven't even thought of any other ways around it. My mind has been churning, constantly with too much to focus on. I curse myself for being so fucking stupid. At least my brain seems to be keeping up with my gut feelings now that Lucille is back home with us where she belongs. As for Cole, I sigh heavily, unable to even begin to comprehend what he's dealing with in his own mind, I'll just have to deal with him later. I'm just glad he's alive so that, providing Silas hasn't already killed him, I can throttle him myself when this is all over. I click play on the live feed from that day and watch as Teddy skips happily through Max's front door and out of view, followed by Max himself. Everything seems completely normal. The only movement that follows for the rest of the video are the cars and people who pass by unaware of the situation that unfurls at some point throughout the night. I continue watching until I see Silas and Lucille appear on the screen and, already knowing what happens next, I rewind it back to the beginning to start it again. I notice the glitch and make a note of it on the notepad next to me. The time jump is an hour exactly, making it harder to notice. Whoever altered this footage knows what they're doing.

I run my hands across my face feeling frustrated that this is taking me so long. My eyes are already burning and I think the lack of sleep might be slowly driving me insane, so much so that I'm almost convinced that I've hallucinated once I see it, what it is I've been searching for. I have to blink my eyes and will them to adjust as I narrow in on a truck, stationary in the traffic opposite Max's front door. The truck is a flatbed, usually used when transporting heavy goods, and what this is transporting makes my heart leap into my throat. Mirrors. Tonnes of mirrors. I pause the footage and zoom in on what I think is, no, I'm sure it's an ATM in the reflection of the mirror opposite the house. "FUCKING JACKPOT!" I shout, slamming my fits into the desk. I switch over to the satellite map and locate the ATM. Quickly loading the location coordinates into the bar at the top of the screen. My screen instantly floods with code. Times, dates, transactions, and what I'm really looking for; the fitted camera feed. I override the security codes after a few moments and access the archived footage, setting the time a few moments ahead of the erased CCTV footage. I hold my breath and zoom in on the front of the house as far as the camera will allow, willing this to work, because honestly, it just has to. The seconds speed by and my stomach bottoms out as a blacked out custom Cargo van pulls onto Max's driveway.

My ears are loud with the sound of my own blood pumping through my body as I watch four men dressed in all black, including the balaclavas covering their faces, jump out of the van and creep towards the front door. It's late enough that they're under the cover of darkness but they still aren't stupid enough to reveal their faces. Two of the group stand either side of the front door and draw out their guns before the third in the group moves forward and kneels at the door and the fourth takes up the rear with their body facing the road incase of any interruptions. The guy on the floor must be picking the lock as moments later he stands and opens the door before pulling his own gun and stepping into the house while the rest of them follow, closing the door behind them. The thought of Teddy being woken up, scared for his life like this makes me so angry I want to spill blood. Not just any blood, but theirs.

Not even ten minutes has passed and the front door opens again, but this time instead of four bodies, there are six. I lean towards the screen narrowing my eyes as I notice an unconscious looking Max being dragged by two of the intruders as another runs for the drivers side of the van, the last man runs from the house with a small limp body swinging from his shoulder. Teddy. My heart breaks as I watch Teddy and Max get thrown in through the back doors of the van and all three remaining men haul themselves in before the driver takes off. I click back through the feed and watch it repeatedly, letting the knowledge sink in that Max was as innocent in this as Teddy was. I internally vow to apologize for ever doubting the Irish prick if he makes it out of this alive, as a disgustingly sympathetic veil clouds my judgment. His father is as much to blame for this as mine was, and he will be punished. Slowly and painfully.

It takes me the rest of the evening to follow the van, tracking it through multiple archives of traffic camera footage until it eventually leaves the city and I lose sight of it heading towards Mountain Springs. The sun is barely piercing the sky as I lose hope. I know I need sleep to be able to function properly and no doubt a fresh set of eyes might be able to pick up on something I may have missed. I just can't bear the thought of seeing Lucille's face when I tell her we still don't know where Teddy is. Although I've been able to regain the missing footage which lets us know Max definitely wasn't involved, we're still no closer to finding out what the fuck happened after. All we know is that Teddy was taken to the warehouse to Vinny, after that, we have nothing. We need to get word on Ronan's next delivery pronto. I grab for my phone and ring Felix. It's early but I know he'll already be at the casino, that is, if he left at all.

"Boss," he answers after the second ring.

"Felix, where are we with the incoming shipment for the Irish?" I question, rubbing my thumb and finger into my eyes.

"I have it on good word that there will be an incoming delivery tomorrow night, Boss."

"How good?"

"Well, he lost two fingers and half of the third before Sully got him to squeal so I'd say pretty good, Boss." I can practically hear his satisfaction dripping through the phone. "I will send you the location now."

"Thank you, Felix. There's something else I need you to do for me before I put my head through the wall." I desperately need to get some sleep if I'm going to be any help at all.

"Anything, Boss."

"I've managed to hack into the ATM across the street from Costello's house and gained access to the archived camera footage. It shows the whole night, the erased footage, all of it. It's grainy using the full zoom but it's all we've got. Whoever did this was smart but not smart

54

enough to check there, too. I've managed to follow the van through the city to the outskirts but I lose it heading towards Mountain Springs so I need you to see if you can get me anything as to the whereabouts of that van now or the men who were inside it. It's all we've got to go off right now and we can't fuck it up." I breathe heavily down the phone, exhaustion suddenly weighing down my eyelids. "I'll send you everything I've got, the footage, the make and model of the van and the coordinates of the last camera sighting of it before heading out of town." I say already attaching everything to an encrypted email before clicking send.

"Sure thing, don't worry, Boss. The email has come through. Get some rest and I'll call you if I find anything." Felix reassures me before I hang up. I contemplate waking Silas, but the thought lasts only for a second as I'm no further forward with any new information on Teddy, and Felix has given me his words that he will ring if he finds anything. I drag myself over to the couch and collapse, letting the weight of the last few days drag me under.

Chapter 6

Max

The entire room is encased in darkness when I finally come round. I'm not even sure my eyes are fully open, or if I've possibly been blinded in my attack, I can't see a fucking thing. I roll my head back stretching out the tension in my neck and groan at the tightening of every single muscle in my body as I try to move. The ache through my arms feels mind-bendingly numb, almost like the entire upper half of my body has been dropped into an acid bath. I can feel my skin burning so much it's like a thousand wasps going rabid on my flesh. I can tell from the awkward angle of my shoulders that my hands are strung up above my head, but the circulation is well past gone as I struggle to wiggle my fingers against the chains holding me upright, this may explain the numbness and tightness across my upper body if I've been strung up for however long. I try to tug on the restraints, testing the strength of the chain as well as myself but a blinding pain down my left side and a sharp inward breath lets me know I have most definitely acquired some internal damage too. Probably a couple of broken ribs, definitely some bruising at least, but hopefully no punctures. I blink a few times, desperately willing my eyes to adjust to the darkness that surrounds me so I can figure out where the hell I am and try to get out of here. My legs feel as if they're barely there, having been suspended for too long. I'd be sure to collapse if it weren't for the chains keeping me up.

I try to compose myself and ignore the constant throb of pain throughout my body, the smell of damp and decay thick in the air leads me to think I'm maybe in a basement of some sort, or a cellar perhaps. I strain myself, listening out for anything that may give me some sort of clue, distant traffic, trainlines, footfall outside, anything to narrow down my location, but there's nothing for what feels like hours as I dangle, just blackness and a deafening quiet that's so loud it's practically screaming at me, rattling inside my skull. I must slip back out of consciousness for a few hours for when I rouse again, I can hear muffled voices from the floor above. They're quiet, definitely male from their tone but I can't make out what they're saying or who the voices belong to. It's undoubtedly the ones responsible for what happened to me. I just wish I could remember. How the fuck did I get here? I try to think back now that I'm in a higher state of consciousness, willing my brain to push past the pain, but the last thing I can clearly recall was putting Teddy to bed...OH SHIT! TEDDY! A feral inhumane scream punctures the air before I realize it's my own. I pull harder against the chains wrapped around my wrist to no avail as the pain splinters across my chest, it becomes too strong to handle and I have to give in. "FUCK!" I gasp, unable to break free, trying to regain my composure and get my breathing under control. I need to get to Teddy, I need to know who's behind this. Jesus Christ, LUCILLE! I hear the scraping of chair legs across the floor from above, but there is nothing that could prepare me more for who walks down into the darkness to join me.

The lights snap on, blinding me before my vision filters back through to reveal what I suspected, a damp and disgusting cellar. There really is nothing else to it, the walls are the same color as the cemented floor and the only things decorating them are thick dusty cobwebs falling corner to corner across the walls. How the fuck am I going to get out of this? I can feel my heartbeat in my eardrum as the footsteps begin their descent but I am completely blindsided by the man who steps into view a mere four feet in front of me. "Hello, Son." he smirks, pure acid dripping from every pore in his venomous face. The ringing in my ears increases and I'm sure something has popped deep inside my brain. His lips continue moving but I can't hear a fucking word that he's saying as my vision momentarily blurs over. Everything in my body burns, the pain, the anger, the betrayal. There are no words that I can conjure in this moment to express the fucking hatred I feel for this snake. My brain has short circuited, and completely fried out. A sharp strike across my cheek snaps my head to the side a second later and I have to blink away the shock before it registers on my face. "ARE YOU FUCKING LISTENING TO ME!?" my father snaps as I slowly turn my face back towards him baring my teeth as if it were to deter him from hitting me again. "That's better," he nods as he begins his speech again, only this time, I focus myself, cutting out the pain, and listen to every single word he says, to make sure that when I kill him for what he's done. I can list one by one all of the reasons as he begs for mercy before I drain the life from his eyes.

I watch in silence as my father stalks back and forth across the damp space in front of me, his three piece suit flawlessly cut across his broad shoulders. Most men age horribly and lose their strength but not him, at the age of fifty-eight he could still put most grown men on their asses before they even knew what was happening. However, I knew he didn't like to be the deliverer and on most occasions gave the orders to his enforcers, Fionn and Cillian.

"You've been such a fucking disappointment to me from the moment you were born. Do you know that? All I ever wanted was a son to carry on the family name. An heir to be proud of. For people to fear whenever they heard talk of him. To run the business, to eradicate those fucking Italian pricks and bathe in their blood while we held the entire city in our hands. But you, you went fucking soft the moment you let a woman become the priority, you wrote your own fucking death note. And what makes it worse is that it was your own fucking whore of a sister that you let bring you down."

"Where is she?" I snarl through gritted teeth, barely holding onto the anger that threatens my vision once more. His laughter rattles in his throat as he stops pacing.

"Oh, so you can speak? For a moment there I thought Cillian had fucked you up so much he'd left you mute." He laughs again and shakes his head. "Shame really," he pouts, tilting his head while he glares at me.

"I said, where is she?" I bark, refusing to break his eye contact.

"Dead, hopefully. I have what I need, there was no use for her anymore so I let her psycho husband do whatever fucked up revenge shit he was planning for her. She was no longer a concern of mine. I didn't care to know, so I didn't ask."

"She's your fucking daughter, you sick bastard! What did Vinny do to her!?" I snap, lunging forward only to be reminded that I'm still strung to the ceiling. Ronan chuckles, a deep demonic sound, at my attempt to get to him, stepping closer with the knowledge that I'm unable to reach him. I can't contain the onslaught of images that stampede their way through my mind at Lucille having to face Vinny after what he did to her. I only hope that she found a way to save herself before it was too late.

"She was never *my own* blood, Son. She was just an unnecessary add on when I regrettably married her slut of a mother. Nothing more, nothing less." He continues to pace once more until he comes to stand before me, his face mere inches from my own. "That was until I realized just how much of a fucking liability you were and how much better of an opportunity my beloved grandson would be to me." His smile is cruel, laced with greed and something else I can't quite decipher when the reality of his words fully etch themselves into my consciousness. I know he notices the moment his words finally sink in, the realization and anger carved into my features.

"You took him? You took Teddy?" I gasp, almost choking on the words as they settle into the air.

"I took him and I intend to break him until he has absolutely nothing left in this world but me. He will be groomed into leadership, trained to reject love, kindness and friendship and unlike you, you pitiful fucking excuse of a son, he will reign when I am no longer able and I will know my kingdom is safe."

"You fucking psycho. You won't get away with this." I shout, trying to gain the strength to pull my arms free, but he simply laughs, a loud menacing cackle, throwing his head back in delight.

"Oh my boy, I already have. You see, after Theo Rossi contacted me about his plan to snub the Salvatore scum from their thrones by using your beloved sister and Teddy as bait, I knew that I finally had my green light. So I struck up a deal to deliver the boy to the warehouse where his father would be waiting while Theo took care of the brothers so he could take back the crown he believed he was owed and I took over running drugs for the city. But

Theo is stupid and weak. He would never make it as a leader, and I knew that as soon as his son found out about his betrayal, that he would kill him anyway…So I put in motion my own plan, one where I end up on top. And I'm afraid son, that you're not part of it" he sneers.

I panic as he retreats up the stairs back to the ground floor of the building, the door opens when he reaches the top and I hear his orders to finish me off before the door closes and I'm left alone once more. Fuck fuck fuck. That treacherous prick. I have to fucking get out of here. I can't think straight anymore as I yank on the chains trying desperately to loosen something, anything that I could work with to help me escape. My inner thoughts are screaming at me and my injuries are screaming louder. Is Teddy in this building too? No, my father wouldn't be stupid enough to keep us both together. Lucille, God I hope she's okay, she is never going to forgive me for letting Teddy get taken. This is all my fault.

Before my brain can overload itself with questions the room is thrown into darkness and I freeze. I steady my breathing, holding as still as I can, trying to prepare myself for whatever happens next. I need all the strength I've got if I'm going to at least try and get out of this one alive, I owe it to Teddy to try. He can't have this life, it will kill him.

A quiet shuffle behind me sends a trail of goosebumps the entire way down my spine leaving a horrible taste of dread at the back of my throat.

"Don't make me fucking regret this," a low voice whispers through the silence and a sharp pain pierces against my skull as I fall into the abyss.

Chapter 7

Cole

Twisting the knife into the flesh beneath me has never felt so good, my demons are feeding on the poor souls I'm eradicating from this earth, one by fucking one. I twist the knife once more, the screams are echoing around me, they are my symphony and I am the conductor for this masterpiece. I feel the blood trickle down the blade, into my hand painting my skin a beautiful shade of crimson red. It begins to pool on the floor, my knees have gone numb from the position I'm in but straddling a person and changing their body into a masterpiece is priceless. My victim has gone limp now, I watch his life draining right in front of my eyes, his once blue eyes now a boring shade of gray are they stare lifelessly into my own. I smile, he deserved much worse.

Tonight I picked my victims carefully, each one has committed a crime that can not go unpunished and I have assigned myself their executioner. Behind me I hear footsteps crunching into the gravel. I had not anticipated having an audience, but as I turned my head, I am met with a face that I had been led to believe was burnt to ashes by my brother.

"My oh my, this is a scene that is going to cost you, Mr Salvatore. The question is how much are you willing to sacrifice to win the game? Are you willing to become a true monster and keeper of secrets to those you would give the heart beating in your chest for?"

I must finally be going mad, hallucinating the man who caused my little mouse so much pain. I guess I'm just as bad as him now. Taking in this vile creature's appearance, I start to notice subtle differences, his eyes aren't as dark, his hair is cut differently and there is a mole on his right cheek.

I frown at the man standing over me in question, pointing my bloodied knife at him, "My brothers gutted you, unless I've gone mad, which is quite possible. Who are you?"

"Ahhh, no, you haven't gone mad quite yet, but the details of who I am are not important. You have two choices, make a deal with me and assist me in infiltrating Ronan Costello's gang or we can lock you, your brother and Mr. Rossi up for good. Then your poor little mouse will be prime picking for the leeches of this world," he replies with an evil smirk lifting his lips.

"How do you know about my little mouse?" I snap, glaring at him with pure hatred. The man raises his eyebrows as I continue my rant, waving my knife in front of him. "I'm game to take down those scumbags but I need more assurances." Like why this fucker is here and who he is, what is in this for him?

"I know a great many things about your life, Cole. I have been watching, biding my time until an opportunity, such as this, presented itself to us. I will answer all of your questions, but maybe we can get this cleared up before we have that conversation." he advises, flicking his gaze over the lifeless body. He clicks his fingers and the deserted alley immediately swarms with men. They are all heavily armed with their guns pointed directly at me. I cannot help but smirk, looking this man in the eyes.

"Well, this conversation really has spoiled all my fun. I was enjoying bleeding these cunts dry. I guess you and your friends aren't giving me many options here."

"Yes, I had noticed you were thoroughly enjoying painting the town red this evening, Mr Salvatore. It's what made finding you so much easier. Now, you have options, Cole. But the one that will allow you to remain breathing is to come with us. So, what do you say Mr Salvatore? Are you ready to save the boy and get the girl?" he asks, tilting his head to one side.

"You have me in a bind. I'll play along, tell me this plan you have," I say, knowing I have no choice but to comply at the moment with so many guns aimed at my head.

"Well, Cole, on your feet then," he orders with a smirk on his face that I'm not sure I can trust. He extends his hand out to me which I take with slight trepidation before placing my hand in his own. As I rise to my feet, I move to take his hand. Though my judgment is severely lacking because the next moment a searing pain pulses through my skull and I barely have time to register it before slamming to the ground as I lose consciousness. The fucker knocked me out cold.

As I come to, a bright light stings my eyes, making me flinch into the hardback of the seat I am attached to. I can feel my wrist restricted by cold metal handcuffs behind my back and my ankles that are tied to the chair legs I am sitting on. Squinting around the room as I adjust to my surroundings, I see him. The one who claims to hold all of the cards, for now.

"Welcome back to the land of the living, Cole," he drawls casually.

"Where am I? What is this place?" I grunt, my voice hoarse.

"Want a drink? Just water, I'm afraid I can't offer

more until we have had our discussion."

"Answer my questions," I say, struggling against my restraints.

"You know better than that, Cole. You aren't going anywhere until you agree to my terms and conditions. How many times have you been on the other side of this? You agree or face the consequences. Surely you know that?" he laughs. The anger is boiling inside of me, bubbling to the surface and I feel like I'm barely holding myself together, but he's right, I need to play the long game and find out who he is, why he's doing this and what he has planned for Ronan and his men.

Forcing myself to swallow my anger, I turn to face the person who holds my fate and the fate of those I love in his hands. "I'll agree to all of your terms and conditions if you promise me to keep those I care for safe."

A smug smile creeps upon his face, his teeth showing like the wolf finally catching its kill. "I'm so glad you are able to see sense, let's get this facade started, Mr Salvatore. You are going to have to put on one hell of a show."

Holding his stare, I flex my jaw and nod, my choice has been made. I'm not the hero in this story, I am the villain and I'll burn the world down to save those that I love.

Chapter 8

Lucille

I sleep for the majority of the following day, prising my eyes open when it's already way past noon. My body feels tense, my limbs somewhat exhausted. One look around the room reminds me why, but I don't feel guilty about it. If Silas didn't want me to destroy his furniture then he shouldn't have locked me in his room. Asshole. I sit up slowly, fighting the little swirl of disappointment I have creeping in that they've left me on my own. If there's any danger to me right now, it's going to be from myself. They may be able to save me from physical danger, but the damage that's happening inside my own head will be irreparable. Vivid flashbacks of Teddy running from Vinny in the warehouse force me to shut my eyes, shaking away the horrid intrusion.

A sudden wave of nausea rolls over me and I almost don't make it to the ensuite in time to shove my head over the toilet before I puke. The acid burns its way up my throat as I fall to my knees, trying to control my breathing while holding onto either side of the toilet bowl. I feel a little better after dry heaving a few more times but the knowledge that I can't remember the last time I ate anything isn't lost on me as my stomach growls loudly to remind me of the fact. I turn towards the sink to get some water and catch sight of my reflection. "Fuck!" I whisper, taken back by the stranger staring back at me. I stand shocked as I take in the black circles under my eyes, the greasy hair scraped back from my face and the sickly pale tone of my skin that highlights the bruises that are still yet to fade. I shake my head, enough is enough. I quickly strip before standing under a scalding hot shower, relishing in the sting it leaves across my body until the water begins to run cold.

I hop from the shower and after running the towel briefly over my hair, I manage to find a clean pair of Silas's sweatpants with drawstring that I can pull tight enough to fit me without the risk of them falling down. I pull on a clean t-shirt out of his wardrobe and, feeling much fresher than I did before, I decide to try my luck, skeptically twisting the door handle. To my surprise, it opens immediately so I quickly make my way down to the kitchen, hoping to find either Silas or Linc so that I can find out what the next steps are in relation to finding Teddy, but as I enter the kitchen I freeze at the large figure sat with his back to me at the breakfast bar. My knees begin to buckle and my head swims as graphic and terrifying images of Vinny looming above me penetrate my vision so vividly that I have to lean against the doorframe to keep myself upright. This is not something I can just shake off. It's as if I'm no longer in control of my own body. My mind is reeling with images, like an old style movie playing in black and white, flicking through the scene, dissecting each and every move he makes over and over again. Only, it's not black and white, the only color I see is red. Blood red. My blood.

I feel a hand settle on my shoulder and the minuscule hold I feel like I have on the situation snaps.
"DON'T TOUCH ME!" I scream, sliding down to the floor and covering my head with my arms to protect myself.

"Shit, Miss Holland, I'm so sorry, I didn't mean to frighten you... I just... Are you OK?" The voice asks as I will myself to believe that I'm safe. Vinny is dead. I saw it happen with my own eyes. "I'll ring Silas," the voice says, causing my stomach to lurch.

"Please don't," I whisper, with my head still under my arms.

"Sorry Miss, he told me to ring when you were awake," he replies, his tone gentle and calm.

"I said, don't!" I bite back, raising my head this time. It takes me a moment to realize that the man is no stranger at all, it's Enzo, Cole's lapdog he stuck on me not long ago when Vinny first reared his ugly head. I almost feel bad for snapping at him, but then I remember the hurtful words that Cole spat at me in the hospital. I stand up slowly, the lack of food and sudden flashbacks making me sway a little as I straighten myself. "I would appreciate it if this," I wave my hands towards the spot on the floor where I was just sitting, "stays between us, Enzo. I'm sorry I overreacted. As you can imagine I'm a little on edge. Where is Silas anyway?" I ask, willing him to put his phone back into his pocket as I try to act more put together than I'm feeling.

"He's with Linc, Miss Holland."

"Please stop calling me Miss Holland," I interrupt. Enzo looks at me curiously then clears his throat and begins again.

"He's with Lincoln. They had a bit of business they needed to attend to and asked if I would stay with you for the day to escort you back to your house to collect your things when you are ready." He looks away momentarily and I know there's something he's not telling me.

"What is it?" I ask, narrowing my eyes at him.

"What is what, Miss Hol– I mean Lucille?"

"I'm not fucking stupid, Enzo. There's something you're not telling me and I want to know what it is."

"I'm sorry, Lucille. It's not my place to discuss business."

"I DON'T GIVE A SHIT, ENZO. IF THIS IS ABOUT MY SON, I DESERVE TO KNOW!" I half shout, half scream at him, my voice cracking slightly at the end as I point a finger into his face. "Please, Enzo, I just need to know if they've found him. I can't live like this, not knowing where he is, or if he's … hurt." I choke out the last word in barely a whisper as tears begin to burn at the back of my eyes. A long silence passes between us and with every second that goes by my heart shatters all over again. I move towards the breakfast bar to prop myself up, scared that my legs will give way beneath me again.

"They haven't found him yet, but they will Lucille. They won't stop until they've found him," he says in the same calm and gentle tone he used before, only this time it doesn't make me feel any better. I suck in a deep breath and wipe the tears from my eyes nodding my head. I know they'll find him. They have to find him. I close my eyes for a while, mentally preparing myself for what must happen next.

I decided to forgo food, the thought of eating making me feel more sick than the obvious hunger was. I don't think I would be able to stomach anything right now and Enzo didn't question it while I poured myself a glass of juice, gulping it down quickly before slipping my feet into the Converse I wore back from the hospital yesterday. "I'm ready to go now, Enzo. Take me home, please." I say with pure conviction, squaring my shoulders to show how ready I am to face it. He narrows his eyes slightly but I don't miss the small movement. I wonder whether he is questioning himself as to whether or not I should be eating, but I ignore him and make my way to the front door.

Before we leave the house, Enzo makes a call to let Silas know we will be leaving. Apparently he wanted to speak to me too but I declined the offer when Enzo held out the phone to me. No way was I speaking to him yet, I was still pissed at him and he deserved to suffer. We had to wait for Dario to arrive, the man I met outside of Silas's stripclub, before we could leave. As if one huge hunk of a gun-wielding bodyguard wasn't enough, Silas thought I needed two to escort me back home and pick up some clean underwear. If he really was so worried, he should be here with me himself. They all should. The thought lighting that spark of fury inside of me once more, and I make sure to let both Enzo and Dario know how pissed off I am that they're having to babysit.

During the drive I stay quiet, trying desperately to listen in on what Enzo and Dario are talking about, to see if I can get any news on what is happening in their search for Teddy, but once they realize I'm eavesdropping, they began to speak in Italian, so I sit back, close my eyes and take myself back to the time that Teddy and I went to the beach for the day with Katrina and Isabella. Christ. I must speak with Kat. I bet she's worried sick. The memories of that day fill my heart with so much love it physically hurts to think about it any longer, and so as I sit in the back of the car, I make a promise to myself that when we get Teddy back, I will take him to that same beach and relive the memory.

We pull up through the gates of my apartment complex and onto my drive and with a shaky hand and even shakier legs, I manage to get out of the car and slowly, step by step, I make my way over to my front door. I freeze as I reach out for the door knob. "I don't think I can do this," I whisper, hanging my head in defeat. I don't want to have to do this alone, even though I'm not truly alone, but Enzo and Dario are not who I want here with me to face this. My grip on the door handle tightens and a burst of anger at the fact that all three of the men who swore to me that they loved me have left me to deal with this by myself. Well fuck them all. I unlock the door and step inside. Both Enzo and Dario step behind me before I spin around and block their path with my hand. "I need to do this on my own." I snap, looking from one to the other, though doing it on my own is the last thing I really want. I needed support with this and none of the men I want it from are here with me. They give each other a quick glance, no doubt contemplating if Silas will have their heads for letting me go in alone, or not listening to what I say. Either way, right now, I don't care and so before they can object I slam the door in their faces and walk into my open plan living space.

As soon as I'm alone, it hits me. The coldness that spreads throughout my body is something I've never experienced before. Like I've been plunged into a frozen lake with no way out and no air. The room begins to spin around me and my vision darkens at the edges. I lean against my couch, grabbing the back cushion hard enough for my knuckles to bleed white. I shake my head, willing the pain in my chest to subside, I just have to get a few things and then I can leave. I repeat my mission like a mantra, keeping my mind busy to distract myself from the onslaught of another panic attack. Taking a few deep breaths until my vision corrects itself and I can see again. I try to itemize what I need and where it is so I can grab it faster and get the hell out. I don't want to be here any longer than I have to. It's too much. I knew it would be difficult but this pain, it's suffocating. I can't breathe. I can't concentrate.

I make my way on trembling legs towards my bedroom and grab my overnight bag from beneath my bed to start packing a few essentials. As I open my wardrobe a low thud from the direction of Teddy's room makes me jump, a sharp gasp escaping my throat. I freeze, my heart thumping hard against my chest. Did I imagine that? Another small thud confirms that I didn't. There's somebody in here with me. Without even thinking about it, I reach to the top shelf of my wardrobe and slide my hand between the pile of blankets, releasing my breath as my hand connects with the cold metal of the gun Max gave me when I first left Vinny. I hold the gun firmly in my hand, getting myself familiarized with it again after all these years and making sure the safety's off, just as he taught me if I ever needed to use it. The rational part of my brain is telling me to shout for help and get the fuck out as quickly as possible but my legs are already walking towards the bedroom door. If there is somebody in here that is responsible for taking my son, I'm going to face them and then kill them myself.

I push the door open with a surprisingly steady hand and aim the gun into the room, pointing it towards the figure on the edge of the bed. "Don't fucking move!" I warn as I step past the bedroom door. When I move further forward my whole body freezes at who I see. "Max!?" I choke as I take in the sight of him. He's covered in blood, some fresh, some old and dried into his clothes and skin, his arms and face are badly beaten and as he attempts to stand himself I notice how he favors his right side, cradling his left arm across his waist.

"Yeah, it's me," he says, barely holding up his own weight.

"What happened? Where the fuck is Teddy!?" I blurt out moving towards him, uncaring of his injuries, only interested in Teddy's whereabouts. My arms remain locked as I continue pointing my gun towards him, following his movements as he straightens himself to the best of his ability. If he noticed the gun at all he doesn't seem bothered by it. He shuffles on his feet slightly and winces at the discomfort it causes but right now, he could be in all the pain in the world, I need a goddamn answer. "WHERE IS MY SON!?" I shout. A white hot rage filling my senses has me grabbing a lamp from the bookcase and throwing it just above Max's head where it shatters against the wall. He doesn't even move and it infuriates me even more as I'm trying to hold back my tears yet again. I hear the front door crash open, they no doubt heard the commotion and within seconds both Enzo and Dario come barrelling into the room, guns drawn and ready.

I watch from the corner of my eye as they take in the scene before them. They must be somewhat surprised to see me holding a gun, thinking I'm weak and unable to protect myself. I chuckle inwardly. But then I notice how their eyes narrow and their nostrils flare as they notice Max leaning against a small chest of drawers, undoubtedly stopping himself from falling over.

"What the fuck?" Dario exhales as he looks me up and down, his eyes bulging at the sight of me holding out my gun.

"Get your fucking hands up, Costello!" Enzo demands, shifting his own gun towards Max and I don't like that one bit. He's still my brother after all.

"Enough!" I interrupt, turning my gun on the two men, leaving Max behind me. "Get the fuck out, NOW!" I rage at them, barely able to keep my hands from shaking now that the anger coursing through me is palpable. Enzo narrows his eyes at Max but neither of them make any attempt to move.

"Lucille, there's no fucking way that's happening." Dario states, staring wide eyed between Max and I, still trying to get his head around the situation.

"I think you'll find there is, unless you want me to shoot you. Now go on, get out, call your fucking boss and leave me alone with my brother." I demand, aiming my gun at his head. I don't feel bad about the desperate look he gives me, even if I did shoot, I have no idea if I'd hit him, I only ever took a few lessons. But the power it gives me feels incredible at this moment. Enzo taps Dario on the shoulder ordering him to stand down but he refuses to lower his gun. I pull back the hammer with my thumb, rotating the cylinder and locking the cartridge in place, clearly stating my warning. It has the desired effect as Dario's pupils flare at me while he slowly lowers his arms.

"You're fucking dead Costello." He spits towards Max as Enzo now drags him from the room, already with his phone in his free hand, no doubt calling Silas.

With a deep breath I turn back to face my brother who looks much worse than he did just a moment ago, but I catch the faintest smirk pulling up the corner of his mouth. I lower my gun, clicking the safety back on and slipping it into the waistband at the back of my sweatpants.

"Where is Teddy, Max?" I ask, all of my momentary bravado now diminished, the after effects of the adrenaline leaving me jittery and unstable. I move forward on wobbly legs until I'm standing an arms length from Max, completely unafraid that he will hurt me. I know deep down in my heart that he never would, not after everything we've been through together. But the look on his face makes me recoil.

"Don't look at me like that." I choke, trying to look deeper into his eyes, unwilling to accept the truth.

"Like what?" he asks, rubbing his hand across the back of his neck.

"Like I'm not going to like what it is you're going to tell me." I say, hot tears burning the back of my eyes once again. This can not be happening. Max hangs his head in defeat, his legs buckle underneath him as he crumples to the floor and begins to sob. I've never seen him cry before, not even when we were children, and his sudden vulnerability catches me off guard. It makes him seem so exposed and my heart breaks for more than just my son while I watch him struggle to catch his breath as he sobs into his hands with a painfully strangled scream.

"He's gone, Luc... we were sleeping... I couldn't get to him... they beat me... knocked me out... and when I woke... I'm so sorry Luc... This is all my fault... I couldn't..." His broken speech cripples me. What he went through, what they both went through, I can't even bear to think about it. Nausea rolls in my stomach at the thought of Teddy being held in a cellar somewhere, beaten, starved and... I lunge quickly, picking up the small trash can next to Teddy's bed before dry heaving myself to the floor where I then begin to cry for everything I've lost. A firm arm sweeps across my shoulders and just like he used to while

I cried myself to sleep after I ran from Vinny, he cradles me against his chest, stroking his hand across my hair and rocking us gently back and forth. The motion used to be so soothing, but now it feels tainted. I notice the stiffness in his movements, and have to try hard to blink away my tears, narrowing my eyes at the large welts around both of his wrists. I gasp, instantly bringing my hands to the wounds and gently grazing my fingers across the raised skin.

"Who did this to you?" my voice is barely above a whisper. "Who took Teddy?" I ask, unsure if I truly want to hear the answer. Max stills and I all but hear the tension crackle through the room between us before the door to the room is kicked from its hinges.

Chapter 9

Silas

"Go long!" I shout across the park to a blonde haired boy. I launch the ball into the air, and watch as he smiles back at me before sprinting in the direction of the football. Beside me I hear giggling, I smile at the sound, it's music to my ears. I cast my gaze to my right where the melody is coming from and see the most mesmerizing woman, with blonde hair and deep emerald eyes in my best friend's arms as my younger brother, Cole is feeding her grapes and smiling at her like she is the world and he is the moon.

"Uncle Si, where is Teddy?" Alesso asks, snapping my focus from the beautiful sight before me. I look around and he's nowhere to be seen. He's gone. My heart thumps frantically in my chest as I begin to panic and I take off running in the direction that Teddy was in just moments ago. Finally, I see him, but he's not alone. He's being held with a knife to his throat by a monster. My father.

"Letting your heart get involved never ends well, my boy. Have you learnt nothing from what happened to your mother?" He taunts and before I can stop him he draws the knife closer to Teddys neck and slits his throat, spraying his blood and covering me in a sickly warm red liquid. I cry out, barely recognizing the sounds coming from within me as Lucille's blood curdling scream pierces my ears while my father laughs menacingly, baring his teeth at me.

My eyes snap open, I'm sweating and my heart is

pounding in my chest like a freight train. It was just a nightmare. It wasn't real. My father is dead. He's not behind this, I remind myself. I gaze next to me as I hear Lucille mumble incoherent noises in her sleep and before I can stop myself I reach over to gently stroke her cheek, desperate to feel her to make sure she's real. Her skin is soft beneath my rough calloused hands, it looks like porcelain, delicate and easily breakable to a monster like me. She's the most beautiful thing I have ever seen. I love her, and I would gladly give my life to make her happy. It's an effort to drag myself from the bed without waking her, but I know she needs her rest. Quietly, I walk over to the window and peek beneath the curtains, it's still dark out. I glance down at my watch, it's still early. I can't have slept more than five hours. I don't see much point in going back to sleep now, not when there is so much to do, so instead I grab some loose fitting sweatpants and a towel, and decide to make my way down to the gym. A work out will help me erase the demons in my head until I can get the revenge I so desperately need. I take one last look at my girl sleeping peacefully beneath my sheets and head out, closing the door as quietly as I can behind me.

I head down the stairs to our home gym and open the door, making my way over to the weight bench. I'd normally want to get in the ring when I feel this much tension but I'm sure Lincoln has had even less sleep than me, and I don't trust myself to stop with any other fucker in this house with my mood. Just as I start to bench a few reps the door swings open, Lincoln looks like he's going to burst as he bounds over to me. I take in his appearance, it's clear he's had hardly any sleep and with the state of him, he clearly hasn't changed his clothes since last night either. I slowly lower the weights and sit up, lifting my eyebrows, silently telling him he looks like shit.

"Don't comment on my appearance, Silas. I've just had a call from Felix, we need to move now. The van has been sighted. Let's go!" He says like he's reading my thoughts about his clothes from yesterday. But what I'm really confused about is what he's actually rambling on about.

"Lincoln, slow down. What are you talking about? What van?" I ask him, hoping he'll explain.

"Fuck, I'll fill you in on the way, but we need to move, NOW!" he yells. Lincoln is always the calm and collected one of the three of us. Whatever he's desperate to find is important and I'll never doubt him.

"This better be worth it, I was planning on taking Lucille to her apartment this morning." I mumble, grabbing a sweatshirt from the rack on the wall on the way out.

I pull my phone from my pocket and shoot a quick text to Enzo and Dario, ordering them to take Lucille to her apartment if I am not back by the time she wakes up. Giving strict instructions to collect any clothes or items she needs and above all, to keep her safe. As we approach the car Linc jumps in the driving seat and I head to the passenger side.

"This could be it, we could have found Teddy, Si."

I look over at Linc in shock, surely I heard him wrong. "What do you mean? Explain NOW, Brother."

Linc lets out an exasperated breath as he starts the engine and races the car down the driveway. He's already hooked his tracking system up to the display across the dash and I can see a direct link to the vehicle we are tracking. It's on the other side of the city but it's moving towards our territory.

"So, last night I combed over every piece of evidence we had from the abduction of Teddy and Max." Lincoln begins to tell me. I'm too eager to know what the hell we are doing and interrupt him.

"Tell me what I need to know, Linc. If there is a chance we can bring Teddy home to our girl today, tell me for the love of God, don't string this out!" I say firmly.

"I'm getting there, Silas. I need to explain everything, it's not as simple as you think. God I hope we can bring him home to her today but first you need to listen to me." I can tell he's riding his own fears with Teddy being taken. He's a father and out of all of us he must understand the way Lucille is feeling the most.

"I'm sorry. Please continue. I'm just as desperate to find him as you are." I admit, running my hands through my hair.

He nods, "OK, so as I was saying, I went through everything again in detail, anything I thought was suspicious, I checked, triple checked until I found it. What I'd fucking missed. The short version is I ended up hacking into an ATM camera feed and I saw first hand how it all went down at Max's. A van pulled onto Max's driveway, custom design with completely blacked out windows. Four men, head to toe in cover, snuck in and took Max and Teddy by force. All I know is the evidence points to Max being innocent. He was unconscious when they carried him from the house, he is as much a victim as Teddy." I clench my fist at the thought of them doing this whilst Teddy was asleep. Or worse having him witnessing the whole thing after what happened with his cunt of a father.

Lincoln continues to relay what he has found. "The van disappeared towards Mountain Springs, but I had Felix keep his eyes and ears to the ground looking out for any sightings of it. And low and behold he called not 30 minutes ago, the van had flagged one of the speed cameras on the city border. He's sent a tracking signal for us to follow and where ever the van is headed we are going to intercept and we are going to find out where the fuck they have taken Teddy and Max and who's behind all of this. These fuckers are going to wish they were never born Silas." he seethes, his eyes burning bright with the rage thats evident in the tone of his voice.

My palms are sweating as I think about all the scenarios that could happen when we find this van. We are one step closer to finding out the truth and finding out where they have Teddy. I cannot fail my love. I will not allow it.

"Good job, Lincoln." I nod, but something about what he's saying still doesn't add up. "How sure are we that whoever it was that took Teddy from Max's was the same person that took him from the warehouse?" I ask "What the fuck does Ronan have to do with all of this?"

I notice Lincoln's knuckles turn a ghostly shade of white against the leather of the steering wheel and his jaw tighten at my questioning. "I don't know brother. But this is the best lead we've had in days" he sighs, visibly loosening the tension in his shoulders. I simply nod and praise him again for his work.

Linc has always there for me, so I feel it my duty to return the favor when his demons rise as he does when mine come out to play. He simply nods. I can't help thinking how today could be the day we fix my love's broken heart, putting every piece back together and making her whole once more. We will avenge her and everything they threatened to take from us all. My mind drifts to where my brother is, he's been AWOL for longer in the past but something just doesn't sit right with me about his behavior this time.

Lincoln is quiet, focused intently on the tracker on the screen but his sharp tone cuts through the silence of the car, "What the fuck, why is it going there?"

I look at the live feed seeing what Linc sees, the confusion in Lincs eyes is mirrored in my own. The van appears to be stationary in the parking lot at Cole's restaurant, and we are three minutes out.

"Put your fucking foot down Lincoln, NOW!" I half shout, half scream. Linc is already speeding to the destination, and as we arrive the tires screech loudly on the tarmac. I'm out of the car before it's even stopped, Lincoln is right behind me. Closing in on the van, I rip the driver's door open, almost taking it off the hinges. It's empty, the fucking van is empty. Rage is bubbling to the surface. I punch the steering wheel and turn to Lincoln, I see the disappointment and anger in his eyes. I can't fucking believe we got so close, I slam the van door shut, snapping my orders through my anger. "Get somebody here to come and collect this van NOW. I want every single square inch of it inspected, raked over with a fine tooth fucking comb, immediately. Nothing gets missed! I need to call Dario. Him and Enzo were meant to escort Lucille to her apartment today but it looks like Cole, Enzo and Benji have some fucking explaining to do as to why this van has shown up on their front door step of all places." I risk a glance over at Linc who merely nods, already getting his phone out before barking his orders into the hand piece.

Pulling my own phone from my pocket I dial Dario, it rings once before he answers. "Boss, how can I help?"

"Dario, I need you to keep an eye on Enzo until myself and Lincoln get to you. Are you at Lucille's apartment already?"

"Yes Boss, she's just in there now getting some clothes together, she ordered us to stay outside so we thought it best to give her the space..." he begins before a muffled shout comes through the phone.

"What the fuck is going on Dario?" I shout, my body stricken with fear at whatever is happening on the other end of the line. Linc is in my eyeline now, silently pleading with me to let him know what's happening, no doubt worried by the tone of my voice. I hear raised voices, one of them definitely being Lucille's, a few scuffles, and then silence before Dario starts talking again.

"Boss, we have a situation. Max Costello is here and she just threatened to fucking shoot me. She won't let us near him. What do you want me to do?" He recalls frantically, I can hear the frustration in his tone, I know he isn't happy Lucille has threatened him with a gun. I'll have to deal with her later for that.

"I want no harm to come to her, do you understand me Dario? We will be there in five minutes. Not a hair on her head is to be hurt, do you understand me?" I threaten, I am not in the mood for incompetence.

"Yes Boss," he replies through gritted teeth.

"Good. See to it you keep to your word, Dario." I snap before hanging up the phone. "We need to get to Lucille's apartment. Tell Felix to get the van taken back to the warehouse, he can work on it in the garage around the back. It'll be better than taking it to the casino or the club, especially if they've still got eyes on it." I say, turning my attention back to the van.

"I really thought we had something here, I can't believe we are back to square one," he exhales in despair raking his fingers through his hair before we both get back into the car, only this time, I'm in the driver's seat.

"We can focus on the van later, Brother. As for now, Max Costello is back from the dead and Lucille's threatening the guys with a gun if they go near him" I say so matter of factly that I almost appear calm as we race out of the restaurant's parking lot. Only I know what's really going on inside of my own head, and it isn't pretty. Max may be Lucille's blood, but if he hurts her in any way, if he is responsible for what has happened with Teddy, that will only spare his life. It doesn't mean he will ever get to walk again after I'm through with him. And that's a promise.

"Once this situation is dealt with, we'll get all of Cole's men in and question them one by one, see if we have an even bigger problem than we thought. And we can try to figure out why the hell the van that was involved with Teddy's kidnapping has ended up at the restaurant." I am trying to make sense of the whole thing as I say it. But I only end up with even more questions than before. Linc grunts disapprovingly beside me.

"Why the hell indeed. Cole has so many things to answer for and this is just the tip of the fucking iceberg Si," he says with malice in his words before calling our men to relay the new instructions.

On the quick drive over I'm on edge the whole time, my knuckles white on the steering wheel as I plough through the traffic, worrying about what's happening. Is Lucille safe? Has she shot anybody yet? Why does she have a gun in the first place? Why is Max there and is he going to hurt her? Does Max have Teddy? I don't trust the Irish prick even if Lincoln thinks he's innocent. Being family doesn't automatically grant you innocence, we've learnt

84

that the fucking hard way. He won't get off easy if I have anything to do with it.

As I park up outside the complex, I'm not even convinced I've switched off the engine before we both rush inside of Lucille's apartment, completely abandoning the car at the bottom of the driveway. We unholster our guns and I nod to Dario who moves swiftly to the side as we enter in a wave of fury. In one fluid motion, Lincoln grabs Enzo by the throat and pins him to the nearest wall, knocking his gun from his hand and consequently expelling the air from his lungs at the same time. Enzo's eyes flare immediately, shock and instant recognition dilating his pupils.

"What the fuck is this?" he rasps, grabbing hold of Lincs forearm and trying desperately to remove his fingers from around his throat. Lincoln leans forwards, his face an inch from Enzo's while I watch his fingertips sink into the flesh of his already reddening neck.

"Are you a fucking RAT, Enzo? If you even for a second consider lying to me, I will cut your treacherous tongue from your mouth and make you fucking eat it." Lincoln spits into his face. Enzo struggles against the wall, fighting for his breath. The panic rising in his eyes is like adrenaline to me spurring me on as I watch Linc show absolutely no remorse as he almost chokes the life out of him before he's able to respond.

"Answer the goddamn question, Enzo!" I snap, pressing my gun into his temple.

"Are you working with Ronan? Has Cole betrayed us!?" Linc hisses at him, desperate for answers. He releases his hold on Enzo's neck only slightly, eliciting a desperate gasp for air as beads of sweat streak down across Enzo's face.

"I haven't heard from Cole since before Teddy was taken, I swear. And I wouldn't work with that filth, take my tongue but I am telling you the truth!" Enzo states. "If Cole has turned, he's as dead to me as he is to you." The room falls silent besides Enzo's heavy breathing. The air tense with what should be decided. I share a momentary glance with Linc and lower my gun. If there's anybody that's going to be able to tell if he's lying, it's going to be Lincoln. The man owns a casino for christ sake. He can read a man's *tell* from a mile away, so I am entrusting this decision over to him.

"You better not be lying to me Enzo, because so help me God, I will take more than just your fucking tongue if you are!" Linc snarls before shoving Enzo roughly against the wall, grabbing the lamp nearest to him and smacking it into the side of Enzo's head, knocking him out cold and breaking the lamp into several pieces. Enzo's body slumps forward as a gush of blood soaks into his hair and to my surprise, Linc catches him before he hits the ground. If it were me, I'd have let him fucking drop, maybe kicked him while he was there too.

"Get him to the club, I'm not finished with him." Linc orders Dario, shoving him over into Dario's chest where he quickly hoists him up over his shoulder and moves to leave the room, but not before he turns back around. "I wouldn't go in there unprepared, Boss. She looked deadly pointing that gun at me. I thought I was a goner," he adds, tipping his chin towards Teddy's bedroom.

"Thanks Dario, we've got it from here." I nod, waving him out dismissively. The thought of Lucille with a gun in her hand both angers me and scares me, the mere thought of her putting herself in such a dangerous situation that she needed to find a weapon to protect herself sends a deathly shiver throughout my body and I fucking hate it.

But also, the thought of my brave but disobedient little light wielding a gun at my men has my cock growing solid, twitching against my zipper and it takes all of my self restraint to grit my teeth and try to ignore it. "Let's go." I all but growl as Linc and I head towards the bedroom, startled only to find the door locked.

"Not today!" I grunt as I use all of my pent up rage and frustration to kick down the locked door, not only did she put herself in a dangerous situation but she locked herself in a room with a potential threat, too. I have already wasted enough time on Enzo, I will not be kept from her a moment longer. I need to make sure she's safe, and the only way to do that is to have her back in my arms, and then I can punish her for her stupidity.

I kick my foot into the solid wood and as the door hits the ground, my eyes snap towards the enemy, Max Costello, sitting on the edge of Teddy's bed holding onto Lucille's hands. Blood red anger instantly clouds my vision, and I dive forwards. I'm unaware of what I'm doing until her screams break through my fiery haze and all I can hear is the sound of her voice begging me to stop.

"STOP IT SILAS, STOP HURTING HIM, HE'S INNOCENT. PLEASE SILAS, STOP."

My breathing comes fast and heavy as I blink myself back to the present, my fists still tightly gripping the front of Max's shirt as he lies motionless beneath me. I shake my head. I crossed the entire room and almost beat him to death and don't even remember stepping through the door. Fuck. I bring my eyes to Lucille's and the horrified expression makes my heart lurch. I have to look away. Max shifts slightly beneath me bringing my attention back down to him and my anger returns.

"Were you involved in Teddy's kidnapping?" I snarl lifting the top half of his body off the floor, he groans at the sudden movement but doesn't respond to my question. I lean his wrecked frame against the bed and inspect him closer, his face and body is covered with bruises that look already a few days old, and wounds that look like they are sure to scar. His lip and eyebrow are bleeding from my assault and his shirt is saturated in blood, both old and fresh. He looks like hell, like if he were any ordinary Joe, whatever he's been through would be sure to have killed him and I almost feel sorry for him as he clearly struggles to breathe without it causing him too much pain. But then I remember that Teddy was taken while in his care and I feel like he deserved worse than what he was dealt.

Max is yet to open his eyes, but his face is laced with pain, his features are unforgiving as he whispers so low I barely catch it. "I would lay my life down for that boy. I had no part in my fathers sick and twisted delusions." I suck in a breath as his confession about his father hits me.

"If that were true, Costello, then you would be dead. And the only reason I am not going to kill you now myself, is because of that angel behind me. She is the reason you live to see another day, stronzo." I snarl, removing myself from the floor before turning to face Lucille.

"Linc, take Mr Costello to the Club, he will join Enzo in answering our many, many questions." I instruct, rolling the sleeves of my shirt up and wiping the blood from my knuckles. Lincoln hesitates momentarily, obviously noting the tension between Lucille and I before he walks in and grabs Max, hauling him up over his shoulders, but before he leaves the room the silent threat he gives me to be gentle with our girl is not something that goes unnoticed. I nod my understanding, not daring to look away from Lucille for a moment longer than completely necessary. She locked herself in this room with someone that might have meant her harm, and she can argue that he might be her brother but she is my world and I vow to keep her safe from anyone who is a threat to her, be they blood or not.

As soon as the sound of the front door shutting snaps through the room, Lucille's whole demeanor snaps with it and she immediately releases her anger onto me.

"Silas, how could you do that to him? He's my brother! You almost killed him. He meant no harm to me, you're an animal!" she rages at me, flying towards me with her fists raised. Before I know what I'm doing I grab her hands and push her against the wall. She squeals as I pin her hands above her and use my hips to keep her still. Fuck, I've waited long enough, la mia luce needs to be taught a lesson. Capturing her mouth with mine, I force my tongue between her lips where I instantly feel her own fighting against me, her sharp strikes battling for dominance. She's angry and all it does is spur me on. I tighten my hand around her wrists, tasting the moan that escapes her mouth before I pull my lips away.

"Don't ever lock yourself away with someone that could potentially cause you harm again." I murmur against her mouth. Lucille wriggles beneath me and shakes her head.

"Fuck you Silas, he's my brother I can deal with him however I see fit, he would never hurt me, and if it wasn't for you leaving me alone this morning then this wouldn't have been a problem," she snarls, baring her teeth at me like a wild animal.

"Ah, my little kitten has come out to play." I tease, leaning down to place a gentle kiss on her neck, sucking lightly at the skin. Her entire body flushes with goosebumps and I bite back my smile knowing exactly

89

what this is doing to her. "Don't fight with me on this, Lucille." I whisper, sucking the space just below her ear then nicking my teeth into the lobe. Her attempts to get free persist but it only makes me harder the more that she tries. I chuckle low into her ear and she stills, realizing the effect all of her squirming is having on me and I push my solid cock against her groin. "Are you as turned on for me as I am for you, la mia luce?" I smirk, pulling back to look into her eyes.

She looks like she wants to murder me and in truth, maybe she does but her reply is simple and a downright lie. "I wouldn't bet on it," she seethes through gritted teeth before turning her head away from me.

"Don't lie to me, Lucille. I know your cunt is dripping for me between those legs," I insist, bringing one hand down to her throat while still holding both of her wrists firmly in the other. I feel the nervous swallow of her throat as I rake my finger across her skin leaving a shiver in its path. Lucille's low groan shoots a spasm straight to my crotch and the ache in my balls becomes almost unbearable. "Would you like me to find out? I can ease that ache if you want my angel, you only have to say the word." I continue to bite and kiss down her neck, gently tracing my index finger down and over the outline of her breasts. I'm pleased to see she isn't wearing a bra and her nipples are readily hardening beneath my touch, pulling the fabric of her shirt taut across her chest.

"Silas, we can't…" she begins before her breathing hitches as I suck her nipple over her shirt into my mouth, pinching it between my teeth. "SILAS!" she gasps, arching her back and pushing her chest further into my face. The sound is like pure ecstasy to my ears, almost bringing me to my knees right there.

"Fuck Lucille, the way you say my name." I groan, and like a man possessed I flip her around in one fluid movement and pin her against the wall with her arms now bent at the elbow and pinned behind her back. "Do you promise to never put yourself in danger again, Lucille?" I ask as I begin to pull at the waistband of my sweatpants she has on. Thank God they're way too big so they don't give much resistance and they're falling to her ankles a moment later, leaving her lower half exposed to me. I take a glance down at her ass, the creamy pale globes of her cheeks so perfectly round and tempting me to fuck them, but that's for another time. Not now, this needs to be quick and punishing. "I need answers baby girl, otherwise you don't get to milk my cock." Lucille shakes her head, defying me. I tut loudly, then slowly graze my fingers between her legs from behind, inserting two fingers into her eagerly accepting pussy, feeling her body tense around me as I push myself knuckle deep inside of her. She writhes at the slight intrusion, but this is nothing compared to what I really want to do to her, to fuck her raw until she's begging me to stop, until she can no longer speak and I've fucked the disobedience out of her. I can feel myself losing my control, my vision is seeping to red again and I'm suddenly scared that I'll flip a switch and never be able to recover from this. I pull my fingers from her pussy and use her wetness to stimulate her clit, gently circling my fingers over her most sensitive area. "Are you sure of that answer, Lucille? I can edge you all night long until you agree."

"Silas, don't," she whimpers, arching her back, pushing her ass into my crotch. Her words are telling me one thing but the way her body is responding is the ultimate betrayal. I know she wants this, she needs it just as much as I do.

"I need the correct answer baby girl, you give me that and I'll give you what you want." I growl low into her ear, rocking my hips forwards and pushing my cock into her ass, circling her clit softly, applying pressure every few seconds.

I know this is torturing her, her body is shaking beneath me, small droplets of sweat are beginning to form at the base of her neck and she's trying desperately not to grind herself against my hand.

A moment later her shoulders drop in defeat before her strangled voice lights my insides on fire. "I promise Silas, now fuck me like you mean it," she chokes, glancing back at me over her shoulder, her eyes hooded and lust filled. I release her wrists, allowing her the ability to steady herself against the wall, knowing she'll need it as I make swift work of shoving my sweatpants down my thighs. Like a horny fucking teenager, I fumble with my underwear before freeing my aching cock from it's restraints and wasting no more time, I force myself into her deliciously wet pussy, grabbing a handful of her hair with one hand and her hip with the other I trust myself deep inside of her, evoking the most erotic scream from her lips I've ever heard.

"Fuck, Lucille!" I growl, yanking her head back so her face angles towards mine as I pull out of her then snap my hips forwards again, sliding myself all the way in over and over again.

Lucille spreads her hands against the wall, supporting her upper body as best she can against my brutal thrusts, her sweet cries, the perfect melody to soothe my inner beast. "Silas, ohhh God!" she chokes out as I release her hair and her head falls forwards against the wall. I place my hand between her shoulder blades and push her upper body down to a ninety degree angle, grabbing onto her hips to give myself better traction.

"Not God, my angel. You either call me Silas or husband because one day I'll be calling you wife." I grunt as I hold my pace fucking her hard and fast, just the way she needs it, digging my fingers into the flesh of her hips. I glance down, watching as my cock gets swallowed over and over again by her hungry pussy, like it was made to fit and the sight is my undoing. I can feel the tightness of my balls as my release draws close.

"Silas, fuck… I'm going to come!" Lucille cries, her words barely audible between her throaty moans. Fuck, thats it, her words tip me over the edge and with a final trust, Lucille's walls tighten around my cock as she screams her climax and I'm fucking freefalling as I fill her up, letting her milk me of everything I've got. I collapse forwards, bringing us both to our knees with my dick still inside of her and place my head against her back, peppering kisses across her sweat covered skin.

Lucille stays silent other than her rapid breathing as she comes down from her high and I continue to kiss every inch of her beautiful body. I lean back, slipping my spent cock from between her legs, pulling my pants back up and reveling in the sight of my cum dripping from her gaping hole. Fuck, that's got to be the sexiest thing I've ever seen. I lean forwards and pull Lucille back into my chest before kissing her on the forehead. No other woman has ever felt so perfect in my arms. I would crawl over broken glass to the end of the earth and back again if it meant I knew she was safe. I close my eyes at the thought of losing her, a thought that's been all too real lately and it has me tightening my arms around her. "I was so scared when I got that phone call. I can't lose you Lucille, I just can't." I whisper, wearing my vulnerability on my sleeve. I shift Lucille onto my lap and bring my hands up to either side of her face. Her eyes dart around the room, like she's just remembered where she is, I see the recognition hit her and the tears that well in the corner of her eyes. "I'm sorry, la mia luce." I confess, dropping my head between my shoulders. I shouldn't have done that. Fuck, what the fuck was I thinking? I should have listened to her when she said no.

"Silas," Lucille places a gentle hand on my shoulder then onto my cheek, bringing me back to face her.

"Yes, Angel?" I ask, searching her eyes for the hatred she must feel towards me for what I've just put her through, but there is nothing but sadness in those big wild eyes that stare directly through to my soul.

"Take me home," she whispers, stroking her thumb against my cheek as a lone tear falls across her own.

I silently oblige, lifting her up with me as I stand, making sure to pull her sweatpants back up before cradling her against my chest and leaving the room. "I love you," I whisper gently against her hair as I walk us into the sitting room.

"The words I love you aren't enough, Silas. I feel so much more than just that. You are in my soul, etched into my very being. The reason I am still alive is because of you." Lucille replies quietly.

I lower myself down onto the sofa with Lucille still cradled in my lap then call Marcello to come and collect us. We stay there until he arrives, neither of us talking, neither of us moving, all the while I'm repeating her words in my head, making sure they're embedded into my memories. As soon as Marcello arrives, I carry Lucille out to the car and secure her safely into the backseat before sliding in

94

next to her. "The club, Marcello. We have some interrogating to do." I instruct from the back of the car. Marcello nods and begins the drive back to the club where I know Linc will have already started getting some answers out of Max and Enzo. I just pray that they're the answers we need.

Chapter 10

Lincoln

On the drive back to the club my mind races with the thought of Silas and Lucille alone in that room, the way she screamed for him to stop when he almost beat the life from Max right before her eyes broke my heart. It notched something deep within my subconscious and all I could picture was my mother, so I froze. My whole body was stuck, like a sleep paralysis demon was sitting heavy on my chest. I stood still as that demon constricted around my body and disabled my ability to move while I watched the scene unfold before me and there was nothing I could do in that moment but wait until Lucille snapped us both out of the nightmares we had both succumbed to. Before I left, I saw the wicked glint in Silas' eyes, the same one he had on fight night when he fucked her in the locker room and she ran crying from the building. I know he would never intentionally hurt her, but right now she's already broken, she doesn't need to be made to feel any worse. And especially not by any of us. I slam my fists into the steering wheel, screaming a slur of profanities that fall on deaf ears.

This entire situation is dire. I look back over my shoulder at Max who soon surrendered himself to unconsciousness after I lumbered him into the back of the car. There's no way he had a part to play in this, other than not being able to fight off four men who came into his home unannounced. The poor fucker looks like he's on death's door already. I know I won't be able to use brute force for this round of questioning, not without accidentally killing him. Though I already know, it would never come to that anyway. He is innocent, he has to be.

I pull into the club parking lot and slowly creep the car around the back of the building where the emergency exit is. We don't often use it, only when we need to keep business out of the eye of the punters, and considering it's still broad daylight outside, it may look a bit suspicious if I'm seen hauling a badly beaten, half dead man through the club in the middle of the day. I notice Enzo's car is already parked up as I pull around the corner and Dario is leaning against the back wall smoking a cigarette. I switch off the ignition, taking a deep breath before exiting the car and striding over to where Dario stands and without a word he offers me his pack of smokes. I smirk at him, taking one from the pack and lighting it up.

"Where is he?" I ask, taking a long deep drag on my cigarette.

"In the stockroom at the moment, still unconscious but shouldn't be much longer till he wakes," he says, staring out into the deserted space around us. I nod at his words, trying to think of the easiest way around this. "You really think he's in on this?" Dario asks, nodding to my car, interrupting my chain of thought.

"I don't think he is, no. But I owe it to Lucille to try and find out what the fuck's going on and right now, he's one of the only two leads we've got." I sigh, slapping his shoulder. "Move Enzo into the holding room, that one won't be waking up anytime soon, so he can wait." I say, lifting my chin in the direction of my car. Dario nods, stubbing his cigarette out against the wall before he walks back into the club, leaving me alone. I finish my cigarette in peace, enjoying the only bit of solitude I'm sure to be getting for the next few hours. I glance at my watch, trying to make a mental plan of what needs to be done and how long I have to do it. There's no chance I'll be finished and be presentable enough to pick Alesso up from school so I type out a quick message to the nanny; Cassandra, to make sure she's available for pick up and to stay at ours until I'm back home later this evening. I've got a lot of making up to do to my son, these past few days haven't been easy on him either and I keep forgetting that. He's facing his own battles too. Almost losing Cole brought back so much for him that I wasn't even sure he remembered. But like all of our own scars, they penetrate into the darkest depths of our minds, haunting us when we least expect it. I wait a few moments until I receive her confirmation then make my way back to my car. I'd better get this party started.

Max is still unconscious so it makes it a little easier for me to carry him over my shoulder like firemen do with the people they save from burning buildings, and into the club. I haul him into one of the private hire rooms at the back side of the building, laying him onto the leather couch that covers the wall. I watch him for a few seconds longer before I leave, making sure he is in fact still breathing. I don't know what Silas thinks I'm going to be able to do with him, he's fucked as it is. I run my fingers through my hair, debating with myself what to do. Lucille won't like us using force against him when she's pleading his innocence, but if he knows something we don't then all bets are off. I'll guarantee his last dying breath doesn't go to waste. I ensure to lock the door behind me on my way out, switching the vacant sign to *occupied* on the door sign.

I swiftly and silently make my way back through the club, noticing a group of several deeply intoxicated men, lined up around the two raised platforms watching Cherry and Mercedes swing themselves around the metal poles fixed to the ceiling, while they shout loud and grotesque obscenities at them when they refuse to partake in a lapdance. Fucking vultures. I would never let Lucille do anything like that in front of another group of men. I meet Dario who stands guard in front of the holding room that's situated underneath the main floor of the club, next to the store room where we have the alcohol stowed under lock and key. I nod my head as he greets me.

"Dario, make sure to keep an eye on the party out front, it's early and they're already far too fucking loud for my liking." I sigh, rubbing my thumb and forefinger into my temples.

"On it, Boss," he nods before stepping to the side. "He's just coming round now, I secured him to the table."

"Thank you Dario, you can go now." I thank him, slapping his shoulder as I move past. "Also, keep an eye on the camera in room three, I put Costello in there until we're done here. I don't think he'll be back with the land of the living anytime soon but I want to be the first to know when he does." I add, giving him a narrowing stare.

Dario does nothing to show any hostility and merely nods his head again. "You'll be the first to know when he wakes up," he says before turning his back and walking away to keep an eye on the main floor. I almost want to say, "that's *if* he wakes up," but I bite my tongue, not wishing that just yet for Lucille's sake.

I enter the holding room and glance around with a smile. It's our kitted out version of an interrogation room, clean and sterile with bright fluorescent lighting making such a stark difference to the darkness that swamps the rest of the club. We use the room mainly to hold those who have had a few too many to drink and need to cool off before leaving the premises. It's not very often we have to bring other work back here. Silas prefers to keep those parts of the job separate, and with good reason. However, the room is still kitted for all intents and purposes whenever we may need it. A large stainless steel table sits central to the room with a welded ring housed in the middle to secure restraints if needed. And in this case, it is. Enzo is fully conscious now, the split I caused from smashing the lamp into his head is no longer oozing but there is plenty of dried blood matted into his hair and staining his shirt. I don't feel the least bit regretful of my decision though.

Enzo sits facing the door as I walk into the room with his hands securely fastened by a pair of handcuffs that loop straight through the metal ring, giving him very little wriggle room. I study him closely as I take the seat on the opposite side of the table. He looks rough, as any person would, had they just been knocked unconscious with a piece of ceramic decor, but his demeanor does not change, he tries to straighten himself however the metal cutting into his wrists limits his movement. I stay silent for a few moments while I lean back in my chair, wondering if he'll bite and confess to everything, but he doesn't, he simply stares straight back at me, no anger or animosity in his features. He's weighing me up as much as I am him but Enzo isn't stupid, he knows and respects the rules of this game. I am his superior, and in our world, I make the first move.

"What happened, Enzo? Did they offer you something you couldn't refuse? Have some sort of hold on you that you can't back down from?" I ask calmly, keeping my eyes trained on his. I learned many years ago how to decipher if a person was lying. Not everybody is the same, but everybody has a tell and it became my job to know what that was and whether or not they were bluffing.

"I don't know what you think I've done, Linc, but I assure you, whatever it is, I have had nothing to do with it. I live and breathe for this business, this family. I did not get my position and rank handed to me on a platter and I'm as good as dead if you brand me a liar. So slit my throat now and be done with it if you have your doubts." he replies in an almost serene tone, grinding his teeth as the metal pinches into his skin. I purse my lips thinking to myself very briefly about the details that have come to light. No, Enzo most certainly did not get his position handed to him like Silas, Cole and I did. For us, it was already in our bloodline and we were destined to take the reins from our fathers, but for him it took many years to gain our trust, most especially Cole's trust, because he gives that away to nobody for free.

"Why did you volunteer to watch over Lucille today? We asked all of our men, and you were the only one to rise to the occasion. Your boss has gone AWOL which subsequently leaves you in charge as his right hand man and the van that was involved in Teddy's kidnapping has suddenly been dumped at Salvatore's Cucina. Don't you think that looks a little bit suspicious to you?" I sit forwards, linking my fingers together and resting my hands onto the table top. Enzo's face flickers with annoyance at my questioning but still there's no hint of deception.

"I volunteered *because* Cole has gone AWOL. I am his second in command, I know what I have to do in his absence. He entrusted me to watch over Lucille and Teddy when there was a threat of her ex-husband coming for her so why would now be any different? She needed a familiar face. I stepped up, like any of the others should have."

There's annoyance in his tone now but it's not directly aimed at me.

"Has Cole reached out to you since he left?" I ask, now changing my direction of questioning which leaves Enzo furrowing his brow at me before he shakes his head.

"The last I heard from Cole was the day he was shot. Since then it's been radio silence. I've tried to reach out since he left the hospital but I've had nothing in return," he sighs, hanging his head. I can tell he's bothered that Cole hasn't tried to contact him, but it doesn't surprise me in the least.

"What about the rest of your men?" I enquire. "Afterall, with Cole gone, you are their boss now. Do you trust them?" Enzo thinks for a moment before raising his head to meet my stare dead on.

"There is no one I would question. Cogliere la notte." He states, with pure conviction in his tone. I mull over this for a second, already settled with the belief that he knows nothing about the van or where Teddy is being held. I slowly nod my head as I rise from the table.

"Get your men in line Enzo. This is your one and only warning. It's hard work being at the top." I advise, before unlocking his cuffs and leaving the room.

Well that went a lot better than I expected. I didn't suspect Enzo of ratting on us or being involved with Teddy's kidnapping due to his reaction back at Lucille's apartment, but I did expect him to piss me off so that I'd end up knocking him out again, and enjoy getting my knuckles bloody. However, it wasn't necessary, not this time at least. I'm not sure how Silas would have wanted me to handle it but there was no need to beat the truth out of him when he offered it so freely. Enzo's a good man, and we'd be fucked if we lost him. I close my eyes and roll my neck, cracking the tension that strains through my body before walking back towards the room I'd left Max in, noticeably a little less tense than I was a few hours ago. As I pass by the bar again, I clock Dario on my way through, catching his eye as he nods in my direction. I shake my head, a silent communication to let him know that Enzo has not fucked us over, he dips his chin, acknowledging the information before turning his attention back towards the club, which is now housing more than one rowdy stag party.

I unlock the door to the private room I'd left Max in and hesitantly push it open. Instead of lying in the recovery position which I'd left him in, I notice he's now lying across the leather couch with his knees bent up and his feet planted into the fabric, with one arm draped over his eyes while the other hangs limp across the couch edge. I walk forward and close the door behind me.

"You know for a moment there, I thought he'd fucking killed you." I say out loud, sighing heavily as I lower myself onto the couch on the opposite side of the room.

"I almost wish that he had," he croaks, swiping his tongue out across his lips, trying to alleviate the dryness.

"You need to tell us what you know Max, we still have no clue where Teddy is," I explain, hoping to God that whatever information he does have helps us get a little closer to retribution, but that hope is about to be short lived. Max shifts his body slightly, obviously in an extreme amount of pain as he winces at the movement. Whoever did this wanted him dead.

"I have no idea where he is, don't you get that?" he chokes, sucking in a large breath of air as he snaps himself up right to face me. I'm a little taken back by the horrific state of his face as he stares at me, blood and bruises cover his skin like a marbled painting, both eyes are almost completely swollen shut and his eyebrow and lip look like they could do with a few stitches. I've seen beaten men before, but the way his eyes bore into me, broken and almost lost is what sucker punches me in the gut. I tear my eyes from his, standing to relieve the feeling as I shake off my jacket, tossing it to the side.

"What do you mean you don't know? What the fuck happened? Where have you been? How did you escape?" I question as I pace the room, needing the answers quicker than I can ask them. I can feel the adrenaline coursing through my veins, the sudden urge to smash my fists into something, or somebody is rising by the second.

"We were asleep when four men entered the house. It was too late by the time I knew they were there. I was hit from behind and blacked out instantly. I have no idea where I was taken, all I know is that Teddy wasn't there. I woke up hanging from the rafters in a cellar for fucksake." He tries to take a deep breath but his ribs are obviously busted because he gives up and holds his head in his hands. "It was my father." Max whispers, his eyes watch me carefully as I come to a stop to face him while I let the information sink in.

"Why?" was the only fathomable word I could muster, trying to understand what he was telling me.

"He wants Teddy to take over the business when he's ready to give it up. Said he was going to turn him into everything I'm not, groom him to be the boss. He said that he left Lucille to Vinny. Wanted her dead for all he cared."

It's obvious that the words are only just settling in for him as he speaks them outloud but I can't think straight, my brain is hotwiring and all I can see is Lucille on the floor with that fucker standing over the top of her about to rape her. I roar, grabbing a fistful of Max's shirt as I haul him to his feet. My face is close enough that I can feel his strangled breath against my cheeks.

"Where the fuck are they!?" I growl, tightening the fabric of his shirt in my fists. Max pulls his head back away from me but doesn't have the strength to put up a fight. He feebly bats at my arms trying to loosen my hold but it does nothing to deter me.

"I don't fucking know, Lincoln!" he shouts back in my face, causing my anger to spike. He's got to be lying. Every logical explanation tells me that he's lying, even when his eyes are telling me something else.

"Don't give me that bullshit." I snarl, as I drag him across the room before slamming his already broken body against the wall, pinning him up just below his neckline, he hisses loudly as the pain shoots through his body and it only infuriates me more. "How the fuck did you get out?" I snarl, pulling him forwards only to slam him back into the wall again. His eyes close for a second and I suddenly remember what the fuck I'm doing. I release his shirt, lowering him back to the floor but continuing to hold his body weight up against the wall, afraid that if I don't support him he'll collapse. I watch as he wills his eyes back open before shaking his head at me. His face is full of despair but I will him to go on.

"I don't know. I was in a cellar somewhere, my father told me that he had Teddy and what he intended to do with him. He left but someone else was down there with me. The last thing I remember was a male voice threatening me not to make them regret what they were about to do. They must've hit me over the head and then drugged me because I woke up on the outskirts of the city. I had to know if Lucille was safe so I made my way to her apartment, hoping she'd show up sooner or later." Fuck.

"FUCK!" I roar, balling my fists once again and slamming them into the wall either side of Max's head. "Nothing. You've given me NOTHING!" I rage into his face before pushing myself away from him in case the urge to kill him becomes too much for me to handle. I stride over to the other side of the room giving myself enough distance not to let temptation drag me under but as I place my head against the wall trying to remain calm, I hear a loud thud behind me, and at the same time the door opens and an unmistakable scream pierces my ears.

I whip my body round to see Lucille running into the room towards Max, who is now lying in a heap on the floor. What the fuck? I snap my eyes to Silas who merely stands in the doorway taking in the scene before he looks at me, his eyes narrowing with a hint of a warning.

"What the fuck did you do!?" Lucille cries, bringing my attention back to her and Max on the ground. She's shaking his body, furiously pleading with him to wake up but he's limp and lifeless as her tears soak into his shirt.

"Silas, get her the fuck out of here," I say calmly while inside all I want to do is vomit. He better not be dead, for fuck sake, he can not be dead this time. Silas moves quickly, pulling Lucille as she screams at us both, flailing her arms and legs at him to get free, though he makes little work of getting her back through the door. I rush forwards, falling to my knees as I check Max's pulse point. "Fuck fuck fuck!" I curse out loud. It's there but it's extremely low. What am I meant to do? There is no way we can get him to a hospital. Ronan will know he's escaped by now and be looking for blood. I wrack my brain, desperately trying to come up with an idea that will work without us having to take Max out of the building. Jesus Christ, a lightbulb practically explodes inside of my head and I'm already reaching for my phone to call in that favor.

The longest hour of my life passes as I pace the room, continuously checking to make sure Max still has a pulse. I reach for my phone again and just as I'm about to ring for an ETA on the doc a knock at the door startles me. I pocket my phone and reach for the door, opening it wide to reveal Dario who's standing next to a slimy weasel of a man that I could happily have gone the rest of my life without ever looking at again, but he owed us for sparing his life and in this moment, I've never been more relieved to have let somebody live.

"You took your fucking time!" I snap, pulling him into the room by his jacket. Dario steps in behind him and closes the door.

"Yes, well you didn't exactly give me much time to get everything I needed so it was a bit of a rush," he remarks, dropping a large duffel bag at my feet and glaring at me with hatred in his eyes as I push him away from me and shake my head.

"Now is not the time to piss me off, Doc. It's time to cash in on that favor for letting you live after the shit you pulled on Miss Holland." I snarl, the memory of Cole catching this fucking waste of a man trying to drug Lucille to take her home makes me feel sick just imagining what would have happened had he not followed her that night and intercepted when he did. "Now, for your life Doctor Graves, you save his." I direct, pointing towards Max.

Tom turns to look at Max then shakes his head. "You have got to be joking," he startles. "He looks dead already. There's no way I can help without taking him to a hospital. I have no idea of the severity of his wounds without running tests, and scans, and he might possibly need surgery by the look of him. I don't have that kind of equipment here." His voice is desperate as he looks between Dario and I, backing away from us slightly as he objects.

"If I could take him to a fucking hospital, do you think that *you* would be here, you fucking idiot? I will get you whatever you need to patch him up. But take this as my one and only warning doctor. If he doesn't survive, neither do you." I warn, watching the bob of his throat as he swallows down his fear. A small smile creeps up my lips. Good, I want him to be fucking scared. Tom turns back towards Max and throws his jacket off before rolling up his sleeves one arm at a time. I watch anxiously as he opens up his duffel bag and pulls out a stethoscope and some scissors. I brace myself slightly, suddenly acutely aware that he could easily end Max's life right now with those scissors and I would not be fast enough to stop him, even though it would be his own execution if he did. I realize I'm holding my breath as he cuts the shirt from Max's body, revealing severe bruising across his stomach and ribs.

"Jesus Christ. We need to get him onto a table." Tom curses while he begins to press the stethoscope across his chest, listening intently before making his way further down across his stomach.

I nudge Dario, implying for him to follow my lead. "Let's get him into the holding room, there's a table in there he can lie on." I offer, hoping it will be good enough for the doctor to work around. Dario and I both kneel down and carefully place our hands underneath Max's body, lifting his deadweight between us as we carry him out of the room to the now vacated holding room I'd questioned Enzo in not too long ago. We lower his body carefully onto the stainless steel tabletop, avoiding the metal ring in the middle as best we can.

"I'm going to need supplies, Mr Rossi. I take it you can get me those considering what you're asking of me?" Tom questions, glaring at me as he empties the contents of his duffel bag onto the table next to Max's body. If I didn't desperately need his help right now I'd shove him into that fucking bag and throw him in the river.

"Write me a list." I snarl through gritted teeth, barely containing myself.

Once Tom has given me an extensive list of everything he'll need to work with I call Felix, because if anybody is going to be able to get all of this at the drop of a hat, it's going to be him, and boy does he come through. Within the hour multiple deliveries are being dropped off at the back door to the club where Dario meets them to bring them, one by one, back into the now makeshift emergency room. In all my years in this business, I've never seen anything quite like it and I have to take my hat off to the doctor and what he has accomplished. There are monitoring machines, sutures, bags of blood, a massive amount of bandages and a weird looking hat with a light fixed to the front of it. The next few hours are a complete blur to me, all sense of time is completely lost as I watch the doctor work his way over Max's body. He starts by cleaning and disinfecting all of the cuts and grazes, making sure to give stitches to the deeper wounds that won't heal on their own, before he begins drawing blood and inserting cannulas into the crook of Costello's elbow. I flinch involuntarily as the needles pierce the skin, bringing back haunting images of Alesso's mother. I shake my head to rid them, running my hands down my face in frustration.

Before long, Max's body has been hooked up to multiple machines with bags of blood, antibiotics and other fluids slowly infusing their way into his system as they hang above the table. I daren't think of Lucille right now, the look in her eyes has singed itself to memory. I can't fucking leave this room until her brother wakes up, and I don't plan to. I still don't trust this prick to be alone with Max while he's unconscious so I plan on staying for however long this takes. I had already shot out a text to Silas to let him know my plan on bringing the doctor in and suggested it best if Lucille remained oblivious of that piece of information too.

"There isn't much more I can do for him here," Tom sighs as he turns to face me, pulling my spiraling thoughts back into the room. "He most definitely needs a hospital."

"Not possible, Doc, you're his only hope right now." I admit, trying to sound much more pleased about it than I feel.

"I have done all I can. He lost a lot of blood and has sustained some severe blunt force trauma to his head and body. I've hooked him up with some blood to replace what he's lost but he needs to be pumped with fluid and antibiotics for a couple of days at least." His voice is so matter of fact, like he's talking to one of his patients and it's pissing me off the more that he continues. "There really is nothing else I can do for him until he wakes up, and there's no telling when that will be."

My whole body stiffens at those words. "But he *will* wake up, right?" I demand, suddenly feeling like I'm about to pass out as I stare down at Max's body, having to brace myself against the wall. Dr Graves turns back towards the table and lifts up Max's eyelids one at a time, shining the light from the hat into his eyes, checking his pupil reaction.

"His pupil reactions are normal, and he hasn't stopped breathing so I have no reason to believe he won't wake up. But, Mr Rossi, I do not know the extent of his internal injuries. From the look of the bruising on his stomach, he could very well be bleeding internally, and without a hospital or a surgeon, he will die."

I swallow the bile that's rising in my throat. I will never be able to look at Lucille again if I am the reason her brother dies. I've failed already at being unable to retrieve her missing son. What the fuck am I meant to say? Dr Graves stares at me while I have my internal breakdown but he doesn't say anything. Apparently he does know when to keep his mouth shut, because another snarky remark from his mouth and I'd have to knock his fucking teeth out and shove them down his throat.

Chapter 11

Lucille

Seconds, minutes, hours. I have no idea how long it's been since Silas dragged me away from my brother's body. If I hadn't managed to find his pulse before I was hauled into the air it would be impossible to convince myself that he wasn't actually dead. But that's all I can do. It's all I can do to convince myself that I haven't lost my son and my brother within a week. The thought is petrifying, so much so, that I don't think I'll survive it. Lincoln's face as I was forced out through the door was distraught, broken even. He looked completely helpless, but in that moment, I wished pain on him I had never thought possible. How could he do that to me? After everything we'd already been through, I thought he was the most reasonable.

"La mia luce?" Silas croons next to me, gently stroking his fingers against my arm. He had carried me kicking and screaming all the way to his office through a crowd of drunken men and women who all watched wide eyed as I fought against his restraint, and not a single one of them offered to help me or ask if I was alright. As soon as we entered he all but threw me onto the leather couch and locked the door so I couldn't get out. I flinch away from him automatically and shrug his hand from my arm. "Lucille, don't shut me out!" he snaps, keeping his tone low and authoritative.

"Fuck you, Silas." I all but whisper into myself. I no longer have the fight in me after staring into the dark hardwood floor of the room for what felt like an eternity, praying that every time somebody knocked on the door, they were coming to tell me that Max was awake, but instead, every time Silas stepped out of the room and spoke in private before he returned, giving me little to no information at all. I bow my head and give in, the overwhelming guilt swallows me as I exhale, unable to stop the tears as they burn their way down my face. I don't fight back this time as I feel the couch shift before Silas wraps his arms around my body and pulls me into his lap. He holds me, stroking his fingers up and down the length of my spine as I nestle my face into the crook of his neck.

"It's going to be alright baby, I promise," Silas whispers, kissing into my hair and squeezing me tighter as it becomes a little harder to breathe. "Shhh, baby shhhhhhh," he soothes, constantly running his hand up and down my back. I try desperately to concentrate on the movement, scrunching my eyes tight as I breathe in while Silas' hand moves up, and exhaling as it moves down, blocking out every other thought from my brain. I will never come back from this if I let the dark thoughts win. I am more than this and I am stronger, even if it doesn't feel like it right now. As my breathing slows, Silas loosens his arms and shifts me carefully back onto the couch before laying his whole body across it and pulling me down with him so my back is pressed firmly against his chest.

"You need to get some rest sweetheart," he instructs softly into my ear, pulling the chenille blanket from the back of the couch to cover my body.

"I can't," I whisper, already trying to fight off the exhaustion as my eyelids become heavy and the room instantly becomes darker.

"I will wake you up if there's any news," I hear before my body gives in to what it needs.

The room is drowned in complete darkness when several taps at the door bring me back to semi-consciousness. For a moment I forget where I am until a large body shifts behind me and I instantly relax, taking in his distinctive smell. I'm in Silas's office, I remember now. And then I remember why. Max. Silas carefully moves himself from behind me, trying not to wake me, not knowing I am already wide awake. Maybe I should just tell him and make it a little easier for him but I'm hoping he'll be more inclined to reveal some information in front of me if he thinks I'm still asleep. I make sure to keep my breathing slow and steady as I hear him open the office door. I feel the light from outside hit my face but I try to ignore it as well as the thumping bass coming from the club downstairs. The door closes a moment later and along with the music, the light fades, pitching the room back to blackness. I jump up from the couch and tiptoe my way across the room, pressing my ear flat to the door to hear the conversation between Silas and whoever it was that knocked, but all I can hear is the low beat of the bass.

"Well fuck this!" I curse out loud to the room before opening the door. Only, it doesn't open. Silas has locked me in, again! "Fucking asshole. Open the door!" I shout, but it's no luck. If he wasn't standing on the other side, nobody would hear me over the music, and if he was still close by, he wouldn't have locked me inside. Prick. I glance around the room looking for something I can use to pry the door open with but instead I find myself sitting in his desk chair staring at his desktop. I nudge the mouse curiously, for the whole screen to light up just like I hoped it would. This fucker really should lock his computer when he's not in here. I have no idea what I'm looking for but if they won't give me any information, then I'll just have to find it myself. I search through several different apps on the display screen and flick my way through tonnes upon tonnes of receipt documentation but that is no use to me. I know there won't be much on here but I have to try. A small camera lens icon in the bottom right corner of the screen catches my eye but when I click to open it a security blocker opens, prompting me for a password. "Oh for fuck sake!" I groan, closing my eyes to think of anything at all that would have enough meaning behind it for Silas to use as a password. I type my own name in for it to be rejected and I all but laugh at the thought of it. Like he would have my name as his fucking password, we're not in high school. No. This needs to mean something to him, something important. I pull open the desk drawers and filter through paperwork, typing in anything that seems like a possible option, but like my first attempt, they all get rejected. A sudden burst of anger has me launching one of the crystal cut tumblers into the bookcase on the opposite wall, smashing against a photo frame before exploding across the floor. "Shit!" I run across the room, bending down to pick the photo off the floor, feeling instantly guilty for my sudden outburst as I look down into the eyes of a beautiful golden eyed boy, nestled delicately into a woman's arms as she swaddles a baby into her chest. My heart palpitates rapidly against my chest as the woman's eyes bore deep into my own. She looks so happy yet she holds a certain sadness about her that makes me wonder what had happened to her. I flip the photo over in my hands. The names Valentina, Silas and Cole are all hand written in beautiful cursive black ink on the back with the date the photograph was taken underneath. I carefully place the photo back onto the bookshelf after staring at it a little longer then I sit back in front of the desktop willing for this to work. I type in Silas' mothers name and press enter. It fucking worked.

The screen is divided into six sections, each playing a live video from the camera's point of view. I'm so overwhelmed at the new power I possess as I'm able to watch what's happening throughout the club that I forget I'm locked in Silas' office until I hear somebody attempting to get in from the other side of the door. My body's fight or flight response is truly fucked as I sit stoic in my position. There's no way anybody could get up here without somebody seeing them. But my heart falters as the door opens and Cole steps into the room. His eyes immediately burn into mine as he stands in the doorway, looking just as shocked to see me as I am him. Our stare off lasts a lifetime as neither of us dares to move. He studies my face, his eyes flicking back and forth between my own. I can see the inner turmoil practically oozing out of his head as he questions what his next move should be. I take in his appearance, dressed completely in black from head to toe. His jeans pull tightly across his muscular thighs and the slightly low cut of his vest underneath the hoodie he has on makes me feel annoyingly uncomfortable. I'm not used to seeing any of them out of their suits and jackets but everytime I caught Cole in his casual biker gear, my brain seemed to lack the capacity to function properly, just like it is now. I take a deep breath and swallow my trepidation, bringing my gaze slowly back to his face.

"Cole." Is all I manage, like a breath of wind, my voice sounded so damn weak when I wanted it to be strong but I don't miss how Cole's eyes shut for the briefest of seconds before he strides towards me. I move back in the chair, unable to read the situation and needing to give myself some space before he gets too close. His steps falter immediately, a flash of uncertainty burrowing into the harsh lines of his face as he comes to a stop. He's close enough now to see what I've been looking at on Silas' desktop but he remains silent as he stalks around the desk to stand between me and the screen. My inner devil is screaming at me to touch him, but I refuse. I won't be the one to make the first move here, not after the horrible things he said to me at the hospital and the way he's abandoned us all, especially me when I need him the most. The memories of his spiteful words make it hard to look him directly in the face without wanting to slap him.

"Somebody's been snooping," he says, tilting his head to the side while his eyes rake lower over my body. He leans himself back against the desk, placing his hands behind him as he leans against the wood, apparently having no intention of leaving any time soon.

"I wasn't snooping," I say quietly, looking down into my lap. I all of a sudden feel very miniscule in his presence, like he's here only to belittle me some more and cause me more pain. I hear him tut at my feeble lie before his finger is under my chin, bringing my face back up to look at him.

"Now, now Lucille, don't lie to me," he mocks, squeezing my chin between his thumb and forefinger. "I don't like liars." How dare he.

"Get your hands off me!" I snap, jumping from my chair and knocking his hands away from my face. "You don't get to fucking touch me, Cole. Not after what you did to me." I hurl, throwing my hands in the air. "You don't get to fucking do that to me." I add, my voice cracking slightly at the end. I can feel my eyes burning again, a sure and familiar warning that I'm going to cry. But I won't let him get the satisfaction, even if I have to turn around, I won't let him see me cry.

Cole's demeanor shifts, and like those horrible films I've seen where somebody gets possessed by the devil, his eyes turn almost black, painting him in his most menacing form. I take a tentative step backwards, only for him to counter and take one forwards, taunting me. My eyes involuntarily flick towards the door and I know by the cruel smirk now pulling at his lips that he caught the action. I launch myself forwards, aiming straight for my exit but Cole is much faster and stronger than I am. I'm certain he let me get so close on purpose before I felt him grab onto my wrist. Before I know what's happening, Cole spins me to face him and slams me back into the door with both hands secured above my head. The movement was so quick I have to close my eyes to regain my balance. I can smell the spiced whiskey on his breath and feel the warmth of his words as he leans into my body.

"Open your eyes," he orders. The words are so loud in this empty room that he could have whispered them and they still would have been loud enough to make me startle. I scrunch up my face, and turn my head to the side. Unwilling to look at this unfamiliar creature, because this was not the Cole I had grown to know, and it most definitely wasn't the Cole that I loved. "Look at me, Lucille." He snaps, losing his patience as he secures both wrists with one hand and brings the other down to caress my cheek. Not long ago there was a time when this would have been everything I could ask for, but right now this isn't what I want. I open my eyes and bring my face back to look at him, earning a satisfied grin in response. "Still so obedient for me," he smirks.

I was always taught that it was un-lady like to spit, but fuck it if I'm a lady. I lean my head back and spit into his face, though the satisfaction it gives me is short-lived when Cole immediately presses my body further into the door, digging his fingers into my cheeks as he holds my head in place.

"That wasn't nice Lucille," he goads. "After everything I've done for you, you just spit it all back in my face."

"You left me," I choke, fighting hard not to let the tears spill. Cole closes his eyes as the deep contemplation that haunted him earlier returns and his fingers loosen ever so slightly on my face. I'm not sure whose heart is beating faster but I can feel them both fighting to break out of their cages against my chest as his body is flush against mine. Cole looks back up at me, anger, confusion and regret swimming through his eyes before he forces his lips to mine, slamming my head back against the door and taking me completely off guard. I try to push him away from me but he only kisses me harder, biting and sucking on my lower lip until I relinquish my restraint and open my mouth to his. His tongue is on mine in an instant and I relish in the way that he tastes. With a mind of its own my own tongue fights back for dominance as I descend into the depth of hell right alongside him, using all of my anger to sink my teeth into his lip. I feel his smile against my mouth as the coppery tang of blood seeps onto my tongue and I can't help the ache that's materializing between my legs. I never want this to end, I'll forgive him for everything right here right now if he just gives me more of what my body is craving, but Cole breaks away, leaving me gasping. I catch my breath for a second before his body tenses, putting me back on edge and, bringing his lips to my ear he whispers three words that rip my still beating heart from my chest.

"You deserved it," he breathes.

My breathing hitches in my throat at his words. I deserved what he did to me? To hurt me in such a way when I was already so vulnerable and then to leave me without another look back? I collapse to the floor as Cole releases me, my knees unable to bear my own weight any longer as my heart seizes in my chest.

I'm not sure how long I had been laying on the floor of the office for after that before Silas came back in and found me.

Chapter 12

Silas

I can feel Lucille's breathing change ever so slightly beneath me. I know she's no longer asleep, her body oozes tension. She's overthinking everything again, seeing Max and then Lincoln losing his temper in front of her really knocked her for six. She's used to seeing my temper getting the best of me, she almost expects it from me and on some level accepts that it is just how I am. In that regard I have never lied to her, I have always shown her my true self. Lincoln however hides that side of him. Out of the three of us, he has always been the best at being able to keep his demons at bay, only releasing them when he deems necessary. But tonight Lucille saw the Lincoln Rossi that our enemies fear.

I close my eyes and breathe in her scent of sweet roses and a hint of cinnamon, letting myself relax with her resting against my chest. My peaceful doze doesn't last long though as a quiet but urgent tap sounds from the door. Fuck. Slowly removing myself from behind her, instantly missing the warmth of her body against mine, I pull the blanket back up over her body, half expecting her to open her eyes as I do, but she remains still and continues to pretend to sleep as I leave the room. I decide to lock the door behind me, the state Lucille has been in today, I wouldn't put it past her to run for the hills, and we have too many enemies around for that. Even if I would quite enjoy the chase under other circumstances.

Dario stands a little further away at the top level of stairs just outside of my office, raising a brow at me as the sounds of Lucille trying to open the door sound out from behind me, just about audible over the club music downstairs.

"You sure that's a good idea?" he smirks.

"She hates me right now anyway so it can't make it any worse." I laugh. I feel relieved that she still has this fight in her with everything she is going through right now. She truly is the queen to my kingdom. "Is everything OK?" I ask.

"Yes…Well sort of. I'm getting worried about Rossi. He hasn't stopped since the doc got here—"

I hold up my hand and Dario immediately pauses. "I'll check on him. Thank you Dario" I nod, giving Dario the reassurance and sending him on his way. I know he means well. Linc is already running on less fumes than the rest of us, he'll crash and burn if he isn't careful. But I know how stubborn he is, and he will want to see that Max is OK before he gets any rest himself.

I make my way downstairs and silently enter the holding room. Lincoln is pacing the room while Max looks like something out of a sci-fi movie with multiple fluid lines hooked up to his barely alive looking body. I am pissed at Lincoln for letting his temper get the best of him, but in reality I am as much to blame as he is. I almost killed him earlier today, and I think I would have too if it weren't for Lucille pulling me out of my trance. I shake my head, taking another look around the room and locking my eyes on the parasite that is lurking in the corner. Lincoln gave me warning of his plan to bring the doctor here, but seeing him in the flesh makes me want to set his fucking skin on fire. I can feel my blood beginning to bubble at the mere thought of the creep being in the same building as Lucille.

He shouldn't even be able to breathe the same air as her. She still, to this day, doesn't know what he had planned for her that night and I will be forever thankful for my brother and the way that he protected her, at a time when she didn't even know how much she really needed him. That's what really confuses me about his sudden behavior. He wanted nothing more than to keep her out of harm's way, but now he is the one causing her all the harm. Cole is the one damaging her by staying away. I still haven't heard from him. I've tried countless times to contact him. But everytime he evades me.

"What the FUCK is going on, Lin?" I bellow, making my presence known. Dr Thomas Graves stills at my voice before he nervously shifts towards Max's body.

"Si, he owes us, he owes Lucille," Lincoln responds as he stops pacing, looking tense and immediately sensing how much I want to slit the man's throat as I ball up my fists. He's trying to make me see reason before doing something I'll regret.

"He does owe us, and if Mr Costello here doesn't pull through, he will pay the fucking price. I hope you've made him aware of that" I seethe through tightly gritted teeth.

"He knows exactly what will happen if Max doesn't pull through" he responds with a matter of fact tone, narrowing his eyes as the doctor fumbles nervously with his equipment. I glance over to Linc who eyes me warily, the dark lines of exhaustion hollowing out his usually sharply sculpted face.

"Does she hate me?" he asks, his voice betraying his previous aggression.

"No, she doesn't hate you. She's upset and frightened, sure, but I don't think she could ever hate you, Lincoln." I huff out before moving closer to the good Dr.

123

Graves. "So Doc, are you going to live another day?" I ask with a menacing smirk on my face. If there is one thing I hate, it is when someone preys on a woman who is incapacitated.

"Whhhatt do you mean? You mean Max? He's—" He starts to stutter but I cut him off.

"No, Tom, I mean you. If Max here dies, so do you. Your fate is linked to his now. Isn't it ironic?" I taunt him.

Tom's face has gone pale and I love it. He looks as though he might faint but he simply nods. "I have told Lincoln I'm sorry for what happened with Lucille…"

Before he can even get a word out of his dirty mouth, I grab him by the throat, tightening my grip around it until I can feel his windpipe crushing beneath my fingers. I can feel his panic, my desire to end him here and now is causing me conflict as he sputters and tries to get free, desperately clawing his nails into my hands and arms.

Leaning into his face a feral growl escapes me, "You do not speak her name, you do not think of her, she is not to entertain any of your thoughts. Because if she does, I'll take great pleasure in removing your vile tongue from your mouth then I will remove each of your fingers, slowly and painfully, for every person that you have ever preyed on, and when I finally run out of fingers to play with, that's when things will really start to get messy. Remember, Dr. Graves, I know all about your activities, so you will do well not to test my patience." I release him before I cut off his airway completely and he immediately collapses to the floor, holding his neck and rasping heavily, trying to pull the air back into his lungs. "Now, tell me when Mr. Costello will be fit and awake for our questioning."

"I told Lincoln, without going to the hospital, I

cannot decipher all of his injuries. He might not survive without scans and equipment I don't have here."

"Well, Tom, I just need him to be awake for long enough to answer a few more questions." I smirk at him.

"Well, I would say from his vital signs, he'll be awake by morning. All the observations are looking good so far. But only time will tell." he explains.

"That's good news for you both then. I'll be back later to check his progress. Don't fuck this up, Doctor" I inform him. Then I turn to Lincoln, who's sitting in the chair opposite glaring darkly at Dr. Graves.

"I'm going back to check on Lucille and the club. I'll be back in an hour. If he wakes before that, ring me. I want to be present while you interrogate him again"

Before leaving the room I take one last glance at the scum that is Dr. Graves and nod to Lincoln. "Ensure he is gone before Lucille comes to see her brother, Lincoln." I instruct him vehemently. I do not trust this doctor.

Leaving the room, I walk down the corridor back towards my office where I left Lucille. As I approach the door, I notice that it's slightly open. I know full well I locked this door when I left. I frantically panic that Lucille has been taken, but when I push through the door my stomach bottoms out as I find Lucille slumped on the floor, shaking with silent cries while tears fall endlessly down her cheeks. Before I know what I'm doing, I'm on the floor in front of her, pulling her into my body. "Lucille, it's okay. Max is fine. He's just resting." I tell her, trying to reassure her. I gently place my hands on her cheeks and lift her face to mine. Her green eyes are full of sadness, broken and dull, lacking that emerald green glow they once held.
What she says next shocks me.

"Your brother was here, I don't know how he got in here but I think he came looking for something. I'm sorry, I don't know what it was," she shakes her head trying to contain her emotions. Her shakes turn into trembles and I can't tell if it's through anger or sadness, but maybe it's both. She wipes away her tears and continues, "I let him get to me again, I just want him to come back to us. This is not him, Silas. I refuse to give up on him even if he's given up on us. But this is breaking me even more"

"It's okay la mia luce, we won't give up on either of them. Teddy or Cole. If I have to beat some sense into Cole, I will. But he will come back to us and we will find Teddy. I promise you, everything will be okay." I assure her, hoping that I can keep to my word.

"I just want to wake up from his nightmare, Silas," she whimpers. It feels as though hours pass as I hold her close to me, in that exact position on the floor, and comfort her the best way that I can, when eventually a knock at the door startles us both.

"Boss, Lincoln sent me to inform you that he's awake," grunts Dario at the door, he knows better than to come in whilst Lucille is here with me.

"Tell him I'll be right with him," I instruct Dario, not making any attempt to move from Lucille. Her eyes search mine and she's about to ask for something I would normally deny her. I can see the determination in her eyes.

"Please, Silas, let me see him. Let me come with you. I know he's got a lot to answer for. But please don't leave me here alone again."

Her eyes are wide and hopeful waiting for me to give her exactly what she wants. The thought of her on her knees begging me pops into my mind. I tell myself it is not the right time for that. But somehow my cock doesn't get the message as I feel it harden beneath my trousers. I

126

choke slightly as I reply. "Okay la mia luce, but just promise me that you'll let us do what is needed."

She moves so fast wrapping her arms around me tightly. "Thank you, Silas" she all but whispers. I smile as I kiss the top of her head, then lead her from the room to where Max is being treated.

As we enter the room I hear Lucille suck in a gasp as she locks eyes on Max laying on the table, taking tentative sips of water from Lincoln as he helps him to lean forward. I chuckle at the sight.

"New occupation, Linc? Suits you. Maybe Lucille can lend you her uniform next time you play nurse." Lucille pushes past me to get to the table, she immediately takes the drink from Lincoln's hand and continues to assist Max, leaving Linc redundant.

"Fuck off! I'd prefer to be the patient, and Lucille be my nurse." Lincoln grunts, not making eye contact with her.

Lucille glares at him before scoffing at his comment. "You'll need a nurse if my brother doesn't make a full recovery, Lincoln. You have a lot of groveling to do." I smirk at Lincoln as I see the side of his mouth lift up in a smile, but he adjusts his face quickly. He loves her sass as much as I do and it's pleasing to see she hasn't lost it..

I watch him as he turns to her and places his hand gently over hers. "I'm sorry, Love, I let my anger and fear get the best of me. I will spend the rest of my days proving to you that I can be better, I will be better for you." Lucille does not respond in words but she doesn't have to, her hand squeezes his hand and then she directs all her attention to her brother once more.

"Max..." she starts to say before he cuts her off.

"Luce, I'm okay. I'm not sure you should be here though. I know what they need to do. It's what I would do."

his voice crackles as he glances at me.

"Well they aren't you, Max. They will give me a choice to be here or God help them." Lucille says assertively. I can't help the smile that forms on my face at that. My girl may stumble but she rises to any challenge put in front of her.

"She's right, if she chooses to be here for our chat, then she can be. I won't hide her away any longer. She deserves to know the truth more than any of us." Linc replies. Max glances over at Lincoln and then at me again.

And as the penny drops, he frowns and looks to his sister. "Both of them? Really Luce?"

She giggles and turns to me and winks, I can't help but beam at her. I haven't seen her look like that in awhile. "Not that it's any of your business Max, but yes." She tells him firmly.

Max closes his eyes and mutters "fuckers" under his breath which only makes me laugh out loud causing him to glare once more in my direction.

"What we really need to know, Max, is what happened? Where is Teddy?" Lincoln asks, getting us back on track. I can tell he's beginning to get impatient. He wants answers, as do we all.

Max coughs and I can tell he must have some broken ribs, or at least severe bruising from the way he winces as the motion, placing his hand onto his chest.

"Like I already told you. I don't know where Teddy is. All I know is they came like thieves in the night. We were asleep when they ambushed us. My men, men I trusted, turned on me and decided to do their dealings with the devil instead." His voice shakes with anger at the betrayal and he pauses for a second, gazing directly at Lucille before grasping her hands in his own. "I woke up alone in a cellar, Teddy was nowhere in sight. Ronan and his men arrived after and he admitted to the break in. He admitted he had worked alongside Theo in Theo's plan to use you as bait with Vinny to enable him to take the head spot in the club once he snuffed out the three of you" he adds, casting his eyes to Linc and me before he continues. "That was until he betrayed Theo and took off with Teddy to groom him to take over the family business in my place."

Lucille gasps, her bottom lip trembling slightly as she asks "How did you get free?"

"I... I don't know exactly. Someone helped me. I think... unless I was too delirious at that point. Ronan had given his order to finish me off but I was knocked out soon after. As soon as I came round, I found my way to your apartment, needing to know that you were safe." Max's eyes begin to close as his words become more and more drawn out. Lucille must notice too as she turns to me with a fierce and meaningful look in her eyes.

"Get some rest Max, we will pick apart your story in more depth another time. You have your sister to thank that it's not our usual form of interrogation." I tell him with a light chuckle. He barely nods before closing his eyes completely.

"What are we going to do?" Lucille asks with desperation in her voice.

"Lincoln and I need to check on a few business issues, you need to rest, la mia luce." I inform her.

"But who's going to take care of Max?" She questions, like she's the one doing the interrogating now. God I love this woman.

"We have a doctor who owes us a favor. He will watch over Max until he's fit enough to leave, don't worry." She frowns but nods, accepting my honest answer.

My phone begins to ring before we leave the room. I look down at the screen and frown.

"Hello?" I answer firmly, why the hell is Benji calling me?

"Boss, we need backup at the restaurant. I couldn't get hold of Enzo, some of the Costello gang have shown up." Benji sputters desperately before being interrupted by gunshots in the background. The line immediately goes dead.

"FUCK!" I shout, gripping the phone so tight I fear I'll crack the screen. The restaurant is where we keep our drug shipments just before they are transported to the distributors. Lincoln looks at me, he's ready for me to direct him on how to proceed. Lucille can't be involved in this. I need her somewhere safe, in case Cole comes back for whatever it is he's looking for.

"Lucille, you need to go to a safe house. The doctor and Dario will stay here and look after Max. Sully will accompany you," I order.

Lucille tuts at me. "No, I'm not going to run and hide Silas." She protests. This really isn't the time for her to argue with me, we need to move. "I'll go to Katrinas. Whoever Sully is, he can stand guard if he must but I need to be with someone familiar to me right now, please." Lucille sighs, her eyes softening around the edges. I can't deny her that request. She's being reasonable at least.

"Fine, but don't leave her apartment unless Sully tells you too. If you want updates on Max, Sully will call Dario to feed back, do you understand?" I relay to her as I stroke her cheek, hovering my thumb over her bottom lip. Her eyes meet mine and she nods. I capture her lips with mine and kiss her like a wild animal. My tongue fights against hers, I want to devour her. This woman has me wrapped around her little finger and isn't even aware of it.

Lincoln coughs in the background which makes me pull away leaving Lucille panting for breath, but before she can recover Lincoln spins her around and pulls her into his embrace, whispering that he's sorry before seizing her lips as well. His kiss is short and sweet, tender but affirmative, and once more she's left panting as she brings her fingers to trace the lines of her lips that are deliciously swollen from us.

"Inform Sully of his duties Lincoln," I instruct him. Lincoln leaves the room to inform his head of security, and all things brutal, of the duties he needs to fulfill.

"Silas, please keep Lincoln safe, I might be mad at him but I need him back whole." Lucille admits..

"Always mi luce, anything else you wish for me to do?" I grin at her, a fool in love type of grin and she blushes. I like that color in her cheeks, a delicate pink for my feisty woman. I like her being bratty, bossy and all things sassy.

"No, no I think that's all," she says as Lincoln returns with Sully following close behind.

"Keep her safe." Lincoln practically growls at Sully as he moves to stand behind Lucille. My glare at him should be enough for him to understand, without my words, that he is to keep her from harm at all costs.

Just as Lucille gets to the door, she stops and turns to face me. "Actually there is one last thing. Silas, make sure you come back in one piece, too. I'd miss arguing with you." Without another glance she is out the door with Sully in her shadow and hopefully out of harm's way.

Lincoln turns eagerly to face me, knowing the news isn't good. "We need to get to the restaurant ASAP. Ronan's men have ambushed Benji and his guys." Lincoln's face drops as he realizes what this means and I hear the murmur of profanities under his breath as he rakes his fingers through his hair. "Also, where the fuck is Enzo?" I snap making my way through the house to the armory.

"He took a run up town to settle a dispute over some dodgy handguns. He rang me not long after his own interrogation but I didn't think much of it. He said he'd left Benji in charge. Figured he just wanted to let me know what was happening considering he's leading them now so this was his first task he wanted to deal with himself." Linc divulges, shrugging his shoulders. I guess it makes sense that he wanted to go himself to sort the problem. It also accounts for why Benji couldn't get hold of him when he tried to ring. Though, I don't think Enzo being there would have made much of a difference from the way that phone call sounded.

We grab as much ammunition as we can before we race across town to Salvatore's Cucina to head off Ronan and his men. I have a total of five firearms concealed in my suit, not to mention the knives I have strapped to me. I will relish using them to cut the hearts out of those that have chosen the wrong side of this war. Lincoln is no different, he grabbed as many weapons as he could tuck away. We are anticipating a fight on our hands and many casualties. I only hope Benji and the rest of the men are holding on until we arrive.

"I don't think I've seen you drive this fast before, Linc." I remark as he speeds toward the restaurant. He doesn't get a chance to respond to me because of what is awaiting us. The sight before us is shocking and I feel devastatingly angry, too angry to form a sentence. Thick black smog seeps out of the building, the raging flames visible from our vantage point, they are wild and uncontrollable. Lincoln doesn't waste any time parking, he hand brake turns the car into the lot, and we jump out of the car as fast as we can to assess the damage. I evaluate the area as we move closer to the building, the air is unbreathable as we approach, both myself and Lincoln cover our faces with our jackets. The closer to the building we get, we can hear voices, Lincoln runs off ahead. Benji and two others are trying to salvage some of our supplies.

"What the fuck happened?" Lincoln barks at them, snapping their attention to our arrival.

"Boss... He... Cole... We..." Benji stutters and coughs trying to explain what the fuck has gone on. How has our inventory burnt to a fucking crisp? Just as I am about to say as much, a familiar voice cackles through the chaos.

"Welcome Brothers, to my reign of fire." Cole grins maliciously. I'm not sure if I am ready for what happens next.

Chapter 13

Cole

Seeing her, feeling mio topolino's lips against mine, I almost gave in to it. My resolve wavered, I couldn't leave my brother's strip club fast enough, but I had to get my hands on the shipment details. Lucille was just a complication at that point. One that I craved beyond anything. Now standing outside of the place that I had made my own, my safe haven until her. I'm grieving as I know that I must now destroy it. I need to do this or I'll never find him. My phone buzzes from my pocket. Glancing at the number, it's him, I have to take it even though he is the last person I want to talk to right now.Taking a deep breath I put the phone to my ear.

"Cole, have you got the details Ronan has asked for? he asks.

"Yes, there was a complication but I dealt with it." I explain truthfully.

"Well it will be your head on the chopping block if they find out what you are doing," he taunts me. I have more to lose than anyone who is in on this operation.

"It's fine, it's sorted. I'm about to put the nail in the coffin so to speak. So as riveting as this conversation is, I have to get the dirty work done, unlike some." I sneer back at him. He's really pissing me off with his orders. My temper can only withstand so much bullshit from him.

"Now, now Cole, you want pretty little Lucille to come to no harm? Do as I say otherwise she'll be finding herself in some trouble that not even your brother's lawyer can get her out of, mark my words." He chastises me.

"Fuck you, I'm just your pawn in this game, they

survive as long as I do as you ask. You never said I needed to be polite about it," I snap.

"Maybe I should change my terms and conditions then. You need to learn to show some respect otherwise this whole operation will go up in flames," he hisses. Well that gives me food for thought. It's time I ignite the fire and leave no one questioning me as to where my loyalties lie.

"As you wish," I say, hanging up the phone. He can get fucked if he wants me to say goodbye politely.

Walking towards Salvatore Cucina, I don't even bother to creep into the place. I have to get this done as quickly as possible. As I enter the establishment, I hope I don't run into Enzo, because that would make this even harder than it's already going to be.

I see Benji at the bar, talking to one of our lower leveled men. Tod or something. Knowing Benji, he will have two others in the back packing and sorting the goods for pick up tonight. It's a well oiled machine. I always liked a good work ethic, get the shit done efficiently and we won't have problems, the men here are the same. No nonsense. Benji's eyes met mine, he looks unsure of me, as he should be. I trained him, not even I am to be trusted when it comes to this world. Good Benji, my brother has you as loyal at least, otherwise I'd have to kill you, maybe not today but at some point.

Benji motions to Tod to go out back. I'll bet to inform Silas, good I want them here to witness this. They have to believe this as much as Ronan. "Boss, where have you been?" Benji asks, I see him move his hand, he's got his hand on his gun. I'm kind of proud of him right now, not many men would have the balls to even reach for it in my presence.

"Benji, Benji, Benji. Do you remember the night I

135

first met you?" I ask. The crazy manic is coming out to play.

"Yes, you were taking the eyes out of one of our enemies, the fact it was in broad daylight made no difference to you." he responds comically.

"Ahhh yes, that fucker deserved worse. He raped his step daughter repeatedly. But alas, I'm glad you remember. I bet you're wondering why I am here? It's the same as that day. I've come for retribution." I smirk.

Benji pulls his gun out but I'm too quick for him and lunge over the bar. He struggles but I overpower him easily. He releases his gun, and it drops to the floor. That is disappointing, he has been slacking on the weights. No change there but that will cost him. I might not plan to kill him but he's going to have to carry some wounds away with him today. I push all of my weight down on his arm until I hear the bone snap beneath my weight and he screams in agony. The doors fly open seconds later, two men rushing in, looking more green than the money in my pocket.

"Get the fuck out of here, get the supplies out!!" Benji snaps, they retreat quickly. Benji struggles out of my grip, and crawls to the doors of the kitchen. I let him get a head start. My plan isn't for him to die, it's to show Silas and Lincoln I am not on their side.

"Run away boys, you won't get far," I taunt, laughing menacingly.

I follow Benji to the kitchen, the guys are already out of the door with the bags of cocaine. I begin to make my way over to the stove, running my fingers across the stainless steel. It's a shame this will all be ruined. I turn the gas hobs to full, letting the smell engulf my nostrils. I take in one last look at the kitchen, before leaving out the door to follow Benji. Benji is shouting down the phone, to my brother I assume. I smirk, "Benjiiiii, it's time to play." That gets his attention, his eyes meet mine, I see the panic in them. I pull my gun out of its holster and shoot at his upper leg making him drop to the ground. His phone slides across the tarmac towards me, I smile as I see the name on the screen before stamping on it, we don't need them to hear what is going to happen next.

"So, Benji, here is what is going to happen. You and the rest of the men here are going to fuck off unless you want to become chargrilled. Understand? Gather that up and fuck off. You have two minutes otherwise, I can't say that I like your chances of survival."

Benji glares at me before I turn and enter the building once again. The smell of gas is so strong now that I have to cover my hand over my face as I stroll through, taking one last look at the place that means so much to me. Stopping at the door I finally light the match to one of the curtains, watching the flames begin to dance up the walls like wildfire. I make quick work of leaving the restaurant before the flames ignite the leaking gas.

Watching from outside as the building begins to smoke, thick smog rises into the air. I hear the screeching sound of a car pulling up around the back of the restaurant. They have arrived. Silas and Lincoln. It's time for me to put on a show.

I make my way around the building, the smoke is getting thicker with every minute that passes. It's becoming difficult to breathe. That's when I see them, questioning Benji, who is clutching leg, desperately trying to stem the bleeding. I don't even think Silas in his rage has noticed that he's hurt.

Laughing wildly, I finally gain their attention.

"Welcome Brothers, to my reign of fire."

The look on their faces is priceless, I kind of wish I had a camera.

"Get out of here, NOW!" Lincoln demands to Benji and the rest of the team, and they don't have to be asked twice.

"What the fuck is going on, Cole?" Silas asks.

I smirk at him, "Well, what do you think is going on?"

"Don't play games, Cole, why are you doing this?" Lincoln coughs through the smoke.

It's getting more and more toxic the longer we are here. I want nothing more than to tell Lincoln and Silas the truth but too much is on the line.

"Why do we do anything in this life, Lincoln? We do it for our own gain. Maybe I'm fed up with being second to you when it comes to my brother. I was second to him in my fathers eyes. I can already see that I am second or most likely third for Lucille." I sneer at them both. It's all bullshit, I don't feel any of this. I never have but I know they worry about such things. It's the only way for me to convince them of my betrayal.

Before they can reply to my deception, a bright flash blinds my eyes as the force of the building exploding knocks us off our feet. The air is so full of smoke, it's hard to see exactly where they are. I ignore the panic inside of me that wants to check that they're okay. It's time to get out of here before I do something stupid.

Running towards my bike, I jump on, looking back one last time. As I do, I see Silas and Lincoln running towards me shouting my name. Relief washes over me at the knowledge that they are safe. I press the pedal down and speed away from the suffocating air, but no matter how far away I ride away, I still feel the weight of my actions. They may never forgive me for what I'm about to do, let alone what I have already done.

Watching the flames engulf my restaurant hit hard, it was the place I could lose myself in without inflicting pain on anyone. My demons rarely reached me when I submersed myself in the kitchen. It felt like losing a piece of my sanity, as the fire burnt the building down, the ash filled the air quickly and flooded the sky with its thick gray smoke. But as bad as that felt, walking away from mio topolino again was a hundred times worse. The kiss we shared is cemented into my memory, I can still taste her on my lips, her sweet mouth felt so good. She fought me, but I felt her softness before I came to my senses and pulled away. I knew as soon as the words left my lips to tell her she deserved it, I'd regret it. She crumbled and all I wanted to do in that moment was to hold her and tell her everything. But I couldn't, not yet. I need to ensure my plan would work, and in order to do that, they must all hate me. I managed to get what I needed from the office, but I wasn't expecting her to be there, it made my mission more difficult. It was the hardest thing I've had to do, see her and leave her, make her believe I am the monster. It's the second time I've had to abandon her, and I feel like each time my soul is being ripped from my body, it's fighting to get back to her. She is the other half of me, the air to my lungs. I try to push away the overwhelming feelings of despair and regret at how I have had to treat her. It is for her own good, I keep reminding myself, no matter how much I wish to keep her, I want her safe more than I want to be selfish.

I pull up to the abandoned house on the outskirts of town. It's the address that Ronan has arranged to meet me at once I had burnt bridges with Silas and Lincoln. It's funny that it's exactly what I've done. I have done as Ronan has asked, I've even gone the extra mile and secured my brother's next shipment plans. All so Ronan can intercept them and steal them from him. Silas is not going to take this well. I know my brother and his temper, he will want to kill me or he will kill some poor soul in a fit of rage. Silas sees everything as black and white. You are on his side or you are the enemy. Lincoln however will be his level headed self, always looking at the picture as a whole. He's the one I have to fool. He will not believe I can be this disloyal to them. It breaks me that I have to deceive him. He might not be blood but he has always had faith in my tarnished soul. He might never forgive me for this.

Taking a deep breath, I dismount from my bike, and make my way to the front door. This house is old, the front yard is overgrown and full of weeds. The fence that surrounds the house is broken in parts and the paint that looks to have been white once upon a time has faded away. As I begin to walk up the steps leading to the porch, I hear raised voices.

"You will not question my authority unless you want me to cut that tongue from your mouth, do you hear me? Now keep the boy happy until I have dealt with this psychopath." Ronan bellows. Is Teddy here I wonder? But before I even make it to the top of the steps, the front door flies open. Ronan is standing with one of his men smirking at me. "Cole, is the deed done?" he smirks.

I take in my surroundings, knowing that I must play this game, I must survive and ensure everyone else will too.

140

"Yes," I respond shortly.

"Let's go inside then and break bread as they say," Ronan chuckles.

I follow him into the old house, it looks even more run down in here than it does from the outside. The curtains are barely holding up, some of the windows are boarded and there is a smell that I recognize. The smell of rotting flesh. This is a torture house. I wonder if Max was kept here before he escaped. Ronan isn't aware he's letting not only myself into his circle but he has another mole scurrying around, picking the pieces from his table, collecting all the little bits of information they need to make their move. The trouble is, that person isn't on my team either, he's not an ally, he's someone I need to watch carefully. I scan the room, making a mental note of all the exits in case this is an ambush. I don't trust him, but I need him to trust me.

Ronan takes a seat in the only chair worth sitting in, and glares at me.

"What exactly did you do? I can see the smoke from here. I wanted their stock! Not to burn it to the ground and start a war Cole!"

"I think it's a little late for not starting a war, Ronan. You pulled the pin on that one. I lit the place up, burnt my bridges and let the ash linger to remind them exactly what I can do." I tell him. This guy must see that he's already started a war by taking Teddy but he is missing a few brain cells so maybe he doesn't.

"Well yes, I suppose I have." he says, as if the penny has just dropped. My patience for this is going to be tested, Lincoln would have been more suited for this. He would have played this so much better than me.

Snapping me from my thoughts Ronan continues. "I want to intercept their next shipment, you will do it for me and I expect to see a profit. Otherwise the boy may have a nasty accident." he begins to laugh. I contain myself knowing he's goading me. He's trying to get me to crack.

"You know the deal, Ronan. You keep him from harm and I will help you take everything from my brother and his territory. I have their plans for when the next shipment will land." I say coolly.

"Yes, well I will keep to my end as long as you keep yours. How did your dear brother and his lap dog look when you dropped the match?" he asks gleefully.

"As you would expect. Violent. Betrayed. Vengeful. Pick one and I'm sure any will fit. Besides, it doesn't matter what they feel." I say keeping my voice low and calm all whilst my inner turmoil is raging to kill this bastard and be done with it. I have to remind myself of the deal I made with the devil to take him down his way and keep Teddy safe in the process.

He laughs, "I bet that bitch is distraught that her knight in shining armor has betrayed her too." His shadow, weedy fuck of a bodyguard smirks at me as he says this. Bastards, I'll gut them all before this is over for daring to even speak of Lucille. But I smile, keeping the murderous thoughts to myself. Little do they know, my grin is genuine as I fantasize about ripping their hearts from their chests and giving them to my little mouse as her trophies one day very soon.

"I'm sure she has plenty of cock to keep her from being too distraught." I mutter to them. I have to make them believe I don't care for her and my reason for being here is because I only care for the boy as I don't want what happened to me to happen to him. While that is a huge part of this, I also love her so much that I will sacrifice myself for her in the end. My love is poison to her, she deserves to be treated like the queen she is. I trust Lincoln and my brother with that. Ronan and his men can never be aware of this. So everyone must believe the worst of me, that I am unredeemable.

They laugh and continue to make disgusting jokes about her as I stand quietly losing myself to the void to keep from snapping their necks. It would be all too easy as they have relaxed now and even poured themselves a drink.

"Well as fun as this is Ronan, I need my assurances about the boy." I explain.

"You will get those assurance once I have your filthy fucking brothers shipment!" Ronan bellows at me, rising from his chair. I feel my shadows creeping inside, they want to come out and play. But I take a breath and respond politely through gritted teeth.

"After I get the shipment, you will take me to the boy, Ronan. That is the deal. Now, if you'll excuse me, I have to get the stench of smoke from my clothes." I add, making my excuse to leave before I can no longer keep my anger at bay. Ronan waves me off not realizing the danger he's so close to getting himself in.

Leaving the house, I take in the view in the distance of the smog floating from the inner city. I wish we weren't in this mess, I would give anything to be with my little mouse, holding her, devouring her, comforting her, instead of how we left things. She looked as though she had given up on me, I can't say I blame her. The look on her face will haunt me forever, but if I can keep Teddy safe and sound then it will be worth it, and for right now, I have to focus on the fact that he's alive. I just hope wherever Ronan has him that he's not suffering.

143

I saddle my bike, revving the engine before speeding off to find the devil himself, so we can plan our next move.

Chapter 14

Lucille

"Jesus Christ girl! Get over here!" Are the first words to spill from Katrina's mouth as she opens the door to her apartment. "I've been so fucking worried Luce." I all but break right there as she pulls me into her chest, wrapping her arms around me in a hold so tight and comforting that I never want her to release me. "It's ok baby girl, it's ok," she mumbles repeatedly into my hair as she kisses the top of my head, trying to soothe the distraught tangle of sobs that wrack my body.

"You can leave now, I'll take it from here." I hear her say with a snide tone in her voice before she closes the door and drags me into her pristine but well-lived-in home. I go with her willingly and let her drag me onto the couch as she holds me tightly into her chest. With everything that has been happening, I hadn't realized just how much I needed Kat in my life and how much I'd missed her until this moment right here, where all of my secrets can come spilling out and the very ugly truth that is my life right now can be laid bare.

Kat has been a constant in my life since I ran from Vinny and turned up on Max's doorstep only a few years ago. We hit it off instantly as we both found our feet within the hustle and bustle of the nursing world while simultaneously raising our babies as single parents. I let her into the dark depths that were my past on a drunken night together when the kids were about two years old. We drank and we cried while we put our worlds to rights and badmouthed our so-called baby daddies. Though my own experience of this was something completely different to Kats, opposite ends of the spectrum entirely.

Isabella, Kats daughter had a father, and he was around in the very beginning until he, all of a sudden, decided to shack up with somebody else and refuse to pay child support. My child's father had no idea where the fuck I was or that I had even given birth. I had fully intended for it to stay that way too, until the monster that I so naively thought I'd buried came back to not only turn my life on its axis, but completely rip my soul to pieces in the process.

"You need to tell me what's happened," Kat encourages, bringing my thoughts straight back into the room. "I knew something was wrong as soon as you didn't turn up to work. Girl, I rang you so many times and then your phone just stopped ringing. I've tried getting as much information as I could out of your bloody henchmen but that's like drawing blood from a stone, and Max isn't returning my calls either." Kat goes on as she cups my face into both palms and swipes her thumbs over my cheeks, attempting to swipe the tears that continue to fall freely. I stare into her eyes, her deep, beautifully colored mahogany eyes that once were so bright and joyful but now they hold such sorrow and despair as she stares straight back into my own. How far back do I go? Silas and Lincoln must have at least kept her at bay with some of the information. I know Kat and when she wants something, she won't let up until she's got it so she no doubt annoyed the information out of them until they broke and gave in to her incessant pestering.

I straighten myself away from Kat's hands, ignoring the hurt look in her eyes as I lean back against the couch cushions. You'd think I'd have cried out everything by now, but still the tears keep coming, it seems almost a waste of time to try and wipe them all away for only more to keep falling in their wake. I'm not entirely sure what to say as I feel Kat's eyes bore into the side of my face, so intensely that I have to turn away, focusing on a photo across the room of the four of us last summer at the beach. Teddy is laughing, his eyes are all scrunched up and his mouth open wide, capturing the moment. I can hear it now as the room around me blurs, the high-pitched happy squeals as he and Isabella wriggle their way in between Kat and I as we try to take a selfie. The memory seizes my heart with the most painful reminder of what's been taken from me.

In a trance-like state, I begin to explain everything that has happened since the last time I spoke to Kat, detailing everything from Lincoln's father being the reason Vinny showed up, to Max and Teddy being taken by my own step-father, to Cole being shot and then walking out on us and Max turning up at my apartment almost beaten to death. Kats reaction to this was horrifying so I made sure to reassure her that he is fine after Linc basically saved his life by calling in a private doctor after I accused him of trying to kill him. And then finally, I explain the phone call that Silas received before I came over. The phone call that was such a matter of urgency that he and Lincoln needed to leave immediately, refusing to take me with them and so here I am. Other than her outburst as I told her about Max, she stays quiet the whole time, holding my hands in her own and delivering reassuring squeezes every now and again when she realizes I'm finding it too hard to get the words out.

I think I've managed to cover everything when I finally breathe out, feeling like a huge monumental weight has been lifted from my chest at the thought of no longer having to deal with this alone. I force myself to meet her gaze again, only to realize, maybe I was not the only one who needed comforting as I relived the events of the last few days. Kat's face is tear-stained and swollen with eyes so puffy and red she looks like she's been crying for just as long as I have. The sight forms a guilty knot in the pit of my stomach.

"Teddy," she sobs, "do they think that he's alive?" The question itself makes my stomach churn again, tightening that fast growing tangle of anxiety, fear and guilt tearing up my insides. On what earth is that a question you should ever have to ask your best friend, or anybody for that matter? Is your child still alive? Have his kidnappers killed him? I have to believe that he is alive. It's the only thing that's keeping me going right now. The promising thought that I'll have him back in my arms again soon.

Scrunching my eyes closed as I try to banish the thoughts that conjure themselves from the darkest corners of my imagination, I answer her with much more confidence in my voice than I truly feel. "Max told us that Ronan wants to groom him to take over the business." I say firmly, as if to convince myself more than anything else. "I believe he is alive and I believe they will keep him alive too." I add. Kats grasp on my hands tightens and just as she opens her mouth to say whatever she thought might comfort me, the door behind us opens, making us both jump up to our feet. Isabella stands in the door frame for a beat, yawning, before her eyes grow wide when she looks over at me.

"Auntie Luci," she screams excitedly as her whole face lights up. She runs towards me into my already outstretched arms and lunges herself into my chest.

"Baby girl," I whisper into her hair. "I've missed you so, so much."

"Is Teddy here, too?" she asks, causing the air in my lungs to expel. I squeeze her hard then bring her back to an arms length in front of me while I run my fingers over her head, hair, cheeks, taking in every beautiful feature of her innocent face.

"No baby, he's not." That's all I can manage. I feel Kat place her hand onto my shoulder in a comforting gesture before she clears her throat, grabbing Isabella's attention.

"Come on sweetheart, let's get you back to bed." Kat sighs, holding out her hand for her to take but she does not move.

"Auntie Luci, will you put me to bed?" She asks, smiling wide from ear to ear with her eyes large and round, mimicking the cat from Shrek. The look reminds me so much of Teddy when he asks for chocolates before bed time, something he knows he shouldn't have, but when he looks at me like that, he knows he's won me over instantly. I close my eyes, capturing the memory before I sweep her up off the floor and cradle her into my arms.

"Of course my sweet baby Bella, I will put you to bed." I agree, turning to Kat who simply looks at me and nods with raw sympathy nestled deep within her eyes.

I wrap Bella up under the comforter of her princess castle bed and kiss her gently against her hair, making sure to tuck her favorite teddy in next to her and give them a kiss too.

"Goodnight angel," I whisper.

"Will Teddy be back tomorrow?" she asks, completely oblivious to the full impact her question has upon my heart. It's all I can do to keep my resolve in check, I will not break in front of her. I close my eyes and take a breath.

"He'll be back soon," I say, forcing a small smile for her hopeful gleaming eyes. "Now, the sooner you sleep, the sooner you can see him." I promise, for I know that to be true, wishing only I could just sleep the days away until my knights can bring him back to me. Isabella yawns and closes her eyes, sighing heavily as I stroke my fingers gently through her hair, the way Teddy likes me to when he is falling asleep in my arms.

"I love you, Auntie Luci," she mumbles quietly, before her breathing becomes deeper and her lips part ever so slightly as she dreams of a world so less fucked up than it really is. I place another gentle kiss against the top of her head and whisper my I love you before quietly slipping out of the room.

When I make my way back into the lounge, Kat has a steaming mug of coffee already waiting for me in her outstretched hand. "Thought you might need this," she offers with a small smile.

"Thank you. Is it alright if I stay the night?" I ask, slumping myself back onto the couch and pulling a cushion into my lap for comfort, something I've done ever since I left Vinny everytime I'm feeling anxious or insecure. I don't know what it is about it being there, but it makes me feel more secure. Like that cushion, or blanket could protect me from harm and without it, I'm left feeling fully exposed and vulnerable.

"I've already pulled you out some of my pajamas, girl. You were never leaving, even if you wanted to." Kat smiles at me over the rim of her coffee mug.

"I can't be here when Bella wakes up in the morning though. That was hard... I can't..."

Kats hand on my knee stops me before my lip starts to quiver. "I know," is all she says. "Also, I want you to take this," she offers, retrieving a small black flip phone from the pocket of her jeans. I eye it warily for a moment, and her, before picking the phone up and flipping it around in my palm.

"Kat, is this a burner phone?" I ask, raising my eyebrows to her, but she simply shrugs her shoulders like it's no big deal.

"You never know when you might need one Lucille. But right now you need a phone so I'm giving it to you. I've already put your three amigos' numbers in for you, as well as Max's and my own so you're ready to go," she trails on, like it's no big deal that she has a second phone ready to hand like this. It's like something my so-called three amigos should have already given me. Come to think of it, why haven't they? I'll be sure to bring it up to them tomorrow.

"Stop overthinking it, babe. My dad gave it to me in case I ever needed it a long time ago. I've kept it topped up and until now, I've never had a use for it so it's yours." I'm still skeptical. Why would her dad give her a phone in case she ever needed it. Kat never has explained much to me about her family. Whenever we've raised the subject of parents in the past, she just said there were always differences in the way they believed things should be handled and me being the non-intrusive person that I am, I never questioned her anymore on it. I slip the phone into my pocket and take a long sip on my coffee, trying not to think that my best friend could also be hiding secrets of her own.

The rest of the evening passes by in somewhat of a blur. Kat tries desperately to take my mind off Teddy by putting old reruns of RuPaul's Drag Race on the TV, something we used to watch religiously when the kids were babies, as that and strong black coffee were the only things that would get us through those long sleepless nights. But before long, she switches the screen to mute and turns to face me.

"Explain it all to me again. From the beginning. There must be something we're missing. Something that could lead us back to where Ronan is keeping Teddy."

I stare at her blankly for a heartbeat, but she's right. I need to think, I need to try and process it all to see if anything sparks some sort of revelation. So I do, I repeat everything that has happened from the beginning and we sit for hours trying to pick apart every piece of information that I know, even Cole's decision to detach himself from us, to just be reminded that we have little to no advantage on the situation at all. Wherever Teddy is, I just hope he's holding on better than I am. We've rarely spent nights apart from each other, only when he has stayed over at Kat's or Max's for a sleepover, and even then I miss him so much it hurts. But this kind of hurt is deep rooted, something I fear I will never recover from.

We retire to bed eventually after I check in with Sully, who, under orders from Lincoln, is to stand guard at Kat's front door for the entire night. The old me would have felt sympathy for him having to be out there all night, but now I just remind myself that that is his job, and it is men like him that are the reason my son is still missing and being groomed into some sort of fucking criminal mastermind. I shudder at the thought as I slide under the comforter on Kat's bed.

"Why do you think they had to rush off so quickly?" I ask absentmindedly into the dark of the room. I hear Kat sigh heavily beside me before I feel her shuffle a little closer.

"I don't know, babe," she admits defeatedly. "Maybe they've had some word on Teddy." I shake my head.

"No, I don't think that's what it is. I'm not sure what's happened, but something's telling me that whatever it was that had Silas so on edge isn't good at all." I say, staring up into the pitch black void above me. I relax slightly as Kat entwines her fingers with my own and strokes her thumb over my knuckles.

"They'll find him babe and they'll bring him home," she whispers.

"I know. I just wish... I just wish they'd hurry up." I choke out, feeling that familiar burn at the back of my eyes as I am once again drowned in tears.

A gentle nudge against my shoulder pulls me from my sleep. I fight the intrusion but Kat's voice forces me to open my eyes.

"Wake up babe. I got you a coffee before you go," she smiles as I pull myself up against the headboard, giving my thanks as I take the first welcoming sip. "Bella hasn't woken up yet but it won't be long if you want to get out first," she says, watching me carefully. "You're free to stay for as long as you need you know."

"I know, but I can't sit back and wait any longer Katrina. I need them to involve me or I'll find Teddy on my own." I say with more determination that I've felt before.

"You will not do anything so stupid." Kat scolds me, giving me a fierce look with her hands resting on her hips that I can only smile at.

"They'll do well not to keep treating me like I'm going to break then won't they. There's nothing more powerful than a mother who must protect her child and they're about to find out that I'm no longer the weakest link." I declare as I pull on a clean pair of clothes Kat had left out for me. I guess it's a good job we're the same size.

"If you need my help, Lucille, you know you only have to ask." Kat comments, noticeably a little nervous about my sudden change overnight. "I will do anything I can to help you babe, you know that don't you?" She queries, furrowing her brows. I reach forwards and pull her into my arms, holding her tight like it could possibly be for the very last time.

"I love you," I whisper, squeezing her once more before leaving her, ignoring the concern within her eyes. When I leave the apartment, Sully jumps to attention at once, eyeing me up as I take in deep breaths now that I'm outside.

"Miss Holland?" He questions, but it's not concern I can hear in his voice, it's anticipation and one look on his face is all I need to see to know that he, this massive hulk of a man, is waiting for me to give him instructions for what happens next. I raise my head and straighten my back. I will not crumble today and I will give no more tears.

"Take me to them," I say firmly before making my way to the car with him following closely behind.

Chapter 15

Silas

Neither Lincoln or myself have spoken a word to each other about yesterday's events. The blaze from Salvatore Cucina could be seen all over the city. We were lucky to get out alive after the explosion. We had to make tracks quickly before the cops came storming in. Now I have insurance paperwork to fill out and file. It's messy and it's something we could definitely do without. But it needs doing so the feds keep off our backs.

The words Cole spoke are ringing in my mind over and over. How can he truly believe what he said? I wanted to reassure him it's not true. We are a unit, we always have been, nothing could change that. How can he not see how much Lucille cares for him? How can he not see there is no competition for her, she is ours. He himself wanted to share but now he has this feeling of what, insecurity? Then he runs for the hills. This is really not like him, it doesn't make sense, I have so many unanswered questions as I'm sure Lincoln does, too. I don't want to believe Cole is betraying us but when all evidence is pointing his way, I have to accept it. Or at least be on my guard. The inner turmoil is raging inside of me, if this was anyone else I would have been putting out a death warrant, he wouldn't get away with the disrespect. Snapping me from my thoughts of anguish, I hear a knock at my door.

"Come in," I shout, rubbing my eyes before laying them on my visitor. It's Linc, he looks as tired as I feel, he probably slept less than me last night. We both wanted nothing more than to fetch our girl after all the events that had passed but we knew she needed time with her friend, she needed someone who was neutral to hear how she felt. And as much as I wish I could have soothed all her worries away, I am glad she has Katrina. Lincoln settles himself down on the chair opposite me, leaning his head back looking to the ceiling before speaking

"What the fuck, Si? I've been over it so many times in my head. What is he thinking?" He breathes out a heavy sigh. He's exhausted by it all.

"I don't know, Lincoln. I'm struggling to get my head around it, around what he said." I tell him as I run my hands through my hair. I don't have the answers that I wish I knew, but I have to make the decisions and as much as I hate what I'm about to say, we have to accept the facts in front of us.

"I hate it but Linc, we have to be real about this. The evidence of his actions, not only yesterday, but since he woke up in hospital suggest that he's no longer someone we can trust."

"What? You can't honestly think that he would betray us? He's our brother." Lincoln protests.

"I have to be pragmatic about this Linc. If it was anyone else, I'd have ripped their fucking throat out by now. You know I can't let this slide, he's made big moves against us, for God knows why." I argue back.

"I don't agree, Si. You do this, you make him a known enemy, we may never get him back." Lincoln shakes his head at me and continues, "and what about Luci? She isn't going to agree with this, she loves him for fuck sake!" he says, swiping his hand down his face.

"This is my job, Linc. I have to make the decisions that no one else wants to make. It's not easy, he's my little brother. But I can't risk you, Lucille, Alesso or any more of our men just because he is my brother. Next time we might not be so lucky. He shot Benji for fuck sake, who's to say he won't do it to you? Lucille will have to just not agree, I can take the heat of her disapproval if it keeps her safe and we get Teddy back. I can't take losing her."

"I get it Si, I do. I just don't like it. I don't like anything about this situation," Linc says, exhaling a deep breath of defeat.

I nod, nothing I can say now will change the facts. Cole has gone too far, too public against us by blowing up Salvatore Cucina. His reasons might not add up but I can't put our organization at risk or our loved ones for his behavior.

"Okay, so let's get down to some business. With Cole not on the forefront accepting shipments, I need to make sure the one today goes smoothly, it should arrive in an hour. Also we need somebody to run point on the restaurant. We need to rebuild. Maybe even look for somewhere new" I tell him.

Lincoln nods. "No problem, I can sort that out and then I'll meet Cassandra and take Alesso out for dinner." I can tell he's not happy about my decision. But he will accept it. He purses his lips momentarily before continuing. "Enzo can take point when he's back from the settlement. Benji will need to recover so he can take Tod as back up. I don't think we should send anybody out alone at the moment". I nod, completely agreeing with what he's saying.

"I agree. I have to finish up filing these fucking insurance claims before I check in with Sully too. I'll give Enzo a call later and let him know what's happened. If he hasn't already seen it all over the news he's going to be devastated." Enzo loved that place just as much as Cole did, and I know he'll take responsibility for this due to his

157

absence last night. I turn my thoughts quickly to Lucille as it falls silent between us. If she wants to stay with Katrina longer, I will not stop her, especially now, but my God I miss her presence. Lincoln shifts in his chair, looking as if he's about to say something as the office door opens and speak of the devil, or angel in her case, Lucille saunters in with Sully not far behind her.

"Lucille," I gasp as I rise from my chair. Lincoln turns in his seat and smiles at her.

"Hello, Love." He smirks at her with a cocky smile. I shake my head at his attempt to flirt with her as soon as he sees her.

She rolls her eyes at him, "Don't love me, Lincoln Rossi. You are still on my shit list after what you did." Lincoln stands and moves closer to her, taking her in as he looks at her standing strong.

"Sully you can go." Linc orders as he reaches for Lucille moving her further into the room and shutting the door behind her in Sully's face. "You are so right, my love, but I'll be on my knees for you everyday until I have that forgiveness of yours," he tells her.

Ignoring him, Lucille looks over to me. "So, Boss, are you going to tell me exactly what your plans are for finding my son? I am fed up with being kept out of the loop," she demands.
She is something else when she's sassy, I can't help but admire her right now. She is fierce and strong. And she is ours.

"Mi luce, it was never our intention to ever keep you out of the loop as you put it. But we do intend on keeping you out of harm's way." She's still glaring at me. Lincoln reaches his hand out and tucks a piece of loose hair behind her ear, making her attention snap back to him.

"Lucille, I have to go. Business still needs to continue. Silas will go over our next move with you and Max once he wakes up." Lincoln tells her, and I notice the way her face softens ever so slightly.

"Just stay safe, please Lincoln. I like your pretty face" she croons. Lincoln smirks before taking her face in his hands and kissing her passionately, wrapping his arms around her waist. Lucille brings her hands to his hair and runs them though it, pulling him closer before bringing her knee swiftly to his groin making him double over in pain.

"Fuckkkk!!" Linc groans clutching at his cock. I have to stifle my laugh.

Lucille looks mischievous, "That was for hurting my brother, you are lucky I didn't go for your face." I can't help myself, I laugh out loud this time causing Linc to glare in my direction.

"Well played la mia luce, I think Lincoln has learnt his lesson." I tell her, smirking at Lincoln and I swear she almost beams at the praise.

"He deserves worse, but like I said, I like his pretty face too much to scar him," Lucille teases him. Now it's me beaming at her.

"You fucker, Si! I might have roughed him up, but I wasn't the one that punched him so hard he needed a doctor to put him back together. I'm not the only one who deserves some punishment." Lincoln grumbles, throwing me under the bus.

The smile that was on my face has fallen, Lucille turns to me. "Umm yes, well he will definitely be serving his time soon. But I need you both to find my son. What is the plan?" she demands.

I let out a huff. "The plan is for you to stay safe. But we have many leads to go over. I had hoped your brother would be up to helping go over some of the details of

Ronan's operations in order to find some cracks." I will always be honest with her about how we plan to execute things. She's just not going to be in harm's way when we actually implement them. "Linc, you need to get going otherwise you'll be late." We can't afford to miss this one after the loss of inventory from the fire.

Lincoln looks at his watch and nods. "Okay, stay safe, and Si, watch out for her right hook. I have a feeling she's saving that one for you." He smirks at me before leaving. That fucker.

"Come on big guy, we need to go and wake my wounded brother. And find my son." She follows Lincoln out the door leaving me stunned at her assertiveness, and I'd be lying if it didn't turn me on.

I follow after Lucille like a puppy on a leash. She makes her way up the staircase and to the spare bedroom where Max is recovering. We had him moved in the early hours of the morning after the incident at the restaurant. We deemed the club to be an unsafe place of healing, all things considered As I climb the stairs two at a time after her, I hope to God that Max will be able to give us some more information about Ronan's safe houses. Then we can make plans to search for Teddy from there. As I approach the spare room, I see Lucille already standing at the side of the bed looking at Max. He's sitting up, he definitely looks better than he did yesterday.

"Luci, I'm fine, I swear," Max huffs with frustration in his voice.

"No, you're not. You keep wincing everytime you move!" Lucille exclaims, matching his irritation. Max's eyes meet mine with a flash of anger as he notices I have entered the room.

"Oh great, here comes the reason I'm here" he growls in my direction. And in truth I am partly to blame for his predicament but the main reason for his injuries is his scumbag father. And just as I'm about to remind him of this, my angel beats me to it.

"No Max, don't you go deflecting this on to him. Yes, he's an ass for all he has done but the fact is he isn't the one whose fault this really is. You're hurt and recovering. You'll do more harm than good trying to be a one man army, so stop getting all worked up" she lectures him. He scoffs at her but seems to have accepted defeat, or maybe not.

"Right, so now you're trusting them to find Teddy? You know what he means to me, Luci. I don't trust them, you shouldn't either."

"You don't get to tell me who I do and don't trust, Max. Your judgment isn't exactly faultless." She snarks back at him and I can't help but laugh aloud at their sibling bickering because it reminds me so much of myself, Cole and Lincoln. They both turn to me and frown.

"And what is so funny?" Lucille snaps in my direction.

"La mia luce, I just enjoy your fierce attitude. But I enjoy it even more when it's aimed at this stronzo." I chuckle.

"Pfft, well enjoy it all you like, you're next on my hit list, Silas Salvatore, just you wait." Pointing her finger in my direction as she hisses at me.

"I'll welcome and embrace all you have to give me, la mia luce." I flirt back at her.

She rolls her eyes at me as Max pipes up. "Right, as touching and sickening as this all is, we have more important things to discuss."

"Finally, something we can all agree on. So, if your beautiful sister wouldn't mind changing your dressings, then we can go to the kitchen and have some breakfast." I suggest. He nods silently and Lucille begins to hover over him as I leave the room and make my way down to the kitchen to prepare something for them both. It's not my usual expertise, this is where Cole excels but I will try my best.

As I am flipping the bacon and eggs in the pan, I'm in a world of my own, trying to fathom how I'm going to explain last night to Lucille. After seeing Cole at the club, I'm just not sure how she'll react. Will she hate him? Will she hate me for having to mark him as the enemy or will she agree and say he has lost all his chances.

Snapping me from my reverie, my phone vibrates in my pocket. I turn the stove down so the food doesn't burn and check who is calling me. It is Marcello, he's looking after the club in my absence. Making sure all of the girls are provided for and it continues to run like a well oiled machine.

"Marcello, what can I do for you?" I answer. He doesn't call often so I know he will have a good reason.

"Boss, I'm just calling with an update," he explains. "The new girls, Trish and Scarlett are settling in well. The sets are bringing in new customers, it was a good decision to take them on as a double act." Trish and Scarlett used to work at a rival strip club. They are twins, which a few of our customers have a fetish for. I'm waiting for him to talk about our other newest recruit when he continues. "Julio, he's getting a lot of attention from the girls, too. But I can't fault his work ethic. He is professional and hasn't even looked at any of the girls unless it's to check on their safety. And I'm not going to lie, no one wants to mess with him. He's built like a fucking giant." I laugh at that. Julio is a big guy, I wouldn't fancy many people's chances on his bad side. I'm happy he's settling well. At least with all the shit going on here the club is still standing.

"Good job, Marcello, I know I have the right guy watching over my empire." I tell him

"Thanks Boss," he says before I hear someone smashing a glass. "For fuck sake, sorry Boss I've got to go, this stag is going to need an ambulance from me beating the shit out of him for breaking one of our don't touch rules."

I chuckle, Marcello doesn't like anyone breaking the rules, especially that one. It's what makes him so good at his job. I pity anyone who gets on his bad side. I doubt they'd even find the body if he wished for them not to. "Do what you think is best, just don't attract too much attention, Marce." I say, hanging up as I start to plate the food up ready for Max and Lucille to join me.

As if on cue they enter the room, chatting about how Max needs a check up at some point, he's fighting a losing battle in my opinion, because if she wants him checked over that's what will happen.

"I've made some eggs and bacon for you both." I explain as I set the plates down at the table and they take their seats opposite each other. I opt for the seat next to Lucille.

Max looks tentatively at his food, though I'm not entirely sure if it's because he doesn't trust my cooking or he's still feeling fragile. After a couple of mouthfuls from her own plate, Lucille asks, "So any ideas where they would keep Teddy, Max?" This new confidence she has since seeing Kat has done her good. Katrina will have my thanks for building my girl up.

"Ronan has a few safe houses scattered over the city we can try. But he's not stupid, it's unlikely he'll be

163

using one of those knowing you'll be looking for him, and honestly I didn't recognise the cellar from where they were holding me." He replies not breaking eye contact.
Truthfully, he has a point but anything is worth trying.

"That's true, but we might be able to find one of his men to question at the very least." I suggest tapping my fingers on the table, Max nods agreeing with me.

"I'd say it's the best opinion we have right now, we have two houses over on the south side of the city and one on the east. My only concern is if the word gets out that we have gone to one, they may empty the others. I think if you have the men we should ambush them all at the same time." Max explains. It's a strong plan and I agree, but with the recent events I'm down a good handful of men. Can I trust Costello to step up?

"I would agree, in normal circumstances I'd have myself take one house, Lincoln another and Cole the final house. But there are some decisions that I've had to make after last night's events." I say, taking a drink of water before eyeing both Max and Lucille who frown and place their cutlery down to listen. Clearing my throat I try to explain the complete clusterfuck of last night.
"Unfortunately Cole can no longer be trusted." As soon as the words leave my mouth, my stomach curdles with a mixture of disappointment and frustration. I hate this. Lucille looks concerned but Max doesn't seem bothered. I mean, why would he? Cole comes across as a psychotic serial killer to everyone outside of our tight family unit. Why would anyone trust him? For me, it's simple, he's my brother and I would do anything for him, that's why the sting of betrayal hurts so much more.

"What happened, Silas? What has he done now?" Lucille snaps at me. I can tell she's angry with him but I detect some concern in her voice. The way her hands clench together as she fidgets in her seat tells me she's fighting conflict with her feelings for him just as I am.

"He burnt down Salvatore Cucina. He openly shot and attacked our men in Ronan's name." I explain.

"That's why you had to rush off last night?" Lucille gasps.

"Yes, he's openly switched sides. I have to think pragmatically about this, and if he wasn't my brother I'd have hunted him down and torn out his eyes for this. I have given the order, if he makes any attempt to get near us, they can use any means necessary to capture him." I sigh, letting out a deep breath as the frustration builds in me. Lucille's features morph into shock but she doesn't argue about it as I thought she might. Max continues to look uninterested as he begins picking at the food on his plate again.

I continue, making suggestions in dividing the teams to be able to take Ronan's safe houses at the same time when my phone blasts from the work top. It can't be Marcello again. Leaving the table I see Lincoln's number flashing on the screen, without hesitation I answer.

"Fratello," I say.

"Silas…" he snarls. I hear gunshots in the background that makes my heart pound in my chest with panic. "It's an ambush, Ronan's men are here!"

Fuck!!! This is not good. I need to get to Lincoln, I look in Max's direction and see he's already on his feet, as is Lucille. They can see the anger in my face. When Linc suggested nobody should be going out alone at the moment, I knew the idiot wouldn't have bothered to think of himself in that scenario.

"Cole is leading them, they want the shipment. I can't take them on my own, there's too many" he states.

The next thing I hear is muffled noises before the line cuts off. My heart sinks. I knew it was true but I hadn't let myself truly believe it until this moment.

"LIncoln!" I shout more in frustration at myself that I let him go alone. The fear, anger and frustration explodes inside of me like a volcano erupting after being dormant for years. Before I can even stop myself, I punch the wall next to me leaving a large hole behind. The anger and fear racing through my veins has me in a blind rage until I hear her voice.

"Silas, we need to help him. Save the anger for your brother because he will have not only your fury to deal with but mine too." Lucille says vengefully.

Chapter 16

Cole

As the data loads on my laptop, I am bombarded with the dates and details of this month's expected shipments. I look at the next anticipated date for the drugs haul. Checking my watch, I realize that the next drop off is due in 45 minutes. Reaching into my jacket pocket, I dial Ronan's number on my phone. I am predicting him being in a foul mood. He doesn't like to be disturbed, especially when he is getting his end away, which seems to be a lot of the fucking time.

"What the fuck do you want?" He answers in annoyance at me. Honestly, he wants to rule this city but he's a lazy fuck and I can't wait to take his beating heart in my hand and feel the life drain from it between my fingers.

Begrudgingly, I respond as politely as I can, "I have the information for the next delivery of cargo to my brother."

"Great, I'm busy. Why don't you call me in an hour," he grunts as I can hear the music pulsating and girls giggling as they clink glasses in the background. I'll take a stabbing guess that he is at a strip club.

"Well, I would love to call you at a more convenient time, but the next load is due in about 45 minutes on the east side of town." I tell him.

"For fuck sake, take some men with you and make sure you steal it all from them. I expect good results Cole," he demands. It's like he doesn't know how ruthless I am, and how I am containing my need to slit someone's throat for his naivety.

"No problem, Boss." I respond, hating that I have just called him that. "But you did make a promise. I do this, you tell me where you are keeping the boy."

"A deal is a deal, Cole. I'll give Marcus here the information on the boy. Once you have completed your task, you can have your reward. Get it done quickly. I don't want any complications." He warns.

I don't completely trust Marcus to give me what I want but once this is over, he will have no choice, I am done waiting after this.

"Consider it done, Ronan." I tell him before I hang up the phone.

Gathering my things, I grab some weapons, including my switch blade that I strap to my right thigh and a Glock 19. Though it's still early the sky is dark as I leave Ronan's building, I can hear chatting and joking from the back of the parking lot. Spotting three of Ronan's men, whom I don't know the names of, so I decide it's easier to nickname them in my head as Baldy, Fatty and Ugly. I don't care to ask their names because in truth, I don't care who they are.

"Boss has a mission for us boys." I shout to get their attention. They turn to me, I see the slight flicker of apprehension in their eyes. They have heard the rumors that surround me. The whispers of what I have done and will do when I lose myself.

"Why should we listen to you?" Fatty grumbles. I roll my eyes, thinking how stupid they are.

The other guy, who I named Ugly, chimes in. "Yeah, we don't trust you."

They are fucking brainless. I'm tempted to take one of their tongues. They won't need to talk for Ronan's demands. I walk up to them, none of the three of them flinch as I get closer.

Unfortunately, Fatty is in the middle making it unlikely he will be the one that I make mute. So I grab Ugly, who happens to be closest to me, by the arm and twist it behind his back before smirking at the other two. "Let this be a lesson boys, you watch how you speak to me from now on." Both of them back away instantly, shouting for help. Idiots, it's only us here.

Yanking Ugly to the floor, I press my weight on top of him and bring my blade around the back of his head to his mouth. "Would you like a new smile as well?" I cackle. Reminding me of that film with The Joker in. He can't see the delight I'm gaining from this, but I can feel him shaking as he's screaming at me to stop.

I lean in and whisper my warning, "I would stop moving if I were you. Otherwise you might lose more than just your tongue."

He stills instantly, whimpering, "Please stop, I'm sorry."

These types of men wouldn't make it in our outfit. They'd be eaten alive.

Just as I bring my knife to the side of his face, the kill joy that is Marcus arrives. "Cole, put the damn blade down. We need him to help us with the heist." He bellows.

For fuck sake, I've felt blood thirsty all day. I huff as I remove my knife from his face, but I can't help myself as I stand, I stomp down on Ugly's dirty hand, hearing the crunch beneath my boot, giving me some satisfaction.

Marcus is a bloody pain in my arse, ruining my fun. "So good to see you," I say sarcastically.

"I should think so, especially as I have the information you're so desperate for. Just so we're clear, I will be tagging along, ensuring you do what needs to be done, Cole." he threatens. Fucking great.

"Let's get going then or do you still want to defy Ronans orders?" I ask the three stooges. They look between myself and Marcus assessing what to do. They are pissing themselves after my little outburst so the decision really shouldn't be too hard for them. I miss my men, they wouldn't blink twice at the stunt I just pulled.

They all nod silently and follow Marcus to his car, I opt for my bike. Marcus raises his eyebrows at me. "Not joining us?" he asks.

"I prefer my bike, I'll race you." I grin, putting my helmet on and jumping on my bike, kick starting it and speeding away from them. Marcus can babysit those fuckers. I agreed to help, not socialize.

I arrive at the yard a full ten minutes before Marcus and the three stooges. I have already spotted the supplier, leaning on the bonnet of his car waiting for one of my brother's men to meet him. What I don't anticipate though, is that Lincoln is the one collecting this shipment as I spot him lurking behind a large shipping container. This makes it tricky, I do not want him to get hurt but he might have to for this to be believable. Fuck.

Pushing my hands through my hair, Marcus pulls up beside my bike and him and the three stooges jump to action, firing shots into the air. Fucking great, bring attention to a drugs trade. Fucking amateurs. Why did we have to bring them? I look over to Lincoln, he's trying to assess the threat as he quickly pulls his phone out, likely to call for backup. I move quickly across the yard to catch the supplier before he makes a run for it, we need that shipment. I need it for Teddy's location.

As I sprint over towards him, I notice Marcus approach Lincoln from behind, my eyes go wide because I do not trust that man, and if he tries to kill my friend then the deal is off and I'll be reigning a hell down on him so fierce that he won't know what fucking century he's in. And I will let nobody stand in my way. I watch as Marcus picks up a brick and without any sort of hesitation, he smashes it over Lincoln's head.

Instinctively, I shout at Marcus, making him look up at me. I need to stop the supplier from getting away before the cops get here but I am fighting my gut instinct to help Linc. I shake my head, Teddy is who he would want me to prioritize, so I cut off the supplier and hope I don't live to regret my choice.

Tackling the supplier to the ground, I pull my knife from my thigh halter and bring it to his throat.

"You will do better if you do not fight me. We are taking your supplies with you dead or alive. Do I make myself clear?" I threaten as I dig the knife into his neck, blood begins to trickle down his throat, bright crimson paints my blade as he gulps nervously.

"Just please don't kill me," he whines. I smile at him and nod, digging the knife just a little bit more as he winces beneath me. Taking my knife away, I use the handle and whack him in the side of the head, knocking him out cold. I stand and leave him on the floor as blood continues to trickle from his neck, returning my attention to Lincoln and Marcus. Linc is still on the ground unmoving but Marcus has moved with the three stooges to the car the supplier arrived in. They are moving the cocaine shipment from the crates into Marcus's van as I make my way over to them.

Marcus glares at me. "You made a good choice, I wasn't sure you would for a second." He hands me a small front door plaque that has an address on it. I grasp it in my hand and memorize the address before turning around and pulling my switchblade out and carving a message on it for them to find. Looking around to ensure nobody is watching, I quickly wrap the small wooden plaque in a layer of packing plastic that's been discarded during the commotion and conceal the plaque in the depths of the remaining crate, deep within the ice, hoping that Lincoln will find this once he wakes up.

As soon as the drugs are all securely placed in the van, I speak to Marcus while the three stooges are getting settled inside.

"What now?" I ask, my voice low and uncertain. I am eager to make my way to Teddy but I need to ensure it is safe to do so.

"Go to the boy but don't do anything foolish, they will be expecting it, Cole." He says, glaring at me before turning and getting in the vehicle. He doesn't linger or say goodbye.

I look over at Lincoln, still unconscious, but I see he is breathing. I am sure my brother will come with an army soon enough and my name will be on the top of that list to take out. Walking away from my friend one last time, I jump on my bike once more and take off to where they have Teddy.

I pray the whole way there that he is okay and that no harm has come to him and I have to block out the burning rage that's building inside of me once I finally arrive at the location of the house address. I drive around the area and conceal my bike almost a block away, deciding that it's probably a better idea to keep it out of sight in case I need a quick get away, so I make my way to the front door on foot. I want to enter the property undetected. I want to see Teddy without anybody else around.

As I make my way over the wall of the garden in the backyard, I quickly hide behind a tree, watching the night guards patrol the house. Fuck this is like a prison, my little man is being held captive. It only makes me all the more determined to get him out of this quickly. I hope Lincoln found the tip off from me and will be on his way with Silas soon. I am not sure how I'll get him out otherwise. I need the distraction of them breaking in to cover our escape. Once the guards are out of sight, I make my way across the lawn and into the house. Listening out for any voices or movement, I find the stairwell and silently make my way upstairs and begin checking all of the rooms for any sign of Teddy. The room to the furthest end of the house is the one I check first. I try to open the door, realizing it is locked. Shit. This must be where they're keeping him. I try the door handle again to make sure it isn't just stuck and that's when I hear him. I hear his little voice from behind the door.

"Hello, is anyone there?"

My heart breaks, he sounds so unsure. "Hey little man, are you okay?"

Teddy squeals, "Cole!! Is that you? Please can you find my mommy, I miss her. I don't want to stop with Uncle Ronan anymore."

"I'll get you out, don't worry, Teddy. Silas and Lincoln will be here soon to help me." I reassure him. But I am so focused on trying to reassure Teddy that it will all be OK that I don't hear the footsteps creeping up behind me until it is too late.

"So, you were a rat all along, Cole? I think you'll regret trying to trick me." Ronan snarls from behind me.

Before I can respond to him, the crack of a gun butt hits my temple and everything goes black. Drifting into the void, I pray that my brothers arrive soon.

Chapter 17

Lincoln

I wake to an electric shock like pain pulsing through my skull. That treacherous fucking prick. The smug look on Cole's face is still burned into my memory. He was the last person I saw before I was attacked from behind. I remember talking on the phone to Silas, telling him that the whole thing was an ambush and that our shipment had been infiltrated. I can't believe I decided to make this exchange on my own. I stood behind a large shipping container, keeping cover as a small group of heavily armed men helped themselves to my goddamn drugs.

There was nothing I could do as I watched a huge portion of our profit get stolen right before my eyes. And just as I heard Silas pick up his phone and ask me what the problem was, I spotted a familiar face amongst the crowd, keeping his distance as he watched the carnage unfold. When his eyes locked on mine, my stomach churned as all he did was simply smile.

That was the last thing I saw before my vision went black. And now here I am, pulling myself off of the fucking floor and wiping the blood from the side of my head. I swear to God, whatever this shit is that Cole has gotten himself into, I will personally drag him back out of it just to send him back down into the depths of hell with my own bare hands. I know Silas has branded him a traitor now, and deems him not to be trusted but this isn't Cole. Silas has to make these decisions for the club, I'm the one who see's the bigger picture and none of this makes any fucking sense.

I stand up slowly, regaining my balance as my head woozes in protest. "Jesus Christ," I mutter, glancing down at my feet to see a bloodied rock left behind by my attacker. Fucking prick. Whoever did this will be sorry they didn't check to see that I was still breathing before they left, because when I find them, I'm going to murder them. I'm already pissed that I had to come out to make sure this went off without a hitch. Alot of fucking good that turned out. I should be back at the house with my son and my woman. I scoff at the thought of Lucille ever being just mine. All mine, to do with whatever I pleased. To touch, to kiss, to fuck. To love. I groan at my intrusion of thoughts, wiping my hands over my face as the idea of it being anything like that now seems completely ludicrous so I shove my feelings down, like I have been doing since I met her and kick the rock out of pure frustration as I make my way over to the stack of fishing crates that had been concealing our drug packages. There's nothing left but broken crates, foul smelling fish and melting ice strewn across the floor. And as if that blow to the head had knocked some sort of clear vision into my head, it occurs to me that this is what Cole was snooping around for when he came into Silas's office. The information for our next drug exchange. What the fuck is he playing at? I sift my hands through the only standing box of ice that hasn't been smashed to pieces, double checking they hadn't left any drugs behind that might be found by unsuspecting hands, because I daren't chance this fuck up to possibly get any worse than it already has.

I notice nothing but ice until I hit the bottom and my fingers come into contact with a small, hard package. Too small to be one of ours. I hesitate for a moment, debating whether or not this could be a trap. A small bomb perhaps? But if they were trying to kill me, surely they would have accomplished that by bashing me over the head. This has to be a sign. I swallow down the uncertainty that plagues my mind and quickly wrap my fingers around the unfamiliar object and yank it up through the ice before I can convince myself not to.

The package is small enough to fit in the palm of my hand and wrapped completely in plastic, sodden and freezing against my skin from the ice in the crate. I turn it over a few times in my hands trying to figure out what it is but the wrapping makes it difficult to see what's inside. As I flip it over repeatedly the only thing that comes to mind is Cole. If someone were holding a huge neon flashing light in front of my face, it couldn't have been anymore fucking obvious. He's left a message. He knew I'd check the crates to make sure nothing was left behind so that's where he concealed it for me to find. I catch myself momentarily as the rush of adrenaline to my head makes me sway with a high pitched whistling in my ears. If this is what I think it is, I need to share it with the others. I pocket the object as inconspicuously as possible. The likelihood of someone from Ronan's team watching my every move is high so I make a run for it back to my car, praying that they haven't trashed it while I was unconscious. I turn the final corner and I've never been so grateful to see all four wheels of my Ferrari as they stand untouched where I'd left them. As soon as I pull out of the shipping yard, I floor the gas and head straight back home to see what little breadcrumb our lost boy has left for us.

Drumming my fingers against the leather of the steering wheel, I'm finding it hard not to think about what could be so important to Cole that he would hide it for me in a fish crate, exactly where I'm adamant he knew that I'd find it. I need a distraction before I drive myself insane trying to guess. I should call Silas to let him know I'm OK before he comes looking for me but fuck it, he can wait.I can't explain this over the phone.

"Call Felix!" I bark into the car's handsfree system, deciding that checking in on my casino that I've left in Felix's hands will be the welcome distraction I need for the rest of the drive home. Felix picks up immediately and can't help but smirk as his cool laughter fills the car.

"I was wondering when you'd check up on me again," he says, and I can almost hear the grin in his voice.

"I just want to make sure my kingdom hasn't fallen," I reply, smiling to myself at his cheek.

"So little faith in me, Boss. I can't lie but that hurts," he jokes and I shake my head, stifling my own laughter this time.

"Anything to report?" I ask before the topic of conversation goes completely off course.

"No Boss, nothing out of the ordinary. I hope my earlier medical deliveries were adequate?" He asks, reminding me that I never did thank him for quite literally saving Max's life and mine when he managed to get everything on Dr Graves' list delivered to the club in record time.

"Yes, more than adequate, thank you Felix. I owe you for that one. You saved my ass big time." I pause for a moment. "Dare I ask, how did you manage to pull that off so efficiently?"

"Better not, Boss," he laughs again, "but this is why you employ me, is it not? To pull off the impossible."

I must admit he has me there, it was in fact one of the reasons why I employed him. He is a fucking mastermind in that sense. If I need something, Felix is the one to call to get it done. I keep him around for his brains and computer skills too, and the fact that I trust him, which is more than I could say for most men I know.

"Well there aren't many other people I would trust to run my business, Felix." I admit while listening intently as I hear a scuffle in the background of the call. Before I can ask what's happening Felix's voice echoes through the car again.

"And I am honored, truly Boss, but right now there's a rather loud lady trying to bring her cat to one of the poker tables claiming he's her good luck charm, so if you want your kingdom to still be standing by the time you come back, I suggest I go and deal with that."

"Jesus Christ Felix, don't let it scratch up the velvet!" I shout before he abruptly ends the call leaving me with the perfect distraction as my own wild imaginations picture a cat being chased around the poker lounge of my casino while Felix, Zack and Sully are in toe with a lady swinging her purse at them yelling not to harm her pussy.

Before I know it, I'm pulling in through the gates at the front of the driveway and bombing it down the gravel path towards the house. I don't bother to park in the garage, skidding to a halt outside the door before I kill the engine, hastily making my way inside to find Silas, Lucille and Max in Silas's office. Their raised voices draw me in immediately but I take a moment to listen outside of the door before making my arrival known.

"What do you mean I can't come with you to find him, Silas?" Lucille's voice echoes on the other side of the door. Oh she is feisty today.

"I mean exactly that, Lucille. I don't know what happened. I don't know who's there. It could be a trap." Silas tries to reason with her before she snaps back at him.

"I don't care Silas, I'm coming to help Linc." My heart soars at her words as I walk through the door unannounced, smiling as they all whip up their heads round look at me, a mixture of relief, confusion and anger showering their faces. I hear Lucille gasp before meeting her wide-eyed stare as she takes in my appearance and runs over to me immediately, grabbing hold of my head with both hands to closer inspect the gash where the blood is still slowly oozing through my hair.

"Christ Linc, I thought you were fucking dead! I was just fighting with Rocky over here about coming to get you." Silas shouts from behind her as he brings his hands to his head, releasing a heavy sigh of relief.

"What the hell happened to you?" Lucille gasps, ignoring Silas's joke on her behalf, examining my wound before I pull away, bringing my arms around her back and caging her into my chest.

"Nothing that could keep me from coming back to you, Love." I smile before tracing my hand up her spine to the back of her neck and pulling her in for a kiss. She resists at first, but I almost lose myself the moment she relents all of her built up frustration towards me and she melts into my body. Her lips part as she accepts my tongue so willingly into her mouth. I deepen the kiss, strengthening my hold on her neck and pulling her flush against my chest until a loud cough reminds me that we're not alone, and although it physically pains me to tear my mouth from hers when all I want to do is ravish her, I remember that Lucille might not want to be fucked senseless right here in front of her brother. Unlike Silas, I am able to keep myself in control of my sexual desires. For the time being at least.

"Seriously, this shit is messed up," Max mutters as he looks between Lucille and I and over to Silas who is standing behind his desk watching us with pure lust practically seeping from his body.

"Watch it, Costello. That's your sister you're fucking talking about." I warn, pulling Lucille protectively into my chest as she turns to face her brother.

"This is my choice, Max," she insists, squeezing my arms that are wrapped around her waist before adding, "and I expect you to either get on board with it or there's the door," she says, gesturing her head towards the door.

Max looks a little shocked by her abruptness but I can only smile at how fucking proud I feel in this moment. I know how much Lucille admires her brother, so for her to stand up to him like that for us, makes my heart fucking burst with pride. It must have the same affect on Silas too as he's stood grinning just as fucking proud as I am while Max's jaw all but hit's the floor. Max is silent for a beat before holding his hands up in defeat.

"Alright, alright," he resigns as he slowly moves himself away from Silas who's now staring at him like he wants to rip his head from his shoulders. Can't say I blame him. Lucille breaks free from my arms and walks back over to Silas and her brother, placing her hand onto the middle of Silas' chest.

"Easy big guy," she whispers to him, leaning up to kiss his cheek, "I only just got him back. I won't let you kill him now."

Max looks smug for a moment, knowing Lucille would never let either myself or Silas hurt him with her standing in the way but as I walk over, I can't help myself from smacking him across the head.

"Knock it off you prick. We've got bigger problems today." I snap as Max rubs his hand across his head and spins his body to face me.

"So, are you going to tell us what happened?" Lucille asks, moving again to stand between Max and I this time. She knows exactly what she's doing. Using herself as a human shield, though I'm not sure who it is she's really trying to protect. Us or him? Seconds pass as we stare at each other, sizing each other up and daring the other to make the first move. "LINCOLN!" Lucille barks, snapping my attention straight to her. "What happened?" she asks again.

"The delivery was hijacked. It's all gone, the drugs, the money, all of it. I got a brick to the head before they could take off. Didn't see who delivered it, but I did spot your brother across the lot before I blacked out." I start, turning my attention to Silas now who's gaze just turned a darker shade of murderous.

Lucille's audible choke almost stops me from continuing. I gaze down, her petite frame looks so fragile between the three of us. I can see how much weight she's lost in these few short days. She's hardly eating or sleeping, all she seems to do is cry. It's questionable whether she's even living right now without Teddy back in her arms. Can I really share this package that's now burning a hole through my pocket? Can I get her hopes up just to tear them back down again if this isn't what I think it is? What if I am wrong and Cole has done this to fuck with us? I close my eyes, trying to fight with every instinct in my body that tells me this is what is meant to happen and only when I feel a cold palm rest against my cheek do I open them again to see Lucille's determination and fire burning behind her eyes. She needs this, she needs to know. With a deep breath, I reach into my pocket and retrieve the package, holding it out into the palm of my hand.

"He left me this."

Silas' abrupt tone cuts the tension. "What is it?" he asks, moving closer.

"Give me those," I call over to Max, pointing my head towards the scissors on the desk. Max obliges, immediately bringing them over and we all watch, with bated breath, as I slowly cut through several layers of translucent plastic.

Once I get to the last layer, I freeze, looking over to Lucille who's nestled under Max's arm, with a sickeningly white sheen over her skin.

"Lucille, I don't think you…"

"No Linc. You can't shut me out anymore. Open it. I need to know what it is." She cuts me off before I have a chance to voice my concerns. I share a look between Max and Silas, who both nod their agreements for me to continue. Fuck, here we go. I swallow thickly before fully pulling back the last layer of plastic and throwing it to the side, leaving a wooden plaque in the center of my hand. It's a house number. A brass metal seven adorns the middle of the wooden plaque with a smaller line underneath that reads 'Clifton Rise'.

"It's an address," Max states.

"Do you think that's where Teddy is?" Lucille chokes, ripping the wooden plaque from my hand as she stares at it, like she's willing it to answer her question.

"Silas, get the address up on the computer. We need to know where the fuck this is." I urge, but he's already across the room having the same thought. I knew Cole wouldn't have fucked us over like this if there wasn't a good reason behind it. He's doing this to help us. I look over to Lucille who hasn't moved from her place as she clutches the plaque to her chest, eyes closed and lips moving rapidly but with no sound coming out. I wouldn't have taken her for one who believed in God, but I know she's praying hard as hell to anybody that will listen right now.

"This better not be some sick fucking joke," Max warns as he stands behind me while we wait for Silas to put the address into the search bar, bringing my attention back to the screen.

"Cole left this for me to find. He knew I'd check the crates before I left. This is a message from him," I counter, willing Silas to move faster.

"It's about a fifty minute drive from here, just out of town." Silas says as he narrows in on the pinned location. "It's pretty much deserted by the look of these pictures."

"Fuck." I snap, not believing that Teddy could have been so close to us all this time yet, we hadn't fucking found him. "I'll call Felix, see if he can get his hands on the blueprints so we can see what we're dealing with on the inside." I add, running my fingers through my hair.

"That isn't one of our safe houses, he must've known you would go looking at those first. We need to go now!" Max demands as he begins to pace the floor.

"No, we need to make a plan." Silas snaps, standing from his chair. "We can't go in all guns blazing because of a little fucking house number that we've found. This could be anything. This could be a fucking trap." He says, pulling rank. "And you," he spins, pointing his finger towards Max, "are a fucking dead man walking. You can barely keep yourself upright let alone go into what could potentially be a warzone."

184

Max moves to counter his argument but stops as a piercing cry echoes through the office. We all move as one towards Lucille who's holding her chest like she's just been shot.

"What is it, Love?" I ask urgently, pulling her into my arms, automatically checking her over for injuries, though I know she hasn't sustained any. I feel her whole body begin to shake against my chest as she points to the house plaque on the floor at her feet but no words leave her mouth. Max bends to pick the sign up, faltering slightly as his injuries still are long from healed.

"What the fuck?" he snarls, holding it out to show Silas and I. On the back of the wooden plaque, carved into the wood, read two words that knock the air right out of me. "He's alive."

"We have… we have to bring him home!" Lucille sobs into my arms as the weight of the message rests heavily on us all.

Silas strides over to us and plants a kiss firmly onto Lucille's head before resting his forehead against her own.

"We will bring him home to you, la mia luce. I promise" he whispers.

"I'm coming with you," she says, putting on a strong front as she swipes the tears from her eyes and pulls her head up tall. But Silas just shakes his head in return.

"No, Lucille. If anything were to happen to you I would never forgive myself."

"Silas, you can not keep me from bringing back my son," she argues.

"I said no, Lucille." Silas growls at her, but it does little to deter her.

"I'm coming with you!"

Silas glares at her before he walks from the room slamming the door in his wake so I squeeze my arms tighter around her to gain her attention before bringing my hand up to cup her face. The extensive pools of her emerald green eyes bore into my own and for a moment, I feel like a fucking fraud as I hold this woman in my arms who wields the power to make my heart feel like its being constricting in my chest with just one look. With all of the sins I have ever committed tarnishing my life, she refuses to let it come between us. I don't know what I ever did in this life or a past life of mine to deserve such a woman, even to share just a third of her with my brothers. But for every day that I'm alive I'll give her a reason to know how loved she is, and how special she is.

"Listen to him, Love. You will be more of a distraction to us out there." I whisper softly against her lips, though I'm not sure my words have the desired effect as Lucille scoffs at me, turning her head away. Fuck. I grip her chin between my finger and thumb and bring her back to face me before trying a different route. "What I mean is that Teddy will need you here when we bring him home, he needs to know you're safe too, Lucille." I try to reason, and as her hard features soften ever so slightly under my touch, I know that she agrees with what I'm saying.

"I'll stay behind, too." Max offers, and Lucille snaps her head in his direction. "He's right. I am a deadman walking. If it were the other way round, I'd tell them the exact same thing. They need to be quick and right now I'll be more of a hindrance than a help. We need to get him back, Lucille. Let them do this their way," he says. I stare at him utterly dumbfounded.

"Fuck me, Irish. Are you actually agreeing with me for once?" I ask, raising my eyebrows at him.

186

"Piss off," he murmurs before hobbling back over to Silas's computer.

I chuckle slightly before pressing my lips firmly against Lucille's head, breathing in her scent. That fucking delicious sweet rose scent that makes my mouth water. I hold her close to me, reveling in the feel of her body pressed so tight against my own, willing my cock to disengage from its apparent need to jerk at the most inappropriate of times while I allow Lucille to take the time she needs in order to collect herself.

"I can feel how hard you are for me Linc," Lucille whispers into my chest, catching me completely unprepared as I all but growl into her ear.

"Watch your mouth, sweetheart. Unless you want me to fuck it while your brother watches." Pulling her harder into my body digging my fingers into the flesh beneath her shirt. Lucille looks up at me and as I gaze between her beautifully innocent eyes to her perfectly rounded lips I summon all of my strength to pull myself away from her. The sudden loss of her body on mine practically aches in my chest but I can't do this right now. I need a clear head. And I know she's just looking for a distraction too.

"Lincoln," I hear her call as I turn my back to her. I'm losing myself in all of this, I can feel my sanity slipping through the cracks. I shake off Lucille's advance as she moves to stand in front of me. I daren't look at her face to see whatever it is that's plaguing her right now. All we need to do, and all that I should be concerned about right now, is figuring out a plan to rescue Teddy. I squeeze her hand to let her know I see her and make my way over to Max who has already mapped out our route to the tip off address.

None of us are prepared to acknowledge the fact that this could be a set up and we could be walking into a deathtrap. Even though Cole seems to have abandoned us, I don't believe that he would stand by and watch while we got slaughtered. Though I don't dare voice my concerns in front of Lucille, who seems to be fairing pretty well all things considered. I know Max is on the same wavelength, even suggesting that it may be best for Lucille to leave while we tried to plan out how we would extract Teddy from the house. Obviously she refuses, arguing her point to stay so she knows what is going on, and neither of us have the heart to deny her of that.

"Got everything we need?" I ask as Silas throws a large duffel bag full of ammunition down onto the desk as he re-enters the room.

"And more," he smirks, "fuckers won't know what hit them."

"I thought you said we couldn't go in all guns blazing?" Max states looking a little concerned as he eyes the bag.

"This is just a back up plan." Silas replies, holstering a pair of Glock G19's on either side of his body before strapping a switchblade to his ankle.

I follow suit, walking over to the bag pulling out my own switchblade and shoving it into a leather cuff under my own gun that's already concealed underneath my arm. I catch Lucille's eye as I strap another Glock to my thigh but the look on her face is void of emotion.

"Felix has sent over the most recent blueprint he could find. By the look of it they've done some extensive remodeling to the basement level but there's a few places they could be keeping him." I inform Silas, holding up my phone to show him the images.

He nods his head slowly, taking in the blueprint, formulating the best plan of attack for this particular mission. His brain works like a goddamn machine when it comes to work like this. If there was anybody I'd want to get lost in a maze with, it would definitely be Silas, because his problem solving brain would get us out of there without issue.

"We go in through the back door, because if this isn't a set up, they won't be expecting us but I'm sure they're not stupid enough to not have somebody watching the front door. We move room to room and sweep the place floor by floor, working our way up. I think they'll have him locked in one of the bedrooms rather than the basement considering Ronan's objective. We need to stay silent, undetected and we need to stay vigilant." Silas rolls off, switching fully into his leadership role.

He glances over to Lucille as he continues. "Our main goal is to find Teddy and bring him home, and we do not leave that house until we've secured him. Do I make myself clear?" His eyes are on me now and the room is completely silent.

"We're not coming home without him." I nod, ignoring the searing gaze coming from Lucille's direction.

At my words, Silas strides over to Lucille, capturing her face with both hands and slamming his lips down onto hers.

"I promise you we'll bring him home," he affirms before kissing her again.

"I need you all home," Lucille states. "Promise me that."

I look towards Max who understands as well as we do that sometimes, you don't always make it back from a fight like this. And with a silent message passing between us, he simply nods his head in my direction before I make my way to the office door.

"Let's go." I call over my shoulder.

"Linc, wait." Lucille calls after me as she runs to the door, but Max is already in front of her, holding her back as Silas grabs the bag from the table and we slip out of the room while she begins to struggle against his arms.

"Promise me you'll all come back to me," she shouts desperately as we walk away.

"You could have at least said goodbye to her," Silas sighs, shaking his head at me.

"This isn't goodbye." I state matter of factly. We will make it home to her.

Chapter 18

Silas

We pull up a few blocks away from the address and my mind is racing. Is Cole in on this? Is this a set up? Will we be bringing Teddy home for our girl? So many things are on the line with this all going to plan.

We make our way on foot towards the address. I look at Lincoln who is determined this is it, and we will all come back from this. He believes there is no other option. I have to look at the bigger picture. Being the one in charge has always made me see all angles, even if I am headstrong and rash at times.

Reaching out and touching Lincoln's arm I stop him from rushing in, I sigh. "Lincoln, let's just think about this. You go in and get Teddy out at all costs. That has to be your priority. Leave Ronan, Cole or any other fucker to me. I need him safe for her and I trust no one else to do that now."

He looks at me and smiles before it fades from his face. "Don't go being the hero, Si. She needs us both to come back to her, heck she needs Cole too and I'm determined to make that happen."

He's so confident this won't be the end of us. That this won't be our last fight. I am confident that Teddy and Lincoln will return to her. Beyond that I have to be realistic, casualties are going to happen, I just hope we aren't going to meet our end in the process.

As we round the corner, I finally set eyes on the building we have been searching for. The security is tight. Behind the face, armed guards and dogs stand in our way. Assessing the area, I notice the back yard backs on to a wooded area. Nudging Lincoln, I nod in the direction, he sees what I see and we move to check if we can get in that way. We need to be strategic with this. Going in all guns blazing will get us nowhere with the amount of security they have. There are only two of us, and God only knows how many there are of them.

Fumbling through the hedges, we see a broken wired fence which looks to have been recently cut.

My heart is beating hard as I whisper to Lincoln. "Do you think someone else has tried this way before?"

Lincoln frowns as he crouches down, touching the edges of the snipped wire.

"Maybe, I don't know for sure." Lincoln starts before we hear shouting from inside as all the guards in the yard leave their posts to run inside the house. We look at each other, it looks like we don't have much time to get in and out. Whoever came before us has been found or is making a diversion for us.

"Let's go, we aren't going to have long." I tell Lincoln, carefully making our way through the yard and to the back of the house. As we enter the patio doors, we hear the raised voices on the level above us.

"So you were a rat all along, Cole? I think you'll regret trying to trick me." Ronan's voice bellows through the house. A loud thud above us has me moving quickly toward the staircase before Lincoln grabs my arm, pulling me back behind the archway that separates the kitchen and seating area. We are concealed, unless you come in through the patio or the kitchen you wouldn't know we were here.

In a hushed voice Lincoln whispers, "No, Silas. As much as I want to run out there and save Cole, we both agreed that Teddy is the priority. I need you to help me with that. And you are leaving with us and not staying back to be the goddamn hero. We are not losing you too! We need to get him first. We can come back for Cole." I see the conflict in him. I feel it inside of me. He's right, I know he is. I nod, I can't promise him that I'll not stay to save Cole. He's my brother. But I will get Teddy out first.

Hearing footsteps making their way down the stairs, we brace ourselves, both of us ready with our guns drawn.
"Take him to the van, he will be made an example of what happens to traitors." Ronan sneers as we hear them stomping and banging around the room. I lean slightly, taking a glance around the corner to see them carrying Cole's unconscious body out of the door. Ronan is facing the opposite way to us and I fight every urge in my body to kill him where he stands. I know we can't, we have to remove Teddy as quietly and quickly as possible.
"All of you back to your stations!" Ronan orders. "You two find out how that cunt got past you all. I want this place tighter than Fort Knox. I bet his brother and that scum Rossi are on their way here. We might have to move the boy, but I'd like to see their faces when they realize they can't breach our fortress."
I hear a gunshot ring through the air. "For fuck sake! What is going on out there? They best not have killed him. I want him to suffer." Ronan screeches as he stomps out of the room and we hear the door slam shut. Knowing we are about to be severely outnumbered, we wait for the element of surprise. We need to take them out with little noise. This means making sure our silencers are on. As one of Ronan's men rounds the corner, he doesn't

notice us there, however the second guy does but before he can shout, Lincoln has taken his switchblade and stabbed him in the side of the neck. He's gargling blood as his eyes roll into the back of his head and Linc slowly lowers him to the floor. The first guy is mine and I jump him from behind, choking him in a headlock before he passes out. I can't leave him alive incase he wakes up and alerts the others so I take my knife from my leg strap and slam it into the occipital bone of his skull, killing him instantly.

More guards are moving around on this floor but no others come our way. I look around the archway again as we hear voice's trail through the front room. The guards make their way up the stairs completely oblivious to the bloodbath that has occurred in the kitchen. They obviously have something worth protecting up there. Once the coast is clear, we make a move to follow them upstairs. I go first, climbing the stairs two by two until I reach the top. At the end of the hallway, I see two guards stationed by a door. I have no choice but to use my Glock and take them out before they have a chance to make a sound. I aim and take the first one out, blood splattering across the door behind him as I land a bullet between his eyes. Lincoln is just as fast taking the second one down with an equally impressive shot, first to the chest and the second hits the guy's head, painting an equally impressive piece of art against the wood. Unfortunately, the thump of their bodies hitting the floor couldn't be avoided from this distance, we don't have long to get in and get back out of here without detection.

"Hello?" a small voice calls from behind the blood-covered door. It's Teddy. We've found him. We rush forward immediately, my heart pounding wildly in my chest.

"Little guy, it's Silas and Linc, your mommy's friends. We are going to get you out but we have to ask you, when we get out of this room, we need you to shut your eyes. You mustn't look, promise us?" I tell him.

"Is Mommy with you? I heard Cole, is he with you too? Uncle Ronan came and shouted at him." Teddy says.

"Your mommy is at home with Alesso, we are going to take you to her. Just sit tight Ted." Linc reassures him.

I look at Lincoln, we need to do this fast. The door is locked and I'm not wasting time finding the key.

"Teddy, stand as far away from the door as you can, OK? I need to break it down as we don't have the key." I tell him, hoping he'll listen and do as I ask.

"OK. Uncle Ronan is the only one with the key, you could ask him for it." He says naively

I smile at his innocence before nodding to Linc. He positions himself at the top of the staircase to cover me. Bringing my foot up and extending it above the handle I kick the door, putting my full weight behind my boot as it connects with the wood, making it snap open with the force.

I see Teddy standing over by the bed. He looks so small, his face looks puffy from crying which breaks my heart as much as it angers me but he looks to be unharmed. He runs over to me, immediately wrapping his arms around my legs, and without a second thought I pick him up and shield him from the scene behind us.

"Little man, you remember what I said? Close those eyes for us, I'm going to pass you to Lincoln, OK? He is going to carry you. Make sure you don't peek. We will get you back to your mommy soon."

"You promise I'll see her?"

"We promise on our lives, Teddy," Lincoln tells him as he takes him from me cradling him protectively into his chest.

"Lincoln, whatever happens next, you get him out." I glare at him. I'm not going to be the hero but I will be a distraction for him to get out with Teddy and whether he likes it or not Linc knows this needs to happen.

Lincoln nods in agreement.

With Teddy wrapped in Lincoln's arms, we move from the bedroom, stepping over the guards bodies. As we get to the staircase, we hear voices start to filter through. Lincoln darts behind an alcove in the hallway to keep Teddy covered and protected. As the voices near us, two of Ronan's men stop right in front of me, completely unaware of the danger they're in. I grab the first one and head butt him, knocking him to the ground. And as he lands, I bring my knife up and slam it underneath the other's chin, causing him to fall back against the wall. Blood pours from his wound, coating his shirt in seconds and booking him a one way ticket to hell. As I watch the blood pour out I am slammed into a door as the first guard rushes me. I punch and block him before I feel his body instantly still on top of me before falling to the floor. Lincoln stands over him with Teddy in one arm and his gun outstretched in the other. The smirk on his face is annoying. I know I'm not going to enjoy hearing about that one over the next couple of months.

Pushing the fucker off of me, I retrieve my blade from the other guard's jugular before I take the lead and we quietly make our way downstairs. There are no signs of Ronan or his men and that makes me feel a little uneasy. I wave for Lincoln and Teddy to follow. As we enter the seating area near the back patio, I check the garden and notice only one guard patrolling. This isn't right. Quickly deciding we need to make quick work of this, I aim and shoot the fucker dead on the spot. All those target practice sessions as a kid are paying off. I suppose my father was good for something.

As soon his body hits the grass I signal to Linc to make a break for it. We make a run for the gap in the treeline where the broken fence is knowing that will be our only way to escape.

"Silas Salvatore, running away from a fight!" Ronan mocks from behind me.

"Lincoln, keep going with Teddy, I'll be right behind you." I snap.

Lincoln attempts to object but I stop him. "Please!" I beg, glancing at Teddy in his arms. His lips thin into a disapproving line but he nods and continues to move forward through the trees all while reassuring Teddy that they will be with Lucille soon.

I turn from them and finally face the fucker who has ripped my world apart, walking towards him to put more space between them and Teddy. "Name a time and a place Ronan, I'll happily take you on. I'll happily fight you on neutral ground when you don't have an army of men to fight for you." I say as I stand a few feet away from him and his gang of men appearing behind him as he grins maliciously at me. I hope I can give Lincoln and Teddy enough time to get away.

"Don't fancy your chances against me now then?" He cackles. "Neither do I," he smiles, bringing his gun up before he and the six men stood beside him open fire in my direction. I've already turned and made a sprint for it back to the trees, zigzagging as I go to avoid being hit before the bullets barrel past me. I almost can't believe my luck until I feel a sharp pain pierce through my rib and the air is completely expelled from my lungs. I do my best to move as quickly as I can to follow the trail Lincoln and Teddy took back to our car, making sure to apply pressure to the wound that's already emitted too much blood.

Lincoln is already in the driving seat with the engine running and as I slump myself into the seat beside him he puts his foot down on the accelerator before I even have a chance to shut the door.

"Silas, that was a close one," Linc laughs, but when I don't answer he looks over at me, his eyes quickly taking in the sight of my blood stained shirt. "Fuck" he spits, reaching his hand into the backseat with his eyes still on the road before throwing a jacket over me. "Don't let him see" he whispers.

I'm unable to speak as my body fights the shock settling into my bones. I tighten the jacket around my stomach, pressing it onto my ribs and swallowing down the pain. My skin is sweating but I can feel my body growing colder. The last thing I see is the worried look on Lincs face as he races us back home before I close my eyes.

Chapter 19

Lucille

It's been three painstakingly long hours since Lincoln refused to say goodbye before he and Silas left, promising that they would deliver Teddy back home to me. I haven't been able to sit down for more than a few minutes at a time while I watch the seconds on the clock pass by.

"What's taking them so long?" I exhale. A question I had started asking about an hour and a half ago, which was noticeably starting to annoy my brother now.

"Luc, we knew this wasn't going to be quick. The house is almost an hour away. Just give them time." Max scolds, like I should know better.

"But what if something's gone wrong Max!?" I plead, feeling nothing but utter uselessness flood throughout my body. "I can't take this much longer, we should have heard from them by now. They should be on their way home at least." I sigh, sinking down to my knees to take in a few deep breaths. I have so many emotions fighting for the top spot, all battling their way through, making this whole waiting game a whole lot worse. Every possible outcome in my head is wrong, something always goes wrong and the anxiety of it all is too overwhelming for me to think straight any longer. Teddy is coming home. I can't let the seed of doubt creep its way through my body, like an infestation, weeding its way into every single cell, making it almost impossible to fight against. I close my eyes and concentrate on my breathing, silently praying that everything will be OK. If Linc believes this is the real deal, like he says he does, then that's good enough reason for me to believe it, too. Right?

As I shake my hands, willing the pins and needles stabbing their way through my fingers to disperse, the door swings open with a bang. I stand so fast that my vision blurs when all the blood rushes to my head. I blink away the stars for a second until my vision clears, and I see the small body of a child standing in the doorway.

"Dad?" I hear the child call before I can fully register who it is.

"Alessandro, you shouldn't run through the house like that." I hear a female voice call from not too far behind him. Lincoln's son is staring at me from the door.

"Did you hear me?" the female voice calls again, closer this time.

"Sorry, Cassandra," Alesso replies, turning to face the middle aged woman dressed casually in pencil leg trousers and a cream blouse. She is now standing behind him, seeming slightly out of breath. I notice her tense immediately as she notices Max and I in Silas's office and her hand rests out on Alesso's shoulder.

"Is my dad here, Lucille?" Alesso asks, snapping me out of my bizarre need to question this woman for feeling like she has the right to put her hands on his shoulder. At the mention of my name I see her features soften slightly.

"Lucille," Cassandra walks into the room, holding her hand out for me to shake. As she gets closer, I realize she is older than I first thought. Though her body looks neither old nor young, the age lines on her face tell me that she has been through much of her life with worry and that her soft hazel eyes had seen things no normal woman should see. It crosses my mind that if I end up with the chance to get to know this woman, there would be many stories she could tell me. But for now, I'm in no state to start sharing experiences. "I'm sorry, I should have realized who you were. Forgive me for being so rude. Only, when Alesso noticed Mr Rossi's car outside, he assumed his father would be here and took off in search of him," she explains. I take her offered hand in my own and give her a gentle, reassuring squeeze, nodding my head to let her know I accept her apology before turning back towards the door.

"I'm sorry Alesso, he isn't here at the moment." I sigh, giving him a feeble smile.

"Has he gone to find Teddy?" Alesso asks, sucking the air right from my lungs. I notice Max moving closer to me in my peripheral vision but Alesso doesn't move. He watches me and I can't blink fast enough to urge away the tears that pool in the corner of my eyes. I admit defeat and nod my head, letting a single track of tears fall across both cheeks. Alesso walks over without another word and wraps his arms around my waist holding onto me tightly.

"He'll come back," he whispers. "He always does." As the words register, I realize it wasn't Teddy he was referring to, and that thought alone, that this innocent little boy who has already lost so much in his life also has moments where he's left wondering when, or if his father will ever return to him and it breaks what little resolve I have left. If my soul hadn't already been splintered beyond repair, the enormity of those words would have struck me down. I place a hand onto Alesso's head, stroking my fingers absentmindedly through his hair as I look back to Cassandra who's watching the moment pass between us with one hand raised, clutching above her heart and the other touching her lips. Her eyebrows are raised slightly, but the sympathy in her eyes forces me to swallow a thick band of guilt that's tightening across my throat. If Lincoln doesn't make it home, I've left this little boy without a mother and a father.

"I'll get started on some dinner," Cassandra mumbles before she leaves the room leaving Alessandro, Max and I in a horribly uncomfortable silence before I feel the burner phone Kat gave me, start to vibrate in my back pocket. Alesso drops his arms for me to retrieve it, watching me expectantly to see who's calling. My own heart drums rapidly against my chest as I flip open the device and it's only when an audible sigh passes my lips that Alesso releases his own breath too.

"It's Kat. Would you mind?" I ask, holding the phone out to Max. I don't have the strength in me to try and explain what's happened, and I know she'll have hundreds of questions. He hesitates slightly, not having spoken to Kat since their awkward encounter in his kitchen which feels like decades ago. But as the vibrating stops to then immediately start back up again he gives in knowing she won't stop ringing until somebody answers.

"I'll take it outside," he says, glancing down at Alesso before he leaves the room. As I watch him step outside, I'm left wondering if that was for Alesso's sake so he didn't have to hear Max explain where his dad had gone or the fact that Kat might bite his head off and he didn't want either of us there to witness it.

"Do you want to watch a movie?" Alesso asks shyly. "Whenever I am sad, Dad makes a den on the couch with my duvet and we get snacks and watch a movie together. It always cheers me up," he explains.

Little does he know, I do the exact same thing with Teddy too. Our favorite afternoons are spent on the couch under the duvet together watching Disney movies on repeat.

"I'd love that very much," I smile, watching as his eyes light up, for him to take my hand in his and lead me though the house to a small but cozy room housing a large flat screen TV mounted on the wall and a huge couch scattered with cushions and blankets. I let Alesso lead me to the couch and follow his instruction as he tells me to sit and wait while he runs to his room to grab his duvet from his bed. Hopefully this will be the distraction I need to keep me sane until Silas and Linc bring Teddy back.

Alesso comes running back into the room a few minutes later with his duvet bundled into his arms and over his head, laughing as he dives with it head first into the couch.

"Are you alright?" I laugh as he untangles himself from the material and begins to arrange the cushions and other blankets, making a little nest of comfort in the middle of the couch.

"Yeah, I'm alright," he answers, fully absorbed in his task.

"Do you want to pick the movie?" I ask, feeling a little helpless as he does all of the hard work to get the blankets exactly where he wants them.

"No, it's OK. I'll let you pick," he says, finally falling back against the couch cushions. "All done. Come on," he grins, holding his arms out wide, showing off his work before he pats the space next to him signaling for me to sit beside him.

"Alright then, how about we watch Spider-Man?" I ask, knowing that's one of Teddy's favorites so I'm hoping Alesso likes it too. And with the loud cheer that erupts next to me, I'd say that that was a yes.

"I love Spider-Man!"

As we settle down into the cozy nest of fabrics Alesso leans into my side just as Teddy does and without even thinking about it, my arm comes up automatically to rest around his back so I can pull him closer to me.

"I think my dad really likes you," Alesso divulges as the movie begins to play. I stifle a laugh at his words, bringing my eyebrows up in a mock shocked expression.

"What makes you think that?" I ask, on a serious note I'm purely invested in how he's gotten to this conclusion. I wonder if he talks about me.

"He's different since he met you," he says quietly, almost in a sort of daydream, but his words are filled with sadness as he stares at the TV screen, not really paying attention to the images. My stomach knots at the vacant expression, wondering if his imagination has taken him back to a dark place in his childhood.

"Is it OK that he likes me?" I ask, mentally preparing myself to be told by a child that's so much like my own in so many ways, that he doesn't like me at all.

"Do you like him?" Alesso asks, catching me unprepared for that specific question but I can't help but smile at him as he stares wide eyed at me, waiting for my answer.

"I do like him." I nod, watching his expression turn from worry to one of joy as he grins widely at me. "I like him a lot." I add, ruffling my fingers through his hair which earns a playfully delighted giggle from him.

"Then yes, it's OK that he likes you," he nods, enthusiastically. "Teddy is lucky to have a mom like you," he smiles, lunging towards me and wrapping his arms around my neck. The statement winds me coming from such a precious little boy whose own mother thought he wasn't worth the fight to survive. I could never stop fighting for my boy. I bring my arms around his body and hold him close, feeling his heart beating rapidly against my own.

"Thank you, Alessandro," I whisper, not knowing how much I truly needed to hear those words today.

Out of the corner of my eye I notice Max standing against the door frame. I'm not sure how much of the conversation he'd heard but he doesn't let on, instead he watches our embrace with sympathy in his eyes before dipping his head and walking away. I hope Kat wasn't too harsh on him over the phone. He's been through his own shit, and although he's hiding it well, I can read my brother like a book. I know he's blaming himself for this. I know he's taking this personally; this attack his father has conducted. But he isn't to blame. I need to make sure he knows that. But right now, I can't bring myself to go after him. Not when Alesso needs me to be here with him, to comfort him and stay with him until his dad comes home.

I must have been more exhausted than I thought as I jolt awake to a pitch black room and see the movie has long since finished. I can still feel Alesso laying beside me and hear his deep rhythmic breathing as he sleeps soundly wrapped under his duvet. I try not to jostle him but even though the room is shrouded in shadows, my eyes automatically zone in on the dark figure lurking in the doorway, causing the hair's on the back of my neck to stand on edge. I gasp, louder than anticipated and the figure immediately moves towards me, covering the space in two large strides.

"Shhh Love, it's only me," a familiar voice melts through my fear.

"Jesus Christ, Linc! You scared the shit out of me!" I whisper-shout, running my fingers down my face. I take in the slight smirk of his lips as he brings his hand to mine, entwining our fingers and although the room is dark, my eyes have adjusted to the shadows enough to notice his eyes flick between Alesso and I.

"Come with me," he whispers, tugging at my hand.

My nerves and excitement of finally seeing Teddy again are making it hard to function and I feel the need to lean against him in the hopes of standing up straight.

"Teddy… is he?…" I whisper, unable to finish my question as Linc leads me through the house, unsure if I honestly want to hear the answer. What if they hurt him? I will never forgive myself. I shudder at the thought, with a threatening wave of nausea rolling through my body.

"He's scared mostly. He fell asleep on the drive back, but he was asking for you from the moment we got to him." Linc responds, not daring to look at me as we come to a halt in front of a closed bedroom door that I've not been into before. "I sat with him while he slept. I didn't want him to be alone when he woke up. He was exhausted and when we realized you were asleep too, we figured it was best to let you both rest. He's in here, he woke up a few minutes ago asking for you but I think he fell back asleep. I thought you could both use a bit of privacy after what he's been through." Linc says sincerely, dipping his head and squeezing my hand.

"Thank you for bringing him back to me. I will never be able to repay you for this." I breathe out slowly before entering the room, leaving Linc in the hallway. Before I close the door, I glance back, noting the unsettled look in his eyes before he turns his head and strides away. That look troubled me, but I can't think straight right now, my entire body seems to have detached from itself as soon as my eyes fall on the sleeping boy across the room.

I made my way across the room in some form of trance. I was unaware of my own movements, or the fact that I had moved at all. That was until my hand reached out so I could stroke my fingers across his perfectly rounded cheeks. The ache in my chest was all too real as I stood watching his chest rising and falling while he slept, but this time it did not hurt. No, this time it encompassed me and pulled me under its weight. I could feel it, the weight of this moment traveling throughout my soul. My body hummed and throbbed and tingled straight through to my fingertips. I could feel every follicle of hair on my scalp as my skin prickled and warmth spread throughout my veins. My mouth opened, but only a silent scream was released as I collapsed to my knees beside the bed. Was this real or was I only dreaming? I couldn't control the violation of thoughts that ravaged me. All I had wanted was to have my son back but now he was here in front of me, without warning, my brain was trying to convince me it wasn't real. It couldn't be real.

I close my eyes so tight I can see white swirls of patterns dancing in my mind as I ball my fists into my hair and will myself to get it together. I can hear Teddy calling for me. This had to be a dream.

"Mommy," he calls as I watch him reach over to me. His voice is faint and far away and I can't quite decipher his features. This isn't real. None of this is real. "Mommy," he calls again, only a little louder this time as his image moves closer in my mind. "Mommy, wake up!" He calls once more, and as the image in my mind grows clearer, his hand reaches out to touch my face. "Mommy," he cries, and I feel a small but firm pair of hands pull on my face. My eyes snap open. It wasn't a dream. Teddy is here, and he was pulling me back from that dark place.

The moment his eyes meet mine everything happens all at once, the oxygen in my lungs replenishes itself as I breathe him in and hold him close. I stand quickly, scooping him into my arms and holding him into my chest as he begins to cry.

"I missed you, Mommy," he sobs into my body.

"Teddy, baby, I'm so sorry!" I plead as my emotions overwhelm me and unwelcome tears blur my vision. "I'm so so sorry." I kiss his head, his face, his hair, anything I could get access to. "I'm so sorry baby."

We cradle together, crying into each other with my constant apologies, the only words spoken as I rock us back and forth. I can't fathom how he felt through all of this, scared and alone. The thought of what they were planning to do to him makes me almost retch as I pull back from our embrace and hold Teddy at arms length, raking my eyes over his entire body. "Did they hurt you? Did they touch you at all sweetheart?" I urge, fumbling my hands over his body, ensuring I haven't missed any bruising or open wounds.

"They didn't hurt me, Mom. Uncle Ronan just shouted a lot and locked me in my room." Teddy recalls, but the relief I feel at his words make it seem a little easier to breathe.

"Thank God." I whisper, pulling him back to my chest and kissing his forehead. "I missed you so much baby. So much. I'm sorry we couldn't find you sooner." I mumble regretfully.

Teddy yawns and rubs his eyes that are already red and swollen from crying. "I missed you too, Mommy," he sniffs, nestling further into my chest and closing his eyes. I continue to rock back and forth, absentmindedly stroking my fingers over his hair while I hum his favorite bedtime lullaby, soothing both of us to sleep.

When daylight finally pierces through the crack in the curtains I'm already wide awake. I've laid as still as possible for the last few hours, simply holding Teddy in my arms as I listened to the soothing sound of his soft snores while he sleeps, delighting in the feel of having him back in my arms. I have no idea what our plan is from here on out, but I do know that I need to properly thank Silas and Lincoln for fulfilling their promise and bringing my boy home safely. But more than that, I need to know what happened. The more I think of their arrival back home, the more it dawns on me that I never saw Silas last night, and even in the brief moment that I saw Linc, he never even mentioned him, and the look on Linc's face before he left me with Teddy keeps playing on repeat in my mind. Something isn't right. I can feel a sickening unease beginning to nestle in the pit of my stomach again and I don't like it one bit.

By the time Teddy starts squirming, signaling he's waking up, I've talked myself out of every possibly bad situation that my brain has conjured up. If something significantly bad had happened, Linc would have told me. Surely. I convince myself I'm imagining things. Silas was probably busy dealing with the fallout of rescuing Teddy, who I should be concentrating on, not fretting over somebody I know is more than capable of looking after himself, and is most probably doing whatever the hell it is he does when he's being a mafia boss.

Drawing my attention, Teddy reaches his arm out as if to check I'm still here, the small gesture forms a lump in my throat at how many times he woke up scared and alone in that unfamiliar space.

"I'm here, baby." I whisper, stroking my fingers through his hair before he twists his body to look at me. The looks of utter relief as his body visibly relaxes catches me off guard. I can't ignore the way his eyes roam my face as he brings his tiny hand to my cheek and utters the word "Mommy."

"I'm here, and I'm not going anywhere." I promise him, kissing his hand. "Are you hungry?" I ask, sitting up and pulling him into my lap for him to nod in response. "OK, let's get you some breakfast. Pancakes sound good?"

At the mention of pancakes Teddy lifts his head, beaming at me. "Yes please," he grins.

The kitchen is suspiciously empty by the time I manage to coax Teddy out of bed and we make it out of the bedroom. Teddy notices it too and as he pulls himself onto the stool at the breakfast bar and glances around the room.

"Where is everybody?" he asks, looking somewhat nervous as his fidgets in his chair. I busy myself with finding the ingredients to whip up some fresh pancake batter, ignoring the irrational feelings of hurt that are manifesting themselves inside me.

"They must be busy, baby. I'm sure we'll see them soon, don't worry." I say, reassuring myself more than anything else. But the next words that leave Teddy's mouth shatter my resolve and the bowl that slipped through my fingers.

"Did Cole get out?"

I'm sure the world spun on its axis for a split second before the glass shattered across the floor making me jump from shock. "SHIT!" I curse, jumping back as a shard of glass slashes my ankle, slicing straight through the skin.

"MOMMY!" Teddy shrieks jumping down from the stool.

"Don't come over here, Teddy, there's glass all over the floor." I warn him, trying to make my way across the space so I can hoist myself up onto the kitchen counter.

As I take a tentative step forwards a deep voice causes me to wobble. "Stop moving!" Linc orders as he advances on me, paying no attention to the floor littered with glass. "Get back up on the stool, Teddy," he instructs while literally sweeping me off my feet with one arm under the back of my knees and the other supporting my lower back. Instinctively, I wrap my arms around his neck as he carries me to the bar stool next to Teddy and places me down. "Are you hurt?" he asks, looking between Teddy and I. "Either of you?"

"I'm fine." Teddy says, nodding his head enthusiastically. "Are you OK, Mom?" he asks, with a worried look on his face.

"I'm alright. I'm so sorry Teddy, it just slipped." I sigh, shaking my head. Not wanting to tell him his question caught me off guard. Cole's name was the last thing I thought would come out of his mouth. Why was he asking if he got out? I catch Linc's eye wondering if there is something he's hiding but I know he couldn't have heard Teddy's question.

Raking my eyes down his body I notice how tense he is, he looks sleepless and distracted but my concern is quickly snubbed as he grabs my ankle firmly in his hand, lifting my foot onto the bartop.

"Lucille, you're bleeding," he states, furrowing his brow before pressing his thumb into the small cut above my ankle bone. I hiss out in protest as the pressure stings but he doesn't let me pull away, he only tightens his hold, and when I finally look back to meet his eyes again, his heated stare welds me to the seat and only when Teddy interrupts asking if I need a bandaid do I manage to look away.

"I'll get the first aid kit," Linc grumbles as he turns to one of the kitchen drawers and pulls out a small white box, opening it up to reveal an assortment of bandages, tapes and various sizes of bandaids. "Alesso is always injuring himself while he cooks with..." the rest of the sentence immediately dies on his tongue, leaving a sour taste at the back of my throat at the thought of what he almost said. I open my mouth to ask after Cole to try and understand what Teddy meant by asking if he got out, but without another word to either of us, Linc grabs a broom from the utility cupboard and starts clearing up the shattered glass while Teddy watches me bandage my ankle. There's definitely something he's not telling me.

After Linc finished clearing the floor and I'd given him the hardest stare down of my life, he left the room again, but not before promising that he'd fill me in with everything I needed to know later on this evening. I didn't want to argue with him while Teddy was here so I let him go with little objection while I start on a fresh batch of pancake batter for breakfast.

I serve up two stacks of pancakes, topped with a mountain of fresh fruit, drizzled with syrup and sprinkled with a generous helping of chocolate chips and Teddy practically inhales the plate within a matter of minutes. Which intrusively has me thinking that they'd been starving him for the last few days. The guilt is almost impalpable, making it difficult to finish my own meal.

"Aren't you going to finish that, Mommy?" Teddy asks, as though he can see it written all over my face.

I smile and shake my head. "No baby, you can finish it if you want. But don't eat it so fast, you'll give yourself a stomach ache." I try to warn him as he shovels forkfuls of pancake and fruit into his mouth like I may suddenly change my mind and take it away from him.

I sit and watch him, taking in every small and perfect detail of his beautiful little face, smiling when I notice the chocolate smeared across his chin. I lick the pad of my thumb and laugh, "I'm not sure how you managed to miss your mouth little man, but you've given yourself a chocolate beard," swiping my thumb across his face to wipe away the chocolate. He laughs and the sound warms my entire body from the inside and I instantly need to hear more of it. In a swift move, I tip him back off his stool, keeping him seated but cradling him into my arms as I rain down on him with a shower of kisses, something I know he finds incredibly hilarious. "You're just so scrummy, I could eat you all up!" I tease as I begin to blow raspberries into his cheek, earning me a high pitched squeal of delight.

"You can't eat me, Mommy!" he wails between fits of giggles. It's the best sound in the entire world and if I could bottle it up, I would.

A low cough from behind pauses my movements. "What's all this noise I can hear?" Max calls from the doorway.

Teddy immediately removes himself from my hold and jumps from the stool. "UNCLE MAX!" he shouts excitedly as he runs over to Max with his arms stretched as wide as they'll go. Max catches him, swinging him up over his head.

"Tedster, I'm so happy to see you little man. I missed you so much." Max states, and I can hear the emotion in his voice. While he lowers Teddy back to the ground, I also notice the flash of pain as his face scrunches and he immediately snaps his arm around his midsection. Fool. He's still healing. He catches my disapproving glare but shrugs it off, kneeling down so that he's eye to eye with Teddy now. "I'm sorry Ted. I'M SO SO SORRY…" his voice cracks as he pulls him into his body. "This was all my fault." I hear him croak as he hangs his head, drowning in the weight of the guilt he carries.
Oh no. I'm not having this. He is not going to take the blame for this one and tell Teddy that what happened was all his fault. Over my dead body.

"Max," I warn, lowering my tone and cutting him off before he says too much. He should know better. But when his eyes meet mine, there is nothing of the man I know lying behind them. He looks empty. The reality of what could have been for both of them overwhelms me with such intense ferocity that I have to steady myself against the counter.

"Are you sad, Uncle Max?" I hear Teddy whisper as Max refuses to let him go.

"No Ted, I'm not sad," Max sighs.

"Then why are you crying?"

Max sucks in a deep breath of air, turning his lips up into an unconvincing smile as he pulls back and looks into Teddy's face. "I'm just happy to have you back little man," he sighs, squeezing him again before standing up and lifting Teddy from the floor. He walks over to where I stand, silently watching, holding back all of the emotions that are running riot, fighting to break free from the inner

214

cyclone that's raging inside of me. The anger, the sadness, the resentment, the love, but even more so, the forgiveness. I never for a moment thought that Max could have been involved in something like this. Never doubted his love for both Teddy and myself. And my god, I would have gone to the ends of the world to ensure justice was served if he had never made it out alive.

You know when you hear the quote that it doesn't do well to dwell on the past? Well, maybe it's right, maybe I shouldn't be purging myself with thoughts of what if and plotting a revenge so sweet that it tastes bitter against my tongue. I should be enjoying these moments while I can. And so with no effort at all, I embrace my son and my brother in my arms and hold them tight, whispering my love to them both.

Max spent the entire day with us after that, not willing to let either of us out of his sight now that we were all seemingly safe from harm. I hadn't seen much from Lincoln and literally nothing from Silas though and the small pit of unease in my stomach grew with each passing hour.

"Earth to Lucille," Max's voice echoes through my thoughts and I blink myself back to focus.

"I'm sorry, what did you say?" I ask, feeling the warmth of the steaming cup of coffee burn through my palms as I nestle onto the couch.

Max frowns slightly, questioning me with his glare. "Have you spoken with Katrina?"

"No. Not yet. She's been texting me all day though." I smile, with the thought of my friend being left on read and the knowledge that it will be pissing her off. "I'll call her tomorrow." I concede, taking a long sip of coffee to which he simply nods.

"Are you alright?" Max asks, crooning his head to the side.

The question seems somewhat alarming given the circumstances recently and I fail to hide the incredulous tsk that involuntarily leaves my lips.

"Are *you* alright?" I counter, knowing full well that he is not. We're both fighting our own demons, and the way he refuses to look me in the eye after I ask only solidifies that knowledge. "That's exactly what I thought," I snap, regretting my tone as soon as I said it. "Fuck, I'm sorry. I just don't know how I'm supposed to feel right now. I'm so fucking happy that we finally got Teddy back, but everything else feels so wrong. I don't know what I'm meant to do now." I admit, turning my attention to Teddy who sits quietly coloring in some of Alessandro's books.

"You live, Lucille. For him. You move on. Christ, you pack your shit and get out of town."

I let the shock of his words slowly sink in, taking a long procrastinating drink of my coffee before I answer. How does he still not understand? "How can you even suggest that to me right now?" I whisper.

"Because it's what's best for you, and if you can't see it for yourself, somebody in their right mind needs to tell you," he states, neither irate nor belittling. I think he genuinely believes this would be the best thing for me to do. To run. "Hell, I will pack your bags for you to get you out of here," he adds while he begins pacing the room.

"I won't run away from this Max."

"This is not your fight to face Luc."

"Not my fight? He took my son Max. He almost killed you because of me. How is this not *my* fight?" I scoff.

Max shakes his head in response, noticeably irritated with me now as he runs his fingers through his hair. "What exactly are you planning on doing, Lucille? You won't ever get one foot out of this place without your boyfriends hot on your tail. You think you will be able to pull the wool over their eyes and you'll somehow find yourself in a position with Ronan where you have the upper hand? Do you think you'll be able to pull the trigger when the time comes? He was your father once upon a time. Don't pretend that doesn't still mean something to you." His words are fast and full of more than just anger. It's fear that riles him so much. I can see it in his eyes and in the way his body tenses as he mentions Ronan's name, but I am not the same woman I was five years ago when I ended up on his doorstep, hell I'm not even sure I'm the same woman I was two days ago. This last week has been the longest, most grueling time of my life and no doubt it has aged me another ten years, but it's also hardened me in ways I could never comprehend. I cast my gaze to Teddy who currently seems to be uninterrupted by our heated conversation with his tongue sticking out as he concentrates on his drawings.

I snap my head back to Max whose eyes have traveled the path of my own. "I will not do this here in front of him." I state, straightening my shoulders and raising my chin.

Max opens his mouth to respond but closes it again in quick succession. I can see the clench of his jaw as he battles with himself on what to say until finally he grunts defeatedly and through gritted teeth says, "Just don't do anything fucking stupid, Lucille," as he leaves the room.

Come bedtime that evening, I hadn't seen Lincoln since this morning and was still yet to hear or see Silas. It didn't take long for me to sing Teddy off to sleep in the same guest room we slept in last night, but my overworked brain was unable to give me the rest I so eagerly hoped for, so I lay awake staring up at the darkened ceiling until I could no longer stand the increasing pitch of the deafening scream that infested my mind.

Making as little noise as possible, I carefully slide myself out of bed and make my way to Silas' office, hoping I'll find one of them in there. The house is completely silent and mostly dark, the moonlight through the windows leading my way. But as I push open the door to be met with a dark and empty room, my hopefulness slowly begins to distinguish. Where the heck are they?

I move into the room, unsure what I'm looking for. Maybe something on the desk or the computer will give me some clue as to where they are. I begin to flick through the mountainous stack of papers that sit on the desk, not really paying attention to what's written on them as the hair's rise on the back of my neck, sending a shiver down the entire length of my spine.

"Find what you're looking for, Love?" Linc's voice calls through the darkness, making me jump, the papers slipping through my fingers and littering the floor.

"I have now that you're here," I answer, though I can't clearly see his face.

"I've been here the whole time, Lucille. Giving you and Teddy the space I thought you needed together. But I've been watching." His voice is closer this time as I watch the shadow of his body stalk slowly towards me, narrowing my eyes as the moonlight bathes his half naked body in an almost glowing, bluish hue. It's breathtaking and I'm completely unprepared for it as an audible gasp escapes my lips before I can silence it.

Chapter 20

Lincoln

That fucking sound has my cock throbbing already. I've been watching the monitors around the house all day and the moment I noticed my little love make her way to Silas' office, I knew I couldn't ignore her any longer. I have tested my patience, pushed myself beyond boundaries I would never normally tolerate and almost broke my goddamn teeth with the force of restraint I've bared.

Forcing myself to concentrate on something other than tearing her clothes off whenever she's around me, but right now I'm not myself, not after hearing the conversation between Lucille and her brother earlier this afternoon. I almost bulldozed my way straight into that room just to fuck the words about this being her fight right out of her mouth. Not wanting to show my anger in front of Teddy was the only thing that kept me from showing her what I really thought about her ever leaving us. But that small little sexy whimper that just slipped its way past her perfectly rounded lips, has cracked every last bit of the self restraint I had left.

I creep meaningfully slow around Silas' desk, taking my time until I come to a stop behind her, taking in the curvature of her body against the light from the moon. Ugh. So fucking perfect. I reach a hand up, slowly running my finger from the base of her spine to the back of her neck, tickling the skin beneath her shirt.

"Is that why you came into the kitchen this morning?" I hear her ask in a hushed tone as my fingers work their way along her shoulder and down the length of her arm, leaving a trail of goosebumps in their wake. I know the effect I'm having on her body already and I've barely touched her yet.

I step closer to her, pressing her hips into the desk as I lower my mouth to her ear, teasing her lobe between my teeth. "Mhmm," I mumble, as I begin kissing and sucking at her neck.

I hear the audible gulp as she swallows her trepidation but I also feel the way her hips automatically push back as she grinds her ass into my crotch. "You mean, you've heard everything?" she gasps as I lean against her more, pressing my throbbing cock into her backside. I nod slowly, my lips turning up into a smirk at the way her voice and her body betrays her. She's not so brave now. I move my head to the opposite side of her neck, paying close attention to the sweet spot below her ear, earning a sensual moan as my reward.

"So what was your plan, little love? Were you planning on running away from us?" I ask, my tone low and meaningful. Her body jerks underneath my hands that have begun to travel around her waist, my fingertips teasing at the waistband of her pants.

Lucille's head lolls back against my shoulder as she breathes out her response, gripping her hand onto my own, "I would never."

"Good girl." I whisper, slipping my hand the rest of the way into her panties and instantly releasing my own feral groan as the wetness from her pussy coats my fingers.

"Fuck, Lucille. Do you have any idea how much I've missed this pussy?" I hiss, not really caring for an answer as I slide two fingers inside her, easily done with her slick juices already coating my hand. "You have no idea how fucking difficult it's been to hold myself back from you."

Lucille's body shudders as I curl my fingers deeper inside while caressing that sensitive bud with my thumb.

"Then don't," she whimpers, grinding herself back and forth on my hand, chasing the friction she so desperately needs. I bring my free hand to her throat and hold her still, squeezing tightly before she's grabbing at my wrist and gasping for air. Desperate and needy.

"Don't ever think of leaving us, Lucille. It's not an option for you anymore." I whisper, loosening my hold around her throat as I curl my fingers deeper inside of her cunt. I can feel her tightening around me, her juices already spilling out as she draws closer to her release.

My cock is so hard at the thought it physically hurts still being in my pants but this won't be quick. I want her limp by the time I'm finished with her, unable to stand, unable to string a sentence together. "You're ours now to do with as we please." I grip her throat again and bite down hard into her earlobe, eliciting a strangled cry as I fuck her hard with my hand. "To keep." I release her throat. "To protect." I squeeze her neck again as she gasps, still grinding her hips in tandem with my movements with the most beautiful mewls coming from her mouth. "To fuck."

This time I travel my hand to her face, already sheen with sweat as I grip her chin between my fingers and thumb, turning her to look at me through the shadowy darkness of the room. Those fucking eyes, Christ, I almost come undone. "To love." I crash my lips to hers, shoving my tongue into her mouth to swallow down her pleasurable cries as she shatters over my fingers. Her thighs squeeze tightly together around my hand as involuntary shudders wrack her body and she continues to ride me, digging her nails into my arms to steady herself, while she glories in the entirety of her orgasm. But now that I've had my starter, I'm not even close to being finished. I pull my lips away from her own and smirk at her sudden intake of breath. The image of her eyes widening as I lean forwards and whisper, "To punish," is one I'll mentally be storing for later use.

"P… Punish?" she chokes as I slip my hand from her pants. Lucille spins to face me, trailing the movement of my hand as I slowly suck my fingers clean of her juices, smirking at her, tasting her cum on my tongue, savoring it as I swallow it down. So fucking delicious.

"Punish baby. Now get on the desk." I order, stepping into her again until her ass hits the desk behind.

Lucille hesitates for a second, pulling her already swollen lip between her teeth as her emerald eyes catch the moonlight, igniting a fire so deep in the darkest depth of my soul that it takes my breath away and I practically growl as I become all too impatient and do the job for her, lifting her ass onto the desk and pushing her down flat to her back.

"Linc," I hear her whisper but I'm already too distracted to engage.

"Lift your hips, Love." I instruct, pulling her pants and little lace panties off in one full swipe as she obeys my order, eagerly baring her perfectly sweet pussy, which still glistens with the evidence of her release as the moon dances through the window behind me. "Exquisit." I groan, as she widens her legs for me, enticing me in. Like I even needed asking. I drop to my knees, hooking my hands under Lucille's knees and pulling her closer to the edge of the desk, placing both of her feet onto my shoulders.

Lucille shifts her bottom half impatiently as I trace my fingers across the insides of her thighs, so torturously slowly, enjoying every sexually frustrated sound that leaves her mouth. "Lincoln," she mewls, "I need more," rolling her hips trying to gain more friction.

"Such a needy little thing." I smirk at the desperate beg in her voice, glancing up to her pleading eyes before slowly inserting one finger, then another and another into her tight hole, stretching her against her protests until I curl my fingers to find that sweet spot deep inside as she throws her head back releasing an agonizingly sultry cry, letting her legs fall wider apart. "That's it baby, sing for me," I smirk, before pressing my lips to her clit, sucking frantically on the sensitive bud. Like a man starved, the first taste unlocks something feral within me and I need her cum down my throat instantaneously. I lash my tongue over her sweet pussy, applying just the right amount of pressure to her now engorged clit before easing off to only apply when she whined at the denial of my mouth, cupping my fingers deep in her cunt, fucking her hard and fast with my hand in tandem. I can feel her tightening already, already on the edge from her first orgasm. I suck harder, savoring the delicious taste of her, grazing my teeth over her clit in the process.

Lucille's fingers lace into my hair, pulling it hard at the root and I zone in on the deliciously painful sting it leaves across my scalp. "Oh god, I'm going to come," she cries, her pussy clamping around my fingers as an explosion of her addictively sweet, warm juices coat my tongue. She tastes so fucking delicious, I don't think i'll ever get enough of it. I lap her up and drink her down, suckling feverishly at her clit as her body writhes with pleasure, ensuring I get every last drop of her orgasm. "Linc," she gasps, pulling my mouth from her pussy as she tightens her grip on my hair. "I need you inside of me." I snap my head up, her release coating my mouth and dripping from my chin as I slowly stand to tower over her body and regain my breath.

"You don't have to tell me twice baby." I smirk, cocking an eyebrow at her. Lucille sits up immediately, grappling with my pants to push them down. It's cute. Sexy as fuck, but still cute. With quick success she frees my throbbing erection from the painfully constricting fabric and instantly grips her hand around the base, releasing a bead of precum from the tip of which she leans down and swipes away with her tongue.

"Christ Lucille," I groan, throwing my head back hissing out at the feel of her tongue against my solid cock. Fuck being a martyr, I need inside of her now, I've tortured myself enough. I push Lucille back against the desk and pull her legs up around my waist. "Hold them there, Love." I instruct, lining the head of my cock against her pussy, glancing up to meet her gaze.

Lucille's eyes are hooded as she props herself up onto her elbows to watch my movements. "You're going to fuck me here, on Silas's desk?" she asks, raising her eyebrows with a hint of amusement in her voice. Dirty girl, she's enjoying this just as much as I am. Letting me defile her in his office.

"No baby, I'm going to destroy you on it." I growl, thrusting my hips, shoving my cock into her perfectly tight fitting pussy causing her to cry out at the brutality of it. She takes me so fucking well as I bottom out, filling her up until my balls slap against her ass. "God. Fuck Lucille, you feel so good." I groan, leaning down to take her mouth too, enjoying her sultry moans each time my hips connect with hers. I feel like my entire body is on fire, the blood in my veins, replaced with molten liquid as her thighs clench around my body and her nails scratch their path down my naked back.

I lift my head back to watch her eyes roll back as she all but whimpers beneath me. The profuse intrusional thought of her going after Ronan spurs me on with anger and an overwhelming need to protect as I pound her hard into the wood. The slap of our skin mixed with her pleasurable cries are a fucking symphony to my ears ringing throughout the room. Fuck anybody else who hears us.

"You will never put yourself in danger, Lucille. Do you understand?" I seeth, bringing a hand to her throat again and squeezing until her eyes snap open to mine as her face turns a deeper shade of red. "I won't fucking allow it." I grunt, pulling myself up and running my hands up her shirt, bunching it under her chin to expose her perfectly plump tits. I take one in each hand, pinching her nipples hard between my fingers until she arches her back off the desk and hisses at the pain. "Beautiful, so perfectly fucking beautiful" I moan, savoring the sight of her pussy devouring my cock as her tits bounce each time I pound into her. I don't think I'll be able to hold on much longer, I can feel myself snapping, desperate to fill her pussy, to have her dripping over my brother's desk with my own cum. I lift her hips, her legs resting on my shoulders as my nails dig into the flesh of her ass, leaving only her shoulders and head against the desk as I pummel into her harder. The new angle gives me easier access to her g-spot. When I see her face scrunch up in ecstasy I know I'm hitting that slice of heaven just right. "Come for me, Lucille. I have not deprived myself for this fucking long for this to be quick. I want another. Now come for me," I growl, squeezing her ass cheeks with bruising force as I drive myself into her dripping pussy. She explodes immediately, gushing around my twitching cock, crying my name into the darkness of the night. I watch with ravenous eyes as she

225

comes apart with her eyes screwed shut as she bites down hard onto her bottom lip trying her best to stifle her screams. What a beautiful fucking sight to behold as she breaks for me, piece by piece.

I slow my pace slightly, enjoying the way Lucille's chest rises and falls while her body writhes against my own. I carefully lower her backside to the desk and lean forwards to kiss her, nipping her bottom lip between my teeth as I do, causing her to gasp. She's spent, panting and covered in a glistening sheen of sweat but fuck if I leave it there, I may as well be dead. "I'm not done with you yet," I whisper, causing her eyes to widen and my own to dance in delight.

"Linc, I can't," she objects, shaking her head at me, but I've already slipped my cock out as I flip her over, placing her on her knees onto the wooden desk. I trail my hand along her spine before placing them on the inside of her thighs, pushing her knees as far apart as her exhausted body will allow, spreading her wide and showcasing my heart's desire. I step back and marvel at the sight of her, so perfect, so mine. Her ass teases me, coated with her juices. It would be so easy to slam my cock into that taut little ring. But it will hate to wait. I need my cock inside of her pussy. I need my cum to fill her up. "You can and you will." I groan before smacking her ass with a sharp snap and thrusting myself back inside her. This new new angle makes me work to force myself just that much more, stretching her tight hole around the girth of my solid erection while she hisses out at the intrusion. But her moans of pain soon turn to pleasure as I circle my hips. The warmth and wetness a welcome fucking feeling as I allow myself to fully loose control. I fist one hand into her hair, yanking her head back to look at me. "Do you see

226

what you do to me, little love?" I dig my other hand into her hip, being sure to leave indentations in her skin, holding her in place as I feel my balls tightening at the sight of her parted lips and lust fucked face watching me over her shoulder. She draws in a shaky breath as I thrust myself harder into her pussy, eliciting an almost squeaking noise from her throat as our bodies slam together. "You make me feel things no other woman has made me feel before. You drive me fucking crazy, Lucille." I pound her harder, my balls slapping against her clit. I can feel the promising tighten of her pussy around my steel cock. A feeling I will never tire of.

"Say it, Linc!" she gasps, arching her back, pushing her ass further against me. Fuck. Her eyes hold mine with desperation and need swimming in the deep pools of gemstones that lie there and I fuck her like a man possessed. Her moans become feral as she reaches out for the edge of the desk, her white-knuckled hold trying to ground her while I plunge my cock over and over into her desperate pussy. She wants me to tell her I love her, she needs it. My broken little love needs reminding just how fucking loved she is. My cock instantly judders, releasing a torrent of cum deep into her pussy as she screams with her own release, coating my thighs with her deliciously slick cream. I slow my hips, riding us both to the end of our climax and groaning at the now emptiness of my balls. I have never experienced an orgasm like that before. Never had a woman's need for me to tell them I loved them be my ultimate undoing, but it was her, and all of my rules had already been broken.

My body screams at me and beads of sweat slide down the length of my spine as I try to regain my breath. I've released Lucille's hair and as she collapses onto the

227

desk I slip my spent cock out of her gaping pussy, staring in amazement at the sight of my cum oozing out between her swollen lips and down her thighs.

I let her remain on the desk for a few minutes, her body still trembling with aftershocks as she slowly comes back down to earth. "Linc?" her tired voice calls to me.

"Yes, Love?" I ask, stroking my hand across her back before helping her to sit upright, frowning as she flinches slightly while leaning back. "Did I hurt you?"

Lucille smiles and shakes her head. "Just a little sore." I watch her closely, and although she's satiated, her smile does not reach her eyes.

I take her face in my hands, kissing her tenderly, stroking my thumb across her cheek while my tongue delves impatiently between her lips. "Lucille," I whisper, resting my forehead on hers, "never have I ever felt a love like I do for you. A love so strong it scares me, petrifies me even with the thought of having it ripped away. You have come into my life, all of our lives and taken everything I thought I knew about what love was and shown me how fucking wrong I was. You have no idea." I swallow my words, unsure on how exactly I can express the feelings that are so unfamiliar to me. "It's hard for me to express myself, for fear of losing you. I am a damaged man Lucille, a sinner. I do not deserve your love but I will promise that in this lifetime and the next I will spend the rest of my days repenting for all of the evil I have done, to be worthy of your love." I wasn't aware that I'd closed my eyes until her gentle hand came to rest on my cheek and my eyes flew open as her unrelenting gaze bore into me.

"I love you too, Lincoln." she smiles, cocking her head to the side and raising one eyebrow. "Now take me back to bed."

Oh my sneaky little love, she just wanted to have me serve my feelings to her on a platter. A punishment for another night maybe. For right now, I help her dress, steadying her as she wobbles once she's finally back on her feet and pulling on my own pants before carrying her back to the guest room. "Sweet dreams, Love." I coo kissing her softly before she walks through the door.

"Goodnight."

I would have loved nothing more than to cradle her naked body as she slept in my bed with my cum drying between her legs but I know deep down, she would not have risked Teddy waking up alone, or felt comfortable enough to leave him for much longer than we'd already been, so my only option was to return her to him for the rest of the night, and return to my bed alone, with the taste of her cum on my tongue and relishing in the sharp sting of fresh scratch marks that score the length of my back. However before I can call it a night, there's somebody I need to see first and with a satisfied grin plastered on my face I enter Silas' bedroom without stopping to knock first.

He's not asleep, though he lies still in the muted darkness of his room, cocooned within the silken sheets on his bed, with only a dim glow from the light on the opposite side of the room casting a warm blanket across the open space. I move forward and sink myself into the chair that's pulled up beside the bed that I've spent the most part of the last day positioned in when I haven't needed to attend to business elsewhere, and smirk to myself fully encased in euphoria.

Silas's strained voice cuts through the quiet, roping me back into the present. "Were you purposely fucking her loud enough for the entire house to hear? Or were you just trying to piss off Irish?"

I can't contain the laughter that erupts. "Well maybe he'll stop trying to convince her to leave now." I scoff, shaking my head as I hang back to glance at the ceiling.

"He what?!" Silas snaps, pushing himself up in his bed, hissing at the movement as soon as he does it. Shit, I guess I forgot to tell him that. I sit up straight, crossing my arms over my still bare chest, taking in the fragile sight of Silas' bandaged torso. Momentarily thinking what could have happened had the bullet punctured anything major. We were lucky to get out of there, and he's lucky to be alive. Another favor I owe that fucking doctor.

"Lay down you moron, he's just scared of losing her." I snap, as he collapses back into his cushions, obviously exhausted from the minimal strain on his body.

"And you?" He gasps, regaining his breath and tilting his head my way.

I remain unmoved in my chair as I return his gaze. "What about me?"

"That wasn't just a fuck, Linc. I know you brother, do not pretend that I don't. Just because you won't admit your feelings doesn't mean that they're not already known to the rest of us." Silas' words wash over me.

Had I really been that obvious? I look to the window, taking solace in the blackness that ebbs out across the garden. Grimacing as a sudden swell of guilt crashes into me like an expanding wave, licking its way across the rocks.

"I don't think I have ever felt this way about anybody, Si. Not even Cassidy." I admit, not daring to look his way. Only he knew the full extent of my darkness back then. When Alesso was so small he never noticed his father spiraling into a black bottomless pit after his mother took her life.

"Your love could not save her, Lincoln. Nobody could save her, she was too far gone." he states matter of factly with an unfamiliar softness to his voice.

I grit my teeth and nod as I turn my attention back to him, quickly moving the conversation in a different direction. "I'll bring her to see you in the morning. I found her snooping in your office, I think she misses you."

Silas smirks for a moment, before the crease between his eyebrows grows prominent again. "Have you told her?"

"Not yet" I sigh, pursing my lips to the side. "We'll tell her tomorrow." I stand from the chair, making my way back to the door. "Get some rest" I add before turning to leave, not looking forward to that conversation one bit.

"You fucked her on my desk didn't you?" Silas calls before I close the door chuckling to myself as I make my way to my room.

Vividly realistic visions plague my mind through the night, rendering me sleepless and sweaty. Black, white, red. Intricate sparks of color and blood oozes behind my flickering eyelids. The lifeless body of my son's mother lay crumpled across the floor. The tearstained face of my son as his mother didn't respond when he cried for her. The beaten body of Lucille screaming for help beneath Vinny's blade. Cole's limp and bleeding body after he was shot.

"NO!" I shout. Forcing my body upright, throwing off the sheets as I repeatedly fail to save them all. I glance at the clock. My mind has been torturing me for the last several hours but for a few minutes I will allow myself to give in to it.

I get out of bed and stand under a painfully ice cold shower. Willing the nightmares from my mind before dressing and making my way to the kitchen where I know Lucille is already making Teddy breakfast.

As I round the corner, an invasion of fried bacon fills my nostrils, making my mouth water and my stomach growl at its emptiness. I take in the sight of Lucille dancing in front of the stovetop, humming a playful tune as she twirls a set of tongs in one hand, with a mug of coffee in the other. Teddy sits opposite her at the bar, smiling and clapping his hands at her attempt at singing, giggling each time that she spins around and pulls a funny face at him. If this is what my life would be every day with her, I'll take it. Happily and without regret. Suddenly a small hand tugs at my sleeve. "Dad?"

I smile instantly, glancing down at Alesso who still dons his pajamas. "What's going on?" he asks, yawning. I thought it was best to keep Alessandro out of the way for Teddy's first day back yesterday, so in an attempt to let Teddy settle in and for Lucille to be able to spend time with him uninterrupted, I let Cassandra take him for hotdogs and to see a movie after school.

I step sideways, clearing his view to the kitchen. "Look who's home." I smile, placing my hand on his back and gently leading him forwards.

"TEDDY!" Alesso exclaims.
Teddy's head snaps round to us as does Lucille's, coffee and tongs too.

Teddy squeals excitedly "LESSO!" He jumps down from the stool and they both break into a run, embracing each other in a tight brotherly hug as they meet. They haven't spent much time together but when they do their bond is incredible. Lucille's eyes have already started glassing over as she stares at their embrace before glancing over to me. I wink playfully before walking over to both boys.

"How do you two fancy playing a game on the big screen in the games room?" I ask, kneeling down to their height. Their smiling faces light up at my suggestion.

"Yes please!" they call in unison, making me grin like an imbecile.

"OK, breakfast first though," I smile, tipping my chin in Lucille's direction who still hasn't taken her eyes off of us. "That is at least if your mother hasn't burnt the bacon," I tease, ruffling my fingers through Teddy's hair before making my way over to help Lucille finish off breakfast, slyly squeezing her ass as I walk past causing her to yelp.

"You cheeky bastard," Lucille giggles, cursing me quietly enough that only I could hear it and my heart kicks rapidly in my chest at how carefree this moment is. Behind us, the boys talk animatedly about superheroes and crash cars, like no time has passed at all between them and Teddy wasn't being held against his will by his completely deranged uncle.

"We need to talk, Love." I whisper as I plate up rashers of bacon and Lucille finishes frying off some eggs.

Her hands falter slightly and I practically hear the nervous swallow while she tries to pass it off as a small cough, but this needs to be done. Lucille nods her head, I expect she already has some inkling on what the conversation will be about, but I doubt she's going to be ready for the entirety of it.

Alesso and Teddy all but inhale their breakfast, swallowing their food before they'd even chewed, too excited about being reunited and playing their games.

"Slow down you two, you're going to give yourselves a stomach ache," Lucille chides, chuckling softly.

"Don't worry, Mom," Teddy scoffs, speaking with a mouth full of toast. Alesso glances at me and I raise an eyebrow. There isn't much of an age difference between them but Alesso has been brought up in an entirely different world, just as I was when I was younger. Even at a young age, he is expected to show respect.

"Sorry Lucille," Alesso voices, lowering his head slightly.

Lucille frowns at first, not understanding what just happened, but she reaches forward, squeezing Alesso's hand as she shakes her head.

"No, honey. There's nothing to be sorry for," she coos before cutting me a harsh stare. "Now, are you both finished?"

"Yes," Teddy and Alesso both smile wildly at her as I stand to clear the plates.

"You'll be OK with Alesso, baby boy?" Lucille asks Teddy as she walks around the breakfast bar to kiss his hair.

"Yes Mommy," he says, shrugging her off playful and rolling his eyes.

After setting the boys up in the games room playing a racing game on the console Lucille pins me with her eyes as soon as we leave the room.

"Whatever happened back there, don't do it again."

I pull up short, grabbing Lucille by the arm and pushing her against the wall, pinning her there with my hips, growling low into her ear. "Are you telling me what to do, Love?"

Lucille resists me, trying to push me off.

234

"I don't agree with…"

"He must be respectful, Lucille," I cut her off.

"He's just a child,"

"So was I." I grunt.

Lucille gasps like I've just knocked the air from her lungs and it's all I have in me to move back from her body leaving her gaping at me.

"Linc," she whispers softly, holding her hand out to reach for me but I turn away.

"We have business. Come on," I order, pointing my chin in the direction of Silas's bedroom as I continue walking, expecting her to follow.

"He looks worse than he is OK? The doc has cleared him, he just needs to recover." I turn my head to warn Lucille with my hand on the handle of the door. Lucille frowns, her worried eyes flicking between my own.

"What? Who is it Linc? What happened?" Her voice barely registers as it cracks with worry.

I open the door slowly, ushering her inside, waiting for the realization of whose room we're in to register. The last time she was in here she destroyed the place after Silas locked her in. It holds much less furniture now due to it all having to be replaced but as soon as she sees Silas on the bed, Lucille runs to the bed immediately, mithering over his body and I can tell by the smug expression on his face that he's fucking loving it.

"Silas. What. What happened?" She whispers, feathering her fingers over his wrapped torso.

Silas catches her hands in his, making them look so tiny and fragile against his bear like paws. "La mia luce," he hushes her, pressing her fingers to his lips to kiss them. "I am fine, just a little nick."

235

Lucille's eyes grow wide as she pulls her head back "Did this happen when you rescued Teddy? Did Ronan do this to you?" She asks standing up from the bed and pacing the few small steps between the bed and the chair I sat on last night, that I'm not perched on again.

"Sit down, Love." I insist as I see the guilt already eating its way through her. The next part of this is going to be harder than I thought. Lucille ignores my suggestion and continues her back and forth while Silas furrows his brows, biting down his pain as he sits on the edge of the bed. I narrow my eyes at him with warning not to overdo it, but he stands anyway against my advice. Idiot. As soon as he stands he roars out, cradling his arm against his chest, and both Lucille and I lunge forward to catch him.

"You fucking idiot," I curse as I take the weight of his body, lowering him back onto the bed.

"I will stop walking if you get back into bed," Lucille offers gently, giving him a half lipped smile but he shakes his head in refusal.

"No. That's enough now. Lucille, you need to sit down. There's something we need to say," Silas barks, sounding more like the boss than he has in days. Lucille freezes momentarily before silently backing up until her legs hit the bed and she sits down with her hands in her lap, picking her thumbnails to quell her anxiety. I pull up the chair and take my place catching Silas's gaze and nodding for him to take the lead on this one.

Silas pulls her hands into his own. "La mia luce… it's Cole," he begins as she cracks her head to look at him at the mention of Cole's name.

"Teddy," she mouths, her voice just barely above a whisper.

Silas nods his head, answering her unasked question. "He helped us to get Teddy out." There was a

236

long pause and as I looked into Silas' face, I knew that he was still struggling with the fact that Ronan now had Cole and would undoubtedly be releasing a world of pain on to him for double crossing him like he had. In our world, you could die for less. But I don't for a second doubt that Ronan will drag out his punishment for as long as he can to teach Cole a lesson for what he's done.

"It was too late for us to help Cole and get Teddy out safely at the same time." I explain, receiving a grateful nod from Silas. "We almost didn't all make it out either. We had to leave him behind." I add through gritted teeth.

Lucille's face has paled a ghastly white. "We have to get him back," she chokes looking into my eyes, pleading with me in that language we seem to have established between each other.

"We will, Love. We will." I sigh, wishing for it to be as true as I'd like. Even if we do get him out, we have no idea what state he'll be in.

Before any of us can manage another word, loud banging comes from the front of the house.

"What the fuck?" Silas grunts, hauling himself up once again.

"What's going on?" Lucille asks, jumping to her feet "I need to get to Teddy." She gasps, running from the room

"Lucille, wait!" I shout sprinting after her as the bangs continue and a muffled shout can be heard in the distance.

We find the boys entranced in their game, obviously undisturbed by the noise.

"Stay here and don't let them out of your sight." I order, unholstering my gun as I stalk from the room.

Silas meets me in the hallway with his own gun drawn and ready as we stalk the corridor towards the front of the house. I can't ignore the way Silas leans his body against the wall for support, but right now I know better than to berate him. As we round the corner to the front entryway, Max appears on the other side of the room, gun pointing toward the front door.

"What the fuck?" He whisper-shouts to us across the space but we both remain silent.

More banging continues until a loud and clear voice shouts through the door "FBI OPEN UP!"

"FBI?" I repeat out loud, more to myself than anybody else. Why the fuck are the FBI here? And who are they looking for?

Silas stalks forwards towards the door before calling over his shoulder to both Max and I, "Guns away."

Max hesitates for a moment but we both submit and holster out guns as Silas slowly unlocks the front door.

"Gentlemen," Silas greets the group of heavily armed men swarming the driveway but they take no time in rushing through the door.

"Max Costello. You're under arrest for the murder of Vincent Holland. You have the right to remain silent. Anything you say can and will be used against you in a court of law." A stocky man with a handlebar mustache and a black trench coat saunters through the door, carefully eyeing up Silas and then myself before his eyes land on something behind me. I glance over my shoulder to see Lucille in the doorway, her face ashen and worried at the scene before her. She just couldn't listen to a simple instruction. The agent roams his eyes over the entirety of Lucille's body grunting approvingly as he does, causing her to step back before I put myself between them, narrowing my eyes in his direction. "Lets go" he shouts, cocking his eyebrow to me and turning to size up Silas.

Max stays silent through the whole ordeal, as he's right to but I can't pretend that I didn't catch the subtle nod aimed at where Lucille is standing behind me and the unspoken words that pass between us as he hands his trust over to us that we will protect his family, no matter what happens. I dip my chin as he gets pulled away and notice as Silas does the same before looking over to Lucille. They have nothing on him, they're just clutching at straws trying to pin this on whoever they can. How the fuck did they know he was here though? I guess we'll just have to find out. It's just another question to ask to be able to put the pieces of this puzzle back together again. If we all manage to survive this, it will be a fucking miracle.

Chapter 21

Cole

The repeating sound of water dripping through the room wakes me from the darkness. I feel a sharp pulsing in my head as I open my eyes to the bright light of a lamp hanging in the middle of the room. Rubbing my eyes, I remember how close I was to finding and rescuing Teddy, a devastation that weighs heavy in my heart. I failed yet again. After everything I have done, I still couldn't save him. My only hope is that Silas and Lincoln got to him in time and did what I could not.

I shake the ache from my bones as I'm finally able to stand to take in my surroundings. It's cold and damp down here, in what looks like a cellar. Steel bars keep me contained in a small part of the room, a cell. There's an identical section next to me too, but that one is empty. I suppose they sometimes hold more than one prisoner down here. I grimace at the cell, grateful for the moment to be alone down here. I'm not great with people I know, let alone those I don't

The walls and floor are cemented and dirty and there are no windows down here either, only a single door leading to the rest of the house. I assume I'm being held in one of Ronan's torture houses. Great. Getting out of this one might prove difficult, even for me. I don't hold out much hope that Silas and Lincoln will come for me this time. They may come for Ronan though. Revenge is revenge and that's exactly what will drive them. I know the damage I've done, I can only hope they will let me make it up to them in the next life.

Hours seem to pass by until I hear raised voices above. I can't make out what is being said but they don't sound happy. I wonder if Silas and Lincoln got Teddy out, it's the only thing that gives me hope.

As if they can my inner thoughts, the door to the cellar opens. The first through the door is a tall, muscly, dark skinned, bald man. He has a scar over his cheek and a look on his face that instantly lets me know that he's here to deliver some punishment. Next through the door is the person who warned me what would happen if I got caught, Marcus. He narrows his eyes on me as he makes his way closer to my cell. I wonder if he'll keep to his word. It doesn't matter if he does or not, I wouldn't trust him either way. The final person to enter this cesspit is none other than the coward himself, Ronan Costello. He smirks at me as he leisurely takes each step further in the room. He nods silently toward the bald guy and smirks.

"Finn, get our guest a seat would you? We have some talking to do."

Finn, the muscle, heads back out of the room quickly returning with a chair with straps attached to it. A dark chuckle escapes me causing Marcus to narrow his eyes.

"Oh, would you look at that? We shop at the same store! Serial Killers R Us. I have that exact same model. Who would've guessed?" Marcus is glaring at me, threatening me to keep my mouth shut.

"Marcus, Finn, show our traitor to his seat." Ronan orders.

Great, this is where they manhandle me into the seat. I know my chances of surviving this are better if I comply. My cell door swings open as they unlock it and I let Marcus and Finn strap me into the chair easily.

"No struggle, Cole?" Ronan scoffs at me. I ignore him. Once I am strapped in, I try not to meet Ronan's eyes, but I can see they're full of glee and vengefulness. "So Cole, you thought you could infiltrate my gang, and take what is mine?" He bellows in my face, I feel the spit hit my cheek, how fucking disgusting. If they don't end up killing me, I'll definitely need to get my shots.

"Not so close Ronan, please. I prefer not to share bodily fluids with you. Have you ever heard the phrase, 'say it, don't spray it?'" I say with no hint of a smirk.

I turn my head toward Marcus. "Be a lamb Marc and wipe his spit off my face." Marcus doesn't move, waiting on Ronans orders. He won't tell him to do anything. Instead Ronan nods to Finn, who punches me in the ribs, expelling the air from my lungs. Stupid fuck! That's going to leave a bruise!

"Fucking scum!" Finn mumbles as he moves away.

"So Cole, what should I do with you?" Ronan taunts.

"Let's see, you could take your gun and shoot yourself, putting all of us out of this misery." I snap back.

Ronan lunges at me, grabbing my worn out shirt just under my chin. Inches away from my face, he spits again. "Don't joke around with me, you fucking cunt. You're lucky I haven't cut your treacherous tongue from your mouth for your insolence… Not yet anyway."

I begin to laugh out loud, throwing my head back which only infuriates him more. My laughter is quickly snubbed by a piercing pain shooting through my leg. I grit my teeth as I swallow down the pain, glancing down to see the handle of a knife sticking out of my thigh. I flex my muscle, the sting is a welcome distraction to his foul breath

I have to say. But the angle of the blade is sure to cause some nerve damage. My trousers immediately begin to absorb the blood seeping from the wound. Ronan leaves the knife in my leg for a few minutes before grabbing the handle and ripping it out with a salacious grin plastered on his face. I gasp too loudly at the pain it causes and he laughs a deep throaty cackle before walking away. "I had so many ideas of what I'd like to do with you, but there is one that really stuck with me. Would you like to know what it is?" he asks me. He doesn't wait for my reply. "I think your brother deserves a little present after all of his patience with you. What do you reckon, Marcus? Shall we send them something to remember Cole by?" he asks smugly.

Marcus scoffs, "What do you have in mind, Boss?"

"I was thinking of taking a limb or two and having them delivered to the house. That whore stepdaughter of mine will definitely choose the other two over you when you are all fucked up and deformed." he laughs.

I continue to stay silent, he doesn't know my little mouse very well if that's what he thinks of her, but I fear that I have already cemented that door shut myself. I don't give him the satisfaction of knowing that though.

He nods to Marcus who pulls some duct tape from his pocket and tapes it firmly over my mouth, giving me a look I can't quite decipher as he does.

"Nothing to say, Cole?" Ronan sneers. "I wonder what your brother will say, let's see shall we?" Reaching for his phone, he dials a number before he places it down on speaker phone. It doesn't ring for long until I hear him.

"Ronan," the deep voice that belongs to Silas answers, echoing around the room.

"Ahh Mr Salvatore, it's so kind of you to answer my

call." Ronan mocks.

"What do you want, Stronzo!? Are you ready to face me, one on one?" Silas barks. I groan against the tape, trying to tell him to put the goddamn phone down. But he can't hear my pleas. Finn kicks me in the shin to try to silence me.

"No, no I don't need to do any such thing. I have someone here who I think you'd be very interested in keeping alive. But alas you have to do one little thing and maybe I'll send him back to you in one piece." He taunts.

"What exactly do you want in exchange?" he asks. I grunt more to get his attention before Finn slams his fist into my face. I feel the force of the impact crack my nose, and the warm stream of blood that oozes from my nostrils makes my head spin. For a moment I think I might throw up.

"What was that? Cole? If that's you I'll come for you. Just hang in there." he yells. I can tell he's losing his cool. He hates being unable to control the situation.

"Let's put this on video call shall we? So you can see just how well your dear brother is doing, Silas." Ronan smirks, nodding to Finn to hold the phone up to my face. My nose is pouring with blood and the knife wound in my leg isn't looking too great but I refuse to look at the phone.

"Come on now Cole, your brother wants to see you. Maybe hear you, too." Ronan demands as he rips the tape from my mouth, it stings like a motherfucker and I hiss as it rips at my skin. He grabs my face forcing me to look at the phone, I can see Silas, his eyes full of worry as he takes in my wounded state. "I've looked worse, Fratello." I smirk, winking at him. He doesn't look amused, I can't say I blame him.

"Your brother doesn't look so hot." Ronan explains.

Silas interrupts him in a stern tone and I can see the way his jaw tightens as he talks into the video. "I'll ask one more time, what do you want?"

"Simple really. I want your empire. Give me that and he's all yours. I'll let you think it over. 24 hours and we will be in touch." He says before hanging up. I glare at him, I can't wait to kill this fucker.

"Ahh Cole, see how he cares? We're going to make both of you suffer in the end. But first, let's send him a little message shall we? Make sure he understands exactly who is in charge." Ronan snarls at me.

The next instant, Finn grabs my hand securing it for Ronan. He brings the blade to my little finger, forcing the sharp edge of the blade into my flesh. Pushing it hard until I feel the blade cut through bone and cartilage. My little finger is cut clean off from my hand and the scream that erupts from my throat is animalistic. "You motherfucker!" I roar. My previously calm composure is gone as I fight the restraints of the chair, fighting to kill everyone in the room.

Ronan laughs and he picks my finger from the floor, ignoring the blood that's pissing from my hand. He nods to Marcus. "Clean him up and then we need to send this to his little mouse."

I shout at him, throwing insults and threats in his direction but it falls on deaf ears, as Ronan and Finn leave the room leaving me alone with Marcus.

"Cole, I did warn you that if you got caught, I wouldn't be able to help you" Marcus whispers into my ear before I feel the sting of a needle piercing my skin. It doesn't take long for my eyes to close and I fall head first into the abyss, not wanting to know what I will wake up to next.

Chapter 22

Max

I've been sitting in an interrogation room for over an hour now. It's like every other one I've been in in the past. Fixed metal table in the middle with a chair either side. The clock forever ticking on the wall gets louder and louder the longer I'm left in here. The fluorescent strip light is doing nothing to help my pounding head either. It's like a torture chamber, without any physical torture. The one way mirror on the wall reminds me of how bad I look. I know they're watching me, assessing me, waiting for me to crack. Normally they cuff me to the ring on the table but for some reason they cuffed me to my chair. My arms went dead a while ago now. My ribs are twinging from the lack of movement but I refuse to show pain. They can fuck off if they think they're getting anything from me.

I glance up at the clock, watching as the hands tick by and wonder just how long they plan to keep here. They can't possibly pin that cunts murder on me, and no matter how much I wish it was me who choked his last breath from his body for everything he put Lucille through. I have to settle with the fact that it was actually Silas who sent that fucker back to the pit he crawled from. But knowing that sick pervert felt every single hit makes being here worth it.

I'm lost in my reverie, coming up with ways I could've made Vinny suffer before ultimately taking his life when the door slams closed behind me. I only realize someone else is in the room when he clears his throat, bringing me back to reality. The violence and blood clears and I see a man sitting opposite me dressed in black fitted jeans and a casual black shirt. A man I recognize, but I know it can't be him. I'm on my feet and lunging forward with my arms behind my back and the chair in tow. "You fucking cunt! Now I'll give them a reason to fucking arrest me. I'll kill you with my hands behind my back!" I roar, ramming into his body before he's able to sidestep me, pulling my elbow up with enough force to connect with his jaw. But the chair tethering my arms together leaves me at a major disadvantage and he pushes me back with such strength that the chair legs become tangled with my own and I fall backwards, slamming into the floor, knocking the wind right out of my lungs.

"Mr Costello," he says in too calm of a manner before spitting the blood from his mouth at my feet as I choke on nothing but air, trying to regain myself. "I am not who you think I am."

I manage to steady myself on my feet and get my breathing under control before taking a long hard look at the man standing before me. "I KNOW EXACTLY WHO YOU ARE, VINNY!" I snarl, ready to finish the job Silas obviously wasn't able to complete. "You abused my sister. Tried to kill her too and you have the fucking balls to show your face to me, here?"

Vinny huffs out a small chuckle and shakes his head, mirroring my footsteps as I circle the room, like two predators stalking one another before lashing out with their claws. "Like I said, Mr Costello. I am not who you think I am. My name is Marcus... I'm Vinny's twin."

I falter slightly, "Impossible."

"How so?" The Vinny lookalike questions with a smirk, cocking his head to the side as he watches me fight with the possibility of truth behind his statement.

"He never had a brother, Lucille would have said something. I would have known." I blurt out, racking my brains for any sort of memory of Lucille or Vinny mentioning that Vinny was a twin.

At this, he laughs, he actually fucking laughs at me and I have to fight the urge not to ram him through the two way mirror. "Don't be stupid, Mr Costello. You know as well as I do, that if somebody does not *want* to be found. Then you will not find them." He walks over to his chair and sits down, motioning for me to do the same but I remain silent and alert where I'm standing as he continues. "Vincent and I, we never got on, not since we were teenagers. His outlook on life was predominantly full of drugs, alcohol and women. Something that was very different to the life I led myself. I ended up moving away, cutting ties with him completely and leaving him for our parents to deal with. I was sick of bailing him out and I couldn't stand to watch the things he did to the girls he managed to sink his claws into night after night. Always promising them a night of ecstasy but come morning, there was always someone's blood on the sheets."

His words make my stomach churn at the thought of that blood being Lucille's. I will never forget the bruises that covered her when she ran from him or the imprint of his hand across her neck. "You could have fucking stopped him." I snap.

Marcus simply raises one eyebrow at me and tuts loudly. "Now, now, Mr Costello. Let's not get into the blame game here. You left your sister all alone with him. Did you not?"

That's it, I'm going to kill him. I surge forward again, but the chair once again aids to his advantage as he's able to dodge my body.

"That's exactly what I thought, Mr Costello. You are as much to blame as I am for what happened. But I will let you in on a little secret." Marcus taunts, his lips pulling into a devilishly evil grin. "I'm glad he's dead. Because to me, he was merely one more piece of shit that I had left to wipe off this earth."

"You're fucking cracked," I scoff. "What the fuck do you want from me?"

Marcus returns to his chair, holding his hands up in mock defeat. "I'm so glad you asked. You see, I'm here to offer you a deal. One I assure you, you won't want to pass up."

"Why should I trust you?" I laugh maniacally at his stupidity.

Marcus has a sense of calm about him that unnerves me while he casually drums his fingers against the table before once again smiling that animal-like grin at me, baring his teeth and narrowing his eyes. "Because I have the ability to put you behind bars for the rest of your life for a crime you didn't even commit. Is that what you want? To never be able to see your sister and your nephew again? To leave them both in the hands of even more monsters? She was no match for one monster. Do you think she can handle three?"

I feel the air of the room become stiflingly hard to swallow as I drag my chair and sit across from his unyielding gaze. Marcus's eyes darken. "Well done Mr Costello. That wasn't so hard, was it?" he chuckles again, which I'm beginning to lose my patience with.

"Just get on with it. You may not be Vinny but you look exactly like him and I can't fucking stand the sight of you." I spit, reveling in the way his jaw tightens at my insult.

"Very well. I need you to help me take down Ronan Costello," he says, straight to the point, taking me completely off guard. I don't know what I expected from this situation, or what he could possibly need my help with, but that sure as shit was not it.

"You want me to help take down my father?" I ask, scoffing in the process.

Marcus simply nods his head, pursing his lips as he carefully gauges my reaction. "Your father has been on the FBI's radar for years and it hasn't been an easy task to be granted access to his inner circle. I lost four good men at the beginning of this assignment who were all unable to gain his trust and be accepted into the underbelly of the criminal world. So it only seemed fair to take the task on myself when it was time to regroup. It has not been easy to get to the position I am at today with your father, but now I need your help to make my final move." Marcus leans forward, planting his elbows on the table and linking his fingers together as he takes a deep breath.

"What do you need me to do?" I ask, genuinely curious as to what he thinks I can possibly do to help him. "If you're so in with my father, you should know that I am as good as dead to him. He has already given the order to kill me and kidnapped my nephew in return to take over the business when the time comes."

Marcus nods. "Who do you think got you out of that cellar, Mr Costello?" He asks with a one sided smirk.

My eyes grow wide in surprise as the recognition in his voice filters through. "That was you?" I gasp.

"I need information, Mr Costello. All of it. All of the drug transactions, the gun shipments, the names and locations of all of his properties and the name of his associates. I know this is information you have considering you both play big roles in the same organization." Marcus roles off like we're in some sort of business meeting. Not understanding that what he's really asking of me, is that I rat on not only my father, but my men too.

I stay silent for a moment, thinking how I could possibly get out of this situation. Do I agree to do his dirty work and then disappear as soon as I get out of here? Would Lucille ever forgive me? Word will surely get out, and I'll be better off dead than to let anybody from the outfit get their hands on me. "I can see your thoughts, Mr Costello. Your worry for your skin once word gets out that you've ratted out not only one of the largest mafia bosses in the game but also your own father. But listen to me when I say that you will in no way be associated with any of this. You have my word. I have bigger fish to fry. I will clear your name and ensure that you and your family are left alone."

"Your word means nothing to me." I snap.

Marcus assesses me for a long time as I battle back and forth on what to do and how best to ensure that whatever happens doesn't affect Lucille or Teddy. How the fuck our lives got to this point I'll never know, but here we are. Playing mind games and harboring secrets that will get you killed.

"Cole Salvatore seemed to trust me. He was able to look at the bigger picture."

My eyes immediately widen. "You were with Cole?" I ask, trying to fit the pieces of the puzzle together in my mind.

"I have been with him since he decided to alienate himself from his brother. He understood what was at stake and you owe him for the safe return of your nephew." Marcus reveals, narrowing his eyes slightly.

I swallow the dry lump in my throat before swiping my tongue out between my lips as the air from the room threatens to suffocate me.

"If I do this. If I fill in the missing pieces and inform you of everything you need to know to take down my father, you have to give me your word that Lucille and Teddy will be taken care of."

Marcus smiles at me with his eyebrows shooting to his hairline. "You think you're in a position to be making demands?" he laughs, throwing his head back but I ignore it. This will only be done on my terms.

"As far as I can see, yes, you need me. You are the one asking for my help, not the other way around Agent Holland." I snap, wiping the smirk off his face at the formality of his name. And as he sits forward on his chair, intertwining his fingers on the table, I find it incredibly difficult to look past the face of Vinny staring straight back at me with his slick back hair and hardened features.

"They will have no involvement in any of this, you have my word," he acquiesces.

"And both Salvatore brothers along with Lincoln Rossi are to have nothing to do with this either." I demand, straightening my shoulders and lifting my chin. "They are to be redacted from any part of your investigation against Ronan Costello. Whatever crossovers you have, you are to remove them, make sure they never happened." The room falls silent as his features remained unchanged. "Do we have a deal?" I urge my voice with a little more authority this time. Marcus and I both know that I'm the one with the upper hand now.

"You know she really must be something special to have all of these men in such a twist. First my brother, and we all know how that turned out and now look she's got three sadistic men wrapped around her little finger who would kill for her at the snap of her finger. Four including you. The overprotective older brother. Tell me Mr Costello, does it pain you to know your father did this to her?

Kidnapped her son and cut you off without even blinking because you were too much of a pussy to run the business the way he wanted."

I grit my teeth, the strain of my jaw threatening to crack my teeth at any moment as I ignore his taunts. "Do we have a deal?" I ask again, staring him straight in the eye, daring him to give me one more reason to crack my elbow into his face again.

We stare at each other, the ticking of the clock growing louder with every second that passes by before Marcus finally sits back and reaches into the back pocket of his pants, placing a recording device on the table between us. "The only person I am interested in is Ronan Costello. If you give me what I want, nobody else will suffer," he breathes, flicking the switch on the side of the device to record.

With my arms finally free and a hot coffee in front of me, I take my time answering every question and divulging every secret of Ronan's empire. When it really came down to it, I had no regrets in what I was doing. His actions solidified my reasons to talk. His actions prove that he was completely unhinged. Never in my life did I think that he would be capable of the recent events. Lucille was like a daughter to him, and he was a role model to me for the majority of my life. That was until I took over my own portion of the business and he was vocally unhappy with the way I ran it. His methods were old fashioned and brutal, and although I have the blood of many on my hands, his reason to kill became much more of a fetish than a lesson.

After a few hours of back and forth, going over vital details with a fine tooth comb, Marcus agreed to have me returned back to the Salvatore house.

"How did you know where to find me?" I ask as he switches off the recording device and slips it back into his pocket.

"Cole," he simply states as if it should have been obvious. Marcus stands to make his exit. "I will get Josef to take you back." With his hand on the door handle he stops, turning back to look at me with a grim expression on his face. "Mr Costello, I think it's obvious now that who I am must remain between the two of us. It is of great importance that until I am able to make my final move, Ronan suspects nothing and for that to happen the fewer that know, the less chance he has at finding out. I dare say, our lives depend on it." I nod my head in understanding. "Oh and one more thing. Ronan found out about Cole double crossing him to save the boy. I'm sure you can imagine what that means for him. I will do what I can without attracting too much attention to myself, but I've seen first hand what Ronans methods of torture are. Though I feel he may surpass them considering the betrayal he feels with what Cole has done."

I push myself up immediately, my hands fly into my hair with a desperate panic already beginning to settle itself into my bones. "Where is he?" I demand as Marcus watches my brain implode with the news.

"He's at one of Ronan's abandoned properties on the edge of town. But you need to be quick, it's going to be a game of survival for him from here on out." With that he leaves the room and my stomach tightens into such a furious knot that I'm forced to double over in an attempt not to vomit.

Josef, who turns out to be the stocky guy with the mustache who arrested me, walks into the room a few moments later, narrowing his eyes at me, quite obviously unhappy with the fact that he's been lumbered with taxi duty. "This way," he huffs, throwing his head in the direction of the corridor, waiting for me to follow him out.

The entire ride back is spent in silence, though I'm thankful for the time to think. How the fuck am I meant to pass the information about Cole on to Silas without letting on anything about Marcus and his investigation into Ronan? What in the fuck am I meant to do?! I'm exasperated and exhausted by the time Josef orders me to get out of the car at the front of Silas' house and the only thing I know for certain is that Lucille can not know. She's already been through too much.

The front door opens before I have time to reach it and Lucille almost knocks me off my feet as she barrels her way through it and into my chest.

"What the fuck happened?" She gasps, kissing my face and wrapping her arms around my waist.

"Oh you know, the usual good cop, bad cop routine. They have nothing, it's just a power play." I smile, hoping she'll drop it without any further explanation. "Come on, I need a drink." I add, breaking our embrace to see Silas and Linc standing in the doorway, their eyes narrowed at me and standoffish.

"I was almost hoping that would be the last time I'd have to look at your face, Irish." Linc smirks as we all make our way to the kitchen and Lucille tuts loudly at his remark, muttering profanities under her breath.

"Is that because I'm better looking?" I laugh, immediately breaking the tension as we all laugh together. Weirdly enough, being welcomed back here feels almost like home now. I shake off the thought turning to Lucille before a loud knock at the door sends a sense of dread through my body. We look at each other, not knowing what to expect. Silas clears his throat heading for the door with Linc shadowing his footsteps with his gun pulled ready for the possibility of an attack. I stay back with Lucille, her grip on my arm now a deathly tight vice cutting off the blood circulation to my hand. Is this what life is going to be like for her from now on? I was right when I told her to get out of here and I'd gladly tell her again if I knew she'd fucking listen.

Silas and Linc walk back into the room cutting the tension with a knife. "Just a parcel." Silas laughs waving a small cardboard box around as he eyes Lucille's pale complexion and she nervously laughs in response, trying to shake away the nerves I can feel humming through her fingertips.

"I'm going to check on the boys," she whispers, leaving the room before any of us can respond.

"I'll see if she's OK." Linc offers, moving to follow her but before he leaves the room, I know my time to tell them is now or never. They will most likely kill me if they ever find out I knew about Ronan keeping Cole prisoner and didn't tell them.

"Wait," I call loudly enough to catch both of their attention. Linc walks back over to the kitchen island and Silas grabs a knife as he begins to open the package addressed to him. "I need to tell you something," I add, "it's about Cole."

At the same time as the words leave my lips, Silas roars, throwing the package onto the breakfast bar. "I'll fucking murder him!" he rages, flying his fists across the kitchen surfaces, smashing into everything in his path.

"What the fuck?" Linc shouts as we both lunge for the parcel, peeling back the opening to reveal a severed finger on the inside and a handwritten note on the inside of the box.

"Traitors will be punished"

Before I have time to think, Linc slams me against the wall, pinning me by the front of my shirt. "What about Cole?" he seethes, his spit hitting my cheek. Silas stands beside him, obviously fighting a fine line between distraught and outraged.

"Ronan's going to kill him for his betrayal in helping you rescue Teddy." I sigh, finally saying it outloud to not only them, but to myself, making the situation all too real. I was hoping that it would feel better passing on the information, but taking in the grim and helpless expression on both of their faces, it only makes it so much worse.

Chapter 23

Lucille

The evening Max returned back from his interrogation with the FBI went past in a blur with broken glass, raised voices and suspiciously hushed conversations. And since then, the atmosphere around the house has been so tense you could choke on it. Both Silas and Linc have been avoiding me, shutting themselves away in Silas's office from morning until night, only leaving the house to run business errands. I forget sometimes that between the rest of this chaos, they're still running an empire. And although Max has been present, joining in while I play games and watch movies with the boys, his focus is elsewhere. What has them so distracted that I seldom get a hello? They can barely look me in the eye. Could it be Cole? Are they planning on making another rescue mission to get him out and keeping me in the dark about it? If that is the case, I'll be pissed. I thought I made it clear that we needed to be in this together. Not one of them has asked how I'm coping with this. I don't underestimate that it must have been hard for Silas to leave his brother behind but this is what they do isn't it? Live for the cause, die for the cause, or whatever rules they live by. Besides, Cole was the one who turned his back on us. Fuck, what am I even saying? I can't think straight anymore. The mental strain from the last 24 hours has been nothing short of exhausting.

"I need to lie down," I mumble, already on my way out of the room.

Max stands to follow me. "Are you alright?" he asks, reaching out to stop me.

I narrow my eyes at his hand around my wrist which he immediately drops, gauging my reaction with apologetic eyes. "I just need to lie down. Will you keep an eye on them for me? At least until Linc gets back from wherever the hell he's gone to this time?" I ask, motioning to Teddy and Alesso who have emptied the contents of Alesso's art supply box onto the coffee table in the living room.

Max opens his mouth to respond before furrowing his brow. I know there's something they're not telling me, but I'm sick of asking and then being ignored. He simply nods and I walk back to the guest room Teddy and I have been staying in, closing the door behind me and collapsing onto the bed. It doesn't take me long to drift off to sleep, letting the sweet scent of fresh cotton sheets envelop me like a cloud.

"Wake up baby," a smooth voice filters through my dream, sending a warm glow throughout my body. I groan slightly, disorientated from the disruption to sleep but welcoming the invasion as I feel rough hands begin to roam the entirety of my body, applying pressure to my breasts, hips and thighs as they go. A warm breath fans my cheek as I become more aware of what's happening and as I blink my eyes open, the dark of the room confirms that I slept the entire afternoon away. "Wake up, la mia luce," Silas whispers into my ear before trailing his tongue down my neck and across my collar bone where he bites down, causing my eyes to fly open.

"Silas," I gasp, feeling him smile against my skin before he pulls back to look at me.

"Max said you've been out of it all afternoon. I needed to see that you were OK," he whispers, gently cradling my face in one hand while trailing his fingers across my thigh with the other.

I raise my eyebrows, and sit up on the bed. "So now you pay attention to me? Christ If all I had to do was take a nap for you to say more than two words to me, I'd have done it sooner." I scoff, crossing my arms over my chest.

"Don't be a brat, Lucille, it doesn't suit you." Silas rebukes, lowering his tone. I part my lips as my breath catches in my throat at the way his eyes darken and his jaw tenses. "If I were to give you the attention you deserve, you wouldn't even be able to talk more than two words so I suggest you cut that out right now," he snarls, standing at the edge of the bed, all powerful and dominating leaving me with an uncomfortable wetness between my legs. I'd never once thought I'd like being spoken to like this, dirty and degrading but I can't stop the effect it has on my body. And I practically come apart when Silas orders me to my knees.

"Up," he snaps, undoing the belt to his slacks, slipping it in one fluid motion out through the loops.

"Silas," I whisper, hoping I sounded more sultry than it did in my head. I'm still not entirely confident with myself in any sexual situation. Vinny fucked that up for me, but I have learnt that I deserve to be pleasured just as much as they do.

Silas removes his shirt before unfastening his pants but I can't help the sudden intake of air at the sight of his still tightly wrapped chest. The bandages cover the majority of his midsection, wrapping his ribs and stabilizing it by wrapping around his left shoulder. I reach forward, gently stroking my fingers over the bandages. "Silas, you're not healed, we can't." I choke, my libido disappearing faster than a goddamn freight train.

Silas quickly changes that by grabbing my chin, forcing me to look into his molten fire, lust filled eyes before inclining his head just a little and smirking at me so damn deliciously that I have to clench my thighs together. "Don't worry baby, I can still fuck your mouth," he all but purrs and I all but melt, thankful that he still holds me hostage by my chin. "Now open your mouth and let me teach you a lesson," he orders gruffly, pulling down on my chin to do it for me while his other hand releases his solid cock from his briefs and gently strokes the length back and forth. I lick my tongue out over my lips quickly, moistening them. I'm already salivating at the thought of Silas fucking my throat and I eagerly swipe the bead of precum from the tip of his cock with my tongue before leaning forwards and taking his length into my mouth. His arousal is hard to ignore as he moans out in pleasure, thrusting his fingers into my hair to gather it up and away from my face. I glance up, meeting his heated gaze as he slowly pumps his hips, reveling in the feel of my tongue sliding against his cock and swirling around the end each time he pulls back. "Your mouth takes my cock so good, little brat. Are you going to be a good girl and swallow me down?" Silas groans, moving his hips with pure effortless vigor as the tears already pool in my eyes and I struggle to catch my breath.

I steady myself by placing my hands against his thighs and hum my reply with his cock still deep in my throat, never once breaking eye contact as he thrusts into my mouth, concentrating on taking every breath I need through my nose. I've never been fucked in my mouth quite like this before. It's something I never really enjoyed taking part in. But with Silas's girth stretching my mouth so wide, my jaw has begun to ache and I can't ignore the way my pussy clenches with each powerful thrust. I want to make him feel good. If he thought this would be a punishment, he's so very mistaken. I eagerly suck him in, as deep as I can handle without choking, cupping his balls with one hand and wrapping my fingers around the base of his cock with the other, the saliva spilling from my lips aiding my hand as I work it up and down Silas' length in tandem with my mouth.

With his fist pulling painfully tight against my hair I hear him groan as his cock twitches against my tongue.

"Fuck Lucille. Your mouth feels so fucking good on me," he praises loudly. I hum again with my appreciation and hollow my cheeks, sucking him harder. The taste of his salty precum teasing me for the full fill of his cum that I eagerly want to taste. My pussy is throbbing between my legs and I can feel the dampness of my panties start to become unbearable as they chafe on my clit. Maybe this is what he meant by teaching me a lesson? I whimper slightly at the thought as I purposefully move my hand between my legs to relieve the pressure.

"I'll help you with that, Love." Lincs heated whisper brushes against my ear. Fuck, I hadn't even heard him come in the room. How long had he been watching us? The thought makes me clench my thighs together. To have him watch as I swallow Silas's cum. These men truly have broken me and my mind instantly races back to the time Cole watched on from the bedroom chair. My thoughts are soon interrupted by the weight shifting on the bed as Linc kneels behind me and pulls my pants and sodden underwear over my ass in one swift pull. I glance up to Silas who has not relented with his movement as his eyes burn into me like scorching embers as his friend spreads my ass from behind and torturously travels his tongue across my swollen pussy all the way to my asshole before pulling away.

I shift at the unbearable need to cum already, closing my eyes to concentrate before Silas yanks my hair so hard I gasp around his cock making him twitch again.

"Eyes on me, Lucille. I want to see into your eyes the moment that you shatter on Lincoln's tongue."

My pussy clenches at those words alone. I master the art of sucking hard, swirling my tongue and trying to breathe simultaneously as Linc shifts his weight behind me and with his head now buried between my legs as he lies beneath me, I feel his hot, wet tongue caressing my aching pussy, teasing and edging me until the burn becomes too much.

I whine around Silas's cock, pleading with my eyes as he grins maliciously at me. "I think the brat wants to cum, Brother," he smirks and I feel more tears spill over my cheeks before Linc obliges humming a delicious vibration through my body before he sucks my oversensitized clit into his mouth, flicking it vigorously with his tongue. Silas squeezes his fist causing my scalp to sear in pain with a reminder to keep my eyes on his. My muffled scream around his cock is nothing compared to the quake of my thighs. I feel Linc's hands come around my legs as I ride his face. My body shudders violently against his mouth while he continues his skillful attack on my clit and I ride the glorious waves of ecstacy as he devours my juices, fucking my pussy with his tongue, ensuring he releases me of every last drop.

My cries are muffled as my body sags with exhaustion, and although I feel so shattered, my entire body pulses with desire making me feel more alive than I have in days. Silas must have slowed his movements to allow me to breathe through my orgasm because I notice the vicious uptake in his movements now as he fucks me hard, keeping me in place by my hair. My face must be a mess because I can't stop the tears that fall as I choke and splutter around him, but he looks down on me taking his cock so obediently like it's the sexiest thing he's ever seen. His arms ripple and his muscles flex as he lays into me. I've never felt so dirty and so sexy at the same time.

"We're going to fill you up, baby." Linc says from behind me as he traces his finger across my backside. My eyes widen as I feel the sudden pressure at my asshole as he pushes the tip of his cock into the tight ring. My body instantly refuses and I arch my back, whimpering out against Silas's shaft. "You can take it sweetheart," he coos before spitting on me and spreading his saliva against the tight hole. It isn't lost on me that those were the exact same words he spoke the first time he fucked my ass. I try to relax, concentrating on Silas's movements as Linc spreads my cheeks and pushes in again, stretching my asshole around his thick girth causing me to cry out as he forces himself inside, pushing deep into my ass. I all but scream against Silas who curses under his breath at my garbled screams.

"You have no idea how fucking good you look like this Lucille, bent over and helpless between us. Impaled on our cocks." he praises, stroking his thumb over my cheek.

Linc gives me a mere second to relax and adjust to his intrusion before fucking me with feral desperation and need. If I could speak, I'd be begging for them to ruin me even more. Thrusting his hips so violently into my ass that the sharp sound of his hips meeting my backside rings out across the room. "I forgot how fucking tight this ass was," he groans, spanking my ass cheek in one sharp slap as I whimper at the sting. My pussy is already burning with the build up of another orgasm, spasming and desperate to be filled, the thought of having both of their cum inside of me almost tips me over the edge. "You are ours, Lucille." Linc grunts, digging his fingers so deep into the skin on my hips that they're sure to leave bruises for the next few days. Those marks I would gladly carry with me till the end of days. "Show us who you belong to, baby. Come for us with our cocks inside of you and let us fill you up with our cum," he orders, snaking a hand between my legs and pinching my clit, snapping the last string of restraint I had as the room turns black and stars burst across the inside of my eyelids as I experience one of the most intense orgasms I've ever had. I arch my back mumbling my pleads around Silas's cock trying not to bite him as my entire body clenches and my pussy juices coat the inside of my thighs.

All at once Silas explodes against my tongue, a heady, intoxicating mixture of salty musk and cursed words as he fucks his orgasm down my throat, and I swallow it greedily making sure to get every drop.

Linc cries out behind me, his brutal thrusts becoming snappy and quick as his solid cock jerks in my ass before filling me with his cum. "Fuck, Lucille," he groans, pumping himself slowly until he pulls out completely leaving a obscene emptiness from where he was inside me just seconds ago.

Silas slips from between my lips and bends down to kiss me, forcing his tongue into my mouth before I can catch my breath. "Such a good girl. You taste so good with my cum in your mouth," he whispers before pulling up his pants, lifting me up and carrying me to the ensuite. I let him wash me in a post-coital daze before carrying me back to bed where Linc is already lying waiting.

"I don't think I can handle any more guys," I say shyly, not wanting to disappoint them as Silas lays me down in the middle of the bed and settles down next to me, but Lincoln grabs my hand pulling me into his chest where he kisses my head.

"No more tonight, Love. Just sleep," he whispers, tracing his fingers along my back.

"Where are the boys?" I ask, already half asleep listening to the sound of his steady heart beating in his chest.

"They're having a sleepover in Alesso's room. Don't worry. They're safe," he replies, kissing my hair.

"Why have you been avoiding me?" I yawn, but I don't catch an answer before the exhaustion has already pulled me under.

I wake early the next morning entangled in their bodies, feeling blissful and content. But the longer I lay there enjoying the warmth and heaviness of their bodies as they each lay a protective arm or leg over my own, I realize how much I miss Cole. The missing part of our family. I believe Linc when he says he hasn't betrayed us but I can't help feeling so angry at him for leaving when I needed him the most. Out of all of them, I thought he'd be the one to understand considering what he went through as a child. But all he did was shut me out and tear me down. I suddenly feel extremely overwhelmed and stifled with a desperate need to get out of this bed and this house, and I know just the person to do it with.

The plan I had to remove myself with the stealth of a ninja didn't work and I'm pretty sure they had both been awake long before I was anyway, but had simply stayed put in case either of them woke me.

"What are you doing, la mia luce?" Silas quips, raising his eyebrow as I carefully try to climb over his body.

"You two are stifling me. It's hard to breathe with so much body heat in the bed." I sigh, to which Silas simply laughs.

"Well why didn't you just say so?" he asks playfully before tipping his hips and knocking me to the floor.

I squeal as I hit the carpet with my legs still on the bed but Silas rolls back laughing. "Silas, you ass!" I curse loudly, hoisting myself to my feet to see Linc trying to conceal his sniggers behind his hand from the opposite side of the bed. "You bunch of morons," I snap, stomping my foot like a petulant child before grabbing my clothes and locking myself in the ensuite.

"Oh baby don't be like that," I hear Silas call from the opposite side of the door.

"You just look so cute when you're angry," Linc adds, fueling my fire and the overwhelming need to have some fresh air. I can't keep up with their constant mood changes. I thought women were bad but this is something else. I go from avoidance to a fucking spitroast and its confusing and exhausting to figure out what's going on.

"I expect my breakfast and a strong coffee to be ready for me once I'm out of the shower." I call, switching the water on before I hear a response. It's the least they could do for literally pushing me out of the bed. It doesn't escape me that my hunger is back with vengeance.

I leave the en-suite to find a steaming mug of coffee on the dresser and can't help but smile to myself when I bring it to my lips. I towel dry my hair before pulling it into a scrunchie and quickly dress in my go to casual wear, skinnies, an oversized t-shirt with a flannel over the top and pull on my Converse for comfort. I grab my phone from the dresser and dial Kat. Hopefully Silas and Linc won't be too mad that I'm not waiting for their permission to leave to see my friend. She's been pestering me to see Teddy for days and I'm close to suffocating on testosterone here so I dial her number before I have time to chicken out.

Kat picks up on the second ring. "Well it's taken you long enough to call me!" she whisper-shouts down the phone making me laugh.

"What the hell are you whispering for?" I automatically whisper back.

Her voice is clearer now but still more quiet than usual. "I'm at work. Some of us still have to come to work, you know. Everybody here has been asking for you. Nosey bitches trying to get some gossip out of me because you left so suddenly. As far as anybody knows, you're on vacation seeing a sick relative," she replies, instantly making me feel a twinge of guilt that she's been having to lie for me for so long and still continues to do so, no questions asked. "And why are *you* whispering?" she adds.

I laugh again and shake my head. "I'm not, you idiot. Now what time do you get off? I have somebody who wants to see you and I need to get out of this stifling fucking atmosphere." I grin smugly on my end of the phone.

"Don't tell me, too many dicks is too many?" Kat groans, feigning sympathy before breaking into a fit of giggles.

"Christ, you're insufferable," I scoff, rolling my eyes and taking another sip of coffee.

"You wouldn't have me any other way, babe. I'm off at lunch. Shall we take the kids to Oxford Park? Bella has been asking for Teddy nonstop the last couple days. I can pick her up early from Kindy and meet you there?"

I skip excitedly on the spot feeling a rush of happy anticipation bubbling in my belly. "OK babe. See you there."

I practically skip to the kitchen feeling lighter already from a few small sentences with my best friend. I wonder if I could push it for a sleepover at Kat's tonight, too. I'll say it's for the kids to spend more time together, not that I need it more than them. Maybe if I bat my eyelashes fast enough? I giggle to myself at the thought as I round the corner where I find Silas, Linc and Max all sitting around the breakfast bar with their heads together having their hushed conversations while Teddy and Alesso sit at the dining table tucking into a buffet of fruit, pancakes and small breakfast muffins. I slip in quietly, heading straight over to the boys, stealing an untouched muffin from Teddy's plate.

"Heyyyy, that was mine," he whines before looking up at the thief. "Mommmmm," he pushes me playfully as I take a bite, licking my lips and plonking myself down into the chair opposite.

"Mmm, that was delicious," I grin, playfully smacking my lips together making them both burst into a fit of giggles.

"Finish your breakfast Alesso, then get ready for school. I'll be dropping you this morning." Linc calls from the breakfast bar. I snap my head over to him, his hard eyes a stark difference from our moments together last night. I break the gaze and give a reassuring smile to Alesso who shovels in a few more mouthfuls of fruit before hopping from his chair and going to his bedroom to get ready to leave.

I watch Teddy who has since picked up a fresh muffin and taken the first bite, turning and grinning at me with food between his teeth. "You're right, it is delicious," he grins, spitting a little onto the table.

I shake my head, trying not to laugh at his childishness. "Teddy, it's rude to speak with food in your mouth." I lightly scold, trying to stifle my giggle behind my hand. "How do you feel about taking a trip to the park today?" I ask. Seeing the way his eyes immediately light up, I already know the answer is going to be a yes, and the immediate guilt I have for keeping him inside the house since he's been back washes over me like a tidal wave. He hasn't once asked to leave, but mom guilt is an undeniable, inevitable thing that I cannot escape.

"You're leaving the house?" Linc asks, pulling me from my own internal chastising, making me jump.

I stutter my words slightly, momentarily slipping back into that dark space that Vinny held me captive in for so many years. I'm unable to look Linc directly in the eye as I respond. "Uh, umm, yes. I'm taking Teddy to the park for some fresh air."

I hear the scraping of multiple bar stools before a firm hand grips my chin and Silas' voice cuts through my mental barricade. "Lucille, look at me," he instructs and I do as I'm told, snapping my eyes to his. "What's going on?" he asks, narrowing his eyes, trying to examine me from the inside out.

I don't know how to explain it. I don't think he would understand it even if I did. How can I tell him that for so long I was never allowed to leave without granted permission on where, who with and what clothes I wore with a time limit on when I would return. Sometimes I feel myself slip back into those bottomless pits of darkness and it's remarkably difficult to dig myself back out of it.

"What's wrong, Mommy?" Teddy cuts in, causing my attention to stray, and though I can tell there's some hesitation against his fingers, Silas releases his hold on my

270

chin so I can return my attention back to my son but he refuses to move from his position.

I smile softly, gazing into his innocently large round eyes and that's all the reminder I need to know everything will be OK. "I'm fine, baby. Don't worry, finish your breakfast," I sigh, leaning forward to kiss his cheek before standing and signaling for Silas to back off, taking note of Linc and Max eyeing me suspiciously from the breakfast bar as I make my way over with Silas hot on my heels.

"Are you alright?" Max calls tipping his chin. He's seen me zone out a few times so it's not an uncommon occurrence for him, though it has been a while.

"I think so. I just need to get some air. I'm going to meet Kat. I'm desperate for some girl talk and she's bringing Bella for Teddy. I think he needs it too." I admit, turning to face him, making sure I haven't given the surprise away just yet.

"One of us will go with you. It's not—"

"NO!" I snap involuntarily, catching them all off guard before lowering my voice again. "I need some air from all of you, too. You're suffocating me."

Max snorts in an offended manner. "You're not going alone, Lucille," he asserts, standing to his full height. His overbearing posture would have had an effect on me years ago, but now it has very little effect on me coming from him.

"I agree, Lucille. It's too dangerous. You're not going alone without somebody with you." Linc adds.
I scoff, almost offended that they feel like I must have a babysitter with me at all times but I know I won't win this one so I give in to their demands.

"Fine. But I'm not going with either of you three," I snap before turning back to Teddy. "Have you finished your breakfast Ted? Let's go and get dressed."

Teddy and I spend the rest of the morning play-fighting, making arts and craft dinosaurs with feathers and sprinkles and watching back to back episodes of cartoon Spiderman. It's wholesome and I haven't been able to keep the smile from my face all day. I can't wait to see his reaction when he sees Kat and Isabella.

"You ready to get going kiddo?" I ask. It's just turned noon and I know it won't take Kat long to get Bella from Kindergarten with the promise of seeing Teddy.

Teddy beams up at me, looking proud as punch at his sparkly feathered dinosaur creation. "Yeah, let's go!" He shouts, running off to grab his coat and trainers, to which I follow and do the same.

I don't bother letting the others know we're leaving. I've already been given my security detail, who I was politely informed should have been waiting outside the house for me from ten o'clock incase I decided to slip out early.

"Hey Dario, hey Enzo, it seems you have the pleasure of babysitting again today." I joke, trying to keep it as lighthearted as I can between us with Teddy in tow.

"Lucille," they both nod respectfully, but I still notice the faint smile at his lips as Dario dips his head and turns to greet Teddy too. "Hello Teddy, you can call me D," he smiles, transforming his usually hard and scary looking face into a much softer, more approachable appearance.

Teddy looks up, his eyes widening and his mouth falls slack with shock. "Wow, D. You're huge!" he gawps, making Dario chuckle lightly before ushering us into his car.

"Oxford Park, please Dario. But would you mind just parking down the road a little please?" I ask, catching his eyes in the rearview mirror, hoping he'll understand that I'm asking him to make it seem not so suspicious that we're having a private driver. He nods silently, acknowledging my request and I drop a quick text to Kat once we're on our way.

"And what's your name Mr?" Teddy directs at Enzo who turn to face us from the front of the car smiling a goofy grin.

"I'm Enzo, but you can call me Z" he says with a wink.

"D and Z, you can call me T" Teddy beams playfully causing the rest of us to burst out laughing. It's a beautiful moment that fills my heart. I guess these guys aren't too bad afterall. Maybe I should apologize for pointing a gun at them? I'll make sure to do that when we get home.

"Hey, guess what baby boy?" I ask Teddy after the laughter dies down.

"What is it, Mommy?" He smiles back at me,

"Auntie Kat and Isabella are going to be meeting us at the park." I grin wildly at him.

Teddy's response is everything I had hoped for, he audibly gasped as I said the words and his eyes bulged wide with excitement before he squealed animatedly in his seat.

"Oh, I can't wait!" He cries hugging me tightly.

"I know, neither can I. We're going to have lots of fun."

Dario parks at the bottom of the road from the park and insists on checking the area thoroughly first before letting us out of the car, leaving us with Enzo as he scopes the area. Both of them ignore my eye rolls and protests. They both have a gun. What could possibly go wrong? When Dario returns, comfortably satisfied that the surrounding areas are clear of threats, he opens the door to let us out of the car. We make our way down the street with the park in sight and our guards keeping their space between us from behind, always on the lookout for threats. I'm surprised Teddy hasn't asked why they're following us but my thoughts are interrupted as I hear a high pitched squeal in the distance. Without needing to look to know who it belongs to, my grin spreads wide and I can't help the laugh that falls from my lips at the sight of Bella screaming, running with her arms stretched out in our direction.

"Teddy!" she screams excitedly as Kat trails along waving her arms around with a huge grin on her face too.

Teddy instantly pulls on my hand for me to hurry up. "Come on Mom, come on," he insists but the screeching of tires right besides us makes me freeze on the spot.

In a blur, I almost don't see it happening until it's already upon us. A white van squeals to a stop right besides us and the side door flies open revealing four men all armed with AK-47's and balaclavas covering their faces. My world stops in that instant. Everything happens so quickly, yet so slowly all at the same time. "TEDDY!" I scream, who still holds tight onto my hand.

"Mommy, what's happening?" Teddy asks with fear in his voice.

I snap my head in Dario and Enzo's direction who already have their guns drawn and are sprinting the few feet between us to intersect the oncoming attack. I crouch, immediately pulling Teddy into my chest but it does little against the arms that wrap around my body, separating me from him, forcing my feet off the ground. "NO, TEDDY!" I scream, kicking out with my legs trying desperately to gain some sort of advantage, but there's two of them on me now, restraining my legs and arms, leaving me with little movement between them in their vice-like hold. Teddy's desperate cry cuts through the static ringing in my ears and straight to my heart.

"Mommy!"

And then I hear the gunshots that ensue, the fast metallic snap of the bullets that release from their chambers, though they're quickly drowned out by my own piercing screams as I watch helplessly as Dario launches himself onto Teddy's body to shield him from onslaught. The lifeless body of Enzo catches my eyes and my throat feels as though I've swallowed glass, raw and cracked, but I can not stop screaming. I fight with everything I've got, kicking out and screaming until a sharp pain pierces my neck and my vision immediately begins to blur.

"TEDDY!" I shout for the last time watching as Kats blurry silhouette runs over to where Dario's body covers Teddy on the ground before my eyelids become too heavy and I can no longer resist the fight of whatever they've just injected me with.

Chapter 24

Cole

The room is spinning as I open my eyes, I am still being held captive in the same prison by Ronan. Whatever Marcus injected me with has my head pounding. It's like I've done ten rounds with Si in the ring. I laugh out loud, remembering the days we would spar. I was quick but his punches always winded me and I welcomed it on my darkest days. When my demons came forward and I had no way to expel them from my mind, he would demand I fight him until I felt nothing but the pain he had inflicted.

I hear a small groan across the room. I have woken with a companion it would seem. Shaking the vice-like feeling that has my head splitting into a million pieces, I move from the floor to assess the room. Over on the metal cot bed is someone I thought I'd never lay eyes on again. I move closer to the bars to see her eyes fluttering beneath the lids in her unconscious state. Moving slowly over to her, I crouch beside the bars that separate us and slide my arm through the gap, stroking her hair away from her face, lingering ever so slightly with my fingers. I've missed her so much. Seeing her even here, I'm ashamed to be slightly pleased she's back within my reach again. Taking in her beauty, I feel the panic begin to creep in as questions flood my mind. How the hell did she get here? And how can I get her out? My fucking brother and Lincoln best have a good reason that she's ended up here when they should be protecting her.

Just as I feel myself getting lost in the anger, her eyelids flash open and her eyes widen as she takes in my face, simply staring at me like I'm some sort of ghost. I fear she's going to scream and attract unwanted attention from Ronan and his men, so before I know what I'm doing I cover her mouth with my hand to stifle whatever noises she tries to make, hating the way her face looks as she tries to move away from me.

"No my little mouse, don't make a sound, we don't want them coming down here. I am the lesser of the two evils in this place. Please don't scream." I whisper, desperate for her to understand. She freezes for a moment before she nods, obliging my request so I slowly remove my hand from her mouth. She sits herself up on the metal cot and stares at me for a beat before lunging herself at me through the bars. Crying into my shoulder, I do my best to reach my arms around her body and stroke her hair to whisper, "Topolino, it's okay. I'll get you out of here, I promise."

"I was so scared Cole, Kat and Isabella managed to hide. I thought they'd take Teddy again," she sobs, causing my heart to pound in my chest. Please don't say they took him. "Dario, he tried to stop them but they shot him, he sacrificed himself to protect Teddy. I don't know if Teddy was hurt. I couldn't see him under Dario's body before I blacked out. And Enzo" she sobs. "I think he's dead".

"Shh little mouse, it's okay. We will get you back to your son." I promise her. She squeezes my torso tightly causing me to wince as pain radiates through my body.

Lucille immediately pulls back to look at me checking for injuries.

"Cole, are you hurt?" She asks before gasping at the blood soaked bandage that's wrapped around my

277

hand, then trailing her eyes down to the stab wound in my thigh.

I know I look terrible, "I'm OK, it's probably going to get worse the longer we are here. But I'll do everything in my power to get you out, you have my word." I promise her.

She looks scared but equally pissed off, "Fuck I've missed you so much, Cole." she sighs, leaving a painful wave of regret in its wake.

Reaching out to her face, I move the hair that has fallen and tuck it behind her ear. "Mio topolino, I'm so sorry. I wanted you and Teddy safe, even if that meant me being the villian in your story."

"I needed you, Cole. You left me and I fucking needed you," she cries.

My heart shatters at her words. "I failed you." I concede, looking away from her.

She grabs my hand as I shift away. "No. Don't you ever block me out Cole, never again. You won't get another chance." she says, narrowing her eyes at me.

I snap my head back to her. Did I hear that correctly? Surely not, not after everything I've done. "Another chance?"

"Yes, another chance, you still need to grovel but losing a finger and what you did to help Teddy get out, I can't ignore that you had the best intentions even if I don't agree with how you went about them."

I can't help but grab her face with both hands, pulling her into the bars to kiss her with all of the emotions I've kept inside over the last few days. I push my tongue between her lips that part easily for me, allowing my tongue to dance against hers. Fuck, I've wanted this for so long, but now I want more, I need more. I feel myself harden in my pants As I suck her bottom lip between my teeth. I swear I will never let this woman down ever again in my life. I bring a hand under her chin, kissing her softly before my whole body stiffens.

Clap Clap Clap.

"Well isn't this a cozy reunion? I hate to be the one to break this up. But we need to send that brother of yours more incentive to meet my demands." Ronan cackles as he walks into the room. I immediately stand, moving myself to try and cover his gaze from Lucille who has moved as far back in her cell as possible.

"Pffft, you think you will be able to stop me from getting to her, Cole? You are outnumbered, if I want to take her I will, and I'll make you watch." Ronan taunts. "Luckily for you, that isn't the plan... Yet." He waves his hand to the darkness behind him, the shadowed figure behind him emerges forward. Marcus. But before I am able to do anything, Lucille spots him. I spin to face her, her eyes widening as she starts to hyperventilate. Oh shit. A scream escapes her throat as she backs herself away into the bars behind her. I move closer to her, still just about able to reach her from my cell. I reach out to grab her, willing her to look at me as I hold her face to look at me. She immediately tries to fight me away, pushing my arms from her body, trying desperately to escape this prison, but there is no escape. Not right now at least. I need to calm her down. I Can't fucking believe this. "Breath my little mouse, he isn't who you think he is. Trust me. Stay calm."

Lucille's body visibly shakes under my hands as she gasps. "He's... he's Vinny."

"No little mouse, he's not. He's someone else. Someone more dangerous. Trust me and do as I say." I order. Her broken gaze bores into me, the tears glistening in her eyes as she struggles to contain herself. She's hardly holding it together.

"Lucille, you have to trust me." I demand before pulling her face to mine and kissing her quickly. I step away and face Marcus and Ronan again.

"How sweet of you, Cole. Anyone would think you love her." Ronan spits, snarling in Lucille's direction.

"How I feel about her is none of your business." I snap, hatred thick in my voice. I would love to rip his fucking voicebox from his throat with my bare hands.

"Have it your way. But I think your brother would like to see her safe or maybe hear her screams as I torture her dark lover some more. Will you scream when I break his hands, little girl?" Ronan sneers, addressing Lucille. I hear the audible gasp that escapes her throat but she doesn't respond.

"Marcus, secure the girl." Ronan orders.

"No, leave her here." I snap.

"Come willingly or I'll have her as my plaything. Would you like that, stepdaughter? You seem to like being passed around by these dirty bastards." Ronan threatens.

"You are disgusting, how can you do this? I am your stepdaughter. Max is your son. And my boy, he's innocent in all of this!" she finally says, straightening her spine.

Ronan scoffs. "Dear girl, sometimes you have to tread on those in the way to climb to success. Your brother refused to do that. No one is innocent. Now, enough talk. MARCUS!"

Turning quickly to Lucille, I pull her against me once more, desperate to get these words out before she's put through the hell of watching another round of torture i'm subjected to."Mio topolino, stay strong for me. My heart is yours, my soul is yours, in this world and the next. It always will be, "I love you." I whisper before Marcus rips her from my arms.

Marcus walks her from her cell, her arms held securely behind her back, but she does as I tell her and she remains strong. I can see that her breathing has quickened but she isn't screaming, and my pride swells in my chest.

"I am not a patient man Cole, the clock is ticking and if you don't come willingly, I will take my other prisoner for a test drive." He goads me, motioning to Lucille to which she stiffens.

I swallow down my emotions and make my way from my now unlocked cell to the center of the room when the chair still stands..

"Take a seat, Cole." Ronan gestures to the chair. As I settle, he secures me quickly and nods to Marcus. My head snaps to Lucille as she is brought closer. She struggles against Marcus but keeps eye contact with me the entire time.

"So I thought we would show dear Silas what we caught in our little trap today," Ronan smiles darkly at us both. Finn has now arrived in the room with a hammer and some nails, followed by another taller guy I know is named Cillian. They both grin at me as they walk to the chair.

"Silas, what a pleasure it is to talk to you again." Ronan says gleefully. I must have missed him reaching for his phone. I can hear Silas grunting a response.

"Now, now, don't be rude. I think I should share my guests with you." Ronan taunts.

The phone automatically turns to video, on the screen before me I see my brother's grief stricken face as his eyes land on me. I look away focusing on Lucille, she needs me to be strong. Locking eyes with her we both know this isn't going to end well but I'm glad it's me in this chair and not her. And I intend to do everything I can to keep her out of it.

"Have you missed your brother?" Ronan asks Silas. "Or have you noticed your little whore is missing?" He moves the camera to Lucille, I'm not sure that they can see Marcus as he stands behind her but he has his hand fixed around her mouth stopping her cries for help as she struggles with panic flaring in her eyes as Silas roars through the phone.

"Mio topolino, eyes on me." I order. She immediately does as I say. "Good girl, stay with me." I demand.

Ronan cackles in the background but I don't pay him any attention as he taunts Silas. "How does it feel that your brother has the girl and I have them both. I'm tempted to see what all the fuss is about with her. I'm sure torturing your brother will get enough of your attention. And if it doesn't, then maybe I'll have some fun with her later," he goads.

"Leave them alone. Meet me and we will settle this between us like men." Silas growls.

"Not before we have some fun," Ronan announces and nods to Finn. He and Cillian move closer to me, and I'm unable to move thanks to the restraints. Finn brings a nail to my hand, placing it over the top of my hand before wasting no time at all and bringing the hammer down and piercing my skin with the nail as a deep growl escapes my throat. Finn slams the hammer down, again and again with each nail he places on my hand as Cillian restrains my shoulders to stop me from writhing. I stay as still as I can for the majority of the time but the pain becomes unbearable about half way through as each nail pierces me with blinding pain more overwhelming than the last. I keep my eyes locked on Lucille, looking into the deep green abyss of her eyes. I try to ignore the blood that trickles

282

from my hand, dripping patterns of intricate blood work across the floor. Lucille lets out a loud scream each time a nail penetrates my hand, but she does as I ask and keeps her eyes on mine the whole time. I hope I'll get to reward her for that one day. I know I've lost a lot of blood now as my head feels light and woozy and the voices in the room are becoming distant. I try to keep my eyes open, trying so hard to focus on Lucille as I slip into the depths of darkness. Screams echo around me until there's nothing but the black void of unconsciousness enveloping my body.

Chapter 25

Silas

After Lucille's refusal to be accompanied by one of us during her day out I sulked off to my office, not entirely happy with the thought that anybody could do a better job than either Lincoln, myself or even her own brother at keeping her safe. But I wanted to give her trust, and space. She needed to know she had freedom with her choices. Something her fuck of an ex withheld from her.

I have been sitting at my desk, staring at the computer for a while now, trying to figure out how to move forward with everything. How we need to outsmart Ronan and fight the urge to lock Lucille in my bedroom again. And while I wished for her to not leave the house, Lincoln politely reminded me once again that I cannot keep her captive. I scoff a breath to myself thinking of how I'm holding myself back from doing just that. What I would give to have her tied up to use for my pleasure, at my beck and call. A knock at the door halts my thoughts from becoming any more depraved.

"Come in," I shout.

Dario and Enzo enter the room, coming to stand in front of the desk, I gesture for them to take a seat opposite me. While I had time to sit and think of new ways to punish Lucille's petulance, I knew I needed to get somebody I trusted wholly to watch her and Teddy, and who better than the men who already understood her new found sass. She did threaten them with a gun after all. And Enzo was found to be faithful, promising his life for the cause.

"Boss, what can we do for you?" Enzo asks. I watch him, narrowing my eyes until he fidgets slightly under my watch, deciding only then to put him out of his misery.

"I need you to accompany Ms Holland with Teddy to the park, she is visiting a friend and her daughter. I want it to go smoothly, with no hiccups. I want no harm to come to any of them. You are to protect her and the boy with your life." I instruct, glancing between both of them who simply nod their understanding. "I don't trust her not to try and sneak out before their arranged meeting time so I want you manning the door from here on out." I advise. They both stand once I deliver my instructions. "I know you won't let me down."

"Never Boss. After losing my own son to those Irish bastards, I won't let that be anyone else's fate." Dario says solemnly. I notice the way his eyes darken, I know he will never get over it, and how could he? I know I wouldn't. It would be my undoing.

Dario had a ten year old son, Lorenzo. The Irish burnt down one of the apartment blocks we owned in a bid to start a war. Dario's wife and son were not the only casualties that night. But it's the one that hit hardest among us all. We all watch out for him. I may be his boss but I ensure he is never alone at family times. I protect my family, my syndicate. I nod in understanding.

"We'll keep them safe, Boss" Enzo confirms before they both leave, closing the door behind them.

I know that I made the right choice.

With Lucille and Teddy now in capable hands, I am able to concentrate on work. Time ticks on as I dive into finances and new and upcoming events to hold. We still have various businesses to run and I can't neglect them. Since the fire at the restaurant Enzo has already managed to find a new location to rebuild. Enabling us to already have the papers in place to purchase and get started. He's falling into his new role well over the last few days and I am proud of him. Though I won't admit that outloud. My brother would be proud of him too. Another reason I've entrusted him to watch over Lucille and Teddy today.

I glance up from a spreadsheet when I hear shouting coming from outside. Before I'm able to investigate, the door bursts open as Katrina rushes into the room cradling Teddy to her chest with her daughter in her shadow. I'm on my feet immediately, the hairs on the back of my neck prickling at my skin as a horrible sense of dread pools in my stomach. I rush over to Teddy and inspect him thoroughly, he's covered in blood but none of it appears to be his. There are no obvious wounds covering his shaking body and no tears falling from his eyes. He looks empty as I stare into his eyes and pull him to my chest. He's in shock. I look past Kat to see Max whose face has taken on that of a demon. His eyes are full of a blackness I can relate to so much of myself but I see no sight of Lucille. My heart begins to race as I try to remain calm.

"Where is she!?" I demand, glaring at both Katrina and Max. "Where the fuck are Enzo and Dario?" I growl. And for a second, nobody utters a word. The only sounds filling the room are those from Katrina's daughter who whimpers behind her mothers legs.

"They were ambushed before they reached us at the park. There was nothing I could do. I hid myself and Bella from them but they were only interested in Luci and if Dario hadn't hauled himself in front of Teddy they'd have killed him. Dario… Dario, he's…" Katrina chokes, letting out a strangled sob as she reaches out to both Isabella

286

and Teddy bringing them closer to her body.

"WHERE IS HE?" I snap, waiting for them to explain. They better fucking explain quickly, my rage is barely being contained but I have to keep a lid on it for Teddy and Isabella's sake. They don't need to be scared of me. Max moves forward protectively.

Katrina takes a gulp before saying a single word "Dead." I take a step back stumbling into the chair. Dario, dead. Those bastards took his family and now him.

"Riposa in pace," I murmur, clenching my fists. "What about Enzo?" I ask, unsure I want to hear the answer. I raise my eyes to Max this time. "And Lucille?"

Max looks at Katrina, almost pleading, like he thinks I'll hurt her if left alone with her. "Max, you have to let me explain, you weren't there. Take the kids to the kitchen. Get Teddy checked over and into some clean clothes, He's in shock!"

He attempts to open his mouth to argue but snaps it shut.

"Max, Katrina will be fine. We'll join you after. You have my permission to come back if we are too long," I tell him.

He scoffs at me and directs Teddy and Isabella to the kitchen, although I hear him mumble, "Permission, I don't need fucking permission." I shake my head letting that one go as I need to find out exactly what happened.

As soon as they are out of sight, I gesture to the chair opposite for Katrina to take a seat. She moves from the doorway, closing it behind her and taking a seat. I watch her inquisitively, wondering what lies in her past. She knows more of this world than she has led my Lucille to believe. My background check came up with some interesting information about her. One day I'll let Lincoln dive in and dig around a bit more. But that is for another time. Now she needs to answer my questions.

"So what happened?" I start, my stare hard. I'm trying to keep my cool as promised though my insides are a jumble of fucking nerves.

"I don't know, they came from nowhere. One minute we were waving at each other, barely ten yards apart, then a white van pulled up and out jumped four men. They all wore balaclavas so I couldn't get a look at their faces. But they were heavily armed and moving with planned precision. I grabbed Bella, dove for cover and shielded her away from what was happening. She was shaking beneath me, my daughter. You have to understand, I would have done something if I could but I had to keep Bella safe. Lucille tried to shield Teddy but they ripped her away and began shooting before Dario and Enzo could even intervene. Enzo had already gone down, and Dario... He threw himself onto Teddy, shielding his body from the bullets. They didn't stand a chance. I don't think they saw me, but If they did, I wouldn't be here right now. I ran to Teddy as soon as they cleared the street and brought him straight to you." Katrina explains. I watch her as she closes her eyes, a single tear slips from her lashes. She definitely knows more about us than she has ever let on.

"Katrina, I want you to be honest with me. I know exactly who Angelo Moretti is to you and your daughter. I know exactly what he can do. You have little contact with him I understand. But I need you to contact him, I want him to do what he does best and find out where they are keeping my brother and Lucille. We don't have time to wait. Do this and I will never speak of your connection to this world to anyone unless asked. I will not tell anyone your secret, principessa mafiosa." I threaten.

She glares at me, straightening her spine. "No one

can know about me and Isabella. If I contact him, I will not let him come anywhere near my daughter. Do you understand? Do we have an agreement?"

"You have my word Katrina. Your secret will always be safe with me." I nod. And hand her the burner phone I keep in the drawer of my desk.

"Now? You want me to contact him now?" she balks at me.

I raise my eyebrow at her. "Time is of the essence, Katrina. Call him and tell him to do what he does best. I will pay any price he asks." She looks at the phone and back at me before punching in the number aggressively. She places the phone onto loudspeaker and places it on top of the desk between us, for us both to hear. It rings until I hear a male voice answer in Italian.

"Salve, chi è? *Hello, who is it?*

"Ciao, Papa. Bisogno di un favore. Mio amica è stato rapito da Ronan Costello. Io bisogno che tu scopra dove lei." *Hello, Papa. I need a favor. My friend has been kidnapped by Ronan Costello. I need you to find out where she is.* Katrina speaks back in fluent Italian. He responds, demanding to know what she has gotten herself involved in but she continues. "Non sono più affari tuoi, Papà. Trasferirò i soldi una volta che avrai lei posizione." *It's not your business anymore, Father. I'll transfer the money once you have her location...* Katrina breaths out, glancing at me before adding, "Anch'io, ti dovrò un favore." *I will owe you a favor, too.*

Interesting that she has something Angelo Moretti wants. She ends the call saying, "Addio, Papa." *Goodbye, Father."*

I raise my eyebrows at her before she stands. "Not a word to anyone." She snaps before abruptly leaving the

289

room and slamming the door behind her. She has her fathers temper, that's for sure. I have only met the man once but he is not someone I would want to double cross. Whatever favor he asks is not one she will be able to refuse.

Just as I am about to call Lincoln to let him know about Lucille, I can hear raised voices coming from the kitchen. Fuck. Combing my hand though my hair, I guess he's already returned and found out for himself.

I make my way to them quickly, and as I enter I look around the room and see only Katrina, Max and Lincoln. Linc has Max against the wall by the collar of his shirt, while Katrina yells at them to stop.

"Where are Teddy and Isabella?" I ask. They all snap their heads to look at me.

"Alesso took them to play in his room for a little while, while this stronzo explains what the fuck is going on." Lincoln growls, hoisting Max higher off the floor.

"Put him down, Lincoln." I say calmly. He is glaring at Max while I glance at Katrina as her phone buzzes. Her eyes meet mine and she nods. Neither Linc or Max notice our interaction as my phone buzzes with Katrina's information. But then to my surprise my phone begins to ring. The number that is on the screen is one that causes my stomach to twist.

Answering it I snarl, "Ronan!" This makes Linc and Max drop their aggression towards each other and face me.

Ronan taunts me before he switches the phone to video. There I see my brother, strapped to a god damn chair, he's already a bloody mess. My fears are becoming reality as I see who Cole is staring at. Lucille is being held by a man who is so far back in the shadows, I cannot make out his features. The way he holds her makes me want to snap each finger from his dirty fucking hands before shoving them down his throat, forcing him to choke on them. She's visually uncomfortable, and as she hears my voice, her eyes flicker to the camera. I can feel my heart seizing in my chest but I watch on feeling helpless as Ronan continues his taunts. I demand him to meet us and settle this for good like men but of course he refuses. I know exactly what will happen next as he turns his attention to my brother and he gives his order for them to begin. One of his men obliges immediately as they begin another round of brutalizing torture.

One by one he nails my brother's hands to the chair until blood is pooling at his feet. Even throughout the pain he somehow remains calm, barely protesting the pain and never breaking eye contact with our girl whose screams are broken and raw as she begs for them to stop.

It doesn't take long for the pain and blood loss to render Cole unconscious, leaving Ronan cackling into the video as he turns the camera back round to face him. "So Silas, as you can see, I have the upper hand. Give your territory over to me or it will be my darling stepdaughters turn next. I'll contact you in 48 hours to find your answer. How do you Italian filth say bye? Ciao?" he mocks before ending the call.

Chaos erupts behind me as Lincoln and Max argue the best plan to free them both. Katrina stays quiet, contemplating a plan on her own.

I gather myself together and shout for them to stop but they continue to bicker. "STOP!" I shout again, this time with much more conviction than I feel. Linc and Max quickly shut their mouths, turning to face me as the room

291

instantly falls quiet. "I have their location. We need to get a small team of men, armed and ready. We leave at midnight." I say before heading back to my office.

Before I can leave, Linc calls out to question me, "And how exactly do you have the location already?"

I glance at Katrina, her eyes widen slightly at the fear of being found out. I then look at Max who is scowling at me with the same frown before I reply to Lincoln. "I have a source that would like to remain anonymous, and don't even think about pushing this."

Fuck the office, I need to go to the gym and burn off the aggression and this horrifically overwhelming feeling of helplessness as my brain tortures me with repeats of what I just witnessed. I keep reminding myself that we'll be there soon. We'll get them out. As I'm heading down to the gym, there's a heavy knock on the front door.

"For fucksake, that better not be the FBI again." I mutter as I turn back towards the foyer. As I reach the door, I glance out of the side window and see a familiar set of arms holding a duffel bag. I hadn't realized how much I needed him until this moment.

"Nic! Fuck man, you certainly know how to pick your moment!" I say, opening the door wide and pulling the giant in for a hug.

"Si, good to see you too man, what's happened? Who do I have to kill?" He asks jokingly, not realizing how close the truth he is.

"Honestly Nic, I don't even know where to begin. I was just heading down to the gym to work off some frustration. I know you've just got here but do you fancy joining me and I'll fill you in? Everything work out OK with your sister?" I ask.

"Whatever you need, man. What do I call you now? Si feels too informal. And yes she's all good thank you"

"Call me Si, Silas, whatever you like my friend. I'm glad to hear it," I reply, as we head downstairs.

When we reach the gym, the look on Nic's face is priceless.

"Fuck me Si, you weren't kidding when you said the gym inside was shit compared to what you had at home! This is fucking awesome!" Nic says, admiring the room my brothers and I spend a lot of time in.

"Are you feeling OK, Nic? I think that's more words in one sentence than you said the entire time we bunked together." I say, slapping him on the back.

"Fuck you. So tell me, what's happened? You looked like someone had kicked your puppy when you opened the door." Nic asks, placing his duffel bag on the bench before he starts strapping his hands.

"I don't even know where to begin. What I will tell you now though is the quick version. Lucille was kidnapped by her stepfather, Ronan Costello, this afternoon. The same Ronan Costello that's currently torturing my brother in his cellar. I literally found out not even an hour ago. I'm going to need your help, big guy."

"Christ. I have so many questions, but first lets spar and you can fill me in. It sounds like you need it."

"Bring it on, Shrek," I laugh, bouncing on the balls of my feet, relishing the burn and pain that's coming.

"Shrek? I'm not a fucking ogre! Are you sure you want to get that pretty face messed up before you get your girl back?" he taunts.

"You can try, I doubt you'll succeed though," I laugh at hIm.

"Tell me the plan to get Luci back. I take it you have a plan, otherwise you wouldn't be down here." he says, observant as ever.

293

"I do have a plan but I'm not sure you're going to like it." I say, side-stepping a left hook.

"I'll do whatever you need me for Silas, I'm here to help. What do you need?" he ask, sneaking a jab in.

"I need you to stay here with Max, Kat and the kids." I say, watching how he reacts to the mention of Katrina.

"Kat's here is she? What has she got to do with this? I thought she was just Luci's friend, a co-worker." he asks, intrigued already.

"She's a lot more involved than I can tell you but that's for her to say, not me. Just know that she is important to Luci and I need you to help Max keep them safe. If things go sideways, let her deal with it."

"Max? As in Max Costello? Fuck, there is alot more to this story than you're telling me, isn't there?

"There is, but now is not the time. Myself, Lincoln and a small crew plan to hit the location at midnight. Until then, I need to vent this frustration, so come on big guy, I know you're holding back on me." I say, digging Nic in the ribs. "Besides, between you and Max, Kat has her own set of drooling guard dogs." I laugh.

"I'm not a fucking drooling anything. I'll do as you ask but that brother in law of yours better keep his hands to himself." Nic says grumpily.

"Yeah, yeah brother, you keep telling yourself that. Just play nicely until we get back, OK?" I chuckle, raising my eyebrow in question.

"I can play nice," he smiles, landing a decent blow to my center that takes my breath away.

We spend an hour sparring, we are equally matched and it gives me an idea that once all of this is over, to enroll Nicholas in our fight nights at the warehouse, as a trainer and as a contestant.

294

Finally feeling calmer and focused, I return to my room and ready myself before meeting with Lincoln and Max to tell them the plan of action.

Chapter 26

Max

Why the fuck I got left on babysitting duty is completely beyond me. While my sister lies in a cell under the order of my own father, her step father, enduring God knows what sort of treatment. Just the thought of it has my stomach in knots.

It's impossible to keep the disapproving snarl from my face as Silas, Linc and a small group of their trusted men arm themselves for their midnight rescue mission. They leave with no other instruction other than to keep Katrina, Teddy, Isabella and Alessandro safe. Lincoln's words ring true in my ears. *"It's harder when your family is involved for you to make sound decisions."* I know what he's saying is true. I can hardly think straight as it is. We only just got Teddy back, now the deranged fucking man I have the displeasure of being related to has taken Lucille in retaliation. I wouldn't be able to make sane decisions, I'd go in head first, slash throats, then ask questions later.

To aid in my anger, Silas recruited a new member of the team tonight. Nicholas, a stocky, stiff shouldered American man he shared a cell with in jail. It seems they hit it off and became good friends. He turned up on the doorstep a couple of hours ago and has been sparring down in the gym. I couldn't give a shit who he integrated into his family but the way he and Kat looked at each other as Silas gave his introduction, with a knowing recognition in their eyes, stirred something deep inside of me, that up until now, I have been unfamiliar with. That in itself makes me want to put my fist through his sharply defined face. Somehow I don't think it would be a good idea to start a fight with someone just because they looked at the girl I've been secretly lusting over for the last 5 years. Even if it was insanely tempting to take my frustration out on him, I swallow my pride and offer out a hand to embrace his own, squeezing my grip around his knuckles slightly as he obliges.

"Max Costello," I snarl, pulling his body closer to mine so our noses are a breath away though he doesn't falter.

"Nicholas Smith," he grunts, flexing his arm in response before lowering his tone. "You can call me Nic."

"OK boys, that's enough," Kat snaps, pushing between us both. "There are more important things going on right now than you two having a dick measuring competition. Now, I'm going to go and fetch the kids and we're going to take them back to my place." Kat walks over to the door with a sexy swing to her hips. I don't think she realizes the effect she has on people. She stops at the door before turning back to us and smirking that sexy one sided grin I've come to love over the years. "And boys, play nice while I'm gone," she chuckles then leaves us both gawking after her.

"She's a handful," Nicholas chuckles, rubbing his hand over the scruff of hair across his chin. How the fuck would he know anything about her? I resist the urge to knock his teeth into his skull once again as I turn to face him.

"Have you met her before?" I ask, unable to help myself. Nicholas snaps his eyes to mine, smiling a smug fucking smile that shows his perfectly white teeth. Fuck I have never let a man rile me up so much over absolutely nothing before. What is wrong with me?

"Na, we've never met. She just seems like the fiery type, if you know what I mean," he winks, spiking my blood to boiling point. I don't trust him. I know they know each other, I just can't figure out where from.

"Why are you here?" I ask, gauging his reaction carefully to see what he's hiding. "What could possibly be in this for you? You don't know this family." I state matter of factly. Spending a few months in the same jail cell as somebody does not mean you know them.

"Silas offered me a job when we were in the joint. Trust me, when you spend all day, every day with the same person, you get to know them pretty well." He begins as his stance hardens and his face darkens with a threatening promise. "I know everything I need to know about Silas, Cole and Lincoln and what their business entails. I know where my loyalties lie in this situation. Do you?"

Before I have a chance to reply, Kat walks back into the room carrying Teddy on one hip and balancing Isabella on the other while Alesso follows closely behind, rubbing his eyes and yawning. The room falls awkwardly silent as she walks over to me and narrows her eyes briefly before handing Teddy over to me.

"He's tired. They all are. We should get going," she insists, looking between the two of us trying to figure out what was said in her absence.

I ignore her prying eyes and walk over to the door, cradling Teddy against my chest. "We'll take the van, it's in the garage."

It's quiet and tense on the drive back to Katrina's apartment. Teddy and Isabella have fallen asleep with their heads each resting into Kat's lap as she stares absentmindedly out of the window lost to her own thoughts, stroking her fingers through their hair. Alessandro has sprawled out across the seats in the rear. I catch Kat's eye in the mirror and try my best to comfort her with a smile. She quirks her lips ever so slightly in response, returning a soft smile at me before returning her attention to the window once again. I had my reservations about leaving the security of Silas's estate where protection and weapons would have been easily accessible should we need them, but I know Kat would feel safer in her own surroundings with the children in tow and so I refused to voice my concerns. While I agree it will be easier to monitor a smaller area, I would have preferred to keep Kat's home out of this.

We sit in silence for the rest of the journey, each of us battling our own demons.

Finally creeping the car onto Kat's driveway, I pray that the kids stay asleep while we get them into the house. I need time to think, and I doubt I'll be able to do that while trying to keep all three of them entertained.

"They can all get into my bed." Kat pipes up from the back, causing Nicholas and I to turn to face her through the center console.

"And where will you sleep?" I ask, raising a brow.

Kat shakes her head and gives me a tight lipped smile. "I don't think any of us will be getting any shut eye tonight. Come on, I can't carry them all," she says, waiting for us to help.

"Thank you for bringing us back." Kat whispers as I lay Teddy in her large double bed next to Bella's soundly sleeping form. "I know you didn't have to, but it means a lot to me that you have, Max," she adds before placing a soft kiss on my cheek and stepping out of the room.

I stand still, staring after her, mouth open and slightly stunned until Nic strides in with Alessandro wrapped into his thick muscled arms. I watch quietly as he stares down at him before he places him gently onto the bed next to Teddy and leaves the room without saying a word. Fucking weirdo. I hope Silas knows what he's gotten himself into with this one. I pull the comforter over all three kids and flick on the bedside lamp, switching the dimmer to low, knowing that if Teddy woke through the night he'd be scared of the dark.

I make my way to the kitchen where I find Kat making a pot of coffee.

"I think we're going to need something a little stronger than coffee." I laugh, eyeing up her scotch collection on the shelf above the refrigerator. Kat looks over her shoulder at me and rolls her eyes.

"Help yourself. I'd rather keep a clear head," she says, pouring coffee into a mug and handing it over to Nicholas who smiles appreciatively at her.

"Thanks, Sugar," he drawls, reaching for the mug. His fingers linger over hers for just a second too long before I notice the blush creep up from her neck. Yep, I definitely need more than coffee to get through this.

"I'm going to patrol." I snap, swiping a three quarter full bottle of Jack before leaving through the front door to survey the area.

I walk around the entire apartment complex three times before I finally come to the conclusion that I can't wait any longer. Silas and Lincoln won't like it but it's my sister sitting in that cell and I'll do anything in my power to get her back to Teddy. I pull out my phone, dialing the number Marcus gave me after our interview and swallow down the last of the whiskey.

The line rings once before a monotone voice answers, "Hello."

"I need to speak with Marcus." I snap, already impatient.

"Who is this?" The voice asks, with absolutely no urgency.

I run my fingers frustratedly through my hair, trying to keep my calm. Almost regretting guzzling the entirety of the bottle before making this call. "Just put Marcus on the phone. It's Max Costello. I need to speak with him urgently." I urge.

"I'm sorry Mr Costello, but Marcus is on a job right now and can not be contacted. I will get him to contact you as soon as he becomes avail-"

"NO. You don't fucking understand, you absolute jobsworth! I need to speak with him NOW! We need to get to Ronan Costello. He's taken my sister. Marcus needs to make his move now. I know his location. He'll fucking kill her if we don't get there in time!" I shout, hardly able to contain my emotion as I beg into the phone, not caring who overhears me.

"One moment please," is all he replies in the same uninterested tone and while I rip my hair out at the root. The line goes quiet except for mumbling background voices.

"What is your location?" He asks a moment later. I reel off Kat's address, giving them strict instructions not to enter the complex grounds but to ring me when they're outside. I won't have her space invaded by more men with guns. I hang up the phone, feeling an overwhelming mixture of relief that they actually listened and a sickening apprehension to what happens next.

I make my way back to Kat's apartment, battling with the temptation not to go back at all. But she deserves more than that, better than another man leaving without explanation.

I brace myself against the doorframe before entering the house, the alcohol settling deep into my system as I take a deep breath and open the door to be greeted immediately with a pointed finger poking me in the chest.

"Where the hell have you been!?" Kat whisper-shouts aggressively, narrowing her eyes at the empty bottle of Jack in my hand.

"I told you, I was going outside." I shrug, side stepping the rest of her assault on my chest to place the bottle into the trash.

"Do you really think it was a good idea for you to drink the whole fucking bottle, Max?" She hisses, trailing behind me like a shadow. Whether it's the alcohol in me or the alluring smell of coffee mixed with the sweet vanilla of her body, I spin myself around so fast I catch her off guard, wrapping an arm around her waist and pulling her hard into my chest. She gasps slightly, her eyes widening in shock as her hands splay out against my chest, the tips of her fingers tracing dangerously close to my throat.

"Max," she whispers, and I swear I hear it as more of a plea than anything else. I tighten my hold around her waist, trailing the fingers of my free hand up her arm, across her shoulder, collar bone and then stroke them up the column of her neck. She tilts her head further up, closing her eyes and allowing me easier access as I lace my fingers into her hair and place feather soft, meaningful kisses against her throat.

"You have no idea what you do to me, Katrina." I whisper, gliding my lips across her jaw. "But you deserve somebody better than a man like me." I kiss her neck again, breathing in her intoxicating scent, before angling her head with the hold I have in her hair, hovering my lips a mere breath above her own. It takes all of my self restraint to hold back from devouring her against her kitchen counter, leaving it up to her to decide what happens next.

"Max, please," she whimpers impatiently, giving me all the permission I need to crush my lips to hers. I slide my tongue between her already parted lips and collide it against her own. Kat snakes her arms around my neck, pulling us impossibly closer as she kisses me with equal fervor, gliding her tongue expertly across my lips before sucking my bottom lip between her teeth. Fuck, I know that if I don't stop this now, I'll end up fucking her where we stand. But I don't have to restrain myself too much as a loud interrupting cough from the other side of the room makes Kat pull away immediately. I grit my teeth as I turn to face Nicholas who stands with his arms folded and a smug grin pulling up the corners of his mouth.

"Nicholas… we were… I was just," Kat stutters, trying to regain her composure as she flattens her hair. The effect I had from one kiss makes me wonder how much more of a mess I could get her into if I was ever given the chance. I tighten my fists at the thought, willing my cock to stay down. I need a clear head, no distractions.

"Don't sweat it, Sugar." Nicholas smirks, narrowing his eyes as he glances at me. What a tool. My phone buzzes loudly in my pocket, bringing Kat's attention straight back to me. I answer and bring the phone to my ear, already knowing who it is.

"With you in two." The familiar voice states before ending the call. I pocket my phone as Kat stands in front of me, pleading silently for answers.

"I have to go," I say, ignoring the confusion that quickly morphs itself to shock then anger.

"What do you mean you have to go? Go where?" Kat insists.

"I have to make this right," I whisper, grabbing the back of her neck and pulling her into me again, kissing her forehead. Lingering for a beat too long as I take in the feel of her in my arms for what could be the last time. I inhale her scent, filling my lungs with her deliciously sweet aroma before pulling away and striding over to Nicholas who hasn't moved from his position.

"If anything happens to her when I'm gone. I will kill you." I state matter of factly, keeping my emotions void. He will never know how much it angers me to leave her with another man. Especially him. I know there's history there, even if it's small, they know each other and he lied to me about it.

"Max, where are you going?" Kat asks desperately as she comes up beside me, but I remain still with my eyes locked on Nic's.

"Noted," he grunts, glancing at Katrina and clenching his jaw like he's biting back more words but I don't give him a chance to speak them. I make my way to the door as Kat begs behind me, her voice becoming more desperate with each word.

"Max, please don't do anything stupid. Silas and Linc will bring Lucille back. We just need to wait here."

I stop at the front door and look deep into her glossy eyes. "This is all my fault. I need to do this Katrina. Promise me you'll stay here with Nic and the kids?"

Kat pulls her bottom lip between her teeth as a single tear glides down across her cheek. "Max, please," she cries at barely a whisper.

"Promise me, Katrina,".

"I promise," she relents and before I can consider not leaving at all, I push my way through the door and walk the short distance to the community gate where a black unmarked Toyota Camry sits waiting against the sidewalk.

"Are you sure you want to do this?" Asks a stocky, dark haired man with a bullet proof vest wrapped around his chest. He has a bunch of old military style tags hanging around his neck but shows no real sign that he's been in any type of battle himself.

"I've never been more sure of anything in my life." I breathe out slowly, coming to terms with the fact that I'm about to discard everything I was brought up believing in.

Chapter 27

Lucille

I never imagined I could scream for so long but as I helplessly watched Cole's body slump forward against his restraints, the loud smack of the hammer splintered every last piece of my resolve as Ronan's men continued their brutal assault. My legs threatened to give way beneath me as I was made to watch, but the iron grip around my biceps kept me upright, ensuring I didn't miss a thing.

"Marcus, shut her the fuck up would you or I'll make sure she's next in the chair." Ronan's order cuts through, sending me into a white panic, making me scream even louder. Suddenly the vice-like hold on my arm intensifies and sharp nails pierce into the flesh of my arms causing me to wince.

"For your own sake Lucille, you need to do as he says. He will fuck you in that chair while everybody else here watches and he won't even bat an eyelid about it when they each take their turn after, no matter how loudly you scream. Now shut the fuck up." His voice hisses just behind my ear, forcing me to snap my mouth shut. I quickly gaze around the room, nobody makes any indication that they heard his whisper of warning as they try to bring Cole back to consciousness.

"What do you want from me? I thought you were dead. I don't understand what's going on. Is your name really Marcus?" I whimper, trying to pull myself from his body.

"I thought you were smarter than this. I am nothing like the man you married. The man I once called my brother. You'll do well to remember that," he snaps back at me.

I immediately freeze at his words. I didn't know Vinny had a brother, an identical twin brother to be precise. How could we have been together for so long without him even mentioning any other siblings to me? I go to question him further but catch Ronan glaring in our direction. I clap my mouth shut at once, remaining silent and looking anywhere but at him as he makes his way over to us. He comes to stand in front of me, and I notice Marcus' hands on my arms tense ever so slightly as Ronan grabs hold of my face, digging his thumb and fingers into my cheeks so hard I can taste the blood pool across my tongue. He angles my head, tilting my face to look directly into his snake-like eyes and it takes everything I have in me not to shiver at his touch. I refuse to give him the satisfaction.

"Pretty little thing, aren't you dear daughter. I can see why they all pine after you so much." He licks his lips as he speaks, churning my stomach at the overwhelming stench of cigar mixed with strong liquor on his breath making me feel physically sick. As though my body recognises the intention behind his words, fear settles into my bones. His smirk is enough to show that he got the reaction he wanted. My mother must have been high or off her head to have married this man.

His attention is quickly drawn away, enabling me to fully breathe again as Cole emits a worryingly strained groan after one of Ronan's men appears to have showered him in a bucket of ice water, shocking him back to a questionable state of consciousness.

"Ahh Cole, you have returned to us once again. You missed saying goodbye to your brother, dear friend." Ronan taunts him as he walks over and leans down in front of the chair that both of Cole's hands are now nailed down too. "You're not looking too healthy, Cole. Do you think you'll last long enough to see that beloved brother of yours and his little lapdog take their last breaths? Or will you be taking your own first?" Ronan cackles, shoving Cole's head back, making him hiss at the painful movement that jerks his hands against the nails.

"Fuck you!" Cole spits, using too much of his strength to spit into Ronan's face. "You will never win this," he snaps before Ronan turns his face to look at me. The look on his face turns my blood to ice. His eyes were no longer human, every part of them had bled to black and if anybody had told me that this was a man I knew, a man I'd once called my father, I would never believe them, for there was nothing recognizable left. He was all monster.

His lips slowly and menacingly pull up at the sides, revealing his stained teeth as he lifts his foot above Cole's hand, staring directly into my eyes as he slams his boot down. Cole erupts, screaming in pain as Ronan twists his foot against him, audibly crunching the bones beneath. I flail my body, pulling desperately to get to him but it's no use. I'm not strong enough to break free.

"Stop. Please stop this!" I scream, with fresh tears staining my cheeks but Ronan doesn't relent. "PLEASE! I'll do anything you want. Please, just stop hurting him." I cry, pulling forward to get closer to Cole, and in that moment everything stops. Ronan removes his boot from Cole's obliterated hand. His blood loss is getting worse now. The wounds on his hands are dripping into already formed puddles.

Ronan turns back to Cole and smiles. "It appears I have already won," he snickers loudly, his gang of assailants joined in and an unnerving laughter swamps the room.

"Lu...cille," Cole stuttered, physically fighting through the pain, trying to stay conscious.

"You're fucking worthless, Salvatore. And now your woman is all mine." Ronan taunts, striding over to where Marcus and I are standing. I kick my heels against the floor immediately, trying to push us back and as far away from his touch as possible but he reaches us too quickly. His hands come up to my face and he runs them roughly through my hair, bringing strands through his fingers and up to his nose where he breathes in deeply, closing his eyes, reveling in the smell.

"What do you want from me?" I whisper, trying not to spook him into doing anything.

"I already had what I wanted... A son to raise and rule my empire when I am old and fragile... Somebody I could bend and break and mold into everything I needed them to be... But you, my darling Lucille, took that away from me."

"He wasn't yours to have, you sick fuck. He's my son." I snap back, no longer fearful. A sharp pain shoots across my cheek and the realization that Ronan just slapped me filters through the sudden fogginess. I shake my head, clearing the stars in my vision, barely noticing Cole as he begins to shout for Ronan's attention.

"He was mine, you silly bitch and you took him away from me. So now you get to give me what I want. And this time nobody is going to stop me," he snarls, moving in closer before trailing his hand across my jaw and neck. He pauses, tapping his finger against my throat before tutting loudly. "Get her into the cell," he orders.

Marcus doesn't wait to be told again as he immediately pulls me away from his leering eyes, pulling me against his chest as he leads me back to the cell I woke up in. I'm suddenly grateful for his closeness as my brain fails to figure out how to put one foot in front of the other and I trip several times causing him to take my weight.

"Get in and don't say another word," he whispers low into my ear before shoving me to the floor. I hit the concrete floor with a loud smack, the pain radiating its way up my knees to my hips, hissing out at the shock. I steady myself with my hands against the dusty floor, distracted suddenly by Cole's voice shouting my name across the room.

"Cole, I'm here. I'm still here. I'm OK." I reassure him, pulling myself up on the bars of the cell.

"Oh, how touching," Ronan taunts before giving his next order. "Pull out the nails. And do it one by one, I want to see if he squeals just as much as when they went in."

The taller of the two guards standing either side of Cole move to the other side of the room before returning with a pair of pliers while the smaller of the two flips the hammer in his hand, holding the claw terrifyingly close to Cole's face.

"Hold still, pretty boy. This may hurt just a little." I hear one of them say before Cole's animalistic screams reverberate around the room.

"Cole. Cole, I need you to stay awake for me." I shout, trying to keep him even the slightest bit distracted. To see him withstanding so much pain is more horrifying than the thought of Ronan's hand on my body. I can barely stand to watch but I know he would do the same for me.

"Topolino," Cole murmurs along with other inaudible words as Ronan's men take turns to pull out the nails out of his hands. His voice cracks while his body tenses and I can see the pain he's trying desperately hard to hide from me.

"I'm right here, Cole. I'm not going anywhere." I cry. "Please Ronan. Please stop!" I beg him while he watches on, a shimmer of amusement laced in his eyes. "You sick fuck. You're enjoying this!" I snap, to which he turns his attention back to me and smiles.

"You've seen nothing yet, girly." He states, narrowing his eyes at me before making his way out of the room shouting. "Make sure he doesn't die. I'm not finished with him yet."

Cole's screams become less and less until he's finally rendered unconscious again. When they removed the last nail from his hand with elated cheers at their handiwork, his body slumps to the floor with a loud thud.

"Check his pulse, Boss doesn't want him dead just yet." The smaller of the two guards orders. The taller one kneels down, pulling Cole onto his back and checking his neck.

"He's alive, for now." he laughs, kicking Cole as he stands. They both laugh before walking out of the room, leaving me alone with Cole's unconscious body.

Hours seemed to pass as I sit and wait, watching the rise and fall of Cole's chest to make sure he was still breathing. Although, from behind these bars, I'm not entirely sure what I'd do if he wasn't.

"Cole," I call out to him, careful not to raise my voice too loud incase I was heard. I don't want anyone coming back down here any time soon. "Cole, can you hear me?" A low groan escapes his lips that I almost miss until he raises a bloodied, mangled hand to his face. "You're awake!" I gasp, pulling myself to my knees.

"Am I?" Cole groans again, rolling onto his side and locking eyes with mine. "I'm so fucking sorry, Lucille," he chokes, trying to push himself off the floor.

"Cole don't move, you've lost too much blood." I urge him, but it falls on deaf ears. His elbows buckle under the strain as he collapses back to the floor, grunting at the impact.

"Fuck," he curses before trying again, succeeding this time and precariously crawling over so only the bars of my cell separate us once more.

With a closer look at his wounds, my stomach churns at the sight of his left hand. It was completely mangled from Ronan's boot and the nails had punctured through his palm. With his already missing finger he must be in an incredible amount of pain, but he's hiding it well. Reaching my hands through the bars, desperate to feel him. I grab his face and pull his head to the bars, pushing my lips to his and kissing him so hard it take my own breath away.

"Mio topolino," Cole breathes against my lips. "I can't get close enough to you through these bars for you to keep kissing me like that."

"Half dead yet you still manage to sweet talk me," I laugh, kissing him again.

"Lucille, I will get you out of here. I promise." He says, pulling back to look me in the eyes. His eyes narrow at me and the line between his eyebrows became prominent when I don't respond. But I'm not sure what to say anymore. This situation is fucked. I don't see him being able to survive much more torture and I don't know how long it will take for Silas and Lincoln to get to us. My mind flickers back to Teddy in that street, the helplessly frightened look in his eyes as I was ripped away. I pray that he's alright and that Kat got to him in time. I know she'll look after him like her own if anything happens to me in here and for whatever reason, I don't make it back.

"Where are you little mouse?" Cole asks, pulling me back to the dire reality we're in.

"I was thinking about Teddy," I sigh, closing my eyes as a single tear tracks down my cheek. "I was thinking about what will happen if I don't make it out of here."

Cole kisses my forehead, cheeks, nose and finally my lips before whispering more broken promises. "Don't think like that. You will get back to him. I promise to get you out of here."

We stay embraced in each other's arms through the cold metal bars of the cell with Cole slipping in and out of sleep and my arms way past numb but I couldn't care less. He's here with me and that's all I could ask for.

"Well aren't you two just fucking adorable." A familiar voice shocks me awake from the darkest corner of the room. Marcus creeps forward carrying a small first aid kit and a bottle of water. "You should patch him up before he bleeds to death," he suggests, throwing the kit and bottle of water at my feet. I carefully untangle myself from Cole's arms, managing not to wake him and reach for the kit, only pausing slightly as I pick up the bottle and wonder if it's laced with drugs. Marcus must notice my hesitation as he chuckles, crouching down to my eyeline with only the metal bars between us. "It's safe." he smirks as if he's able to read my mind.

"Why should I trust you?" I whisper, gazing into his all too familiar face. A face I learnt the hard way not to trust.

Marcus huffs a small breath, the corners of his lips curving up, turning his face into something deadly as he puffs out his shoulders, standing to his full height above us.

"Because if I wanted you dead sweetheart, I'd have already made it happen. That goes for your boyfriend, too." He declares, nodding his head in Cole's direction. I swallow the dry lump scratching in my throat, following the direction of Marcus' gaze before I move back to Cole with the first aid kit and water and get to work.

It doesn't take long for Cole to wake after I start cleaning the wounds on his hands. Starting with the worst hand first, I manage to gently wash away most of the blood with some of the water Marcus gave me then stitch what I can before applying some disinfectant spray that was packed in the first aid kit and wrap them tightly with gauze and bandages. I notice, now that I'm closer, the savage wound where Cole's missing finger is and it takes all of the remaining strength I have not to cry when I look at the raw brutality of his wounds. Wounds that have been inflicted because of me. I work as tenderly as I can, clenching my jaw to distract myself from the person behind the pain, though if this is hurting him, he doesn't show it. His eyes burn into me the entire time but he stays quiet while I work. It's a rough job by the time I'm finished, and he most definitely will need medical intervention if we get out of here, maybe even surgery to repair the worst of the injuries but with the tools I have, it's the best I can do right now.

"Mio topolino, look at me," Cole whispers, his voice low and hoarse. I glance up to meet his eyes so full of pain though he tries so hard to hide it. He can't hide it from me, not anymore.

"I'm here," I whisper, placing my hands against his face. "I'm not going anywhere." I pull him into me, crushing my lips to his in a desperate need to be granted with equal brutality as he kisses me back with the same force. I groan into his mouth, parting my lips, allowing his tongue access to mine as we collide. Our hearts. Our souls. Our bodies. We come together as one and in that moment, I know I can't live another day without this man knowing how I truly feel.

"I love you," I gasp against his lips. He freezes for a heartbeat before I feel him smile as he kisses me again.

"I love you, Lucille. I'm in love with you. I have been since the moment I found you. You have always been mine, and I will always be yours," he whispers back so tenderly that my chest seizes at the feelings that flood my body.

"I hope you know you have to share," I giggle, and the playful smile he returns me with lets me know he knows exactly what I'm referring to but before he can respond the cellar door crashes open and Ronan comes barreling in, closely followed by his men in arms.

"Touching, really it is. Now you can call me impatient but I really couldn't give a fuck. Get her out and stand him up. I'm ending this now!" he barks out his orders, narrowing his eyes at Cole and I.

Without needing any further instruction, the two garish brutes from earlier stride towards the cell, grinning maliciously as they unlock the door and drag me out. I kick my legs frantically, screaming for them to let me go but all it does is entice them more.

"We like it more when you fight us," one of them snarls while the other pulls at my hair, yanking my head back to look in Cole's direction while dragging his tongue along my neck to my jaw.

"She tastes so good," he taunts. I recoil at the stench of alcohol on his breath, trying desperately to breathe through my mouth to stop myself from screaming.

Cole has already been hoisted to his feet. "Get your fucking hands off her!" He roars, his rage fuelling him as he shoves against the two men holding him back. He succeeds, his strength catching them off guard and knocking one to the ground but Ronan strides forward, gun raised to his face and Cole freezes.

"NO!" I shout. My voice is barely recognisable, even to myself. "Please. I will do anything." I beg. "Please don't hurt him anymore." I'm desperate now as a white hot fear ignites my chest. I can't lose anybody else. I can't be the reason for anybody else to die, especially him. "Please. I'm begging you."

Ronan keeps his gaze narrowed on Cole. "Get her on the floor," he snaps and before I can process his words I'm being shoved to the ground. Their rough hands are on my body but I'm already disassociating. I know what happens next. My arms are pinned above my head and my feeble attempts to get free are worthless against their strength.

"Don't fucking touch her!" I hear Cole growl. "I will fucking kill you, you sick mother fucker."

I can't look in his direction as violent hands tear my pants down my legs and claw at my exposed skin.

"I wonder if she tastes as good down here," somebody snickers, I can only imagine it's the one who

316

licked my neck but as Ronan walks into view with his gun still pointing at Cole, I repress any thoughts of right now and tune it all out, projecting my mind as far away from this place as it will go. Back to when my life was simple. But when was that, exactly? Could it have been when I was young, striving daily for my mothers affections? Doing everything I possibly could to get her to even say the words I love you. Or when I was struggling to get by with my shitty job between classes? Or when I was scared of my abusive husband? Was it after I ran away and birthed his child in secret? Always looking over my shoulder for him to find us...Or was it when he did eventually catch up to us and Teddy got kidnapped? When has my life been simple?

A sharp pain across my cheek brings me straight back to my reality. I can taste the blood as it floods my mouth, swallowing it down, not wanting to give him the satisfaction of seeing the damage he caused. "I said you wanted to beg, you whore. Now I'll give you something to beg about." Ronan snarls just inches above my face. "Let go of her hands. I want to make sure he has an unrestricted view on what I'm about to do. There are no rules when it comes to survival Cole and for my legacy to survive, there must be an heir."

I can hear Cole's relentless protests but he sounds too far away as Ronan positions himself above my body. I brace myself for what's to come, turning my head away from the room, staring directly into nothing. To blackness. To the gun Ronan had held to Cole's face, sitting on the floor next to my head. I blink away the tears, focusing my vision, thinking at first it was a figment of my imagination, I was sure I could hear Max but surely not, as the blurriness clears so does my mind.

At the same time, a loud explosion shakes the room, plastering the space in a thick layer of dust as three familiar figures force their way through the wreckage. A deafening silence rings through my ears and my soul seems to leave me while I lay beneath the man who was once a father figure to me. In and out of body experience, my hand moves quicker than I can think of what to do next as I reach for the gun. Ronan scrambles at the sudden explosion around us as he tries to retreat but he won't get away. I wrap my fingers around his gun, the coolness of the metal pulling my mind right back where it needs to be. I aim and squeeze, watching as Ronan's body visibly flinches as the shot rings out, his eyes bulge in his head and an animalistic squeal escapes his throat. Blood immediately gushes from the single shot wound in his neck, soaking through his crisp white shirt, staining it a deep shade of crimson as he stumbles forward on his knees, clutching his hands to his throat desperately trying to quell the bleeding. I watch, fixated on the blood that covers his body the more that he struggles to cling to life. He gargles on the blood pooling at the back of his throat, spitting scarlet droplets over my bare legs as he sways, before collapsing on top of my frozen body. An inhuman scream rips from my chest as I realize what I've done.

Chapter 28

Lincoln

Silas, Zack, Marcello, Sully, Quinton and I huddle together on the perimeter of the property, the rain beats down heavily against our backs as we run over the blueprints Felix emailed over to me on our drive here. I can barely manage to stand still to listen to Silas as he gives his orders. My skin feels as if it's physically crawling with anticipation and anger. I shift my weight continuously from one foot to the other, caressing the hilt of my knives sheathed inside of my bulky bullet proof vest, doing a mental stocktake of every weapon concealed on my body. I throw my head to the sky, letting the rain fall across my face, as the sound of loading guns filters through the group and I know the time to move is fast approaching.

"The video call puts them in the cellar." Silas states, holding the phone in his palm so the group can see the layout of the building on the device. He continues, pointing out the path we will take on the screen as I turn my attention back to him and the group of men we handpicked for occasions exactly like this. We are few but we are strong in our ability and by the end of the night, none of our enemies inside that building will be left breathing. When I let myself think of Lucille, and the torture Ronan has undoubtedly subjected Cole to, white hot anger burns beneath my skin, threatening to split me open.

"We will work our way through the building, quickly, quietly and efficiently. We cut down anyone in our path, is that understood? They have taken too much and we will make them pay." Silas' voice thunders through the impending storm. His eyes are dark and blood thirsty as he stares at each of us one by one. "Ronan will be finished at my hand, nobody else's."

I raise my head as his eyes fall to mine. "Cogliere la notte!" I smirk, with him nodding his head in agreement.

"Cogliere la notte!" the group call in unison, raising their guns above their head towards the moon.

"Let's move."

We cover the open ground in a matter of seconds, spreading out along the length of the house, keeping away from the windows. The darkness of nightfall keeps us well hidden as we move as one, a fully armed unit prepared for war. As Silas takes point with Quinton beside him, Zack and Marcello fall in behind them while Sully and I take the rear. Normally I would stand next to my brother but we agreed that in this situation, we need to be the head and tail of the snake.

Silas gives Quinton a nod and he opens the door to the front of the house and they creep inside. Two heavy thuds and a muffled garble can be heard between the claps of thunder filling the night before Quinton appears at the door giving the rest of us the green light to follow.

Three bodies lie still in growing pools of their own blood, their necks slit open and eyes boring into nothingness. The sight would be enough to make any grown man sick to their stomach but my stomach only twists with the need to spill some blood of my own.

The house is small, with scarce furniture but even through the dimly lit rooms, the dampness visibly soaks into the walls, filling the air with a thick musk. I signal Zack and Marcello, instructing them to clear the upper floor before we move on. The ability for us to communicate silently makes it easy to comb through the building, picking off those who lie unprepared for our arrival. The four of us remaining filter through the first level of the house, knives drawn as a first choice of weapon. The quieter, the better. After clearing the floor we circle back round to the kitchen as Zack and Marcello make their way back into the room with a nod to confirm the floor above is clear.

Silas moves towards the cellar door, hesitating slightly with his hand on the knob. I nudge Sully, nodding for him to take over and he does without faltering, pushing his way past Silas and opening the door. The staircase leads onto a narrow corridor. The coldness of the space seeping into our rain soaked clothes sends a blistering chill throughout my body, but it doesn't come close to the soul shattering sound of Lucille's screams filtering through the concrete walls.

"Fuck. We have to get in there!" I snarl, trying desperately not to think of what could be happening on the other side of the wall.

"Why the fuck is the door locked?" Silas seethes as he tries to ram his entire weight against the thick metal of the door.

"Just fucking get it open!" I demand, fisting my hair into my hands as Silas rams the door again with no movement at all.

Sully and Zack both run to the other end of the corridor, searching for another way in. "I saw a crowbar upstairs, I'll get that." Marcello shouts.

"Don't bother. All of you, get out the fucking way." A harsh voice snaps. We all spin towards the direction the voice came from.

"Max? What the fuck are you doing here?" Silas shouts, stepping into his face. Max shoves him back with more force than I thought he possessed, sending Silas into the wall behind him.

"I'm saving my fucking sister, now MOVE!" he snaps back before glancing back up the stairs and yelling for whoever he brought with him to follow him down.

"Where are the kids? Where is Alessandro?" I ask, suddenly distracted as I watch a group of men sporting FBI jackets and vests, all armed ready with M4 Carbines, come filtering down the stairwell. "Max? What the fuck are the FBI doing here?" I spit, rushing his body, fisting his shirt.

"I'll explain later, just get out of the way." Max hisses, shoving my arms away.

I look at Silas whose face looks as furiously confused as my own as Max works together with a couple of FBI agents to set up a small explosive against the metal door.

"Fucking hell Irish, you brought explosives?" Silas snaps moving away from the door.

"Actually, they did." Max smirks, nodding towards the retreating FBI. "Everybody move back."

In the next instant the wall explodes and dust pollutes the small space.

"Lucille!" Max shouts through the thick cloud.

I wade my way forwards through the debris and toward the light shining through the opening, meeting Silas and Max on the way. We step through the broken brick, completely unprepared for the scene before us.

As the dust settles, my eyes zone straight in on Lucille's body with Ronan between her legs, he's fumbling with himself trying to retreat, no doubt shitting himself at the exploding wall behind him. Lucille's face is turned in our direction but she isn't looking at us, her eyes are glazed over, completely unaware of our arrival. I hear a deep threatening growl beside me, unsure to whom it belonged to. I drag my gaze away from her as Cole struggles against three men all trying to detain him. Almost as though they haven't noticed our arrival, as he gives the three grown men a good run for their money. There's blood, a mix of fresh and old dried into his clothes, his hands are bandaged and he sounds feral as he roars at them, spitting death threats to them all as he desperately fights to break free and get to Lucille.

My mind snaps instantly, like an elastic band being pulled all too tight. I move forward with swift precision, swiping my blade from the strap on my vest, and slicing it with a fluid motion across the nearest of Ronan's men who stands dumbfounded having been taken by surprise at the sudden chaos. I catch Silas doing the same, mirroring my movements and striking down another of Ronan's men in his path. Beside me, Max falters at the sight of his father bearing down on Lucille. I keep my eyes locked on her, trying to get to her as my eyes lock on the movement of her hand reaching for a discarded gun. My blade disconnects from the soft flesh of our enemy, expelling his sticky warm blood over my hand. My chest seizes as I watch Lucille's face morph from being void of all emotion, to shock, to pure panic as she squeezes the trigger and Ronan's limp body falls on top of hers. Her piercing scream echoes around the room as she stares down at his lifeless body and the thick crimson blood spilling over her bare legs. It's a sound I will carry with me for the rest of my life.

Suddenly the room erupts as though time has finally caught up. Gunfire reins down around us as the three men failing to secure Cole fire shots at every angle. I move fast, throwing my body to shield Lucille as Silas and Max, who seems to have mentally checked back in, do the same.

"It's OK, Love, I've got you." I groan, hurling Ronan's body from between her legs. My chest aches at the empty void of her eyes as she glances up at me, no longer screaming.

"I thought…I thought he was going to–"

"Shhh, it's over now." I whisper, pulling her trembling body into my chest and cradling her safely in my arms.

"Linc, we'll cover you, just get her out of here," Silas snaps as he pierces a guy's eye with a single shot.

I twist my head, searching for Cole across the room. He's hand to hand with a large tattooed bald man. I don't remember seeing this many bodies when we entered the cellar but they seem to have multiplied since the explosion. Fuck.

"Linc, we can't leave him," Lucille whispers, placing her hand gently on my cheek. "I won't leave unless it's with all of you." I glance down at the woman in my arms, half naked, covered in blood and dirt, with a fresh bruise beginning to blossom across her cheek and bloodied scrapes covering her knees. Her body is so fragile against my own, so beaten and broken, yet still she has the ability to make me question my own instincts. "Lincoln, please!" she pleads, softening her eyes, begging for me to change my mind.

324

I shake my head, what the fuck am I thinking? "I'm getting you out of here." I grunt, readying myself to stand.

"Linc—"

"No, Lucille. I won't have it any other way. I will not risk your life anymore than it already has been." I snap, causing her mouth to clamp shut.

I glance back over to Cole once more who catches my eye as Zack subdues the bald guys by snapping his neck. Cole's eyes flare when he looks at Lucille but he nods, understanding what must be done. He would do the same. Any of us would. There was once a time when neither Silas, Cole or I would have cared if we went into a situation that we stood every chance of not returning from. But now, since Lucille, everything is different. Now we live for her.

"Silas!" I bark, trying to get his attention over the noise, to let him know my intention.

Gunshots continue until silence falls and he shouts, "NOW."

With that I spring to my feet, Lucille's body bouncing against my chest as I make a run for the hole in the wall. Silas and Max fire into the remaining group of Ronan's gang, covering us as we escape. I jump over the fallen rubble, ignoring Lucille's pleas to turn around and wait for everybody else. She can hate me, but I'd rather that than her death. I take the stairs three at a time, breaking out into the kitchen then swiftly making my way through the house to the front door before freezing at the sound of a bullet being chambered.

"Is he dead?" A cool voice has me spinning round to meet a face that has me instinctively holding onto Lucille tighter. I notice her body shift as she places a steadying hand on my chest.

"He's dead," she replies, matter of factly to the ghost standing before me. I'm confused, for the first time in a very long time. I feel completely blindsided. I notice the small flicker in his eyes as his gaze quickly roams over Lucille's exposed legs and it makes me want to put the fucker through the wall behind him.

I tense as he lowers his weapon, shifting his body to remove his shirt, revealing a FBI bullet proof vest.

"What the fuck is going on?" I demand.

He steps forwards, holding out his shirt, looking directly into my eyes.

"Cover her up," he offers. I hesitate, but the thought of any other man looking at Lucille's compromised state has me reaching for the shirt and tucking it over her legs.

"Thank you, Marcus," Lucille whispers softly, unsure of the words as they leave her mouth. I frown at the name, Marcus notices and smirks to himself.

"I'll let Max explain…" he chuckles, waving his hand as he saunters off in the direction of the cellar.

"What the fuck was that about?" I gawp, utterly confused by what just happened.

"I don't fully understand but it turns out Vinny had an identical twin brother." Lucille says slowly, like she's finally realizing the information as she says the words out loud.

I frown, how could we not have known this? How was it not picked up on our background check? Then I realize he probably redacted the information himself when he became part of the FBI. Knowing the true extent of his brother's proclivities and the multiple convictions no doubt left him not wanting to be associated with such a piece of shit.

"I don't like him," I grunt, carrying Lucille out of the house to the van we left beyond the perimeter of the fence.

326

It wasn't long until Silas, Cole and the rest of the group all came clambering back to the van. Cole looked even worse than I remembered, with blood soaking through the ragged bandages wrapped around his hands and multiple lacerations and bruises covering his face and body.

"Jesus Christ!" I curse, noting the pale tinge to his skin and layer of sweat glistening across his face as Zack and Sully hoisted him into the backseat of the van, climbing in after him. Nobody else seemed to have sustained any serious injuries.

"Where…Where is Max?" Lucille asks, the question breaking at the end as she glances back toward the house. Oh fuck.

"He's gone with the FBI to answer some more questions, they said it couldn't wait but he'll be back at the house as soon as it's over." Silas informs her, pulling her into a solid embrace before slamming his lips to hers, letting his emotions break out in one of the only ways he knows how. Lucille gasps as their lips part and I notice the way her skin flushes at the words Silas whispers in her ear before she directs her attention back to Cole.

I turn to Silas, pulling him in closer out of Lucille's earshot as she assesses the damage to Cole's wounded hands. "If we don't get him to a doctor he's going to be in trouble real soon." I whisper hiss, mentally preparing myself to deal with what happens next. "Lucille needs a doctor, too. She needs to be checked over." I add, catching a glimpse of anger in Silas' eyes.

"Is the doctor still contactable?" he asks, rubbing his fingers into his eyes, smearing the blood from them across his face.

"He won't have a choice in the matter." I state, already firing out a message to the good doctor with instructions on where to meet us.

"That's good, he can treat Cole at the house. Lucille will be going to a hospital though. I'll take her there myself. He comes nowhere near her." Silas says out loud, more to himself than me. I would never let Lucille back in the same room as that man let alone let him treat her. The thought of it leaves me tense but before I can ask any further questions, Lucille's desperate voice calls out from the back seat.

"We need to get him to a hospital now!"

Chapter 29 Epilogue

12 months later

Silas

Waking up next to la mia luce most mornings is a dream come true. After all we have gone through in such a short amount of time, the kidnapping, almost losing Cole on multiple occasions and the trauma that Lucille herself went through and still manages to overcome everyday makes my chest swell at how proud of her I am, and only solidifies to me how much I truly love her. Our unit was broken almost one year ago, and we lost two good men in the war against Ronan. Enzo and Dario. And although their deaths were avenged, their lives will live on in the rest of us.

I kiss Lucille's head softly, breathing in the scent of her new coconut shampoo before moving myself out of the warmth of our bed and head straight for the ensuite. Turning the shower on, I let the water temperature build as steam slowly begins to fill the room while I move over to the sink. Looking in the mirror, staring back at me is a different man to who I was a year ago. That man had nothing to live for, but now I have a family, not just my brother's and Alesso but Lucille and Teddy. Even Katrina is becoming like a little sister that just won't quit. She's trouble, with a dark past that only I hold her secret to, but she's Lucille's best friend and as annoying as I find her, I can't help but have respect for how she has always been there for our girl and now I find myself eyeing Max every time he glances her way. Lucille teases me often that I am becoming more of an overbearing big brother to Katrina and that I need to let her and Max be. But I can't help it, he might be Lucille's brother but the hot and cold game he plays with Katrina has me wanting to punch his head through a wall for her.

I place the towel over the radiator, just as I hear the door click open behind me. I smirk, already knowing who it is and what she wants. Standing before me is a golden haired wonder, hair that is tied up in what women call a 'messy bun'. I can't help thinking it looks so damn sexy on her as she pops her hip and smirks at me with a greedy hunger in her eyes. Her skimpy little nightdress that barely covers her thighs leaves little to the imagination and I already know she's bare underneath. Her gaze draws down my body, I am in nothing but my boxer shorts, and I can't help but chuckle at the way her eyes widen as she notices my hard length growing. It's been long enough that you would think she would be used to it by now, I'm always hard around her, but her wanton need is sending an uncomfortable ache straight to my balls. What a woman. She is beautiful, sexy, she's a Goddess that I can never get enough of. She's perfect.

She smirks, cocking an eyebrow at me, "Big guy, we went two rounds last night, you can't possibly be ready for me again."

I shake my head with a deep chuckle rumbling in my chest, before backing her into the door, closing it as I press my body against hers, instinctively bringing my hands to her throat. My thumb pulls on her bottom lip that is caught between her teeth, releasing it with a pop.

Bringing my mouth close to her ear as she closes her eyes and I smile as her body shivers against mine at the warmth of my breath ghosting over her skin. "I'll always be ready for you, I'll always be ready to fill your greedy pussy and have you screaming my name from those pouty lips as I devour every inch of you over and over again." I whisper. She squirms beneath me as I suck her earlobe into my mouth. I can't resist tasting every inch of her body.

"Silas," she gasps.

With her body pinned to the door as I flex my hips, pushing further against her, making her feel how solid my cock is just for her. Parting her legs with my knee, I trail my hand down the side of her delicious curves, gliding my fingers across her hip as I continue to work my hand down her body until I reach between her legs. Her hungry eyes snap open, studying me as I gently rub her clit with my thumb and part her already slick pussy to access her entrance. Knowing how much she hates being teased, I stop at her opening, halting the circulation movement of my thumb causing her to groan out in protest. "Baby girl, I'll never get enough of you." I growl into her ear before inserting two fingers inside her, making her gasp. "Eyes on me, I want your attention on me as your pussy clenches around my fingers and I leave your cum dripping down your thighs." She mewls against me as I kiss her neck, grazing the skin with my teeth, making her cry out for more. Like the perfect little puppet her body responds so well as she begins riding my fingers, begging for more as the waves of her pleasure begin to climax. I have come to recognize the moment just before Lucille's orgasms, and as I see the burn crest and her back arches from the door I tighten my hand around her throat making her gasp out as she comes hard around my fingers, soaking my hand with her cum.

"Silas!!!" She cries as her legs start to shake. I remove my hands from her body, her thighs slick from her cum, and bring my fingers to my mouth, maintaining eye contact as I suck her sweet juices from each finger. She's a fucking delicacy.

Lucille watches me with hooded eyes, regaining her breathing as I suck the last finger into my mouth, releasing it with a resounding pop. "I'm not finished with you yet Lucille." I groan as I grab her thighs and lift her body from the floor, she automatically wraps her legs around me as I carry her out of the ensuite and back to the bed. My lips find hers immediately as I place her down on the sheets, our tongues fighting one anothers for dominance. Lucille's hands reach for me but before she can succeed, I secure both wrists above her head. "Let's have some fun shall we baby girl? Let's see which of my brother's comes running first at your screams as I impale you on my cock." I growl before flipping her onto her front making her gasp at the sudden movement. Holding her down so she's facing the sheets, I part her supple thighs, stroking the insides, teasing her momentarily before I line myself up to her entrance and thrust inside her wet, hungry cunt. She screams out at the intrusion but soon those screams become throaty moans with every thrust as I fuck her into the sheets. I'm so close to exploding inside her I don't know If I can last much longer, and I can already feel her tightening around my cock. "So Lucille, who do you think it will be? Who will come for you first?" I ask her, pulling my solid cock from her gaping pussy before I blow too soon.

"Fuck. I don't know, don't stop!" She shouts at me, shooting a dangerous look over her shoulder.
I chuckle, bringing my palm to her ass with a loud crack that makes her knuckles turn white as she grips the bedsheets.

"No baby girl, answer my question." I demand as I slam back inside her, barely restraining myself from

332

fucking her so hard into this bed that we'll have to buy a new one.

"Linc," she gasps.

Such a good girl. As a reward I thrust into her harder, making her shout out his name as I bottom out inside of her. As if by magic, the bedroom door flies open. To my amusement, both of my brother's have decided to join us, looking just as ravenous as I am for a piece of our girl. I smirk, and continue to fuck Lucille, not relenting in the force of my thrusts.

"Having a party without us, Love?" Lincoln teases, walking up to the bed. Her eyes snap to him as she clenches hard around my cock.

Cole laughs, "Now, I think you need to be punished for teasing us with your screams, little mouse. What do you think, boys?"

Lucille gushes at the suggestion, her pussy contracting around my ready to explode cock. Her cum coats her thighs and my own as I bury myself inside of her.

"Well Lincoln, she guessed you'd be first to come and join us, so I guess that means she wants you to take her mouth." I smirk at Lincoln. His eyes light up in response as he runs his fingers through Lucille's hair. I feel her pussy tighten again causing a deep groan to rumble its way through my body. Fuck. I don't know how much more I can take.

"You want me to fuck your throat, Love?" Lincoln asks as he starts to remove his clothing.

"I want all of you." She pants hopelessly as I slow my pace in a desperate attempt to last longer.

Lincoln climbs in front of her and I re-adjust my position so that she is on all fours, my cock still buried deep inside her tight pussy. Lucille lifts her head to look up at Lincoln as he tenderly strokes her cheek before pressing his cock to her lips, parting them. I see the pleasure in his face as Lucille runs her tongue against his cock and as I thrust harder Linc gasps as she takes his length into her throat. I pick up my pace again, pounding into her, making her shift forward as Lincoln matches my movements and we begin to fuck her mercilessly. The sight of her between us is magnificent. Her taut body glistens with sweat as I dig my fingers into her hips, ensuring I leave my mark and Linc fists into her hair, pulling hard at the root, keeping her restricted and exactly where we want her.

"Your mouth feels like heaven, Lucille. I'm going to come down that pretty little throat of yours as Silas comes in that slick pussy," he groans. Lucille responds with a muffled moan and I lose it. I buck hard, shoving her forward, forcing her to choke on Lincs cock as his body tenses and he shoots his load down her throat, wiping away the tears from her cheeks. "Fuck. I will never get over how good it feels to defile your pretty mouth," he groans as he pulls his cock from between her swollen lips.

She screams and tightens like a vice around me, flooding around my cock as her cum spills around my cock and with her undoing comes my own. My cock immediately pulsates inside of her, unable to take any more, I groan loudly as I cum hard and fast, filling her up. "Fuckkkk!" She feels like heaven. I can feel the sweat trickle down my back as I lean against Lucille's spent body, trying to regain my breath. After a moment, I slip my cock out of her, stepping back to stare at the mixture of her cum and my own seeping from her pussy and painting a beautiful artwork against her thighs as she collapses against Lincoln, her face flushed a rosy pink color. The fact that she has our cum filling her pussy and her mouth leaves me ecstatic and fulfilled as I watch Lucille relax into Lincoln's arms.

Collapsing on the bed next to her, I close my eyes trying to regain my composure when I feel the bed shift. I peer from one eye as Cole lifts Lucille against his chest and carries her to the bathroom. He still prefers to watch and instruct when it comes to group sex but he always gets his way with her in the end. "I'll clean you up, mi topolino," he whispers, turning to wink at me before closing the door behind them.

Cole

I cradle Lucille in my arms, making my way to the bathroom. I smile at the feel of her thoroughly fucked body falling limp against my chest as she sighs heavily sated by her orgasms. She's exhausted, and it's cute. The ensuite is thick with steam as we enter. It seems Silas got too distracted before turning off the water. I can't say I blame him.

I place Lucille onto the edge of the bath quickly ensuring the door is locked behind me. They've had their fun, now I want her all to myself. I round back, tilting her chin up, admiring her natural beauty, reveling at the way her eyes sparkle as they take me in. I lean back as her eyes slowly travel down the length of my naked torso. I was half asleep when I heard the telltale song of Lucille's orgasm calling to me like a siren and a worn pair of jeans were the first thing to hand before I came running. She audibly gulps at the sight of me, her eyes filling with desire, making my lips curl at the edges. "Like what you see, il mio topolino?" I tease, stroking my fingers tenderly across her flushed cheek, before caging my hand firmly at the nape of her neck. She knows how I like to play.

"Yes sir, always."

Her eyes flare as she parts her lips, breathing out a small and steadying breath, letting me know I have her full attention. I'm going to enjoy devouring those perfectly plump lips. I release my hold around her neck, moving towards the basin, where I take my time soaking a clean washcloth before turning back to an eagerly awaiting Lucille. I smile as she waits patiently like a good girl as I begin to gently wipe over her face, removing any residue of Lincoln from her skin. When I'm fully satisfied, I rinse the cloth and kneel between her legs.

"Stay still for me, mio topolino." I order with a hushed tone, blowing a teasing breath across her thighs sending a wave of shiver through her body. She nods, pulling her bottom lip between her teeth. I begin to clean her swollen pussy, slowly stroking the washcloth across her sensitive clit, massaging as I go. Lucille moans as the friction from the cloth as I apply pressure, throwing her head back and opening her legs wider for me. Such a needy thing. I glance up, her eyes are closed, a slightly scrunched up look of pleasure etched into her features as her chest rises and falls frantically. I can't help but chuckle. She's already so sensitive and I'm barely touching her.

Once I've cleaned the remainder of my brother's cum from between her legs, leaving her pussy bare and begging for me, I kiss the inside of her thighs, dropping the cloth and stroking her softly, slowly teasing my fingers across her entrance. I refuse to push my hands too far, the ache in my balls becoming hard to handle. But I need her to feel that way I felt last year when I forced myself away from her. To feel the burning ache to have what is being so cruelly refused to me. I'm torturing her in my own fucked up little way, and I love every moment of it. The way her mouth opens as she subconsciously holds her breath, waiting for me to fulfill her needs.

"Breathe, little mouse."

Lucille instantly does as I say, and slowly exhales the air from her lungs, taking another deep breath. I smirk up at her, her hooded eyes now completely focused on me. I'm the one on my knees but I'm in full control of the situation, and she knows that just as well as I do. "Such a good girl for me, Topolino." I praise her, edging my face closer to her now glistening pussy. It never fails to amaze me how wet she can get from hardly a touch. I inhale her, crushing my lips to her sensitive clit, sucking hard as I grasp my hands firmly onto her thighs, indenting my nails into her skin, leaving my own mark against her milky white skin as I force her legs wider for me. It doesn't take long until her legs begin to shake against my hold as I flick my tongue over her cunt. She tries desperately to shift her lower body against my mouth but I pull away, extinguishing the build of her orgasm before it hits.

"I am going to remove my hands from your thighs, you will keep still for me Topolino or you'll receive a punishment, do you understand?" I inform her, the smell of her arousal thickening around the space between us.

Lucille whines, chewing her bottom lip before batting her thick black lashes at me. "But what if that's what I want?" she replies. She's being a brat and she knows it.

I raise an inquisitive brow at her. "You want to be punished? You want to play that game, my little mouse?"

Lucille's hooded eyes meet mine, full of lust and need, she nods slowly, popping her lip from between her teeth.

337

Well then I guess I must oblige. I move swiftly, grabbing her hips to flip her body, leaving her bent over the bath and spreading her legs apart, exposing her ass and pussy on full display, all for me. Toying her slick folds with my fingers, her wetness coats her upper thighs, as I slowly push one deep inside of her.

Lucille wriggles her ass against my hold, trying to push back onto my hand. So impatient. I tut loudly, shaking my head. "Now, now, mio topolino, I need you to count to ten for me." She continues to move her hips impatiently in front of me, giving me her own version of teasing. Pulling my fingers from her pussy, I bring my palm to her ass, making her wince from the sharp and unexpected contact. I'm suddenly thankful to the surgeons who put my hands back together because the thought of never being able to spank my little mouse again physically pains me. The sight of my glowing handprint marking her skin makes my cock twitch painfully against my jeans.

"One," she squeals, I stroke over the already pink cheek and bring my hand down again, with her screaming out each number. "Ten!" she croaks as I make my final blow, her throat is hoarse from her pleading screams and she pants desperately trying to compose herself.

The way she has come to allow my punishments has been nothing short of a miracle. She truly is the perfect woman. One I can punish and praise, "Good girl. Now would you like your reward?" I stroke over her red raw ass, staring at it like it's a work of fucking art before turning her around, to see the same deep shade of scarlet staining her cheeks. I make quick work of removing my jeans, my solid erection springing free from the restraints before lifting Lucille with my hands at the back of her thighs causing her to squeal in delight as I wrap her legs around my waist and she hooks her feet together at my back while I walk us into the shower.

I take no time in capturing her lips with my own, devouring her tongue as I suck it between my teeth and shifting my hips, lining my cock with her pussy, slamming her back up against the tiled wall as I bury myself ball deep inside of her.

"Cole!" she gasps, groaning with ecstasy, rolling her eyes to the back of her head. I lose myself inside of her, fucking her hard and fast against the tiles, the sound of our wet bodies slapping together as she cries out, digging her nails into the skin of my back.

"Lucille," I growl, sinking my teeth into her collar bone as she screams wildly around me. My cock slides in and out of her easily as I slam my hips against her body, she's so wet and yet her walls cling so fucking tightly to my cock it feels like a vice as she explodes around me, tightening her thighs and screaming her orgasm, her pussy clenching so hard she pulls me right over the edge with her.

"Good girl, take my cock, let me fill you with my cum."

"Yes, Cole!" she cries, riding the waves of ecstasy.

I feel the surge as I shatter inside of her, filling her pussy with my cum, a deep feral rumble ripping from my throat as I thrust my hips forwards one last time. "Fuck, I hope my cum makes you pregnant one day. I'll gladly fuck you every chance I get until your belly is swollen with my child." Lucille moans at my promise, but I notice her eyes full of tears before she snaps her head to the side. I immediately pull back. "Mio topolino, are you okay? What's wrong? Did I hurt you?"

She tries to move, releasing her thighs from my waist but I refuse to let this happen. Instinctively, I lower

339

her feet to the shower floor, grasping her face between both hands before I move her head back to look at me. Her eyes are closed but I can see the pain behind her expression. "Look at me, Lucille." I demand, my voice is soft but authoritative. She does as I ask, her wide eyes pleading with me but not like they were before. No. Now they're begging me for understanding. I narrow my eyes before somehow the pieces come together. "You already are?" I ask, my voice barely above a whisper.

I don't realize that while I wait for her response, as she searches my eyes, desperate to find what she's looking for, that I've held my breath the entire time, and only when she finally nods her head do I breathe again, my head swimming with the revelation as a smile breaks out across her beautiful face.

"This is amazing! How long have you known? Do the others know?" I ask excitedly, grinning from ear to ear like a school kid at Christmas. I kiss her, feverishly planting chaste kisses everywhere I can.

I feel her smile against my lips before he giggles, pushing me away as she shakes her head. "No, but Cole, you need to understand. I don't know which of you is the father." She looks down slightly and fiddles with her hands, and I know she's feeling guilty about it. I take her hands in mine and kiss each one tenderly, bringing her attention back to me.

"Lucille, we will all be the father, like we are to Teddy." I lean in and kiss the top of her head before lifting her out of the shower, wrapping her in a towel and grabbing one for myself. I pick her up again bridal style and carry her out to the bedroom where Lincoln and Silas are now casually laying chatting to each other on the bed. Their attention soon diverted as I place Lucille down in the space between them.

"Tell them." I urge, trying to hold back the excitement I know my brothers will share with me. She nods tentatively, fiddling with her fingers again as they both glare at me like I'm the bad guy.

Holding my hands up I grin, "Woah guys, this is all our fault. It's not just on me this time." They mirror one another with confusion pulling their eyebrows together before Lucille clears her throat.

"Cole's right. This isn't just on him. It's something I have been meaning to say for a few days now, I just haven't known how to." She pauses, flicking her gaze to me but I give her an encouraging nod to let her know it's ok. "I have been feeling a little more tired than usual, and a little nauseous, so I decided to take a pregnancy test—"

Lincoln immediately springs from the bed, lifting her up and twirls her around in the air, laughing a deep hearty, joyful laugh that brightens his entire face. "You're pregnant?" He laughs again, and the excitement in his voice is all Lucille needs to make her burst into tears. "This is wonderful news, Love. We couldn't ask for anything more than you have already given us, and yet you bring us new life, a new little love to cherish and protect." Lincoln sets her down carefully, placing his hands onto her belly, kissing her with a gentleness I've not seen from him in a long time as she continues to cry her happy tears against him. I watch, a feeling of pure joy and contentment settling over my body, resting deep in my bones. Silas moves from the bed and pulls her lovingly from Linc's embrace before lowering down to one knee.

"Lucille Holland, light of my life. I want you to be the first thing I touch every morning, and the last thing I taste every night. You have enchanted each and every one of us, and we could no longer live another day on this earth without you by our side. You are ours to love, ours to protect, ours to share. Will you marry me? Will you marry all of us?" He asks. I knew he'd be the first to do this, he's been threatening me and Lincoln for the past six months that if Lucille ever fell pregnant he'd be marrying her, no doubt about it. Lucille sobs hysterically now, nodding her head profusely as she wipes her tears away and jumps into his arms.

"Silas! Of course I'll marry all of you, but is that legal?" She mumbles through her emotional outpour.

"If it's not, I'll make it so. Nothing will stop us from making you ours in every possible way, not even God himself." Silas says darkly with a small but defiant glint in his eyes.

But he's right, we would burn down the world for her. For our family. God help anybody who stands in our way.

The End.

About the Authors

S.L Wisdom

S.L Wisdom is an aspiring new author, who lives in England. Her favorite color is black, she loves true-crime documentaries and has a soft spot for the bad guys in the books she reads (somebody has to be rooting for them). She's a wife and mother and when she isn't working at the hospital her downtime is spent reading, writing, baking, drinking tea and pretending to be a 'mommy monster' while she chases her daughter around the house.

Without the constant support and words of encouragement from her husband, who has had to do the bedtime routine on more than one occasion so she could keep on writing until early hours in the morning, she knows she would never have got to the end of this series, or even had the confidence to start it, and for that she will forever be grateful to him.

S.J Noble

S.J Noble is an adventurer, reader, dreamer, writer, single mother and Aries star sign. S.J Noble lives in England and spends her days working in the local hospital with S.L Wisdom and rounding up her two strong-willed sons. S.J Noble loves anything fantasy, thriller and crime, whether that is a movie, series or a book. She can often be found reading any book with a shocking plot twist and an anti-hero as the main character. Yes, she's a slut for the villain, feel free to stalk her on the pages below to find out more!

For more information about both S.J Noble and S.L Wisdom upcoming releases please visit the sites listed below:
Facebook readers group:
http://www.facebook.com/groups/760611272268230/?red= share
Instagram: S.JNoble and S.L_Wisdom
Tiktok: WisdomNoble_69

Please check out our amazing editor Ria at Moon and Bloom Editing.
Facebook page:
http://www.facebook.com/moonandbloomediting
Instagram: Moonandbloomediting

Acknowledgements

First and foremost we'd like to give a huge thank you to our friends and colleagues who have been our biggest supporters since the very beginning of this book when the idea first came to life over a lunchtime catch up on what books we were reading. Without your words of encouragement and support this would have been a much more difficult task. So thank you for everything!

Of course a HUGE thank you to our amazing editor Ria. You have been an absolute godsend through this whole process for us. We're super grateful to have you alongside us on our new book journey.

Thank you to Francessca for designing such a beautiful front cover for our book, our promotional images and social media banners and always being so patient with us.

Heather and Erin, a special thank you to you both for not only Beta reading for us but also the constant support, endless amount of giggles and crazy messages that has kept us going and wanting to write more books for you to consume! Thank you for loving us and our books as we love you both so very much. P.s there is a worm at the bottom of the garden, and his name is Timmy toe LMAO!

Lastly, but by no means least, thank you so much to our Arc and Street team who have lifted us and showed us immense love and support throughout this process. We have to pinch ourselves every time you shower us with admiration for our writing, we couldn't have done this without you!

Printed in Great Britain
by Amazon

48249486R00195